Also by Nélida Piñon in English Translation

THE REPUBLIC OF DREAMS

Caetana's Sweet Song

NÉLIDA PIÑON

Caetana's Sweet Song

Translated from the Portuguese by Helen Lane

Alfred A. Knopf   New York

1 9 9 2

THIS IS A BORZOI BOOK
PUBLISHED BY ALFRED A. KNOPF, INC.

Library of Congress Cataloging-in-Publication Data
Piñon, Nélida.
[Doce canção de Caetana. English]
Caetana's sweet song / by Nélida Piñon ; translated from
the Portuguese by Helen Lane. — 1st American ed.
p. cm.
Translation of: A doce canção de Caetana.
ISBN 0-394-58997-1
I. Title.
[PQ9698.26.15D613   1992]
869.3—dc20   91-26409   CIP

Manufactured in the United States of America
First American Edition

Caetana's Sweet Song

ON CROSSING THE SQUARE, Polidoro looked at his wristwatch, a present from his grandfather Eusébio. The hour hand pointed to past five. He was irritated at himself for being late, as though his life depended on an arbitrary punctuality, imposed only by his haste to be all by himself, in front of a bottle of whisky at the bar of the Palace Hotel.

He stepped up his pace in an attempt to recover lost time. His body, however, did not possess the nimbleness of bygone days, thereby giving him reason to curse the passing of the years. He then had a foreboding that that Monday, with its patches of near-yellow sky, threatened to spread discord everywhere. One had to be on one's guard, especially since it was just a few hours before the day would end.

Already that morning, at the sign of the wind sweeping leaves and insects before it, lashing the clothes hanging out to dry, he had felt heavy-handed as he shaved. And rather than confront Dodô across the table, he had fled from her sight. She never missed a chance to keep a sharp eye on him, to make her presence felt at the table, especially over breakfast. Always the first one to wake up, she was proud of having inherited from her father the habit of greeting the sun the moment the first light of day filtered through the window and invaded the room. Polidoro even suspected that in order to meet the challenge that she had set herself of never sleeping a minute more after the sun appeared above the horizon, Dodô surely must keep one eye open while the other rested. That was the only possible explanation for how, during all these many years, he had never entered the dining room without finding her waiting for him, eyes wide open, wary, even if she was busy setting out the trays of salty breakfast dishes and biscuits on the table.

The voracity with which Dodô ate her food, not letting a single breadcrumb fall onto the tablecloth, was evident. Everything was always neat and clean, the table set. No visitor would catch her unprepared.

"And who's going to visit us at this hour of the day, Dodô?" Polidoro protested, seeing before him the clean cups lined up to go back to the kitchen.

"There's no way of knowing who's going to knock on our door. Having the table all set is like having the coffin ordered."

She uttered the phrase in such a serious voice that Polidoro lacked the courage to voice his argument; it might be valid, but it was useless in practice.

That morning Dodô seemed to be on pins and needles. She offered her husband cheese bread, just out of the oven, in an effort to protect him from a plague that was about to descend on them at any moment.

Though the smell of cheese bread awakened his appetite, Polidoro refused an offer that might provoke a sequence of questions, which were such a habit with his wife. The moment he gave her a discreet smile, Dodô boasted of probable victories. She immediately asked him with whom he had dined the night before, since he hadn't swallowed a single grain of the rice she had left in the oven in the hope that her husband would not forget the savor of homemade food. And what time had it been when he put the key in the lock? She reminded him that at last he had a house in Trindade that was his, of which she was co-owner, through a formal deed and family obligation. Questions scarcely concealed her resentment of their having slept in separate bedrooms for many years.

Undaunted, Dodô insisted once again that he have some cheese bread, set before him this time on a silver tray brought from Portugal. Polidoro forbore accepting. With a gesture stemming from a boredom that grew with every hour he spent in the house, he deflected her generosity; it gave him chest pains.

Confronted with another negative answer, Dodô drew herself up proudly, insisting on offering him the sight of a body that for years he had avoided touching, even in pity. As though the flight from the nuptial bed seemed to the husband to be a decision that the two of them had agreed upon after a pleasant discussion.

Once, alone with her eldest daughter, Dodô had protested against their unusual situation.

"He only acts that way to get revenge."

"And why would Father be out for revenge? You gave him five healthy daughters, and landed property as a dowry."

The mother's stinging words came amid a shower of saliva. The daughter placed particular emphasis on the fortune, as a means of launching her mother on the only reflection that would calm her down; in fact, she emerged prepared to take the initiatives necessary to confront her neglectful husband.

Wearing a black dressing gown dotted with purple roses, a trite imitation of the blooms that she herself watered in the flower bed at the back of the house, Dodô challenged him with her eyes. Her look gave forth carving knives, jackknives, imported sabers, and assured him that, in the arsenal of her sentiments, there existed arms of heavier caliber. Many of them, hammered out in the forge with delicate precision, had been plunged in cold water from the river Jordan. Polidoro had no reason to doubt her secret resources. At times he felt like certain stars in the galaxy invisible to the naked eye.

In that contest, Dodô took pleasure in demonstrating to her husband a nonchalance with regard to both their town house and their country estates, a vast fief that belonged to the two of them—almost an entire district. It was difficult to administer, but they never relaxed their guard over its ownership.

After looking him up and down with a deliberately hard gaze, Dodô turned her back on him and left the table. Her house slippers dragged, as though she were sweeping the floor as she crossed it. She used this maneuver to her greatest possible advantage, knowing very well how much Polidoro held certain details against her after the more than thirty years they had spent together.

His eyelids weighted down with grave melancholy, Polidoro

watched his wife disappear into the hallway, taking with her to her room, at the other end of the house, the sound of her slippers, which assailed the rooms of the building from the early-morning hours until lunchtime, when, finally, she would decide to remove those white monsters glued to the soles of her feet. A sound to which throughout their marriage Polidoro had never resigned himself.

He could not resist the urge to let her have it once and for all, to put an end to a situation that made it hard for him to breathe in the morning. He felt tempted to send Dodô a crushing written message, each word inviting her to shut herself up in the country house. All she need do to comply with such an order was to point out, on the map of her feelings and her fantasy, which country house among the five they owned particularly suited her in the month of June. Any one of the properties would welcome her with a wood fire all lit and the bean stew already cooked.

Regretfully, he grabbed paper and pen. He was sorry not to have at hand paper with official stamps affixed, which would lend seriousness to the message. He hesitated as he drafted the text. The first sentence, ordinarily the hardest to write, allowed the others to flow spontaneously. As though impelled by secret ire, they trickled down a streamlet full of pebbles. Ought he to address her as "Dear Dodô," implying that he would come to love her in the future? He resisted this polite formula for suggesting a certain affection.

As a matter of fact, as far as Dodô was concerned, his heart was dried up, exhausted. Despite having frequented her bed and, imprudently, having knocked on the door of her womb, all he wanted was to rid himself of that affection, to blot out forever any temptation to dream that the woman might still cling to.

He composed his first sentence. At a glance, it seemed to him to be discreet and persuasive. But who could tell, whether, far from convincing her to leave, such reserve might not strengthen her resolve to stay, just to fight him?

He put the pen down on the table. Leaning on his elbows, he looked around the room. The walls, decorated with paintings by Venieris the Greek, were beginning to peel. Dodô kept them in that state just to prove that the house, like himself, had grown older, and to remind Polidoro that, close at hand, amid rooms and hallways, an adversary unwilling to grant him the slightest truce was getting fatter and fatter. It would be better to frequent her bed than to remain at the mercy of her pity.

Prudence warned Polidoro to put the piece of paper in his pocket. Dodô ought not to have access to lines written in such a disturbed frame of mind. As a precaution, he tore out the next few pages of the pad, where the imprint of his handwriting was visible. He feared Dodô's wrathful gaze, the poisoned arrows her uncontrolled tongue would hurl at him. She was capable of cursing him for the rest of the week. Above all, he had the vague memory of Dodô's having said to him, a few days before, that on the following day, Tuesday, her husband would find himself free of her presence. She had plans to take refuge at their Suspiro country estate and therefore had much to take care of.

Polidoro slowed down halfway through the square. His lungs, consumed by tobacco smoke, demanded air and caused him to pant. He looked to the right, toward the mango tree planted by his grandfather Eusébio. This trunk threatened to last a long time, to survive him and his grandchildren. That grandfather, shortly before dying, had proclaimed, with darting black eyes, that, as long as Trindade existed, from which mountains could be seen that touched the sky, he would be eternal. To accomplish this goal, he had scattered all about unmistakable signs of his passage. The only way to destroy his memory altogether would be to demolish all of Trindade.

On recalling his grandfather Eusébio, whom he suspected of having introduced distant Negro blood into the family, Polidoro thought, with unexpected relief, that all the Álveses, with the exception of his father, had died in the last few years. He retained uncomfortable memories of those relatives. Some of them invaded his sleep, demanding their return to a reality from which death had banished them, merely to name him spokesman of the desires they had not yet given up.

None of these Álveses had manifested a desire to live beyond the age of eighty. On nearing this mark, they limited themselves to the minimum of polite formulas, avoiding saying good night most of the time, doubting that they would still be alive when morning came. They frequently closed their eyes, in an evident demonstration of their weariness in the face of the monotonous sight of Trindade. At the table, forced to down puréed bean soup, they rebelled against the members of the family by yawning, so that everyone would see how eager they were to be on their way.

Joaquim was the last of that flock. By dint of his health—constantly put to the test in the wild, amid snakes, lianas, swamps, intermittent fevers—he stubbornly proved how difficult it would be to uproot him from this earth without his express consent. Deciding that he had been neglected by the living—above all by Polidoro—he declared, in a more and more feeble voice, his immortal status among so many weak men. As long as he lived, he would pass on the tenor of this message to Polidoro, his firstborn son, and hence in a position of authority.

His father's almost excessive vitality surprised Polidoro. True, the old man's eyes no longer had the wicked gleam they had once had. But even today Polidoro feared the manifestation of his intolerant turn of mind. At the height of fury, Joaquim hid his trembling hands in his armpits, in an effort to exorcise evil spirits. He then took out of his pocket a mother-of-pearl rosary and told it bead by bead, never praying or thanking God for his long life, but instead between imperceptible hisses, reeling off the names of notorious enemies to whose intransigence and cruelty he considered he owed a life spent in endless fights. Obliged to concede that he had made his enemies equally miserable, Joaquim admitted that, as a matter of fact, he had inflicted his ill-omened shadow on them each day. He still enjoyed, however, the voluptuous advantage of being the last remaining one of those names monotonously repeated with every bead of the rosary that passed through his fingers.

"Of all my enemies, Bandeirante was the only one who caused me to feel remorse, because I ended up liking him. But I could never approve of his immense ambition, the desire to rob me of my family's affection."

At the mere mention of Bandeirante, Polidoro was plunged

into a region of dark feelings within himself. He therefore extracted details from his father that dragged on until dinnertime—before six, just as it was getting dark. Joaquim, however, his appetite stimulated by the platters that arrived at the table smoking hot, ended up by becoming irritated. He couldn't bear his son's interest in the rekindled memory of an enemy. At times his temper, hidden only skin-deep, moved him to point to the front door:

"Don't you see how right I was? Even after his death, Bandeirante insists on stealing my own story, just so that I'll tell his mean and petty one. What would become of him without me?" he said, proud as ever, in spite of having to walk with a cane.

Yet, by still telling stories—with a memory continually lubricated by the fat from the pork he ate at every meal—he caused his own life, like a basket of fruit just picked in the orchard, to leap from his pores. He did not fear the responsibilities resulting from his long existence, especially since he had no one to thank for it.

He considered himself to be his own god. He had managed to handle his long span of life all by himself, and regarded everything as being his own handiwork. Each muscle of his body and effort of his will had been worked on by his temperament, which ardor and rage had strengthened so as to make him recognizable from leagues away, amid the dust raised by a herd of mules. Few people in Trindade had escaped his testy, almost disrespectful ways.

At home, he was the first to get up in the morning. He would nervously open his bedroom window, indifferent to the lot of those who were still asleep. As soon as he saw the sun in the back yard, his spirits were renewed till just before dawn. Life would be taken from him only as day broke, when he would again struggle to prolong it.

In his pajamas, leaning on the windowsill, Joaquim pounded his chest repeatedly, stretching his hand out toward the trees.

"You're my witnesses. I've just won another day. Death still hasn't managed to strangle me!" he shouted.

No one dared to suggest that he suppress these outcries, which came forth in a voice badly afflicted by hoarseness, thus giving the entire neighborhood reason to complain.

Polidoro made him see that insulting death so often in public would eventually make death come knocking on his door ahead of time. At this advice, Joaquim threatened his son with his cane. He didn't lack the strength to let fly a well-aimed blow in Polidoro's direction. Old age had not robbed him of his manly bearing.

Sometimes Polidoro tried to disarm his father's animosity with false praise. Here was a man who, going on ninety, proved himself to be still thin-skinned about his dead adversaries. Joaquim, however, adjusting the frames of his glasses—which kept slipping down his nose, causing the reality surrounding him to go out of focus—noted in his son the trace of a smile that mocked his father's situation as an old man. He demanded that Polidoro sit down; he had an urgent need to speak with him.

Polidoro obeyed, keeping his distance. He would have liked to disappear from his father's sight, for the latter gave him a pain right in the pit of his stomach. Joaquim asked him to draw his chair up closer. From that vantage point, each would measure how much the other had aged. Polidoro would see, through his father, that he too was slowly withering away, his wretched pride notwithstanding.

Once he had his son at eye level, the two of them breathing as one, Joaquim let out a great guffaw; his mouth discharged droplets of white, virulent saliva in Polidoro's face.

"Though you're in such a hurry to bury me, I'm resisting death. That whore who lives in the room next to mine, and whose everlasting old bones make noises during the night—I'll get even with you though, because I'm convinced that that actress will come back to Trindade some day just to tear all your hair out. Neither your money nor your cattle will be of any use to you."

His father's breath filled Polidoro with uncontrollable revulsion. It entered his nostrils, almost asphyxiating him. Unable to bear Joaquim's presence a moment longer, he rose defiantly to his feet.

"I'll come back one of these days for your funeral. And I hope not to be a minute late. I wouldn't miss that performance for anything in the world. That's the only way I'll be sure you've left us forever," he said, and stormed out the house.

Joaquim did not resist the exile forced on him by his son. Two hours later, foreseeing a sleepless night fighting with phantoms, he summoned Polidoro back to the house. The hour to die had come, so let their disagreements be forgotten. Dividing up the estate would make the dialogue go more smoothly.

In the bar of the Palace Hotel, where alcohol scarred his heart with unanticipated desperation, Polidoro had refused to think about him. His father deserved the punishment of plunging into the flames of his own hatred. Yet, even now, after he had left him, the spiteful echo of his words predicting the old man's death troubled him. He felt sorry for his father, who roamed up and down the hallways of the house, surrounded by strangers of his own blood, with nothing for his very own but a cane and the fear of dying.

"You never loved me," he said, when he had answered Joaquim's summons. "That's why we're a family of loners and despots."

To all appearances, Joaquim hadn't moved from the armchair in those two hours that Polidoro had been gone. Freed of physiological necessities, he seemed to have turned into a vegetable. With a table napkin tied around his neck, he was chewing on arrowroot cookies. The crumbs were falling on his neck without his removing them. He was longing for a certain degradation, in which the sad profile of his future death could be seen. A man lacking the aid of others.

"Have a cup of coffee with me." The neutral voice was addressed to a stranger.

After the coffee, Polidoro helped himself to the cookies piled in a disorderly heap on a plate on the table. Like his father, he let crumbs fall down his shirt, forgetting to brush himself off until he noted that he was thus dutifully carrying out his father's intentions; he shook them off his shirt.

The son's gestures were a denial of any sort of solidarity. It mattered little to him whether his father drooled or defecated in the middle of the room. He had never been his accomplice.

"And aren't you going to tidy me up too?" Joaquim asked, after a long silence.

Polidoro observed that his father, at the gates of death, was trying to accuse him of being his enemy. As if it weren't enough for Polidoro to endure Dodô, his daughters, and so many bitter scenes steeped in his memory as though in vinegar. He did as he was asked, however. He went about the task carefully, so as not to fracture his father's arm, his jaw, or other parts of him ready to come loose from his exhausted body. It would be difficult for his bones to mend now.

"I've removed the cookie crumbs, Father. In exchange, I demand that you respect me and never mention that woman again."

His father's stare could no longer unleash against him, as it used to, sentiments he really intended for his enemies. The old man had best pay court to death, about to come looking for him, and free the family from his irascible nature.

It was now a matter of months. Then they would bury him alongside Magnólia, who had been content to leave them. His mother had no longer been able to stand a family who kept passing through Trindade with pitiless arrogance, some on horseback, others at the wheels of splendid cars.

Polidoro had the papers in order for his father's burial. Certain measures that would not wound the brothers, always sensitive about his fortune and his primogeniture. Moreover, ever since he'd been a little boy, he had gone to wakes, seen dead people shoved by brute force into their coffins. Their transparent skins and ice-cold innards had never frightened him. They seemed to plead for flowers, masses, and the weeping and wailing of the family. And candles as well, the sort whose wick takes seven days to burn down.

"When I close my eyes, stay at my side. Tell me the story of your love for that woman," Joaquim said in a soft voice.

Polidoro straightened the lapel of his shirt.

"Do you realize that I'm afraid of dying?" Joaquim lowered his head. His son must not catch a glimpse of the tears that had welled up in those craters, awash with terror and incredulity at his status as a mortal.

Tempted to comfort that mountain of muscles about to collapse, Polidoro stretched out his arm. He was impressed by the functions of death, and wanted to drag his father to the kingdom of shadows. What was he doing among the living, if he gave scarcely any signs of life?

Intimacy made him uncomfortable. It was best to efface the scars that his father had imprinted on his heart, so that the latter would have a place there forever. In order to break the spell, he clapped his hands to summon the maid.

"Haven't you noticed that it's already dark outside?" He nervously ordered the woman to turn on the lights in the house. "Then serve dinner. Seu Joaquim is going to bed earlier tonight."

His father nodded his head.

"I'm hungry, it's true. But what about going out to the Suspiro estate tomorrow?"

Polidoro appeared to be stalling for time. He looked at the clock on the wall. Dissatisfied, he consulted his wristwatch.

"What's the time?" Joaquim asked, more calmly.

"There's a difference of three minutes between our timepieces."

"That's nothing, when we've all of eternity before us," Joaquim remarked, showing his worn teeth.

AS SOON as the bus left in a cloud of dust, Ernesto looked at his watch again. He wanted to make sure that Polidoro was late, so that he would have more than enough reason for criticizing him. He'd been leaning against the lamppost since four o'clock, making no effort to hide his eagerness to talk to him.

He was afraid that Polidoro had changed his usual hour for dropping in at the hotel bar. Ernesto could stop him en route, at the corner, which Polidoro passed by each afternoon. He never changed his itinerary, despite his daily threats to follow other routes, more in harmony with the fantasies that he had been weaving recently, in spite of his age and Dodô's bothersome presence.

Ernesto smiled when he caught sight of Polidoro, about to cross the street. He noted his rigid posture, reserved for moments of inexplicable distress, but he didn't see any reason for him to be anxious. Unless he was feeling the impact of having grown older, something that had happened practically without warning.

Polidoro was surprised to see Ernesto on the lookout for him, absorbed as usual in defining his frame of mind, threatening him with dramatic prophecies. In the middle of his verbal outpouring, Ernesto pretended to read Polidoro's heart merely by looking at his face.

"Today, for instance, you woke up in a state of anxiety. Watch out for a heart attack."

Subjected to such examinations, Polidoro rebelled. He made Ernesto see that he alone had access to his own soul, so Ernesto was not to invade his territory, assuming a supposed title of ownership.

Ernesto did not admit defeat. He attributed Polidoro's reaction to a timidity with which he was well acquainted. Ever since childhood he had followed Polidoro up the hillsides of Trindade, chasing after cows and skirts. He was not about to give up the voracious intimacy of that affection now.

The Chinese smile on Ernesto's face was an essential part of the siege to which he was subjecting Polidoro. Resignedly, Polidoro found fault on occasion with his heart's apathy, which did not know how to sing the praises of a friend as faithful as Ernesto.

In recent months Ernesto had acquired an unobtrusive pot-belly, after freeing himself of a persistent case of acid indigestion, attributed to coffee. Once he had regained his health, he fled the pharmacy to spend hours at the bar on the corner. Among his fellow idlers, he deciphered doctors' prescriptions and interpreted the printed instructions that came with medicines. Vivina, however, aloof to his caresses, threatened to clip his wings with the family shears.

"Have you ever thought, woman, what it's like to endure imaginary sick people coming to the door of the shop, year after year?" He used the same sentence in the mornings, with slight variations. His voice, apparently troubled, swore that life was a burden. Anything to touch his wife's heart and broaden her streak of independence.

Polidoro, knowing that he was the target of other people's curiosity, scowled when strangers approached.

"Snoopers like that even follow me to the toilet. What is it they want? For me to open my fly and show them my balls?"

Ernesto smiled. He didn't feel that he was the butt of the remark. It was Polidoro who persisted in following him, so as to secure his friendship or subject him to an outpouring of the kind of confidences which Ernesto received from behind the counter of the pharmacy.

"I'm late, Ernesto. Leave it till later," Polidoro said, dragging Ernesto along with him.

"Why all the hurry? Just to sit at a table in the bar all by yourself?" He kept taking visiting cards and photographs out of his wallet as Polidoro stepped up the pace.

"It's Seu Joaquim." And he waved the instructions for a prescription in the air.

Polidoro gave in. He scrutinized his friend to console himself, and noted resentfully that life had spared Ernesto. The wrinkles that made Polidoro look older had no counterpart in Ernesto's face, even though the two of them had been born in the same year.

As a matter of fact, ever since adolescence he had given himself over to superfluous emotions. He had surely inherited from his mother the fate of possessing a skin-deep sensibility. He suspected that his body was consumed by ardent sentiments, even though he did not allow them to show through for others.

"What does the old man want this time?"

He took pleasure in offending Ernesto by the way he treated his father. According to the pharmacist, who was sensitive to blood relationships, he ought not to disparage any member of the family except the wives, since they did not have the blood of the flock, but only the husband's sperm.

"Seu Joaquim came to the pharmacy this morning, but he refused to come in. He stayed out on the sidewalk, tapping his cane on the cement. He changed his mind and came in only when he saw that the pharmacy was empty. He practically asked me to lower the blinds over the doors."

"Why all that caution, especially since my father is an exhibitionist?" Polidoro remarked, his curiosity aroused.

"He asked me for a poison, one that kills humans and rats. Seeing my surprise, he admitted that he was just joking. He needed to pretend to have a sickness that would keep him in bed for at least two weeks."

"My father's gone mad!"

"I was surprised too. He of all people, who would get rid of half a herd of cows in exchange for a few more days of life! I spoke of the risks of such products. There's always the danger of a cardiac arrest. 'The devil take you, man! Shut your mouth!' he shouted. Finally, he confessed that he didn't want to appear at the unveiling of the bust."

The unveiling of the bronze bust in his honor was planned for the near future. The idea had been Virgílio's, a faithful observer of daily events in the nation, the only citizen in Trindade who cared about the strengthening of a national identity, threatened daily by the inroads of foreign hordes.

"A country devoid of symbols and with a flag whipped by the wind is a pitiful spectacle. It's like a dying man in a room in a boarding house, without anyone to put a candle in his hand and take the chill off his last dream before he dies."

Following the example of the tribunes of the empire, Virgílio waxed enthusiastic about civic expressions. He tightened the knot of his tie, which was dancing about his shirt collar.

"Brazil needs young people who will devote themselves to republican ideals. This country is a gigantic friend, brought by the Portuguese to the back yard of our heart." Moved by an image engendered thanks to his own overblown rhetoric, he concluded forcefully: "But it's owing to this Brazilian giant that we have food and a pleasant climate. We never suffer from typhoons, tornadoes, submarine earthquakes, or tidal waves."

In the beginning, Virgílio fought for a marble pantheon capable of sheltering heroes, who, despite the pettiness of everyday life, conferred grandeur on the human condition.

"Life humiliates us at every moment. From bellyaches and attacks of diarrhea to the gradual decay of our teeth. Not to mention loss of memory and herniated testicles. It even seems as though the only need of life is to benumb us till death comes along. This being so, why don't we fight it through acts that make us believe we have wings and can fly?" he proclaimed, sitting at a table crowded with men.

This proposal gave rise to sarcastic remarks. Those hearts, hardened with mud and cow dung, couldn't tolerate idealism.

"That pantheon of yours runs the risk of being occupied by brigands and scoundrels."

Eager to produce proof to the contrary, Virgílio consulted encyclopedias. "That's slander. Trindade is grazing ground not only for cattle but also for illustrious men. Besides, grandeur is a human function. It is present in all men, even in hearts infested with hatred, pestilence, and insanity."

Confronted with the indifference of his audience, he had a different idea. "How about honoring Seu Joaquim! Since he's going on ninety, we could dedicate a marble bust to him," he said as a challenge to Pentecostes, the mayor, who was sneaking out of the bar.

Urged to stay, Pentecostes took his handkerchief from his coat lapel. With surprising promptness, he shed abundant tears. The gesture earned him great praise. Polidoro himself, despite recent political differences between them, complimented him. But, in order to neutralize the political effects of the gesture, he put his arms around the others in the same strong embrace.

Swiftly counterattacking, Pentecostes came out in defense of an emotion inspired by the merits of the Álves family, which had Polidoro as a distinguished representative. Polidoro's steely gaze stunned Virgílio, thanks to whom Polidoro's adversary won an undisputed victory.

Some days later, in the course of the wedding festivities of a rich landowner who was a friend of his, Pentecostes gave a speech in honor of the bride and groom even before the wedding cake was cut. Besides offering them the usual wishes for a blissful married life, he lost himself in a display of rhetoric that brought in its wake delicate lyrical laurels, immediately followed by a proclamation of how proud the city was to have among its progeny a man such as Joaquim—an illustrious son of Trindade straight out of Plutarch—whose bust would forever adorn the main square.

Ernesto, who had been downing one beer after another, kept going off to the bathroom, from which he returned looking younger somehow. Forgetting the duties of friendship, he applauded the mayor, to Polidoro's even greater irritation.

In a grateful tone of voice, Pentecostes asked, with unrestrained impatience, for silence. "I am a servant of the city and, as such, I am of the opinion that the orchestration of this public festival ought to be handed over to a citizen above all suspicion. As illustrious, moreover, as the man whom we shall be honoring." And his eyes, fixed on Polidoro, were an implicit endorsement of his name.

His trips to the urinal caused Ernesto to miss parts of the speech. Unwilling to approve of decisions made in his absence, he demanded of his neighbor a detailed account, even though, personally, he was suspicious of the uncertainties of the past and the difficulties of bringing oneself up-to-date with regard to events already over and done with. He himself, every time he made a mistake. when describing a distant reality, would say, in a sad voice: "I feel that I arrived late for my own life."

After drinking the last swallow of his mug of beer, Ernesto wiped his mouth with his shirttail. He suddenly took heart; he did not want to disappoint the select audience. "There's only one man in Trindade accustomed to such celebrations. I am referring to the eminent historian Virgílio."

Free of the duty to be silent, the men applauded the professor. His face flushed with pleasure, Virgílio took in these words. However late in coming, they brought recognition to his life, which he had dedicated to providing Trindade with a culture that those same men fought against assimilating.

Virgílio was always carefully dressed. Although he lived by

himself, no one ever saw him looking untidy. Even his hair, dyed the color of mahogany, didn't strike people as odd. It went well with his grenadine-red ties—that being his favorite color.

Obliged to express his thanks for the recommendation, he polished his words, in an effort to make them impeccable. As a matter of fact, his fondness for literary effect was a matter of public knowledge. Pentecostes actually brought him certain speeches to free of stylistic impurities. And, while Virgílio respected the mayor's recherché and repetitive vein, he forced him to decant the Brazilian past by means of a series of historical quotations.

Pentecostes pretended to back his nomination. Obliged to listen to someone else's speech when his aim was to go on with his own, he waited for Virgílio to pause for breath so he could regain the floor.

Virgílio wiped the perspiration from his brow with moderate gestures. That was enough to allow Pentecostes to cut him short. "And who will be responsible for paying for the project?" he inquired, offhandedly, hoping to get Polidoro involved.

Absorbed in doodling on the tablecloth with his fingernails, Polidoro pretended not to have heard. He was not about to finance the political projects of a mayor who hadn't consulted him or presented electoral considerations for naming as building inspector a notorious adversary of his.

Pentecostes's proposal, received in silence, threatened to undermine Virgílio's dreams. In his anxiety to save Joaquim's bust, he interrupted the mayor and took over.

"The money is a subject of lesser importance. What we need, first and foremost, is a sculptor with a sure hand, capable of capturing the heart of Seu Joaquim and eternalizing it in bronze." Slightly tipsy, Ernesto burst out laughing.

"And who might that be?"

Virgílio frowned, forgetting that he owed to Ernesto his being recommended to take charge of the ceremony. "What do you know about such things, Ernesto? Only artists can fly, even without wings."

Pentecostes took the initiative again. The public purse, in a precarious state, managed only to meet the absurd budgets inherited from previous administrations thanks to his talents at management. "After paying the schoolteachers, the functionaries, the building contractors, and the pensioners, whom we rehire so as to skimp on the retirement fund, there's nothing left. Just an empty coffer."

His voice, with sudden sincerity, seemed to express real suffering. It made his words credible as he went on to hint that, should Polidoro refuse to assume the expenses of this sincere homage, he would be slighting his own father. "I have an idea for getting us out of this impasse," he finally proclaimed, deeply distressed.

"Only if it's accompanied by a nice warm meat pie," Ernesto interrupted, as he circulated the tray of appetizers that the lady of the house had entrusted to him to pass around.

Standing alongside Polidoro, who passed up the pie, Ernesto insisted.

"Have you stopped being young, Polidoro? Is there no trace left in your soul of the memories of youth, when we used to eat meat pies made by Dona Amélia?"

Stumbling over the chairs, Ernesto kept Pentecostes from speaking. Such contretemps, far from irritating Polidoro, evoked from him an ironic smile, directed at the mayor standing in the middle of the room, his mouth wide open, wanting to utter words that he'd pickled in brine.

Polidoro turned around. "Pass me a pie, Ernesto." He encouraged the others to imitate him. "Anybody who doesn't appreciate a pie like this has one foot in the grave."

The men flung themselves on the tray and asked for draft beer, fresh out of the cooling coils.

"Long live the newlyweds!" a voice proclaimed.

"Long live pie, long live Brazil!" Ernesto added, as Polidoro gave him a friendly bear-hug. Clasping each other, the two of them blocked Pentecostes from the view of the other guests.

Pentecostes succumbed to the weight of his body and collapsed in the rocking chair. He had hopes of reigning over the room once again. On other occasions, after being banished from speakers' platforms, he had returned to them by loudly protesting. Immersed as he was in this order of thoughts, his attention was attracted by the sound of mouths munching all around him. The smell of the fried dough awakened his greed. His tongue palpitated between his teeth from sheer desire. He made a move toward the tray, and he had very nearly grabbed the very last pie when another, swifter hand reached out past his.

This lack of esteem pained him. It compromised his authority and, above all, it made him suddenly understand the strange renunciation of the rights of progeniture in exchange for a mess of pottage. The Biblical reminiscence irritated him nonetheless. They were all bastards.

Virgílio, whom the hubbub had forced out of his air pocket, noted Pentecostes's dismay and, seeing him in the rocking chair, remembered that he still hadn't finished his speech.

"Your attention, gentlemen, we're about to hear what the mayor has to say!"

Impelled by an invisible spring, Pentecostes rose to his feet. After clearing his throat, he immediately brought forth from his pearly vocal cords the first words.

"At this moment, when Brazil is putting into practice a generous economic model oriented toward progress, under the inspiration of General Médici—who, incidentally, has brought us so much good luck—it is altogether fitting that civil society take up the challenge to render homage to Joaquim Álves. I therefore announce my readiness to share with all of you gentlemen the glories of such a campaign. As a citizen of Trindade, I insist on making a personal contribution. We cannot, by any manner of means, turn over to the state a celebration that belongs to the people."

So that they might sense his emotion, he let his head hang down and, still fearing that his hidden feelings might not be recognized, blew his nose into his sandalwood-scented handkerchief.

Ernesto, who had long been eager to debate questions that might concern him, was enthusiastic. Pentecostes's political vision was at last allowing him to experience an eloquent moment of freedom in that city. In a gesture of repentance, as though he were in church, he placed his contribution on the platter from which the pies had just been served.

Under the pressure of this spectacle, Polidoro muttered: "I'll make up however much we fall short."

Virgílio hurriedly left the wedding feast. By consulting the telephone book, he reached Borelli. This sculptor, who lived in Rio de Janeiro, provided so many proofs of being a perfect master of the art of carving busts that he practically freed the model of the sacrifice of posing for him. He needed only to observe a face for ten minutes in order to reproduce it instantly with a realism considered almost unbearable. To the extent that certain of his bronzes and marbles breathed, suffering from a pain that the medium of the material employed had no way of expressing.

Borelli arrived in Trindade the next morning, on the first bus. Exhausted from the trip, he complained of the lack of an airport.

"It doesn't seem as though this city were a part of Brazil! Where else has anyone seen a city that doesn't have a single place for planes to land? How, then, can Trindade have men who deserve to have their busts in the public square?"

His arrogance irritated Virgílio. Once he had a look, however, at Borelli's bearlike hands, he was moved. They were surely the hands of an artist, capable of doing battle with the signs of eternity. It was necessary to have patience with creatures such as this, touched by grace.

With an understanding quite out of the ordinary, he smiled at Borelli. If life created rough spots for the sculptor, he intended to protect him during his stay in Trindade.

"I want to go back to Rio by car. I'm no longer young enough to take my chances on the road in buses," Borelli said.

Ready and willing to obey his wishes, Virgílio demanded in return the strictest discretion. He was not to reveal to Joaquim the reason for his visit. They would surprise him. In any case, Joaquim was an odd sort.

Borelli rebelled. He would not agree to keep his status as a famous artist secret. He himself had ordered his name and the titles attributed to him printed on his visiting card.

Convinced finally by an additional check, Borelli agreed to pass himself off as a refrigerator salesman. For a long time now, the refrigerator at Seu Joaquim's had been defrosting without warning.

As soon as he had opened the door to let Borelli in, Joaquim ordered him to leave. It was no use coming to him with sales pitches. On the eve of his ninetieth birthday, he had no need of a new refrigerator. There wouldn't be enough years of his life left to wear it out.

"If I'm already having so much trouble leaving life behind on account of all these useless furnishings, how would I sleep forever knowing that I'm leaving behind a yellow refrigerator, the color of gold, that preserves all the food in the world? Food I won't have time to eat!"

Zealously carrying out his mission, Borelli persisted, without hiding his embarrassment. An artist like him had not come from Rio de Janeiro to fill such an inelegant role.

Admitted into the kitchen, he hastily inspected the refrigerator. He didn't even open the door, with its visible rust spots. He was already on his way out, after a fleeting look at Joaquim, when the latter stopped him.

"Where do you think you're going? Before you leave, show me that you know more about refrigerators than I do." And he grabbed his arm in a tight grip.

Borelli struggled against the old man's powerful tongs.

"Let me go. Who do you think I am?"

"An impostor and a liar. Who's been staring at me insistently ever since he came into this house. Have you been hired to kill me?"

Joaquim eyed his every move. He feared the revolver hidden somewhere on him.

"Confess, you chicken thief! Aren't you ashamed of killing an old man like me?"

Borelli could not bear the humiliation. Ever since his first trip to Italy, he had packed pride in his luggage as an essential part of the role of an artist. Wherever he went, he moved his head in a gesture that reminded him of Julius Caesar in marble in the gardens of Hadrian's Villa. He often appropriated memories of Bernini, and strolled about Florence with them tucked under his arm, as though it were up to him to safeguard the glories of a chisel that had been able to bring the cold marble of Carrara to life.

He decided, then, to use the whip that best suited the occasion.

"Do you think you own the world just because they're going to pay you homage with a bronze bust of yourself?" In his vehemence he spattered a shower of saliva along with his words. Out of control, his voice resounded even in the garden.

"What bust are you talking about?" Joaquim's eyes, opened wide, were proof of his innocence. The man wasn't lying.

Joaquim looked around for his cane. Ridiculed in his own house, he had to pay back the insult. Borelli foresaw a blow on the head, with fatal consequences. He headed for the door as Joaquim dragged himself along behind him. The sculptor's body was already halfway out the door when he turned around.

"Thanks to my talent, you're not going to be forgotten. And you can thank your lucky stars that I won't make you uglier than you already are."

Hurriedly summoned, Polidoro listened to his father's scurrilous words. The old man could not bear the idea of being turned into a bronze bust that would only serve as a target for the droppings of the damned pigeons that fouled the benches in the main square of Trindade.

"What have I done to make them get back at me that way?" Exhausted from the effort, he collapsed in the easy chair. "What's more, that confounded tenth-rate sculptor is going to make me uglier than I am. Why didn't they cast my face in bronze when I was twenty!"

And, apparently sobbing, he covered his face with his hands. Polidoro knelt at his side. Joaquim raised his head. Without fear of his son's meticulous scrutiny, he sighed.

"Ah, Polidoro, you don't know what old age is. To be ashamed of one's body, of all these loose folds of skin. When somebody looks at me, I hurt all over."

Polidoro felt inept. He did not know how to console someone in distress. As hard as rock, he had failed to give anyone in this world proof of unpremeditated love. His own father had brought him up in a way that had abolished all demonstrations of feeling.

He awkwardly patted the old man's shoulder. "I too have begun to age, Father."

Joaquim looked at him. There was no comfort in that tense face. Polidoro felt he'd been naïve to try to cheer him up with a useless example. He could not withstand the severity of that gaze.

"The ceremony in your honor will be a quick one, Father. But if you prefer, I'll send Pentecostes and Virgílio to your house with the bust in their hands, and we'll stick it in the garden," he said nervously, already on his feet.

Joaquim got out of the chair without his son's help. He seemed not to be able to see him. He now walked with firm steps to the door that led to the bedrooms. From there he raised his cane on high. The gesture took in the entire room.

"Do you want to know something? Stick the bust up your ass." And he disappeared down the hall, without giving his son time to feel pity for his slow gait.

"What shall I do about Seu Joaquim?" Ernesto persisted, standing in the middle of the street.

Polidoro gave a shrug. To all appearances, Joaquim held to life by a thread, and by memories steeped in bitter displeasures. He could still see his father's member, in front of the mirror, swinging back and forth, withered and defenseless.

"Do whatever he wants." And he headed for the hotel.

Ernesto's feelings were hurt. "Have you forgotten that I was your musketeer in the old days and rescued you from dangers?"

Polidoro willed himself to recall the vital instinct that in bygone days had made them roam all through Trindade in search of adventures and magnificent, moist virgins.

"I'm just a cattle rancher who makes his living from cow's milk and manure," he whispered, stepping up his pace, not wanting to hear the voices inside him or break the strange spell that had brought him, from the depths of his memory, the vision of those musketeers ready to risk their lives for the queen. "Besides, where is the queen?"

Ernesto perked up. "The queen will come back some day. Don't lose hope."

At the mention of a crowned feminine head, Polidoro shivered. He made his face a blank. Ernesto did not have the right to lay claim to any of his dreams.

"What's the matter?" Ernesto asked dolefully, seeing the hostile expression on his friend's face.

"Didn't you have the feeling that this morning's wind was bringing bad omens?"

He assumed a gentler expression, in an attempt to bring Ernesto back to his everyday life. The pharmacist's credulity, however, plunged him into mystery once again.

"Or was it only to my ear that the wind whinnied like a wild colt?"

Polidoro's confidence comforted Ernesto. He wanted to pay him back by sharing secrets with him that would provoke his sensibility. "Vivina too. She woke me up in the middle of the night to warn me that something was about to happen in Trindade. And just to keep me on tenterhooks, she closed her eyes, turning a deaf ear to my insistence. It was only after breakfast that she decided to say anything. Do you know what she told me?"

"Kindly shut your trap!" Polidoro shouted, his legs braced.

Held fast by his domestic memories, Ernesto went on.

"Ever since we've been married, Vivina has had visions. And so, when she confessed that she had dreamed of a woman who had wings on her back and spit out gold coins, a real cornucopia, I shuddered. I ran to have a look at the calendar. But the children had torn off several pages, and we were already at next Friday." Vivina's message escaped Ernesto's grasp when he tried to catch it. He couldn't make out the meaning of it.

Polidoro anxiously grabbed him by the wrist. "Why did it take you all these years to tell me about Vivina's visions?"

"You wouldn't have believed me. What would make you accept the fact that women have extraordinary intuition? And that they were priestesses and members of religious castes at the beginning of several civilizations? Perhaps that's why even today they

lack any notion of the boundary between ordinary household objects and those that are sacred. The two sorts are all mixed up in
the kitchen, in the living room, and in bed. The divinities of
women participate in the daily life of the house, even when it
comes time to season the beans."

Though he was deeply impressed by the message, Polidoro was
in a hurry to get to the Palace Hotel. Assuming an eloquent
attitude, Ernesto threatened to follow him in.

Polidoro cut his gesture short. He needed to knock on the
door of his own heart, without witnesses. He went off by himself,
not noticing Ernesto's disappointment.

THE PALACE HOTEL was ten minutes away from the Bom
Espírito pharmacy. At every alcoholic ruckus in the bar, Ernesto
came running, to be of help.

"Pharmacists are consultants to the human soul, in the absence
of a priest or a doctor. In return for the injections we give, those
who are suffering empty out their bile and tragedies on us."

The Palace, facing the main square, was in sharp contrast to
the other buildings on the block, because of its splendor. The
architecture, inspired by the French style of the early years of the
century, had its origin in the decision of a man from São Paulo
who had arrived in Trindade at the end of the 1920s. By nature a
restless sort, he immediately gave signs of wanting to stay forever.
In a few weeks, challenging the opposition of certain citizens, he
drew up plans for the hotel.

Joaquim was the first to instill in his son, then a small boy,
the idea of the dangers represented by the Paulista. He accused
the architect, as he ate, of settling in Trindade because of the
impulses of a perverse and enigmatic heart.

"That sort of man, driven by a murderous ambition, rides roughshod over Brazil. He wants to strip us of our possessions with that disreputable progress he represents."

Joaquim's unexpected reaction went beyond a mere defense of the local economy. He regarded the subject as a matter of honor.

In order to calm him down, Magnólia offered him sugar water. The mixture, fitting and proper for young ladies, offended him. Especially when his wife described the Paulista in minute detail, doffing his hat to her the moment he saw her in public places. A compliment that made no distinction on the basis of race, money, or religious belief. Not to mention his three-piece suits imported from Paris, which gave rise to arguments and disagreements.

"It's one more reason to drive him out. That Paulista wants to turn us into repulsive dandies. That's what you want too, Magnólia."

The look in Joaquim's eye gave his wife the rare opportunity to declare her love for him. In order to shield the family, she was supposed to insinuate, in the presence of the children, that she had in the house, and particularly in her bed, a man who kept her from having to resort to others' fantasies in order to be happy.

She fled her husband's gaze by furiously dusting the furniture. Accustomed to his easily wounded susceptibilities, she put an end to them by serving a meal with an abundance of spicy dishes.

The family controversy fascinated Polidoro. The Paulista's prestige managed to rock the foundations of a marriage based on an imperturbable daily routine. He had been looking for a long time, as an adolescent, for a legendary figure who would cross the desert, the Amazon Basin, in a khaki outfit, boots, and a horsewhip, without making the least effort or giving up his gallant poses. And who would emerge from such regions only for the pleasure of telling stories never before heard by human ears. A man who, despite visiting stopping-off places where death, amid the exuberant chlorophyll, was sovereign, serenely lay his head down on the pillow at night, without fear of the residual traces of dreams that would linger in his imagination.

Unlike his father, who was acquainted only with cows, the

Paulista had a store of wisdom that opened his visor for him; through it he caught a glimpse of another world, outside of Trindade.

Each day, when he got out of school, Polidoro watched the building going up. Thanks to the Paulista's energy, the bricks, joined one to another, gradually formed endless walls. As he contemplated the construction, Polidoro sometimes forgot that danger might be lurking.

"This time I've caught you playing hooky," his father said, sneaking up on him and threatening to punish him. Above all, his son ought not to ally himself with his father's enemies.

As he spoke, Joaquim kept close watch on the movements of the workers brought in from neighboring towns. "What good is a hotel of this size to us? Are we going to fill the rooms with gamblers, whores, and bandits?" he muttered, forgetting that his son could overhear him.

When he referred to the stranger, Joaquim never mentioned him by name. He called him "Bandeirante," an exploiter of the hinterland, to make fun of him. To entice the others to join his cause, he suggested that Bandeirante had come to Trindade after being driven out of São Paulo.

On a certain sunny Sunday, there was a knock on Joaquim's door. He had decided, that very morning, to conduct a searching investigation of his offspring and his wife, who had long been going adrift.

"Well, then, Magnólia, aren't you going to open the door?"

Attending to her household duties, his wife had not heard his directions. Perhaps she was in the henhouse, collecting the eggs— a task that she never turned over to the children. A systematic observer of details, Magnólia took care to examine the blood-stained shell of the valiant hen. And in her eagerness to ennoble the creature, she spoke of it as though it were a sister brought down by the rigors of a war.

Unresponsive to her arguments, Joaquim retorted: "And what does a hen suffer that a woman doesn't? You, who've already given birth, ought to know how much it hurts to push a baby's head out!"

Joaquim headed for the door. People gave him no rest, even on Sundays.

"It's me," the Paulista said. Dressed in boots and breeches, just dismounted from a light-colored bay left at the door, he carefully adjusted his riding cap, a kind that Joaquim had seen only in foreign magazines, which rarely came his way.

Joaquim hesitated. Since the Paulista's foot was already on the doorsill, it seemed to Joaquim that it would be hard to expel the intruder.

"You may come in," he said stiffly, "but on condition that you keep track of the length of your visit by watching the hand of the clock that goes around the fastest."

He motioned to him to sit down in the overstuffed chair, whose semiexposed springs respected no one's backside. The room, with few adornments, looked like a cloister. Its most impressive piece of furniture was the dining-room table, which had drawers and bowed legs of surprisingly careful workmanship.

The Paulista seated himself with indifferent elegance, giving no signs of suffering. His legs put down roots in the freshly washed floor.

"Very well, the time of your visit has already begun," Joaquim reminded him, fascinated by his polished boots. His intention was to upset the visitor, to break the magic spell that he was trying to cast over Joaquim's family. The visitor leaned his body in Joaquim's direction, without violating the politeness learned in a lordly manor house in São Paulo. His eyes, fixed on his host, devoured the latter's feelings. For a few moments, the life of both of them seemed to slip uselessly away.

"I didn't come to bring progress, Seu Joaquim. Progress is an illusion. And I'm no longer taken in by idle boasts," he finally said.

Joaquim feared that the varnish of words of arrogant urban origin would crush a man with a rural background.

"Be more direct," he replied coldly.

"What I'm trying to say is that the hotel is an illusion for me and for you." After this confession, he assumed once again, with relief, his initial position, leaning back in the chair.

"Don't include me on the list of those hopeless people," Joaquim protested. His strident voice echoed all through the room. Magnólia could hear it.

"You're right. Every illusion robs us of half an inch of our guts. And since I don't know how many feet we have at our disposal, we'd better not sacrifice a single bit of them. For precisely this reason: how are we going to shit without them?" The moment he made use of this surprising language, the Paulista scrutinized Joaquim.

Joaquim's sensibility, governed by the dung of the countryside, resisted the siege of the Paulista, who had just challenged him in his own language, merely to convince him that they belonged to the same spiritual family.

Urged to give up his own dreams, the Paulista decided to fight.

"On the other hand, illusion is the best of remedies. It's a temptation that has its price, and that I'm prepared to pay. I shall disclose to you, then, that, the more deceptions and fictions I construct in front of the main square of Trindade, the better it will be for all of us, including you."

After getting this off his chest, the Paulista sized up his adversary. He bore a tortoiseshell on his back, and in the design of the shell the marks of a thousand years of resistance. The flesh he carried about inside could not be seen.

Joaquim took a roll of tobacco out of his pocket. Before slicing it on the table with his knife, he breathed in the smell of it. He noted that the Paulista, glued to the chair, was forgetting to consult the clock on the wall, which stood next to the commode from Minas. The hands were moving forward in their usual rhythm.

Bandeirante rose to his feet, and looked his host up and down. Joaquim had no idea why a choreography alien to his interests should be forced on him in his own house.

"Did you know that Fernão Paes Leme, the mythical hero of the backlands, ordered his own son killed?" The Paulista gave the impression of speaking candidly about a member of Joaquim's own family.

"Why?" Joaquim asked, startled.

"On account of the emeralds. He had to choose between the stones and his son," the Paulista replied, overwhelmed by pity now.

Joaquim asked permission to go around the man, who was blocking his way. Bandeirante let him pass with a gesture of sheer elegance. By acting as the master of the house, he forced Joaquim to thank him.

At the window, Joaquim took a deep breath. He returned immediately, reinvigorated. But the moment before, he had examined the portrait on the wall out of the corner of his eye. His children and their cousins in a mixed group, dressed in their best clothes, on the occasion of a baptism. Making certain that they all belonged to the family line, he suffered the shock arising from the sense of human community—he had been forced all of a sudden, because of an unexpected act of fate, to use a dagger against a member of his own family. It seemed to him that he saw blood alongside the dust on the floor.

The shadow of Fernão Paes Leme pursued Joaquim. In all of the history of Brazil, he had never heard of such a barbaric case. To him, such incidents could happen only in neighboring countries, of savage ferocity, given to decimating whole families. At the same time, the story served to enhance the evil profile of the Paulista. He was certain that the man had invented the story in order to deprive him of the advantage of being in his own house and, hence, in a position to throw an intruder out.

He cut other chunks off the roll with his knife. His fingers slowly shredded the tobacco over the transparent paper. Confident of each gesture, he rolled it back and forth a number of times, till the cigarette was the right shape. With his rough tongue, he spread a thin thread of saliva across the edge of the bit of paper. Then, laying the cigarette down on the edge of the table, he gave a satisfied sigh.

"It must not have been easy for that Fernão fellow, right?" He looked at the stranger as though seeing him for the first time.

Joaquim's gentle tone of voice seemed to reveal a long friendship with the stranger. The Paulista was not fooled. He must swiftly return the lance thrust of the astute cattle rancher.

Joaquim foresaw the defeat of the Paulista. And he magnanimously readied himself to allow him to remain in the house a few minutes more, so as to make his words wither away and imprint upon his face an irremovable disillusionment. Only in that way, in defeat, would he leave Trindade.

The two men eyed each other amid a solemn suspicion, paying no heed to the sounds produced now by the presence of Magnólia in the room.

"Ah, I didn't know we had a visitor!" The woman set the platter on the table, without looking at the stranger.

The intrusion destroyed the reigning tension. Annoyed, Joaquim gestured to his wife to leave the room. Magnólia, paying no attention to her husband, finally realized, to her surprise, that a total stranger was present: a character whom she had never imagined in her living room, bare of decorations. In her sudden shyness, her body took on a feline grace.

Joaquim noted the change, the solemnity that should be employed only when dealing with the members of the imperial family, who lived in Petrópolis.

"There's no need to put on airs, Magnólia," he announced unceremoniously. "This man is as plebian as we are. He's come from São Paulo, bringing a strongbox full of money." Feigning cordiality, he consulted the visitor. "Isn't it true that you decided to spend the money like the old-time gold prospectors of the Amazon, who lit their cheroots with banknotes worth a thousand *réis?*"

The target of Joaquim's sarcasm, the Paulista, who had introduced himself to Magnólia as Antunes, was relieved. The woman's presence had brought an end to an unfavorable situation. Gratefully, he outdid himself in offering the two of them polite compliments. He paid particular attention to Joaquim.

"You are the one citizen in Trindade to have a sense of reality. I can imagine how difficult it is for you to fall asleep at night when you have a burden such as that on your chest. Isn't it true, Seu Joaquim, that it pains you to be so realistic?"

The words of the Paulista, regarded by her husband as an angel of evil, charmed Magnólia. This man, despite the burden of the fortune he possessed, humbly sat down in the middle of the living room of people as simple as they were, without the least display of false pride. On the contrary, he begged Joaquim's indulgence for any disturbance he might have caused him.

Joaquim tried to interrupt him. Antunes, however, launched into another speech, equally captivating.

"As for myself, I have chosen to remain on the opposite bank of the river, watching reality pass by, as though I were not part of it. For that reason, I need to have recourse to those who—like yourself, sir—are valiant and levelheaded."

Without ridding Joaquim of his fear, he turned to Magnólia.

"May I present my sincerest compliments to Senhora Álves?"

A sentence merely for the sake of politeness: before Joaquim had granted him such a favor, he had not only grabbed Magnólia's hand, but bent toward her from the waist as well, in a bow never before seen in the city.

Such a gesture immediately took Magnólia back to the silver screen of the movie theaters, when Jeanette MacDonald and Nelson Eddy, absorbed in passionate gestures, could scarcely conceal the love they felt, despite its overlay of sin. A passion that had always succeeded in bringing tears to Magnólia's eyes, to the point where Joaquim, in the darkened theater, gave her a jab with his elbow, on the pretext that she would compromise his honor in public. For how could his wife be carried away by the feelings of two lovers who were harming society? Once they got home, he upbraided her for her lack of moral chastity.

She had openly defied him.

"Instead of blaming me, why not imitate them? Don't you see that Trindade lacks men who revere women?"

Magnólia was at last making her dream come true in full view of her husband—and thanks to the stranger, who did not restrain himself from showing in public his admiration for women, those creatures that brought with them, beneath their apparent fragility, the shadow of tragedy, typical of Greek heroes.

She watched her husband out of the corner of her eye. It was taking him some time to get over the scene. Still imprinted on his retina was the image of the Paulista venerating his wife as though she were a saint that Rome had recently enthroned. And all to answer a request that Magnólia, in the intimacy of their bedroom, never failed to ask of Joaquim, once she saw that he was satisfied after having fulfilled his conjugal duties.

Magnólia eagerly approached the stranger, admiring his riding habit. She immediately pointed to the table.

"It's lunchtime. We insist that you eat with us. It's home cooking, but it's been carefully prepared."

Spurred on by the invitation, Antunes walked through the room, never losing sight of Joaquim.

"With the greatest of pleasure, Dona Magnólia. That is to say, if Seu Joaquim doesn't mind having a Paulista at his table."

Before Joaquim could reply, Antunes pushed a chair to the right side of one of the ends of the table. He was cheered by the smells coming from the kitchen, from which he could not predict the dishes that would be served, except for the beans, whose odor arrived in the room intact, after traveling through the kitchen and the hallway—a dish whose flavor was enhanced by garlic, bay leaf, dried beef, pig's feet, potatoes, bacon, pig's tails, all the salty bits forming a harmonious combination just to awaken one's appetite. He realized then that he was hungry. He had arisen very early and forgotten to have coffee at the boarding house in his concern over the forthcoming visit.

Magnólia set the platters out on the table all at once, so that the food wouldn't get cold. Though she was a good cook, she did not vary the menu. Joaquim, conservative by nature, would not have allowed her any culinary ambition. He was suspicious of copious menus, which, leaving room for imagination, seasoned dishes on the pretext that it gave them exotic flavors. If the fare wasn't Minas regional cooking, he scowled.

Magnólia called her husband and children to the table, but Joaquim would not sit down with them. Installed in the easy chair, he stubbornly refused to take a place next to the children. Perhaps he hoped that the family, in their distress, would plead with him to join them. Or give him, in the presence of the Paulista, exuberant proofs of their love, of which he was in dire need.

At the head of the table, next to the guest, Magnólia did not immediately catch her husband's signals. She did not seem to understand the man with whom she had lived for so many years.

Antunes's impatience on seeing the platters before him led him to rub his hands together in anticipation of the pleasure that the meal would offer him.

"So, Seu Joaquim, aren't you inspired yet to come to the table? Look, the food is getting cold." His voice came out well modulated, so as not to hurt the crystal eardrums of the other man.

Magnólia's smile bared a molar with a gold cap. Antunes suspected that the woman was pleased to show off a sign of wealth that at the same time enhanced her beauty.

Joaquim hesitated. Bandeirante, besides disregarding the overall plan for the city and threatening them with a luxury that to them was unthinkable, was invading his house, exacting food from him, and stealing from him his wife's smile and the pleasure of his children's company, submerged as they were in the sphere of admiration that the Paulista was arousing. A spell from which not even Polidoro, a standoffish sort, was escaping.

In those brief instants, he searched his own heart. Inclined in general to blaspheme against anybody and everybody, he restrained himself in the Paulista's presence. Sentences in Antunes's mouth had an almost musical rhythm and prosody. Some of the notes stuck in his memory.

He was unable to go on feeling rancor toward the man. Moreover, he was attracted by anyone who asked him for a plateful of food. Here was a man who, driven by desperation, lived in need of human company. And who, by devoting all his energies to the art of getting rich, had ended up living with no one but the dregs of society. Not to mention his having inherited, as a native of the state of São Paulo—whose separatist bent had always fought for the creation of another country inside of Brazil—that dramatic feeling of repudiating his native land. Hence, without ever finding the time to make a family, he devoted himself to attracting to his solitary, sweating bosom humanity in general, represented first and foremost by the workers who worked on his building projects.

Magnólia went on with the meal, paying no attention to him,

busy keeping order among the members of her undisciplined family. Indifferent, all of them, to their father's lot. Only Bandeirante, of everyone in the room, depended on him in order to survive. Perhaps the Paulista wanted to beg his pardon for abusing his hospitality. Though Joaquim could understand him better now. At an early age, Antunes had gone out into the world in search of what men, with hope in their mouths, call love. As he sought, then, a dwelling place for his weary bones, anyone could see that he was close to exhaustion, about to collapse unless they offered him warm milk, homemade food with a high proportion of lard, and fresh hay in the stable on which to lay his head till death, a beneficent huntress, came looking for him. He feared, however, that those generous measures had come his way too late. Antunes's soul, saturated with pain and fat, had grown as rigid as the skin of a drum, and there was no help for him now.

Meanwhile, on that sunny Sunday, he had come to the house of Joaquim, a man who was obviously impulsive but magnanimous, to ask him, in the name of Christian charity, to prolong his life. Who in Trindade offered more food to the poor than Magnólia? A lady with the name and behavior of a flower, capable of giving up her own happy lot in life, and her bread, in order to save a city. A city doomed to luxury, to waste and sin, thanks to Bandeirante, who had arrived under false pretenses so that they would not notice his presence, despite the important sums he'd spent buying the plot of land that faced the main square. In fact, would it be an exaggeration to imagine that Trindade, like Brazil itself, was severely threatened by English creditors, owners of half the country, and by men like Antunes?

The smell of the bean stew entered Joaquim's uncultured nose. His stomach was undergoing pitiless agony. Nonetheless, the return to the bosom of the family might signify a moral weakness. They had just demonstrated that they did not depend on him to live.

But that certainty, although it displeased him, also gave him the courage to occupy the last vacant chair at the table. He decided to challenge Antunes.

"Let's see if he's skinny because he dreams so much or because he scorns the food of ordinary people." The authoritarian gesture with which he grabbed his fork freed Antunes of the obligation to answer.

Magnólia suddenly lost the spontaneity that had enlivened her. Immersed in doubt, she didn't know whom to serve first. She was afraid that her husband, carried away by jealousy, might ignore the laws of hospitality. She was so perplexed that she just sat impassively in the high-backed chair.

Polidoro noted how ill-at-ease his mother was. Sitting alongside his father, he pulled on the sparse hairs of his beard. His mother's hands, trembling slightly, were holding up, with difficulty, the platter piled high with beefsteaks alla milanese.

Suddenly Polidoro held his empty plate out to her. "May I be the first one served today?"

Joaquim's face flushed. His son failed to show respect for him in the presence of strangers. Greed, stored up in his children, constituted a threat against him. He ought to take precautions. As soon as he spied a dull look in their eyes making murderous designs visible in the iris, he would hasten to punish them.

Since Magnólia failed to react to the plate that her son had held out to her, Joaquim showed the Paulista the sharply honed edge of the carving knife, exactly the right tool for cutting up roast chickens on Sundays, in a clear demonstration that he had his family under control.

"Did you know that the Italian popes who had taken refuge in the south of France made the cardinals eat at separate tables at mealtime? And that the popes forbade them to use knives, out of fear of being assassinated by them?" Joaquim said, pointing at his son. To all appearances, he patiently tolerated certain acts of insubordination.

"Excuse my son. He was born with as impetuous a nature as mine. From his mother he inherited melancholy, which I have never felt, not even when I lost a number of heads of cattle last time the river flooded over. I only hope he doesn't cultivate illusions, the way *you* do."

Magnólia served her son and in the same generous spirit prepared the guest's plate. She placed the rice and the chopped cabbage alongside the beans as she made room for the chunks of salted meat and the toasted manioc. The plateful grew higher and higher beneath the greedy gaze of the others.

"Help yourself to the pepper powder, but be careful, because it's very hot. It was given to me by a woman from Recôncavo, in Bahia, who can spend hours describing the pepper plants that she was familiar with before coming to Trindade on a trip."

She was careful not to overturn the plate. She had gone too far in staging a spectacle that fraternally united the starving people of the earth around her table. She happily calmed the children down, so they wouldn't choke on the manioc flour.

Antunes brought the beans to his mouth with his eyes closed. His discreet smacking of his tongue cleared his palate. Pleasure radiated all through his body in a red glow. He had forgotten that he had company at the table till Joaquim cleared his throat.

Embarrassed, the Paulista reduced the size of his forkfuls and chewed slowly, as though he didn't appreciate the meal. But as Magnólia urged him on and kept supplying him with more food, he became enthusiastic again.

"What marvelous pepper powder! It's an invention of the gods. It's like going through the antechamber of passion without the threat of being banished from it."

Being in the habit of creating images, he kept talking as he downed one forkful after another.

"Have you ever chewed a pepper with your teeth? It's like suffering a sweet death. In return, one comes to know the state of grace. And, doubtless, the spice of passion."

Joaquim pushed the food on his plate around with his bread, which was ready to fall to bits between his teeth, as his wife, who appeared anxious, kept a close watch on him. Antunes again turned his attention to her husband.

"As for the popes, Seu Joaquim, they were right to be on their guard. Otherwise they would have had poison poured into their wine goblets. It was only their mistrust that saved their lives and their power. That's the reason they held out for centuries in Avignon and Rome. And each century was more murderous than the one before."

He turned to Magnólia. "How do you think the cardinals reacted to papal discourtesy?"

She stalled for time, cutting the beefsteak alla milanese in tiny pieces.

"Magnólia is timid," Joaquim said, waving his knife and fork in the air. "What's more, I'm the pope in this house. Isn't that so, Magnólia?"

Polidoro laughed along with his father. This was Joaquim's way of publicly demonstrating that, if given an incentive by his family, he could be brilliant. Joaquim's vanity fed on such details.

"If he's the pope in Trindade, why wouldn't he be the supreme pontiff in his own home?" Antunes said.

Seized by the desire for vengeance, which he had not buried beneath the copious repast, Joaquim turned to the Paulista.

"And how is the construction work going? Will the hotel really get built, or will it be like the unfinished symphony of that Russian composer?"

Magnólia gave a start. Her husband was covering her with humiliation and shame, and she did not know how to protect him from his own impudence. He was unwilling to measure precisely the limited knowledge that he possessed. He kept belching up notions whose source was an alchemy produced by luck and destiny.

The Paulista's face showed no emotion, as Magnólia cast her sorrow into her crumpled napkin.

"It wasn't Tchaikovsky who left an unfinished symphony. In any case, he needed time to complete other work," she said.

"That may well be," her husband answered irritatedly. "There's so much information around nowadays that I don't know how to free my family from the plague of ignorance."

Antunes praised the beefsteak alla milanese to the skies, as a subtle way of thanking Magnólia for her hospitality. And, to prove that he harbored no hurt feelings, he smiled at Joaquim.

"Culture without kindness is a useless adornment," he pontificated.

After a strategic pause, he went on with renewed strength.

"You will be my guests on the day of the official opening of the hotel. I insist on reserving you a suite on the fifth floor on the very first night. You'll sleep in a bed intended for foreign tycoons. From that floor you can see every last house in Trinidade. The view is so panoramic that it takes in part of the Suspiro estate, which belongs to you, doesn't it? I set aside that apartment for my own use. A bachelor like me needs to have a home. I guarantee you'll be happy in those quarters; they get the morning sun."

Joaquim admired his cunning. He carried delicate weapons in his belt, in case of an affront. He was in no hurry to attack. On the contrary, he decanted time so that the minutes would mature slowly, turning gold in the sun like white grapes.

Magnólia brought from the kitchen another pitcher of maracock juice. The fragrance of it, slightly intoxicating, cleared the atmosphere. Her husband's silence, however, indicated to her that he hadn't yet made up his mind about the invitation.

In her eagerness to save the Sunday dinner from ending up a failure, Magnólia solemnly sat down.

"Nothing will give us greater pleasure, Seu Antunes. Isn't that so, Joaquim?"

He drank his maracock juice down in one gulp, cleaning his vocal cords of the detritus that dulled his voice and impeded his breathing.

Antunes feared that a conjugal disagreement was imminent.

"From now on, call me Bandeirante." Seeing Joaquim's amazement, he explained: "That was what they called my forebears, a mixture of natives of São Paulo and Portuguese who were murderers and lyric poets at the same time. Beginning with Fernão Paes Leme. People who killed other people, supposedly over gold and land, as they were transmitting to those of mixed blood the spirit of the new race. Thanks to those men, meddlesome intruders, we became the country of the future. If it hadn't been for them, Brazil today would be the size of France. And with unstable borders in the bargain. Surrounded by enemies, we could hardly manage to get a night's sleep."

And before Joaquim could get over the shock of seeing the

nickname that he himself had given the Paulista come to light in his very house, Antunes responded to the interest shown by Polidoro.

"Some day, you too will be happy in my hotel. Isn't that all anybody wants out of life?" Stricken by an irrepressible memory, he hid part of his face in his napkin.

Polidoro sat up straight in his chair, haughtily.

"I'd rather be your associate, Seu Antunes."

Before Joaquim could check his son's impulse, the Paulista perked up.

"So you want to be my associate? Maybe I'll leave you half the rooms in my will. What floor do you prefer?"

"The apartment on the fifth floor. I want to look at the Suspiro estate from there, since it's going to be mine some day," he said, so resolutely that Joaquim froze, not moving a muscle.

"Before that, however, we have a problem," Antunes said anxiously. "The hotel doesn't have a name yet. How about baptizing it right now?"

Polidoro consulted his mother. With her hands resting on the table, Magnólia winked at him, delighted to be participating in a festive occasion taking place in her heart and the heart of her son.

Polidoro had always dreamed of journeying across the Indian Ocean. In his mind's eye, he could see on these distant voyages women wearing fur coats and raising to their lips glasses of sparkling wine. These images were invariably scenes and details taken from his reading of popular almanacs. It was time, then, to make his desires a reality.

"I already know what we're going to call it: the Palace. That's it, the Palace Hotel."

"But what lack of imagination," Joaquim protested, his son having neglected to ask his opinion. "There's a Palace Hotel in every city in the world!"

Under his mother's protection, Polidoro stood up to his father.

"That's the only thing it can be called."

"And why do we want a palace in Trindade? Its only use would be to keep prisoners in their dungeons," Joaquim said rudely, in the face of the threat from the ambitious Paulista.

"That palace will befriend travelers. It's not being built at the cost of the people's bloodshed." Antunes answered, ignoring Joaquim's moods.

Taking no part in the argument, Magnólia dreamed of monuments that had taken shape in close alliance with eternity. From the photographs that she had seen, those buildings, in their beauty, bade farewell to the duties of this earth and kept human works as a souvenir.

"Beautiful words, Seu Antunes," she said between one sigh and another.

The lethargy brought on by the heavy meal swimming in fat was taking its toll. Joaquim thought the time had come to end the lunch, although Magnólia was ill-humoredly stirring the milk custard with a spoon, as though she were still in the kitchen fighting to keep the milk from curdling.

"It's naptime, Seu Antunes."

Antunes prepared to leave, followed by Polidoro.

"Where are you going, son?" Joaquim said with rare politeness.

Polidoro asked for his father's blessing. He made a move to accompany Bandeirante to the front door. Antunes, for his part, certain that he was facing Magnólia at the head of the table, made the same bow as when he had arrived. Only later did he perceive that she had left the room without saying goodbye.

The useless gesture brought an ironic smile to Joaquim's lips, baring his teeth yellowed by tobacco smoke. Having seen the Paulista blunder, he called to Polidoro:

"Visit Seu Antunes's palace. Isn't that where he promised you that you'd be happy? I only hope that that happiness comes in the form of a woman. As a matter of fact, it's the one form that's of any interest."

Forcing a laugh, he bade Bandeirante farewell at the front door of the house.

POLIDORO headed for the reception desk of the hotel. Mágico was waiting for him, making obvious his disapproval of Polidoro's turning up late for the first time in many years. Dressed in a heavy dark suit with an ash-gray vest, Mágico was pretending to be suffering from the rigors of winter.

He disliked talking. He considered it part of his duty to save his vocal cords, so as to use them on guests of unquestionable prestige. He never defined the criteria he used in establishing such principles. He merely scrutinized the guests with an intolerant eye, looking them over from head to foot, classifying them on the basis of everything from their shoes to their toilet water.

On catching sight of Polidoro, he removed his watch from his pocket without consulting it. He did so deliberately, to make him feel bad. Polidoro, however, ignored the gesture, and leaned on the counter.

"Good afternoon," he said, as though he didn't know Mágico, employing a ritual between them that had long since become hallowed.

"It's a good thing it hasn't rained. There won't be a single vacant room this weekend," Mágico said pompously, forcing Polidoro to believe that the establishment, though suffering the ravages of time, still attracted venturesome travelers and honeymoon couples.

Mágico lied for the sake of defending the honor of the hotel. And because he disguised the death throes of an establishment still alive in his heart too, Polidoro kept him on at the reception desk, forgiving him for his petulance.

"Any day now we'll build another floor just to keep up with the demand," Polidoro said, forestalling the usual question.

Mágico was aware that he owed Polidoro his job and admitted to himself that he never thanked him for the checks he received from him at Christmastime.

"It remains to be seen whether the foundations will support the weight of a sixth floor."

Polidoro placed his hands on the counter as Mágico, avoiding his eye, inspected his fingernails, painted with colorless nail polish.

"Has any mail come for me?" Polidoro asked, ill-at-ease.

Mágico knew the sentences by heart. The rhythm, the labored breath with which they were uttered. For the last twenty years, always in that same position, Polidoro had gathered his strength together to repeat them as night fell and the lobby was plunged into semidarkness, since it never occurred to Mágico to turn on the splendid crystal chandelier hanging from the arched ceiling.

Mágico opened the right-hand drawer and rummaged through the papers, convinced that he had seen, at last, a letter addressed to Polidoro. The cattle rancher also seemed convinced that a letter for him had come in the mail, as a reward for his persistence.

With deliberate slowness, Mágico went through bills, notes, and correspondence never claimed by former guests. In this way he kept Polidoro standing at the counter for several minutes.

The disorder of the drawer leapt to the eye. Mágico's zeal, concentrated on his attire and on the building, relegated the administrative part of his job to the background. On the other hand, because of his collector's temperament he kept even the napkins on which certain guests, inspired by passion, had written down ardent phrases.

Every afternoon, Mágico pawed through the papers, in search of the desired letter. He got through them thanks to the illusion that he was discarding useless records, though he lacked the courage to throw them in the wastebasket. He went from one drawer to the next with the same results.

"This time I could have sworn we received a letter," he informed Polidoro, dejectedly.

"I'll come back tomorrow," Polidoro said, turning his back on Mágico, indifferent to there being no mail for him. He crossed the lobby, heading for the bar, and looked at the crystal chandelier from Bohemia. With the light now on, the pendants gleamed brightly.

Bandeirante, in his day, had forbidden women to visit the bar.

It had more or less the look of an English pub, for Bandeirante had decorated it in accordance with the memories he had retained of the one trip he had taken to Europe. In order to justify his not wanting women to be present amid blasphemies, alcohol, and tobacco, he resorted to a number of considerations.

"They ought not to frequent a place conceived for our male vulgarities. I'm afraid of wounding their delicate souls."

Since Antunes praised feminine virtues so highly, Joaquim was afraid that Polidoro, an adolescent still, would absorb, out of sheer envy, some of the spirit that Magnólia displayed in running the household, that inborn ability of womankind to make everything seem as if it happened by miracle. He was adamantly opposed to such demonstrations. He wished to protect his son's soul from future threats brought upon him simply because he was overly polite. Joaquim wanted to inculcate in his son a code that would prey upon him from inside. Like Carthage, covered with the salt of heroes, so as to keep flowers from budding even in vases.

When the bar had been officially opened, Joaquim had refused the Scotch that Bandeirante was offering on the house. In a certain sense, drinking whisky from Scotland placed in jeopardy their native tongue and the feelings that go with alcohol. Bandeirante, however, mindful of the protests against imported habits to the detriment of national ones, persuaded them that he had no intention of bending them to his will.

"A culture resists only when put to the test," he stated with conviction.

In the bar, Polidoro greeted Francisco. Comfortably settled in the wicker chair that was reserved more or less for his exclusive use, he observed ill-humoredly the bottles set out in disorder on the shelf. The way his shaggy eyebrows knitted together near the bridge of his nose was a sign of his embittered mood. Glued to the table, he pretended not to see Narciso the constable greeting him effusively. Francisco brought Polidoro the whisky, the ice bucket, and the bottle of mineral water, which he drank in another glass.

"Professor Virgílio has just left. He was looking for you." Francisco carefully put the ice in his glass.

"What does he want?" Polidoro asked curtly.

Francisco shifted the toothpick he'd been chewing to the other corner of his mouth. He took pleasure in this dance, twisting words around it that could scarcely be heard, a little trick of his that assured him of the privilege of avoiding, at any time, making any unseemly remark that might wound customers' feelings. His black hair, dyed blacker still, betrayed his fear of growing old. He also wore a satin waistcoat, the one article of clothing he had left from a season spent in a cabaret in the Lapa district in Rio. Every time he mentioned his adventure in the capital, tears came to his eyes.

Nobody knew Trindade as well as Francisco did. In order to keep up-to-date on other people's lives, he resorted to methods that were not always commendable. When it fell to his lot to serve a drunkard, he listened to him all night long, until he had dragged every last one of his secrets out of him. Without ever losing his enthusiasm, he resorted to every sort of cunning. Polidoro himself encouraged Francisco's shrewdness. A vocation like any other, and, furthermore, one that could be useful to him. Francisco, however, foresaw his approaching decline, old age blowing out the beacon in his lighthouse, doing away with his opportunities to listen to malcontents. Polidoro would be the first to abandon him. He had always been Francisco's most rebellious listener. When he failed to captivate his employer with his first phrase, he lost him the very next minute.

"I don't know what the professor wants, but I can guess. I guarantee it's something important." And Francisco cast a glance at him that promised the revelation of secrets hard to come by.

Polidoro felt a strange shock of fear. He controlled himself, nonetheless, in the hope of silencing the waiter.

Francisco, however, was unable to give up dwelling on the hardships of his vocation. "Ever since I came to work this morning, I've been patting my pocket the whole time. I have the feeling I've lost something of value. A ring, for example, that someone has asked me to keep for them. One that has to be restored to its owner at the end of the night. I have no idea why, Seu Polidoro, but today is different from other days. Have you noticed what the clouds look like?"

Polidoro did not encourage him to go on; he never once looked at him. Such disdain would damage the waiter's prestige unless he responded.

"The professor headed for Estação. He had on the blue suit he wears on Mondays, and his Monday cologne. He was surely on his way to the party. You know what party I'm referring to." With his usual wicked smile, Francisco looked closely at Polidoro, who was not always receptive to intimate gossip.

For the moment, Polidoro was keeping his distance from Estação—the Station—the name that Gioconda's "boarding house" went by. He had not knocked on the door of her place for two weeks now—an absence that made the women suppose that Polidoro had gone back to frequenting Dodô's bed, or else had found a new young girl on one or another of his cattle ranches. Despite his sixty years, his vigor in bed never left him lacking for women.

Taking no notice of Polidoro's indifference to this gossip, Francisco continued.

"He went, sure as shooting, to Gioconda's place. He never misses a single Monday."

He enunciated each word clearly, hinting that he knew that Polidoro had not gone there since May 18, a day that, incidentally, had been foggy and dreary. This piece of information had not come to him from Gioconda, whose memo book, in which she wrote down in minuscule handwriting the frequency of the visits of certain gentlemen to her house, she kept as secret as her very soul.

Polidoro closed his eyes, bringing the conversation to an end. Hurt by his lack of interest, Francisco looked at the wrinkles around Polidoro's puffy eyes. He saw him growing old before his very eyes, hardly in a condition to inspire another great passion in any woman in this phase of his life.

He walked slowly away, hoping to be called back. Polidoro stretched his legs out more comfortably below the table. He had not gone straight to sleep the night before, tormented by the fear of dying without seeing once again the woman whose name he took care not to utter. With every year that went by, he felt his life growing shorter.

The hand of the clock pointed to six. The stroke of the church bells pealing fell on his ears in quick succession. Gathered together in the church, the women were surely telling the beads of their rosaries with inevitable nervousness. Each bead was a plea. Polidoro was absorbed in these reflections when a sudden noise brought him to.

"Were you looking for me?" he said to Virgílio, without inviting him to sit down. The professor, leaning his body on the leg of his that was permanently out of joint at the knee, awaited the invitation. Polidoro, embarrassed by the presence of Francisco, made the gesture that promised to make amends for his initial discourtesy.

"If I had known that Virgílio was coming by, I would already have asked for another glass to be brought. We still have time to make up for the omission. What will you have to drink, Professor?"

The tactic touched Virgílio. Polidoro made others believe that he accepted Virgílio only because he could not avoid his company. Francisco had no doubt hastened to divulge the scorn of the owner of huge cattle ranches for a professor whose house was modest but filled with books, and who was lavish with his culture. Polidoro, on the other hand, a reader of popular almanacs and drugstore pamphlets, sinned out of vainglorious ignorance, depending on personal experience alone to size up the world.

"How many years has it been since anybody has asked you for a robust Portuguese wine?" To Polidoro's astonishment, the professor smiled at Francisco. "Bring us the best wine you have in that dusty cellar of yours. And one from a vintage year. Today's a holiday, even though Polidoro forgot that he invited me to have a drink on him."

Virgílio's cheekiness surprised Polidoro. The professor was not in the habit of abusing friendships. Nonetheless, Virgílio did not offer Polidoro his apologies. On the contrary, he carefully inspected the old bottle and the colored label. In the end, the ill-fated Monday, buffeted by whistling winds since the wee hours of the morning, seemed to unite them. They had to proceed with caution.

Francisco did not budge. He was afraid he'd lose out on the

secret that Virgílio was keeping for the cattle rancher's ears alone. If he, Francisco, possessed it, he would be king for a week and would feel compensated for the niggardly tips and the miserable salary he received, too little to allow him to redo the plaster of his house, which had been threatening to fall into ruins since his mother's death. Not to mention that, in recent years, nothing touched the hearts of Trindade. Ever since the advent of television soap opera serials, the neighbors had occupied themselves in forgetting their lives, embroidered once upon a time with colorful threads that went from pink to green, without scorn for the aesthetic.

Today there was not a single soul in Trindade ready and willing to commit wild follies. That duty had simply been delegated to actors. And politics itself, once a public activity, had lost its bedrock of passion after the occupation of Brasília by the military. It was even rumored that in certain large cities cruel tortures were being employed against students and communists. No one, however, believed slander that was circulating against President Médici, the most likable general of the military coup, on the eve of having his name forever associated with the forthcoming third World Cup victory of the Brazilian soccer team in Mexico City.

At home, Francisco fought against his loneliness by gathering gossip intriguing enough to spread throughout the city. This vocation caused him no remorse, since he considered it indispensable to pay attention to human actions, whether great or small. As a matter of fact, he preferred petty acts: inasmuch as their meaning was difficult to decipher. He did not see, therefore, any reason to be discreet, filing secrets away forever in strongboxes. Because of their collective nature, human deeds deserved to return to the society in whose bosom they had been engendered.

"What about the wine, Francisco? Didn't you hear what Polidoro said?" Scowling, Virgílio imitated the cattle baron.

Polidoro sat erect in his chair. He did not want to be the first one to speak. It was up to Virgílio to take the initiative. If he was so devoted to the intrigues of history, let him shed light on what was hidden in the quagmire that the human heart represented.

Virgílio leafed through the book he had with him. As he handed Polidoro the envelope, he sighed with relief.

"The letter came to my house, but it's addressed to you."

Beneath Virgílio's agitated gaze, Polidoro was afraid that the letter would explode in his hands. His chest ached from the sudden influx of blood. He suspected that the letter, written at the time of the discovery of Brazil, had endured for centuries only to fall to dust now in his presence.

Feigning indifference, he examined the envelope. Suddenly he noticed something out of the ordinary.

"How come it's grease-stained?"

Polidoro's ingratitude made Virgílio shudder. Besides failing to thank him for the service rendered, Polidoro was harboring nasty suspicions. "I'll be damned if I know where that stain came from! Those mailmen are slovenly. While they're eating, they keep wiping their fingers right on the letters," he said circumspectly.

Polidoro wasn't convinced.

"This is a recent stain." He sniffed the outside of the envelope inquisitively. "And what's more, it smells like roast chicken."

Virgílio admired such great discernment. In fact, when the mailman had knocked on the door to give him the letter just as he was sucking the thigh bone of the chicken clean, having wiped every last bit off his plate with a bread crust, he did not have time to go to the bathroom to wash his hands. So he took hold of the envelope with two fingers so as not to soil it all over. The explanation he'd come up with had been of no avail, since Polidoro laid the blame on him without the slightest mercy.

Francisco interrupted them, bringing the bottle. Feeling as though he'd been saved, Virgílio waited for the wine to warm their souls. With each sip of the deep-red vintage, their anger would evaporate.

As he took the cork out of the bottle, Francisco bowed lower and lower, a mannerism that betrayed his weariness after so many long years in his job.

"You're going to swallow that toothpick any day now. It'll be written on your tombstone that you died because you choked on a toothpick. Or else like a vampire, who goes to its death with a stake driven through its heart," Polidoro said, irritated.

No matter what the circumstances, Francisco defended good manners. He envied those guests who, in passing through the Palace, left signs of their refined upbringing.

"A wine like this calls for solemnity," he said politely.

"Make it snappy. We don't have all day to down this wine," Polidoro said curtly.

Remembering that he too had been a victim of Polidoro's despotism, Virgílio broke in.

"What we have the most of is time. What difference does it make whether we're someone who's lived in the second century or the twentieth? We only know about past eras from books. And what importance can possibly be attributed to us in them?"

Francisco poured the wine into the Baccarat glasses.

"These are the last of the set of lead crystal. How beautiful they are!" Virgílio noted the cattle rancher's uncommunicative mood. "What's the news from the capital?"

Polidoro was afraid that his sweaty hands would efface the handwriting of the letter, written in ink. In his breast he harbored a viper's nest. Quaking and nervous, they stirred inside the basket, ready to eject the venom of betrayal at any moment. This was how those reptiles, a species condemned in Eden itself, strove for felicity.

He opened the letter. The paper, as thin as a handkerchief, trembled as he began reading. The handwriting, almost a calligraphy, was straight and firm, thanks to a pride whose scent reached his nostrils in the way that the odors of his cows came to him as they pissed urine and milk. Defenseless, he was disarmed by any evidence of feeling.

His elbows on the table scraped against the wood. He read without a sound; the words flew by; Virgílio's curiosity grew keener still. What was knocking at their door at that hour to destroy Polidoro, ordinarily so stonyhearted thanks to the lessons taught him by his father? Without the courage to question him directly, Virgílio saw the cattle rancher lose the vitality that he drew each day from the cows and bulls of his vast landed estates.

He felt sorry, forgetting now the times when he had envied Polidoro at Gioconda's place, when the latter had left the bedroom with an air of triumph, whereas he himself was humiliated by his own weak sexual performance. However, he never envied Polidoro's sad eyes, wandering off to a place unknown even to their owner. As Polidoro stroked the hairs of his beard, he appeared to issue a muffled lament.

On the balcony, Francisco turned the tuning button of the radio. The voice of Maria Bethânia, singing a song devoted to profane love, echoed through the room. As the singer made her dramatic appeal, Polidoro fixed his gaze on the yellowed print of Don Quixote on the wall. Feeling all alone in the world, he waved his hands toward an absent body.

"Kiss my mouth. Kiss my mouth!" His puckered lips moved toward a face close by, which only he discerned, ready to wrest from it its tongue, its teeth, its last breath.

Virgílio got in the way of his gestures. The cattle rancher returned, maimed, to reality.

"The hour has come that I feared and desired most!"

Virgílio was amazed. Had Polidoro so wearied the gods with his dreams that he had finally been heeded? And did he now have the gods as neighbors, thus being able to call to them through the window, to speak their names aloud?

"Is the news from her?"

"Caetana's coming." He was slowly regaining his composure.

"When?"

"On Friday. Read the letter."

Virgílio patted his suit coat. He'd forgotten his glasses. "I'm getting old." He took hold of the letter with the care reserved for manuscripts written on parchment. He finally deciphered the text.

"And who told you that it would be this Friday? Caetana mentions a Friday in June. There are four weeks in June, and she doesn't mention any Friday in particular."

Virgílio's didactic attitude irritated Polidoro. While the other paraded his culture, he for his part compensated for his lack of studies by his knowledge of human passion. Unlike savants, who took little pleasure in the bodies of peasant lasses, he had delightedly grazed on sylvan backs with his blind and enlightened member.

He tried to grab the letter from Virgílio. The professor was reluctant to give it back to him.

"You'll end up tearing it," Polidoro roared.

Virgílio imagined the consequences: Polidoro in pursuit of him, crying out for vengeance, and there would be no use in his taking refuge in the National Library, a redoubt where in bygone days he had dreamed of spending his life. The institution *would* give him sanctuary, on the pretext that with his help they would disentangle the remaining mystery in the history of Brazil. Not counting, naturally, the material buried in the secret files of the Vatican and in the archives of the Jesuits, which the Brazilian people might as well consider lost forever. They would never get it back. It would constitute a part of the memory that vanishes as time goes by, without the hope of leaving any record. The most they would allow him to do, despite Polidoro's pursuit of him, would be to transmit in passing to other historians his suspicions as to the real motives of the Portuguese in bidding such a hasty farewell to the ambitious Dom Manuel, on the banks of the Tagus, on the long-ago day of March 8, 1500, before starting out on the voyage which would result in the discovery of Brazil.

"What's the matter?" Polidoro's voice brought him back to the table.

Virgílio looked down at his empty hands. He had given the letter back without realizing it. Once he had recovered from the shock, he poured himself some wine.

Polidoro readily admitted the mistakes and mishaps for which he was responsible. He would immediately say, contritely, in his eagerness to charm his victim: "I'm a brute; it's a family trait I've inherited!"

"Read it aloud," Polidoro requested.

Francisco hurried over to the table and, to the surprise of the two men, grabbed the letter, which Polidoro was handing back to Virgílio. He began to read in well-modulated tones.

"The letter is for Polidoro and it says: 'I left Trindade by train on a Friday long ago. I remember clearly that it was raining. As soon as the train whistle gave the signal to leave, I forced myself to look through the dirty windowpanes. I saw nothing but the downpour that blended the landscape with those who were standing in the station, frozen to the spot in astonishment, and who, unlike me, would never leave Trindade. Now, however, it is time to return. I am therefore coming back this June, arriving by the same train that I left on. I chose Friday so as to have the illusion that twenty years had not gone by. As for the rest, we'll wait and see. It's life that whispers the message in our ear. Signed, Caetana.' "

"And what year is Caetana referring to? Can it be this present year of grace, 1970?" Virgílio said.

Polidoro did not answer, incapable of the slightest forethought.

Virgílio thought that the most timely move would be to discover where Caetana was. For all they knew, she had written to them at the end of a tour through the Northeast, with her bags all packed and the lids about to be closed. "Where was the letter sent from?" he persisted.

Polidoro could not make out the postmark. In need of a breath of fresh air, he left the bar, followed by the professor.

In the main square, near the mango tree planted by Polidoro's grandfather Eusébio, they looked at each other again. Virgílio deliberately said nothing. The dark night shadows chilled his bones. He didn't want to go home. Nobody was waiting for him in the dining room with a plate of food kept hot for him in the oven. Plunged into despair as he was, it seemed unbearable to him to resort to lying.

"Up until last night, we had the illusion that we were happy. After this letter, it's going to be harder to fool ourselves, isn't it?" asked Virgílio.

He leaned against the mango tree, the one tangible presence in the darkness. Frightened by the sequence of entanglements that life had in store for them, Virgílio had a feeling that his emotions were escaping his control. After struggling for such a long time with books and papers, he had grown inattentive to the feelings that clouded others' faces. He was simply a clumsy bachelor when it came to the dictates of love, which escaped his grasp like mercury. For Polidoro and his circle of friends, however, the recounting of another chapter of an interrupted story was beginning, after a twenty-year wait for which they had never been prepared.

In order to escape the darkness, they walked over to the lamp-post. But the light bothered Polidoro. Wherever she might be, Caetana's shadow was spying on him, knowing, wherever she was, that Polidoro, with the letter in his pocket, wouldn't sleep. Possessed of this certainty, Caetana could pack her bags with extreme care, so as not to forget the belongings in boarding houses and dressing rooms she had passed through, always pressed for time. Along with troupes of performing artists, each actor leaving messages of hope and anguish written on dressing-room mirrors in red greasepaint. In this way they left word for the mountebanks, their successors in those circus rings, that the sweat of performers such as they would in fact be appreciated only if they aroused the audience's applause.

"I'll wager that Caetana already has her bags packed. The only thing she's doing now is waiting for the whistle announcing the departure of the train. She no longer lacks time. She's made us wait for twenty years! I was beginning to get fed up." And with a sigh that cooled Virgílio's face, close beside his own, Polidoro tried to calm down. Where had such an outrage ever been committed?

All of a sudden, not paying attention to what Polidoro was saying to him, Virgílio grabbed the latter's arm.

"What's the matter?" The cattle rancher was startled.

"You forgot about the train."

"What's the train got to do with it?" He couldn't make out why the professor was so distressed.

"Have you forgotten that the train doesn't go through Trindade any longer?"

Polidoro paled. He raised his hands to his face. He was trembling as hard as when he'd had malaria, from head to foot, so that being covered with blankets did him no good at all. Virgílio heard the dull sound that issued from his chest. And he shook with sobs, unable to tell if they were Polidoro's or his own.

OVERCOME now and again with bucolic fervor, Virgílio called the women of the Estação brothel "sacred cows of the Ganges." He wanted them to be proud of the feelings they inspired in the ordinary run of mortals.

"Cows give the impression of being abject creatures, but they can moo for more than twenty hours without showing the slightest sign of fatigue."

Gioconda was not about to let herself be convinced.

"If that's a compliment, how come they call us cows when they want to offend us?"

In the leisure of Mondays, Virgílio persuaded the Three Graces—a trio made up of Diana, Sebastiana, and Palmira—that the crudeness of his epithet did not come from the heart. In India, to the detriment of human beings, cows were an object of worship. "In that country, they gave birth to humanity amid urine and feces. Like women. Moreover, cows are given to madness, like poets," he said dreamily.

Virgílio cooled the tea brought by Gioconda by blowing on it a number of times. But, once revived by its warmth, he complained of the excess of seasoning that reality contained. "I, for instance, have salt, pepper, and garlic in my voice. From having given so many lectures, I have useless vocal cords and the pension of a pariah."

Grateful for so much attention, he tried to honor Gioconda with a noble epithet.

"You're both the queen of cows and a Roman matron."

Suspecting that the professor was relegating her to the category of women lost for love, Gioconda took offense. Such titles treacherously insinuated that days hurriedly ripped off the calendar pad had robbed her of the last vestiges of youth.

"The only reason I'm not offering you manioc-flour tea cakes

is because they're the very last ones," she said avariciously, showing him the nearly empty tin.

Noticing her hurt feelings, Virgílio defended analogies that
came from the heart. After all, the Roman matron had influenced
both the home and the Senate. How many overseas provinces
were there that had been sacked at her request?

"Sometimes I get everything all mixed up, as though I were
shuffling cards. I'm a bad player. I've never had a wild card in my
hands. What's more, the only wild card in Trindade is Polidoro."

As a way of punishing himself for offenses inadvertently inflicted, and feigning modesty, he rid himself, in the presence of
the Three Graces, of the title of zealous observer of daily life and
of the human soul.

Gioconda was satisfied with his explanations. In his dealings
with reality, this man aroused her tenderness. She now saw the
originality of the portrait that he had made of them. And, wanting
to reciprocate his polite attentions, she hailed his virile virtues,
so far from abundant lately.

"Don't ask me who praised you. In this house I am the priestess:
I receive confessions and don't give away their source."

Virgílio blushed. The equipment that nature had given him
never seemed to him to be an enjoyable gift. On the contrary,
because it frequently failed him, he tended to use it sparingly.

"Are you sure they were referring to me?"

He straightened the knot in his tie in the mirror of the salon,
ablaze with the bright red of the walls and sofas. Perhaps his vigor
was due to his mother's milk, from which he wasn't weaned until
he was three years old. Standing up while his mother sat, impatient
to return to her household tasks, he would cling to her nipples,
punishing them with his voracious mouth.

"Ah, Gioconda, never mind all the bad things they say about
women—in fact they're the best fruits of the earth."

Little by little, Gioconda became proficient in the art of fooling
others. For a long time now, she had buried her feelings in favor
of words that came out of her mouth dressed as Harlequin, Colum-
bine, and Pierrot, a festive calling up of memories that hid the
sadness of the forty years that had followed the days of riotous

revelry. On Sundays especially, she succumbed to her feelings of emptiness, despite the succulent dishes of rice, beans, pork loin, fried manioc that came to the table.

On that Monday, for some inexplicable reason, the customers, anxious to return to their homes, kept yawning constantly. The resentment accumulated over time and another dull Sunday with the family had exhausted them; they had put in an appearance at Gioconda's place only out of obedience to a schedule that left room for desire.

Even Virgílio, the moment he appeared, announced his decision to leave again in thirty minutes. Hence they should not use their blandishments on him, or take off his suit coat as though he were someone who had arrived to spend several hours in a row on one of their mattresses. Polidoro was waiting for him at the bar of the Palace. They had a great deal to talk about.

"It's too bad you can't come along, Gioconda. It's an old building, but it's still elegant. Nobody there is in a hurry. It's only this country that's in a hurry. Luckily, Brazil can grow without us!" he said, to cheer her up.

Before giving him back his hat, Gioconda removed the dust from it with a clothes brush.

"Once I've become a respectable old lady, I'll come and have a glass of wine with the two of you. It won't be long now."

He adjusted the brim of his hat. A real Ramenzoni, one of the very last before the factory went bankrupt. He turned to Gioconda and stroked her face with an absent-minded gesture.

"You'll never grow old," he said before he left.

On that afternoon, in spite of the calm enhanced by the weariness of the Three Graces, Gioconda intuited that danger was close at hand. She feared the presence of intruders invading the house, gagging their mouths and their hearts, for no practical purpose. Late that night, she was still hounded by these worries. Feeling not at all sleepy, she sat down in the parlor. Her chest rumbled as though she had caught cold. To calm down, she looked out the window, attracted by the shadows. She spied a man on the sidewalk, leaning against a tree. The light from the streetlamp did not show his face. Overcome with anxiety, she breathed in the smell of freshly percolated coffee coming from the kitchen. The hand of the clock was pointing to three, and she still didn't feel sleepy.

The man on the sidewalk alternately made as if to leave and inspected the bricks of the house, warmed by the heat of the whores. Wearily, Gioconda went back to the easy chair. With her legs resting on the footstool, she thought, uneasily, about the man. The memory immediately fled from her mind, attracted by other memories. On certain nights, she fell asleep right there. She could sense that she was being besieged by ghosts, come specially to strip away her hope and her illusions. They were persistent, bent on enveloping her in a shroud of scorn or indifference. Amid this sort of invasion, Gioconda wondered whether she might not be dreaming of her own death. Between starts of fright, she put such presentiments to flight by insulting them.

She felt cold. With her legs uncovered, she wrapped her negligee around her. She felt too lazy to go get a blanket from the upstairs floor. Then she heard sounds at the door. She suspected that it was the stranger. His tense breathing seemed to come straight through the knots in the wood, as if seeking help. Who could tell if he had holes in the soles of his shoes and hunger pangs gnawing at his belly? Even so, perhaps he could guarantee that far from there, waiting for Gioconda, was an anonymous life and a well-laden table.

Tempted by this consolation, Gioconda opened the door. Polidoro hurried in, the pupils of his eyes dilated. Judging from his breath, he had been drinking.

"You're out of luck. Everybody's gone to sleep. I'm the only night owl in the house."

Familiar with the dramatic splashes of red adorning the easy chairs and the wallpaper of the parlor, Polidoro also took in the smell of sweat and perfume pervading the objects scattered on top of the various pieces of furniture.

"It's the heart of passion," Gioconda would say, justifying the striking touches of red to sensitive customers, when life was draining out of them and their hands had to be stroked.

Polidoro sat down in the easy chair. Gioconda offered him the footstool. She was always careful to treat him well. He was a steady customer. Usually he put in an appearance at Estação twice a week. Thanks to his advice, Gioconda instructed the Three Graces to vary their coiffures and their makeup, to foster the illusion that they were fresh off the boat from Italy and Japan. Otherwise, once their desire had been satisfied, the customers would retreat at an early hour to the marriage bed, forgetting the cosseting that they might have found at Gioconda's place.

Despite all these precautions, for some time now Polidoro had shown signs of being bored. It took him a long time to choose which of the women he'd follow upstairs to her room. And on Fridays, arriving at the same time as Ernesto, he pleaded with him to help him get it up with obscene gestures, never repeated by either of them away from Estação.

On one occasion, Polidoro confessed pitifully: "How tiring it is to be a male. If I don't show up here twice a week, the rumor will spread all through Trindade that I'm impotent."

Gioconda respected his silence. His knitted brow shadowed his face. He made a vague gesture. He seemed worn out.

"How are you, Gioconda?"

She pointed to the little bar, after pouring herself a glass of jabuticaga liqueur.

"We're all growing old, Polidoro. They no longer call us the 'girls of Estação,' the way they used to. We're the only ones left of the old crowd. And there's nobody to take our place on the job. The new generation climbs onto the back of a motorcycle now and clears out of here. We're the only ones left."

He forced himself to continue the conversation.

"We never wanted to leave Trindade." Her melancholy tone of voice was yet another expression of Polidoro's mood.

"You had a reason to stay."

"To me, this town is the whole world in miniature," he said, his eyes fixed on an imaginary horizon. "I haven't gone anywhere else for twenty years."

"Waiting for Caetana, who might turn up at any moment."

And Gioconda headed for the window in an angry stride, affording a glimpse of her legs through the slit in her negligee.

Polidoro observed them without lust. White and gelatinous now, they made him recall the beauty they had once had. His heart melted. This woman's anxieties also had a melancholy origin.

"And what about you? Haven't you ever awaited her return?"

Gripping the window frame, Gioconda pretended not to have heard his question. She gave every appearance of rambling on to an invisible conversational partner.

"Do you remember the way circuses used to come by to visit us in the old days? And how we laughed at any sort of slapstick, even when the clown had no idea how to be amusing?" She turned away from the window to face him directly. "Why did circuses disappear?"

Polidoro pushed the footstool aside. He asked her permission to remove his boots. They were a heavy weight after he'd worn them for so many hours.

"Would you like a sandwich?"

Polidoro had had a bite to eat in the hotel bar, before it closed. At his house, a banquet awaited him in the oven, which Dodô insisted on leaving for him, knowing all the while that her husband wouldn't come home. Just for the pleasure of accusing him the next morning of wasting food. "You're going to make paupers of us yet, Polidoro. The refrigerator chock-full of food you didn't even care to taste. Where have you been that made you come back with such a sad face?"

Dodô's words anticipated his answers, which she needed in order to feel that she was the object of her husband's attention.

"Well, don't make dinner, then. Besides, I have money enough to fill the belly of everyone in Trindade. Stop being so niggardly."

"Don't forget that part of that money is mine too," Dodô answered defiantly, pointing her fan at him, with its several broken slats.

"Do you think I've forgotten? You don't need to keep reminding me every week."

Polidoro went over to the bar cabinet. He rummaged about

among the bottles, opening and closing compartments, as though he were in his own house.

"Since it's so cold outside, I'd like a cane brandy. Will you have one with me?" He smiled, feeling relaxed.

"It's really strong. And I'm still on duty," she replied ironically.

"As far as I'm concerned, you've been relieved."

Polidoro sipped the cane brandy appreciatively. At the first swallow, he sensed that this was from a noble still, the product of which he himself had furnished to Gioconda.

She hid her feelings. She did not want to expose herself. Her voice, however, betrayed her resentment.

"What brought you here? Her disappearance? We could have died and you wouldn't even have known." She was almost close enough to Polidoro to feel his breath, reeking of alcohol.

"You've never forgiven me, isn't that so?" He noted her years-old eagerness for vengeance, long repressed. The two of them exchanged spiteful looks. Polidoro searched her face for a vulnerable point, the better to observe the wounds he was about to cause.

"You've never told me your baptismal name."

Gioconda took the blow in stride, as though the past could not harm her. She drew herself up proudly, oblivious of her negligee, which had opened partway, from her knees down.

"I don't remember any more. The only name I've gone by is the one Caetana gave me. It's the one I want to be buried with."

"Why did Caetana want to change your name?"

Forgetting his adversary, he found himself really intrigued by this episode he knew nothing about. Perhaps it was one of a series of steps that had led to Caetana's departure with no advance notice whatsoever. Impulsive by temperament, she took offense at the merest trifle.

"Caetana had a mania for undoing what she found ugly. As an artist, she didn't accept reality. I remember her saying that a new name could change a person's fate. So I asked her: 'What name do I need, then?' She answered with a smile: 'Gioconda— the one of the dance of the hours.' I was ashamed to ask who it was she meant. What did I know of Caetana's world? Every time she repeated my name, her voice grew grave. A voice that made me

laugh and cry. One day she asked me: 'Are you happy, Gioconda?'
When I said yes, she went to a box lined with velvet, full of
trinkets. And took out this ring."

Gioconda looked down at the ring. The metal had lost its
luster, buried from sight on a finger far fatter now.

"This ring is my fate," she said to herself. And because of the
impetus of the story that she was telling, she felt she was back in
Caetana's dressing room once again.

"Then Caetana said to me . . ."

Too bashful to go on, Gioconda fell silent. She no longer
accepted Polidoro as a conversational partner.

"What was it she said?"

He felt banished from the parlor and from Gioconda's past;
jealousy and alcohol made Polidoro's face burn. He did not approve
of Caetana, who had renounced his tutelage and given herself over
to wanderers who perhaps possessed her now, with no respect for
the marks of sensuality that he had left on her body. He was unable
to bear the idea that she had been happy without him. He wanted
to beat Gioconda, to make her responsible for the pernicious
sentiments that had precipitated Caetana's flight.

Gioconda foresaw the danger, the fumes of the alcohol giving
him a raging fever.

"Why did you come here?" She preferred to plan ahead. His
visit was intended to shake the very framework of her harlot's
home and fireside.

"I came to ask a favor."

He poured himself some more cane brandy. The swallow he
took burned his throat. He confronted the woman then, face to
face. The favor must not turn him into the slave of her whims.

"I need Dr. Mendes, a graduate engineer of the National
Railway Service, to sidetrack the regular train so that it will come
through Trindade next Friday." Relieved, he filled his glass yet
again.

"The train? You're out of your mind. There hasn't been a
single train through here for more than seven years." Gioconda
pondered the situation without hitting on the reasons for his request.

"All he has to do is give orders to switch the locomotive onto our branch line and get it here to us. I'll take care of the rest. I'll have the tracks cleared and the station tidied."

"Is it that important?" She could see his distress, his chest bared for her to trample on it. Greeted by silence, she persisted: "What freight is the train carrying that can't come by road?"

She became more and more distrustful. Unless she knew the real situation, she would be in no position to help.

"I thought we were friends," he said hesitantly.

Gioconda proved to be utterly intransigent. He would have to tell her what the freight was, or else she would refuse to help him.

"It's a friend who needs to get off the train without being recognized."

He didn't want to resort to the governor. A request such as that would arouse suspicion. Polidoro would immediately become an easy target for political intrigues. As for Gioconda, she had nothing to lose. The engineer's steadfast passion for her was well known.

He made a move to leave, assuming that the subject had been settled to his satisfaction. Gioconda, however, did not accompany him to the door.

"Aren't you going to see me out?"

"Tell me the name of that friend first," she insisted, not giving an inch.

"Do you really want to know?" he asked in a merciless, threatening voice.

Gioconda considered backing down. There was still time to safeguard herself from morbid curiosity. Polidoro, however, snapped his fingers demandingly. He sounded like an alarm clock. Her immediate reaction was to take hasty refuge in the kitchen. Polidoro heard water streaming out of the open faucet. When she finally came back, every step, from the kitchen to the parlor, robbed her of a piece of her own body. She had forgotten to dry her wet face.

"May I count on you?" He had regained control of the situation.

"On one condition."

The expression on Polidoro's face did not change.

"I'll go to the station too. I want to be there waiting for Caetana on Friday."

Polidoro headed for the door, disregarding Gioconda. When he opened it, the cold from the street permeated the parlor. He folded his arms across his chest; he mustn't catch cold. His life was focused on Caetana. He patted his wallet, in his suit-coat pocket. Inside it was the only photo he had of his wife. Every so often, he took a look at it so as to refresh his memory with details that with each passing day he was less and less able to recall.

As he crossed the doorsill, Polidoro breathed in the night air. He noted with intense sensual pleasure signs that he was coming back to life. He looked at Gioconda; he owed her a reply.

"All right, Gioconda. We'll go together."

He was in a hurry now to leave the house. Luckily, he had gotten through yet another night. He took the first steps toward the street. It would soon be daylight. There was a great deal to do that Tuesday.

ERNESTO AND VIRGÍLIO contended for the honor of identifying the bed that had been the stage of the love fests of Caetana and Polidoro. The contest had begun that morning in the Bom Espírito pharmacy.

Polidoro had called them together after his morning bath, beneath a hail of protests from Dodô. Standing right next to him, she accused him of hogging the telephone when he was home. He turned a deaf ear to her complaints, and seemed happy.

"What are you up to, Poli?" She called him by his nickname, to stir up his old conjugal fears.

He ate some cheese bread to please her. To divert her suspicions, he patted his pocket with the palm of his hand. "I'm about to close a big deal."

Dodô's eyes gleamed with greed. He had immediately won her over, for nothing made her feel so pampered as the prospect of acquiring land, as though the vast properties she already possessed were not enough for her. She dreamed of seeing her photograph in foreign newspapers, as an example of the lady owner of large Brazilian landed estates, the possessor of thousands of exotic zebus, brought from India by boat, capable of supplying a country such as Belgium all by herself.

"Watch your step, whatever you do," she warned him when her initial euphoria had passed.

In the pharmacy, Polidoro impressed on the others how urgent it was to restore the room of the Palace that he and Caetana had occupied in the past. He demanded unconditional fidelity to the way it had been decorated, so that Caetana, captivated by its magic, would never suspect that she had left Trindade, and time would be suspended, leading them both to believe that they were twenty years younger.

That love moved Virgílio. Forcing himself to prove his solidarity with Polidoro, he touched his arm so that the cattle baron would note his emotion. He could hardly speak.

"Ah, Polidoro! I never imagined that you were sensitive to poetry. Or that you had such a feminine soul!" He wiped the tears from his eyes, anxious for Polidoro to see the monogram embroidered on his handkerchief, the same intertwined letters that marked his underwear.

Ernesto was suspicious of that fit of weeping. It doubtless had to do with the professor's loneliness. In order to console him, he pointed out to him that the assigned destiny of love was to make the flesh burn on the same pyre onto which in bygone days inconsolable widows had flung themselves. Yet, although subject to such follies, love was capable of bringing about its own system of cure. The moment Caetana arrived, the house of love, in disarray for so many years, would promptly be set in order.

Paying no attention to their debate, Polidoro's mind wandered in places that were his alone. The other two discoursed with fervent authority on the caprices of passion. Ernesto himself, neglecting customers who had prescriptions to be filled, impatiently sent them on their way. He assured them, with a few brief words to soothe their hurt feelings, that it was an unsuitable time for consultations. Love was now his patient. Except, of course, that love, once it had settled in the body, immediately revived health.

"Love is the best of remedies. It heals any wound or physical ailment. It is a demiurge that works miracles," he said, devoting all his attention to Virgílio.

Ernesto's thoughtful concern for Virgílio touched Polidoro's heart. At the same time, he was ashamed of himself for remaining unmoved by the professor's lot.

"Ah, Polidoro, how painful these years have been to live through!"

His voice choking, Virgílio kneaded his handkerchief between his fingers. During these years, thanks to Polidoro's generosity, he too had cohabited with Caetana's shadow. And since he lacked a family of his own, engraved on his face was the portrait of Caetana, equally visible to Polidoro and to Ernesto. With what pride he had been the familiar of a love that had sought refuge in the Palace, once Caetana had finished her performance in the circus ring. They were such avid lovers that Virgílio had even dreamed of having on his plate some day a big chunk of meat that he would eat with the passion invented by hunger.

Polidoro did not want to attract attention. Until Friday, they would display in public only the most discreet of gestures. Hence Polidoro would not take more than one man with him to the hotel.

Ernesto wanted to accompany him. But Virgílio, feeling that he had been passed over, put in his claim as a historian, a profession that obliged him to be in the forefront of events.

Ernesto refused to listen to his complaints.

"Do you know how to cure illnesses and injuries the way I do? How to give injections?"

Sentiments based on a person's profession irritated Polidoro.

"Whichever one of you has the keenest memory, come with me."

Virgílio and Ernesto did not disguise their hurt, which they drank from the same cup.

"Tell me straight out, this minute, the day of the month and of the week on which Caetana left Trindade without leaving a single farewell note."

Ernesto's memory was often undependable. In school, when he conjugated Latin verb endings, indispensable to the translation of Cicero's sentences, he struggled in vain to hit on the right one. He got everything garbled, confusing Cicero with Cato. He did have, however, a vague memory of the ill-fated day. He had been at the table having dinner when Polidoro summoned him immediately to the Palace, expressly to tell him of Caetana's desertion with her troupe of assassins of art. The dinner, more elaborate than usual, made Ernesto certain that it was a family birthday. But whose? His own, his wife's, or his eldest son's? His memory betrayed him, refusing him any worthwhile aid. The only things that came to his mind were scattered reminiscences. This sudden lapse of memory kept him from considering himself the owner of his own past; he felt incapable of offering testimony regarding his own life. Hence any unscrupulous neighbor could boast of incidents that in fact belonged to Ernesto's life.

Paying no heed to Ernesto's effort to remember, Virgílio asked permission to put a word in. His excessive politeness hinted at his intellectual superiority.

"It was on Friday, May 3, 1950. On that morning, the train left Trindade ten minutes late, on account of the heavy rain. It left, therefore, at nine-forty-five. The rain had begun the preceding day, before lunch, at the very hour when Polidoro had been hurriedly summoned to Suspiro and went out to the ranch to see at first hand the damages caused by the water tank that had burst in the kitchen, bearing away in the flood the pork-and-black-bean stew that Dodô had ordered made for the baptism of her godson Joãozinho, the offspring of Doçura and Maneco, people from right there on the cattle ranch, in the days when the overseer was Seu . . ."

"That will do," Polidoro said impatiently. "You win."

His victory proclaimed, Virgílio consoled Ernesto, in the same lofty manner.

"If historians didn't have a good memory, who would defend the history of Brazil from the foreigners who put into port here to steal our documents?"

Quite out of the habit of physical exercise, Virgílio had difficulty keeping up with Polidoro.

In the hotel lobby, Mágico seemed to be startled. "What brings you here at this hour?" Yet, despite his show of surprise, Mágico was prevaricating. Francisco had surely informed him the day before that Caetana was coming.

"Isn't it true that you already know?" Polidoro didn't give him time to recover from the shock. "In that case, keep your trap shut. It's a secret, understand? As for Francisco, I'm still going to have his balls cut off some day."

Mágico paled. He wanted to speak up in Francisco's defense.

"It doesn't matter. All I want right now is to know who's occupying the suite on the fifth floor." Polidoro pointed upward, his eyes resting on the unlighted crystal chandelier.

"A honeymoon couple. They're staying till Saturday. From Miracema. The young man's family has a little cottage industry that turns out homemade soap. Probably Portuguese, with the cross of the Knights of Malta. They seem like decent people."

"Get them out of there this minute. Any excuse will do."

"But they're still sleeping. They didn't order breakfast sent up. Honeymooners, as you know, never go to sleep early." He smiled for the first time, hoping to touch Polidoro's heart.

"Anybody who screws all night long needs rest. So I'll give them two more hours. After that, change their room. But since they're from Miracema, where I have friends, the hotel management will pay for their stay. Including meals and drinks."

He headed for the closed door to the right of the reception desk. He knew every inch of the entire hotel. Mágico followed him. Polidoro was insistent about the newlyweds. "If you don't have a word with them, I'll kick them out of here, even if they're in the middle of fucking," he said in a fury as he opened the door that led to the stairs.

"We're going to test your memory now, Virgílio. For Mágico's benefit, in the rear guard. Bring me the key to the cellar."

Polidoro bounded nimbly down the stairs, in contrast to the slow pace of Virgílio, who, lacking light and afraid of falling, kept leaning against the wall for support. "You can count; there are twenty-seven steps," Polidoro explained.

Once they were in the cellar, he tried to open the door. The lock stuck.

"Damn it to hell! What confounded kind of key is this? How many years has it been since this door was used?" Finally, it gave way, creaking in protest as it opened. Polidoro went in first.

"Turn on the light, Mágico."

In the dark, Mágico stumbled over Virgílio, who clung desperately to him. The two of them together found the switch. The light revealed a cemetery of furniture, with gravestones everywhere, in the form of chairs with their legs in the air; there was no indication on the furniture or crates as to their origin. Total confusion reigned. Heaped up from one end of the cellar to the other, the furniture created a labyrinth that could only be surmounted with zeal and determination.

"How are we going to find the furniture and the mattress from Caetana's room in the midst of all this clutter?" Virgílio sighed.

"We won't come out till the job is done. You'd better watch your step," Polidoro warned. Running his hands over the pieces of furniture, he felt the crust of dirt inlaid in them, like lusterless rubies. He forced himself to identify them. He began the excursion through a territory where he had no map at his disposal to orient him. In his persistent effort to overcome obstacles, however, he cleared a path little by little, to force his way through to the other end of the cellar, from which point he would have a broader perspective. He had hopes of seeing his search rewarded.

"Have you some idea at least of what it is you're looking for?" Virgílio asked.

"Don't interrupt me, please." He nervously crossed the Sargasso Sea, followed by Mágico and Virgílio, who gradually fell behind, hanging on to each other so as not to get lost. They were touched by this universe peopled by debris and forgotten memories.

Despite his careful steps, Virgílio, clumsier than Mágico, stumbled over a pile of crates, which began to collapse on top of the historian like a house of cards. Foreseeing disaster, Mágico hastened to his side to save him. His timely gesture did not keep Virgílio from being scared out of his wits.

"To whom do I owe my life?" he said, stupefied.

Mágico took him in his arms and nestled him there. Face to face with the man who had saved him, Virgílio yielded to the attraction of human warmth, forgetting the furniture. The sounds of fellow-feeling alerted Polidoro.

Virgílio, still in Mágico's arms, noted how difficult it was for Polidoro to locate them.

"We're here, next to the pile of mattresses," Virgílio informed him, fearing that he was outside the cattle rancher's field of vision.

Polidoro saw the havoc that had been caused. He was relieved that there were no victims, but Virgílio's carelessness had slowed up the search.

"How long are you two going to linger in that friendly embrace?" he said, reprimanding the pair of clumsy oafs.

Once free of Mágico, Virgílio covered his mouth with his handkerchief, protecting himself from the dust raised by the crates that had fallen. In the midst of such precautions, he looked to his left.

"Look! There are the mattresses we're looking for!" he said, rushing toward the new pile.

Held back by Mágico, who wanted to examine his tibia to see the damage caused by the accident, Virgílio was unable to budge. Polidoro grew impatient at this excessive compassion in wartime.

"Do you two know what time it is? In less than three days, Caetana will be getting off the train in Trindade."

With a shove, Virgílio, forgetting his elegant manners, pushed Mágico away. "I swear I'll find Caetana's mattress. It's the most important furnishing of all." He uttered the words in such a way that they would not hint at anything indecent, though privately he considered it absurd to force Caetana to lie down on any of those mattresses.

"You're out of your mind, Virgílio. How are we going to discover the mattress amid all this filth?" Polidoro shouted in an anger born of his unwillingness to accept the damage wrought by the years.

His feelings wounded by the disbelief of the cattle baron, whom he had served with unconditional loyalty, Virgílio rebelled. In the last analysis, the profession of historian, though modest, had taught him to extract the greatest benefit possible from documents. Good technique recommended inventing whenever he was confronted with unfavorable situations. Therefore, in his eagerness to identify the mattress of the fervent lovers, he would avail himself of similar resources.

He was looking for the mattress where, bare naked and all alone, the two of them had had only each other as the sole reference to human forms. Beneath the primacy of pride, between sighs and caresses, no other bodies had better represented man and woman to them.

On the other hand, it upset Virgílio that Polidoro demanded of him proofs of his long-standing love for him. Puffed up with pride and diligent, the cattle baron, far from resembling a truly romantic character, now had the big potbelly of a buffoon. Yet, led astray by the arrogance that comes from wealth, Polidoro wanted to reconstruct, as he approached his sixties, the passion that had had as its frame the dreams of a golden age.

With his eyes riveted to the mattress, it seemed to Virgílio that he saw Caetana rising up from a zone of shadows, moving her hips with voluptuous determination, so that Polidoro's exhausted but still-magnificent penis would not slip out of her vagina. Her artful wriggling kept the man's appendage squeezed inside her, forcing it to swim agonizingly in the shadowy insides, where salt water had taken possession.

"Grab hold of the edges of this volcano," Virgílio shouted, disconcerted.

Under the sway of memories of a love that had never adhered

to reality, Polidoro too was frightened. In that stuffy cellar, they were subject to fits of delirium.

"Would you like to get a breath of fresh air?" Polidoro suggested.

Virgílio regretted the interruption. The episode would not be repeated. He knelt down on the floor, searching for something. In that position, the cold of the cement penetrated his bones. Mágico and Polidoro joined him in his search.

"What is it we're looking for?" Mágico asked.

"My hat," Virgílio answered. "I lost my hat in the deluge of crates."

Responsible for this tribe inclined toward madness, Polidoro took command.

"Let's go back to work. I'll get you another hat once we're out of here."

The hat was irreplaceable. Virgílio wore it every Monday, when he visited Estação. And at the celebration that the students in the state school had held for him on the occasion of his retirement, they referred to the hat as the symbol of his love for the history of Brazil.

"That was the same hat I wore at my mother's funeral."

Mágico did not take part in the argument. Feeling about on the floor, he went on searching. Finally, he came across an object.

"Isn't it underneath this crate?"

Virgílio bemoaned the crushed hat. He immediately began to shape it, trying his best to return it to its original form, his attention still concentrated, however, on the pile of mattresses. Because he wanted to supply his memory with details that would make it easier to identify the mattress, he went back to roaming through years long past. Certain months came to mind very clearly. Certain sunny days, moreover, had never faded from his memory. Especially the Tuesday when he had knocked on the door of the fifth floor of the Palace to warn Polidoro, who was with Caetana, that Dodô had come back to Trindade before the intended date.

The cattle baron, in a dressing gown purchased in Rio de Janeiro, received him with an air of constraint. His face, sagging with fatigue, indicated that he had no sleep. The living room gave off a fragrance of fresh lavender. The breakfast tray had been picked clean; there was not so much as a crumb of bread left. One of the coffee cups had lipstick stains on the edge, revealing Caetana's habit of painting her lips each time she finished making love. The disorder of the room betrayed their hurry to go back to bed.

Polidoro appeared not to care one way or the other about Dodô's return. He reacted only to the argument that Caetana, once she was exposed to the scandal his wife would raise, would never forgive him.

"In that case, I'll go visit the family."

He disappeared into the bedroom to offer Caetana the traditional vows of love. He would be back in a few hours, ready for passion once more.

The odor of lust, coming from the bedroom, clung to the objects in the living room and to Virgílio's body now, as it trembled with envy. The closed curtains darkened the living room, further exciting his fantasy. He felt certain that Caetana, having come from the other side of Brazil, where there were palm trees, dunes, and macaws, had brought with her an experience that Trindade, such a provincial backwater, didn't even suspect existed.

Nervously, the professor stroked the mound in his trousers that had formed between his thighs at the level of his pelvis. He was whiling away his time in the age-old ritual when Polidoro called to him.

Virgílio halted at the door of the bedroom. He was deeply moved to be picking the apple of the most coveted tree, to be surprising Caetana in bed, her lingerie indiscreetly baring her breasts.

In the spacious room, Polidoro was on his knees, picking up a deck of cards scattered all over the rug. These cards appeared to have witnessed extraordinary scenes, or to have been part of a game in which the amorous advances between the partners were based on previously placed bets. As he picked up each one, Polidoro sought Caetana's conniving glance, which could not fail him at such a moment.

The trajectory of his impenetrable gaze, undermined by remnants of passion, reached Caetana's rounded pubis. Beneath her nightgown, the tufts of bristling hair throbbed, oppressively and continuously. The aim of life there was to reproduce chimeras and obsessions.

Up until then, Virgílio's emotions had been restricted to the Estação brothel and the rare bordellos of nearby towns. At the sight of those plump thighs, however, he turned deathly pale. As though, on a visit to hell, he were licking the flames of genitals that poured out larvae, juices, and other filth.

Having had a strict upbringing that made the "solitary act" a grave transgression, he fingered his genitals furtively, and in great haste. On surprising himself in this shameful act, he forced himself to sneeze several times in a row, to enable him to turn his back on the two of them. When he looked at Caetana again, she gave him a vague smile. Her half-open lips took in wedges, stakes, poles, tree trunks, Polidoro's penis. Virgílio felt he was in a den of wild beasts.

Polidoro's voice cut his delirium short. "I've found the card, the queen of spades," the cattle baron said, laughing.

He went around to the other side of the bed and handed the card to Caetana. "That queen of spades is the pledge of my passion." And, the possessor of an unexpected gift for lyricism, he respectfully bowed to her. "You need only show it to me in the future, and I'll give you everything you ask me for."

Caetana sniffed at the card. Her nostrils brought her the smell of sweat and perfume. Assured of the value of the promise, she put the queen of spades away in the night table, amid drinking glasses, jewels, and medicines.

Polidoro asked Virgílio to pick up the cards. He obeyed, a participant in a passion that did injury to his body. As he held in his hand the first card, warm and damp, he felt a shock that was never to leave him all through the years. He had only to close his eyes as he was feeling the bodies of the women of Estação to call immediately to mind Caetana's breasts, large and flabby, spread out over her own flesh.

"Give me five minutes more and I promise you Caetana's mattress," Virgílio said, freeing himself from such memories.

Comforted by the promise, Polidoro too returned to the scene of his long-ago passion. Caetana's figure, sprawled out between the sheets, was engraved on his face—to Virgílio's joy as he observed it, eager to attain personal gains. That was all it took for the professor, ridding himself of doubts, to point with upraised finger to the oldest mattress in the pile.

"It's this one. Here you have the stage of the loves of Caetana," he said, shaping his hat to fit his head.

It took Polidoro, immersed in the remembrance of Caetana, who at that very moment was sucking on his jugular vein with irresistible ardor, a long time to come back to the cellar.

"Don't give me false hopes," he said forlornly.

His voice, however, grew stronger and stronger, the more he distrusted Virgílio's positive identification of the mattress. He had no remembrance of it that would allow him to contradict Virgílio, but its similarity to the others, all of them dirty and moldy, made it hard for him to accept the verdict. He was dependent, therefore, on Virgílio's sincerity, and the latter had always given him ample evidence of his lack of guile. A decent man, though perplexed in the face of the glaringly obvious facts of reality, owing perhaps to the demands of his profession, which was nurtured by ambiguous and contradictory versions of any sequence of events.

Faithful to his rural origins, a classic example of mistrustfulness, Polidoro carefully examined the mattress.

"Aren't we perhaps exhuming the wrong corpse?" He phrased the question carefully, so as not to hurt Virgílio's feelings.

"If it were necessary, I would locate a butterfly, not to mention a mattress which, in the order of human creation, is no more than a crude piece of handiwork." Virgílio sullenly defended the power of his memory.

"Even so, I need proof. A wine stain, perhaps. Or other stains. When all is said and done, we committed so many excesses," he said ironically.

"A love stain perhaps?" Virgílio was growing bolder and bolder. Thanks to Polidoro, he was passing through a sphere in which love banished modesty and prudence.

At his side, Mágico was feeling resentful. Excluded from the circle of memories of Caetana, he took a step forward with the intention of pulling down the pile of mattresses.

"We'll see if Caetana imprinted the image of her face on it," he said, pleased at taking the lead.

As the keeper of Caetana's image, Virgílio pointed out to him the eighth mattress from the top of the pile. Polidoro cleared a space for it in the dense forest of dusty furniture. Laid out flat in full view of all of them, the mattress proved to be in the worst possible state. Straw was poking out of its ripped sides.

"It's worthless," Mágico said.

Polidoro paid no heed to his employee's disbelief. He had undertaken to recover the mattress, if it was Caetana's.

"By Friday it's going to look as good as new."

"You can take it up to the fifth floor. It's the mattress we've been looking for," Virgílio said.

Trapped in the human contingency that forced so many uncertainties on him, Polidoro was suffering.

"Give me one last proof."

Virgílio resigned himself to the impoverishment hindering human imagination. But how to be a poet of reality if even artists failed to define the soul of the human species? Unhurriedly, he tried to offer the necessary proof.

Exactly twenty years before, in his eagerness to pick the cards up from the carpet in response to Polidoro's request, he had had a close look, from between the rumpled sheets, at the mattress in question. It had not occurred to him to inquire into the reasons why the cards were scattered all over the floor, sent flying one by one from the bed. The fact was that, as he picked each of them up, he kept bumping into the bare mattress, and thus noted in exhaustive detail during these short journeys back and forth in the bedroom its weave, its salmon color, and the places in the left-hand corner where it had been mended by hand.

"Wait—I'll offer you the most convincing proof yet. Tell me, which mattress is the most broken-down one of all?"

"Mine, without the shadow of a doubt," Polidoro answered unhesitatingly.

"And that could make all the difference! What other passion

was there in Trindade as torrid as that? Wasn't it the only one powerful enough to ruin any mattress? And don't try to tell me that this mattress is in the state it is merely on account of the years that have gone by! After all, what are twenty years in comparison with history!"

Polidoro brimmed over with pride.

"What do you think, Mágico?" He seemed to be looking at him for the first time.

An easy prey to a love that had never knocked at his own door, Mágico favored the hypothesis that it was the right mattress.

Virgílio drew himself up proudly. However, the historian lacked words that, born of the heart and devoid of logic, could arouse emotion in its pure state.

"The best way of paying homage to Caetana is to agree that this mattress became the scene of a grand passion," he said, without the slightest conviction.

Polidoro sensed the poverty of Virgílio's description. On the other hand, the historian had made them see the grandeur of a love that had been truly lived, the memory of which would not fade with the years.

"I loved like a desecrator! I fucked like an Oriental potentate!" Polidoro could scarcely believe the vast scope of his amorous exploits.

Polidoro's amazement at his own prowess impressed Virgílio. He had to be scrupulously honest with the cattle baron, yet avoid erasing at the same time the look of ecstasy on his face.

"You never got out of bed. Even your meals were sent up to the room. You looked like zombies who never slept. In the very last days, with impressive circles under your eyes, you weighed yourself on the scale in the storeroom and you'd lost over five kilos. Don't you remember?"

The description excited Mágico, who felt like the protagonist of the episode. He understood, belatedly, that the epic, previously restricted to the handful of romances that he had read, in which the heroes died, was equally within the reach of ordinary human beings.

"What amorous vigor had the men of long ago! Nowadays all

we have is free samples," Mágico said, in such a rush of enthusiasm that it left no chance for his envy to show through.

Surrounded by an admiration that Dodô reduced to nothing in the sanctuary of their home, Polidoro raised his hand to the fly of his trousers, forgetting that he was in the company of others, eager to check and see whether his sturdy cock merited such praise.

Virgílio noted his misgivings. To distract Polidoro, he enfolded him in a friendly embrace.

"Ah, Polidoro, what a shame that Caetana can't testify in your favor just now. Better than anyone else, she would tell us of the marvels of that time."

Polidoro's mind was elsewhere, as he eyed the mattress. Little by little, his overwrought excitement vanished. No inner voice dictated to him feelings capable of taking the place of the one of bygone days, when he was forty years old.

Virgílio feared that because of Polidoro's dejection he would be deprived of the honor he deserved for having discovered the mattress.

"Let's restore this object immediately. It constitutes part of the art of love." He feigned enthusiasm.

Polidoro was unresponsive. Life escaped him through the cracks in the door as he heard Virgílio arranging Caetana's bedroom without forgetting a single detail. Caetana, whose eyes were drained to the last tear by the poverty of Brazil, should lack for nothing. With what delight Virgílio referred to the yellow pitcher whose flowers came from the garden of his house. And the deck of playing cards, which should be close at hand for the two lovers, in case they wanted to entertain themselves with private games! At each recollection, Virgílio, with Mágico's approval, became Caetana's partner in playful pranks, failing only to admit in his flights of fancy that the actress, after getting off the train in Trindade, would automatically substitute Polidoro's name for his as a natural corollary of the story now being recounted.

As the two men labored over this wealth of details, Polidoro felt neglected.

"The bedroom will be ready by Friday, but which of you will

give me back the twenty years I'm in need of? What do I do now with these wrinkles and stiff joints of mine?"

Polidoro covered his face at the memory of a love that in the past had not shunned what were most likely obscene practices in order to express itself.

Faced with the threat of losing Polidoro's trust, Virgílio searched through his repertory for the phrase that would raise his friend's spirits. No word to restore the cattle baron's morale came to mind. Any error, and Polidoro would accuse him, till his dying day, of having only inadequate resources at his disposal. They were arguing over the subject, beneath Mágico's dejected gaze, when a knock on the door drew Polidoro from his apathy.

Ernesto, having forgotten the ill-treatment to which they had subjected him in the pharmacy, asked to come in. He wanted to see Caetana's furniture.

"Why such a long face, Polidoro?" Smiling, he scrutinized the chaotic collection. "And what were these pieces of furniture doing in this damned cellar all this time?"

Polidoro clung fast to his friend. Virgílio had not been able to rid him of the dark veils that were gradually obscuring his vision of the world. Perhaps Ernesto, with his easygoing temperament, a steadfast proponent of the simple, everyday life, would bring him back to the earth's crust, where human passions truly fought it out with one another. Only upon his return to a landscape at times inhospitable would he regain the joyfulness with which to greet Caetana on Friday.

Polidoro showed Ernesto the mattress. There, according to Virgílio, Caetana and he had used tooth and claw to provide an outlet for the desire that took over their conscious awareness. And in the celebration of the amorous ritual they had automatically gone back to pagan times, when humankind had at its disposal a legion of friendly gods and goddesses. At this point, though, he could not deny the dramatic evidence that the twenty years of waiting had exhausted the energy that in the past he had squandered like a despot.

"When I had carnal knowledge of Caetana, I felt I was a god.

My body was a razor. It mutilated anyone and everyone. No one could wrest this sharp-honed sword blade from me. But now, in front of the mirror, what I see does not match my heart, which has the illusion that it is still young."

Ernesto avoided associating himself with Polidoro's recent depression. He too felt his joints growing stiff, death whispering in his ear words that smelled of spikenard, promising him the one embrace that possessed immortality as an attribute.

"So you're not going to save me, then?" Polidoro shouted, pulling himself together.

Ernesto had no way out. Polidoro wanted him as a mirror, even one that was broken and tarnished.

"Tell me, Ernesto, where can the face that Caetana caressed have gone? Look, I'm old and bloated. I no longer arouse anyone's passions. How can a person live without that hope!"

Ernesto decided to do battle with this funeral procession of desperate men in the cellar, led by Virgílio. He had falsehood on his side, to be used kindly and in small doses.

"Enough of all that history of Brazil. By harping on it, we'll doom this country and ourselves," he said.

The professor had to be unmasked. Even at Gioconda's place, on Mondays, he persisted in presenting the whores with bits and pieces of the history of the country that they hadn't had a chance to study in school. And as part of his pedagogy he took them to bed only after questioning them about the transition of Brazil from a monarchy to a republic.

Ernesto pitied Polidoro. Standing there before him, crestfallen, Polidoro needed to have his confidence in himself restored.

"Fight, man! Who is there anywhere around here who has a biography so full to overflowing with love affairs? Even Gioconda is infatuated with you."

This odious expedient, resorted to on the pretext of consoling Polidoro, wounded Virgílio's sensibilities. "Such a lack of respect!" He hastened to defend the honor of the woman who offered him a cup of tea every Monday.

"Why is it impossible for me to be loved? Am I a monster?"

Polidoro awakened from his lethargy, gravely offended. Had the professor forgotten his talent for inspiring sentiments underlaid at one and the same time by nobility and ecstasy?

Virgílio regretted his own imprudence. He gave the field over to Ernesto, who thanked him with a sarcastic smile.

"How to admit any other woman in his life except Caetana, even though she was off on a tour of all of Brazil?" Virgílio responded forthrightly, with the intention of rescuing his friendship with Polidoro.

A plot aimed at discrediting Virgílio was taking shape. Mágico could provide the names of those responsible. He prided himself on being present at the very place and moment of its birth.

"What bad taste to compare Gioconda with Caetana, who's a professional of the seventh art," he said, in his eagerness to take part in the dispute.

Surrounded by enemies, Ernesto admitted that he had spoken impulsively, and that certain of his words vanished in thin air in seconds whereas others, by virtue of their burden of poison, put down roots, contaminated human destiny. It behooved him to rid himself of the latter. They gave the Judas kiss to the very best of sentiments. This being so, his friends should respect his good faith. In the name of this principle, they would be treading on firm ground once again, surrounded by palisades and barbed wire.

Ernesto's defense was based on increasingly minute details. Like Virgílio, he delighted in overwhelming his fellows with his fiery discourse.

"In this entire story, I'm the only one who's been hurt. I lost Caetana, and I feel the mercilessness of the years. Enough of all these apologies," Polidoro broke in, impatient with an outpouring of words that threatened to last till lunchtime.

As he accused them of being thoughtless, or asked them to make amends, he began to experience a sense of unexpected vigor. The memories awakened by the mattress brought back his youth and a tumescent rod, a cock ready to welcome acts of sheer folly.

"After all, what reason do I have to complain if this mattress is the living proof of how happy I can still be!"

Having marked each word with the brand of hope, he fled from the arms of Virgílio and Ernesto, who celebrated his return to the sexual tournament, in jousts they regarded as exemplary.

On his own initiative, Mágico dragged the mattress toward the door, leaving behind a cloud of dust. In the unexpected haze, no one could tell which one of them had voiced a lament that slashed through the cellar like a machete.

"Who's that who's weeping?" murmured a voice that might well have been a collective one.

As the dust settled, Virgílio stifled his sobs with his handkerchief, risking stumbling at any moment over the mattress. Seeing the professor in danger, Polidoro hastened to the rescue, but his gesture came too late. Dragged down by the weight of Virgílio's body, the two of them fell on top of the mattress, struggling in vain to get off it and stand up again. They were trying their best to free themselves from a magic spell coming from the mattress itself that made them scarcely able to move, while Polidoro, for the first time, lay down on it without clasping Caetana's body to his.

Mágico knelt on the mattress, attracted by the scene. Virgílio, already recovered from his fit of weeping, immediately welcomed him. Sitting there, they would be protected from the unpleasantnesses that were clotting the streets of Trindade.

From a distance, Ernesto resisted joining the bizarre party, fearing an unpredictable outcome. He was tempted at the same time to test his status as a man amid those who were wretched. Cautiously, he came closer. Polidoro held out a hand to him, preaching the need to undergo their experience. He gratefully accepted the gesture and allowed himself to be led to the mattress.

The disconsolate air of the four men made their destinies one and the same. They felt cold, because of the dampness of the cellar, but they lacked the courage to break the spell cast by the mattress, and lacked, above all, the will to rise to their feet and together confront once again the burning-hot sun that at that hour beat down on the streets of Trindade.

THE FLOWERS were gathered in the garden, amid the tomatoes, the cabbage, the parsley. Gioconda was partial to magnolias, thinking of Polidoro's mother, who had borne the name of that flower. Gioconda herself cut the blooms, with the rusty pair of shears lying long-forgotten in the kitchen drawer.

On that Friday, contrary to her habits, Gioconda woke up early, anxious to prepare lunch, which was supposed to be on the table at eleven o'clock. The ceremony to welcome Caetana couldn't be one minute late. The arrival of the train in Trindade to let off Caetana and friends was scheduled for two-seventeen that afternoon.

It would definitely be nerve-racking getting off the train. The stoker of the locomotive had orders to remain just two minutes in the station, after which time the passengers could protest the sidetracking of the train, which, in flagrant disrespect of the timetable, was taking off on tracks long out of service, at the risk of their lives.

Locomotive engineer Mendes, despite his fear of an administrative trial that would cut short his careful, cautious career just one step away from his retirement, and despite his doubts about tracks liable to cause a derailment, finally gave in, upon being faced with Gioconda's insistence and the impulses of his own passion. She herself proved to him that the railway tracks, luckily, were still in good shape on the branch line.

Nonetheless, they would do everything quickly, so that the city would not suspect what was happening. After leaving Caetana on the platform, the train would depart, whistling for all it was worth, so hurriedly that the curious, seeing it leave, would think that they were the victims of an illusion brought on by a long siesta after a copious midday meal.

Since the day before, Gioconda had had to cope with the animosity of the Three Graces. By common accord, they had decided to appear at the station, with the intention of offering Caetana the homage that for twenty years had been filling their hearts like the padding of a quilt.

Gioconda was scared. The convoy of whores was going to infuriate Polidoro, who, after so many years, was dreaming of another sort of reception for Caetana. He therefore asked them to sacrifice their ambitions for at least a few hours. Caetana would not fail to visit them under cover of darkness. How happy she would be to settle herself comfortably on the red sofa that in the past had merited her lofty praise. Then the five women, dallying over arrowroot biscuits, cookies, cheese bread, and coffee, would utter the words that on many a night during those long years had set their imaginations on fire. Nights, above all, when they were assailed by the dark world of affections, generally rarefied sentiments that required air shafts, exit doors, so as not to asphyxiate the women.

When crossed, Polidoro could be unpredictable. And they ought not to forget that, besides being a frequent visitor to the establishment, he brought them presents throughout the year. At Christmas, he loaded their table with roast turkey, toasted manioc, and trays of fruits and sweets.

"But even so, Polidoro didn't make us rich or set any of us up as his mistress with her own house. What proofs, then, did he give us of love?" protested Diana, the one in search of a man who would hand her the keys to a furnished house. Her eyelashes, tense from her fear of the future, blinked nervously.

"If he were to take one of us as his mistress, he would be betraying Caetana," Sebastiana said, with the logic of loyalty.

"Anybody who disappears for more than twenty years can no longer count on her lover. He's free to take another mistress," Diana insisted, obsessed by the vision of a little house where she could be at peace some day, without fear of bills to be paid at the end of the month and swollen varicose veins.

Gioconda was peeling potatoes, her eyes meanwhile fixed on the pots boiling on the stove. As the slices dropped into the water, they spattered her angry eyes. Sebastiana tried to console her.

"Diana doesn't know what she's saying. It's that wretched age when we're forced to retire that's threatening us. After all, who's going to take care of us when that time comes?"

Diana was stubborn. She confronted Gioconda rebelliously.

"Just look at what a sad life we lead. Who ever saw the owner of a first-class brothel peeling potatoes? What good did it do you to be all smiles for Polidoro?"

The intrusion of that voice cawing in her ear upset Gioconda, who flung the paring knife into the sink.

"I do certain things out of nostalgia. And out of the pain I bear in my breast that you never suspected."

Palmira begged them all to calm down. The next few hours demanded a concentration befitting the sentiments long sheltered in their bosoms.

"It's to celebrate Caetana's arrival."

The remark, made so kindly, moved Gioconda. And so, especially, did the cup of coffee Palmira brought her. She sipped each drop with the certainty that Polidoro would not forgive the women's presence in the station, clinging to one another, getting mud all over Caetana's red velvet cape, now surely faded and threadbare.

Diana did not give an inch. And, as proof that she would not abandon her convictions, she even refrained from taking Gioconda a glass of water to relieve the thirst caused by their fruitless, endless dispute.

Despite the argument, they rubbed their hair with castor oil. And when it came time to rinse it, they resorted to expedients that made it dance in the wind. Their fingernails, painted a reddish purple, reminded Sebastiana of the liturgical draperies for Good Friday. Meanwhile, on the second floor, Diana hurried to the oval mirror in the hallway, which cruelly enlarged the worn-out pores of her face.

"How we've aged in these years! I only hope that Caetana isn't as sharp-eyed as she once was," Diana muttered, filled with nostalgia for a house of her own that was vanishing on the horizon. She was always embittered when she returned from these excursions to the mirror. Trying to fight time, she immediately changed her hairdo, her makeup, daubed her eyelids and lashes with mascara like a star in silent films, longing to recover the beauty she had had in the days when she had gone to visit Caetana at the circus, in the afternoons, before her act.

Such effort moved Sebastiana. She too—the victim of the bleeding away of the years, which she had no way to stanch—blew her nose into a linen handkerchief, a present from Virgílio.

"Remember the caramels that Caetana gave me when she saw how upset I was at the figures that moved about the circus ring like elves and princes?"

Gioconda drew her close, with the aim of interrupting an outpouring of emotions. Sebastiana, however, drew away from the scrawny arms whose embrace was painful.

"I never managed to find out whether Caetana shared my tears or was saddened by them. All I know is that she began carefully licking them away and I was afraid her tongue would hurt me. And she wouldn't allow Polidoro to rush her to the hotel."

As she listened to the secret that Sebastiana was sharing, Palmira lit her cigarette with a long-stemmed match, set aside for giving an elegant touch some day to the fireplace that Gioconda had promised to build in the parlor. The flames would warm her joints in winter before she disappeared into one of the upstairs rooms.

Gioconda finally gave in. The bared incisors of the women signaled her defeat.

"Polidoro deserves to be peeved. He's a dictator," Diana said, her attention concentrated on enameling her fingernails.

"Aren't all men dictators?" Palmira mused resignedly.

Sebastiana quickly reviewed the history of Brazil. Thanks to Virgílio, who frequented her bed, she could reel off certain fragments of it with relative ease and offhandedness.

"It's always been that way, ever since the first days of the discovery of Brazil. Beginning with the three emperors who lived down in Petrópolis."

The domestic rebellion slowly spread. Gioconda, however, followed these manifestations with a strange sweet-tempered delight. These women were her family, especially Sebastiana, who touched her more than all the others.

"You're mistaken this time, Sebastiana. We had two emperors, that's all, and that's enough, since Pedro I was a real skirt-chaser. There's not one man in Trindade who can hold a candle to him. But what was the use of his going across other men's rooftops like a scalded cat if nobody remembers him today?"

For lunch on that Friday, Gioconda used seasoning with too heavy a hand. Hurriedly put together, the beef hash, loaded with garlic, pepper, and bay leaves, wasn't at all to the women's liking.

"Nobody's going to want to go to bed with me today if I reek of garlic," Diana complained.

Dawn had not yet broken when the Three Graces had beaten the cake batter, with renewed hope. Once they had taken the cake out of the oven, they put the three layers together with the greatest caution, carefully frosting it with egg white they had thickened by beating in sugar and lemon. Since the cake made them think of a religious holiday, they spent the whole time singing liturgical hymns, chiefly the ones devoted to the Virgin and to May, the month of Mary, which brides also remembered.

"If it weren't for Sebastiana and her mania for dates, we would have forgotten Caetana's birthday. She's a Gemini, but she looks like a Leo. A wild African beast without a mane," Palmira said, her attention fixed on the spatula with which she was smoothing the icing on the cake.

"She chose this day on purpose. Just to test us. And to see whether we'd forgotten her." Sebastiana prided herself on a memory that, even though it made her suffer, kept her in close touch with the past, always more favorable than the present.

Sitting at the table, they downed the lunch they found unappetizing. Sebastiana never took her eyes off the cake, which she was afraid might fall.

"Who told Polidoro that it was her birthday, so that he bought a necklace with four strands of cultured pearls, each representing a season of the year?" Palmira sighed dreamily.

Diana immediately attacked her.

"Have you forgotten that spring in Trindade is the same as

summer? And that the breeze in January is the same one that blows in July as a sign that winter has come?"

Gioconda looked at the clock.

"We'd better get going. We'll wash the dirty dishes when we get back."

The station was a long way from the center of town and the brothel, so it took them an hour to get there. If they were lucky, they wouldn't find anybody around the place. The building, its paint peeling, was completely deserted. From inside, Narciso the constable, responsible for keeping order, consulted with ill-disguised impatience the pocket watch attached to one of his suspenders. Each hour brought the illusion that good news was about to arrive by telegraph, informing him of his transfer to a suburb of Rio de Janeiro.

From the knock on the door, Narciso suspected that women were about to visit the place. It was a knock that lacked force and strength of purpose. He had trouble getting the warped door open. When confronted by the retinue, he drew back fearfully. The afternoon heat blurred his sight.

"What are you doing here?" He looked Diana, Palmira, and Sebastiana over from head to foot with a stern gaze. "I have orders to let only Gioconda in." As he mentioned the woman's name, he lowered his voice to a tone of respectful gallantry. "That is because of her queenly bearing."

Against her will, Gioconda stiffened her shoulders. She felt tired. She had gotten out of bed at six o'clock that morning. And the journey from the house to the station had been even longer because of the roundabout path they had taken, to avoid arousing people's suspicions.

"Brazil has no place for queens, officer. Much less for cavaliers." With a resolute gesture, she sought passage for herself and the Three Graces.

"Just a moment." He made as if to keep them from entering.

Gioconda pushed his arm aside with her hand. "It's too late now, officer." With a forced smile, he accepted the gesture. "All of us are in the same boat; we all share the same fate."

The white turban she was wearing that afternoon hid her curly hair and made her look taller. The contrast with her swarthy skin was striking. Narciso had never been able to bring her secrets to light or get to the bottom of her intimate relationship with Polidoro. He decided it was best to give way.

Then, proving the truth of his words despite his great propensity for telling lies, she came into the station, drawn up to her full height, followed by the Three Graces in a row. The walls, covered with dark-purple stains, gave off a strong smell of urine and mold. The damp spots had already reached the ceiling. The diligent cleaning job done by Narciso and the police sergeant early that morning, by candlelight, not making a sound as they rid the building of big dead rats, spider webs, litter on the floor, had not eliminated its look of desolation and squalor.

The women followed Gioconda without ever once opening their mouths, their attention concentrated on the cake now being carried by Palmira, in accordance with the rotation that shifted it to a different pair of hands every ten minutes, Gioconda being spared from this task from the very beginning since she had not taken part in making the cake. Her duty was to cradle the fresh bouquet of magnolias against her bosom. Her hands, thus occupied, kept her from greeting those present.

They had dressed discreetly, except for rhinestone-studded barrettes in their shiny hair. But Polidoro shuddered at the sight of these harlots disguised as respectable matrons. Convinced that Gioconda was responsible for the group's follies, he readied himself to rush at the women, taking care beforehand to alert the professor standing at his side.

"Here I go!"

Virgílio did nothing to hold him back. He was even relieved by Polidoro's providential abandonment of him. It would keep him from having to use force to restrain Polidoro in his furious attack on the women to make them return to Estação. He had no desire whatsoever to be a witness to an act of public humiliation. After all, he drank tea in the company of these women every Monday. Not to mention his setting foot, and then placing the remainder of his body, in the beds of the Three Graces. And Sebastiana granted him not only her intimate favors but made him the beneficiary of her resigned patience as well.

Polidoro modulated his voice in Gioconda's presence. He did not want to call attention to himself in a building with unpredictable acoustics. Life's echo was immoderately loud in that place.

"Apparently you've brought your entire entourage. The one thing that's missing is a band to strike up in celebration of your arrival. Where do you intend to take all these womenfolk, if I may ask?"

Gioconda adjusted her turban; the structure threatened to fall apart at her first careless move. Polidoro looked into her eyes as into a remote shadow on the horizon outside the building. A man prepared to give up his pride the moment Caetana was installed on the fifth floor of the Palace. He would be the first to present her with the keys to the city. With her Eurasian eyes, which opened wide with fury, Caetana could be persuasive, though she was capable, once pacified, of depositing in friendly hands presents that ran the gamut from hairpins to homemade perfumes. By means of such gifts, she had encouraged the Three Graces to give free rein to the roguishness of their hearts, though the heart was an organ, according to her, that encouraged sudden storms and ought to be mistrusted: contrary to what those afflicted with love troubles maintained, the heart had more to do with death than with life, properly speaking.

"Have any of you ever heard of Don José? He's a character in an opera who, in the name of love, regarded himself as the lord and master of Carmen. And, for that reason alone, he knifed the woman. Lovers, in general, are horrible property-owners. They appropriate other people's bodies without acknowledging the rights of their legal owners. Never forget, Gioconda, anyone who loves to excess all the time ends up loving in the wrong way. Cite me just one example of a character in opera and literature who loved in the right way, in the proper proportion," Caetana had said to her in confidence on the eve of her sudden departure from Trindade.

Gioconda's inattentiveness was interpreted by Polidoro as a

discourtesy. He would not allow himself to be affronted in public by a courtesan.

"Besides being a whore, have you become deaf as well?"

This hostile remark mobilized the Three Graces in Gioconda's defense. Sebastiana, whose turn it was to hold the cake, raised it in front of Polidoro's eyes, blocking his vision.

"Stop that, or you're going to cause a disaster," Polidoro said; afraid that the cake was going to end up on the floor, he propped up Sebastiana's arms so they wouldn't give out.

In the struggle, Sebastiana misinterpreted the meaning of his gesture as a threat of gratuitous violence; she called for help.

"Don't ruin our birthday party. Caetana would never forgive you."

The victim of unexpected injustice, Polidoro did his best to clear up the misunderstanding. It was far from his intention to hurt friends whose bodies he had seen growing parched from exposure to the sun and to the years for a long time now. Incapable of listening to him, Gioconda called on the representative of authority who was present.

"Constable Narciso, I need your testimony. That's what the police are for, after all. But if it were necessary, I'd hire a lawyer. Do you think harlots never have lawyers?" She puffed out her chest like a pouter pigeon's.

Polidoro apologized profusely. It was quite true that he had resorted to words tinged with wrath and scorn, but he had no intention of causing mortal wounds. Why, then, were they shooting poisoned darts back at him?

"Don't you think of me as a friend any more? Am I to stop sending you roasts for the month of December? Or cane brandy from my own stills for hot punch in midwinter?" His voice faded beneath the stress of his emotion, to the point where Virgílio, who had now come closer, did not hear what he said.

"What plot are you hatching so stealthily?" the professor asked suspiciously. "I too am part of the company that has lent luster to this celebration! If it weren't for me, the love affair of Caetana and Polidoro would be no more than a second-rate story. Do you remember Romeo and Juliet? If it hadn't been for Shakespeare, those two adolescents wouldn't show up on Brazilian menus so frequently as the name of a very popular dessert. Who among us does not appreciate a slice of guava paste with cream cheese?"

More relaxed now, Gioconda tried to give up her strong feelings and return to the laws of her profession. Her face, again a mask, smiled at Virgílio, as Polidoro, wanting to please her, stepped aside to let her pass. He was the first to recognize the vagaries of friendship, generally mere tides that came in and then went out again, causing disturbances in the lunar heart. It was worth everyone's while, therefore, to back the effort being made by the professor, thanks to whom the secrets of all of them would be recounted in prose and in verse in the future.

"It'd be too bad for us if we didn't have a neighbor who makes us the focal point of his intrigues! Virgílio is right. Who would ever believe that there existed in Trindade people like us, with the same passionate nature as Romeo and Juliet?"

Now that calm was restored, Narciso settled down on the bench. He had not slept a wink that night. Broom in hand, he had not left a speck of dust on the floor. Even though this service undermined his authority, it ought to be rewarded. He had long sought an assignment to the outskirts of Rio de Janeiro. As a constable in Trindade, condemned to oblivion, he would never get his name in the records of the capital.

Absorbed in such thoughts, he took a close look at Gioconda. She was avoiding the sun rays coming in through the skylight. Standing near the window where train tickets had once been sold, she pointed to the wooden benches.

"Take a rest, girls. We still have nine minutes to wait. Let's pray that the cake doesn't collapse. How did you ever come up with the idea of making three layers? Look at the top one. It's crooked."

Palmira, whose turn it was to watch over the cake, felt her arms giving way. What with the heat and the trip to the station, she was afraid the cake was going to collapse. She would prefer that the disaster take place when the one on watch was Sebastiana, who was given to bursting into tears in front of strangers, twisting locks of her hair with ring-laden fingers.

Palmira put the tray down on the bench. In order to make certain that the cake was still all right, she removed the paper protecting it. The five doves made of sugar, poked into the icing for decoration, seemed to be asleep. Three of them still had defiant beaks, but the littlest one of all had a broken wing.

Diana came over to watch the operation. As she walked around the bench, she let her splendid legs show through the side slits in her dress. Their eyes glued to the clock on the wall, none of the men paid any attention to her, however.

Diana harbored a secret envy of women who sprinkled life with sugar in their kitchens, exercising an art in whose name they allowed themselves to be shut up in windowless bedrooms, though they nonetheless sighed with happiness. Jubilation came to them from the red-hot oven where they were baking the most savory fantasies, and that permitted them to be whores like herself.

"Don't be sad, Diana. We'll soon be embracing Caetana," Palmira said, free now of responsibility for the cake. She cautiously opened her handbag. She was afraid of waking up one morning without any resources, without a single penny for soup. Perhaps that was why she avoided giving presents to anybody, her avarice being a fact well known to all of them. She had made an exception only for Caetana, by buying the five little doves to put on the cake.

She took out of her purse a handful of birthday candles, each a different color. Polidoro watched Palmira inserting them in the snow-white surface of the cake.

"Wouldn't it be prettier if they were all the same color?" He pointed to the candles, oblivious of the fact that he had made fun of them in public.

His interest touched Palmira. What was missing, of course, was Caetana, to blend the colors into a harmonious whole.

"Well, anyway, an imitation rainbow is a pretty thing," Palmira answered simply.

Noticing the fragile wick of one of the candles, Polidoro forgot about the train, his attention focused on how carefully the candles must be lit when the time came. The slightest inattention to the rain or the wind would make it impossible to keep them lit until

Caetana could blow them out. "And isn't it bad luck if a candle goes out before it even gets blown on?"

Gioconda's turban threatened to fall off. She was having trouble keeping it properly balanced on her head.

"Enough of your pessimism, Polidoro," she said, carefully readjusting the turban. "Even Venieris, it seems, is so mistrustful of life that he calls upon the gods on the smallest pretext. He at least has the excuse that he's Greek."

Polidoro looked at the clock and trembled to see how little time was left. He threatened to go out onto the train platform. "There are only seven minutes left, and Ernesto still hasn't come," he said, not budging. As though he sensed this plea, Ernesto arrived just then, all out of breath, his face dripping with sweat.

"I almost didn't make it. Vivina was late getting lunch on the table. I couldn't plead with her to hurry it up, or she might have suspected something. She'd already accused me at breakfast of having the face of a horse thief. I asked her what sort of face a thief who specialized in stealing horses had. She answered that it was the face of somebody who's committed a crime. I laughed along with her. So then she put on a face that made her look like a fortuneteller, an expression she always gets exactly right."

Noting Polidoro's pallor, Ernesto forgot his recent troubles.

"What kind of face is *that?*"

Gioconda was upset to see the flowers wilting after being out of water for so long.

"Even magnolias are afraid of minutes that are wasted."

She clapped her hands, grouping the women in a tight formation, well suited to Caetana's theatrical sentiments. When she stepped off the train, she ought to catch them unawares in a harmonious pose. An actress with her perfect poise took notice of any gesture reminiscent of the theater. Anyone who had once trod the boards never again looked on the world in the same way. Even if one's heart was paying no particular attention, it would unexpectedly be overcome by any passing fever.

"Where are you going, Gioconda?" Polidoro asked anxiously.

Gioconda moved her shoulders, freed now of secret burdens.

"I want to hear the train engine puffing in the distance. It sounds like a puppy with its tongue hanging out, or an old man in bed."

Such words affected Polidoro's sense of honor. Gioconda was taking her revenge by painting his portrait. He thought of replying in kind, but controlled his fury, following the hands of the clock, which had moved forward five minutes.

"That whore became refined at my expense, and now she's making fun of me," he said to Ernesto.

The pharmacist saw no reason for complaint. The whole thing had been nothing but a minor cockfight, troubles vented in the back yard as the two of them pecked at each other. He for his part was longing to have his face scratched by a mandarin's fingernails.

"Have you ever thought what it means to make love as an indomitable harlot rakes your face with her nails painted red?" Wherever he was, Ernesto dreamed. He took pleasure in giving free rein to his appetites. For a few seconds, lust set in on his distended features.

Virgílio went back inside the building.

"Don't you want to be closer to the tracks, to get a better view? Before the train arrives?"

Virgílio's insistence made Polidoro uncomfortable. He also felt Narciso's vigilant eye keeping tabs on him.

"When you hear the train whistle, just before it gets to the curve, let me know."

As he sat down in the place that had just been occupied by Sebastiana, Polidoro absorbed the warmth that her panting, voluminous backside had left behind. The sensation that mounted along his thighs did him good. He had the illusion, amid chills and shivers, that he was on top of Caetana's body. The image, though fleeting, made him numb all over.

Ernesto came back inside from the platform, where he'd gone to have a quick look. "Unless it's late, the train will be here in three minutes. You'd better get a move on, Polidoro. Otherwise I'll take Caetana in my arms before you do," he said to needle him.

Polidoro pretended to be suffering from a sudden pain in his jaw.

"Can it be that that miserable tooth of mine has started making my gum swell at precisely this moment?"

As they discussed what procedure to resort to if this were the case, Virgílio too seemed all on edge.

"According to the smell of coal reaching my nose, the locomotive is already almost at the curve. I'll make a bet with anyone who's willing that Caetana will step off the train dressed in yellow, her favorite color."

All their rushing back and forth upset Polidoro. As did the applause that he could hear from the platform. He was afraid that life was unfolding somewhere far from his eyes, but at the same time he could not bear to surprise Caetana in the act of setting foot in the place where she had been happy.

Polidoro was sweating. Ernesto felt his head. He had a fever. Not wanting to arouse people's pity, however, the cattle baron proclaimed in a voice loud enough to be heard by everyone:

"Women are ingrates."

Polidoro's love knew no shame. It set his face and his heart on fire, both at the same time. With such a scene before his eyes, Ernesto had a presentiment that love, under those conditions, could be a dark, cold dungeon. He felt sorry for the rancher, for himself, for the illusion of being happy some day that both of them still cherished.

"The train has reached the curve. Are you listening?" he said one last time.

Polidoro marshaled all his energy. He forced himself to smile. At that moment, he yearned to grow younger.

"I'm not listening, but my heart is. This heart sees Caetana in the last car, with her head out the window, eager to identify each tree, each tiled rooftop of Trindade. And me as well, who will be behind all those people on the platform waving flags, greeting her with outstretched arms. Isn't it true that I've hardly changed in these twenty years?"

The plea, addressed to Ernesto, reached for Caetana, still a long distance away from the spot where Polidoro was standing. Everything about him rejected the truth. As a matter of fact, he forced Ernesto to answer with a white lie. Shielded by fantasy, he would have the courage to go through the door, to join the others.

The whistle of the train, at the curve now, cut through the hot afternoon. Ernesto embraced its shadow.

"Why is it, do you think, that in Brazil progress always robs us of a tradition that was part and parcel of our soul once upon a time? Whatever happened to trains, for instance? How can we get to the Northeast or the South if they yank out the tracks the way dentists extract rotten teeth?" Polidoro said, in an effort to fill the emptiness between fear and illusion.

An adherent of the progress that opened up narrow forest trails, Ernesto waxed enthusiastic.

"Consider the size of Brazil if you use nothing but cars, buses, and airplanes. That damned Andreazza is pulling up the tracks with his very own hands while everyone is asleep. That's why God made him as stout as a bull."

Led out to the platform, Polidoro took his place directly beside Virgílio, who was looking at the train windows as it pulled in, searching for a head that he knew well.

"Who knows whether the fireman aboard is still Pedro, who used to bring me books and scholarly journals from Rio de Janeiro?" Virgílio said, enveloped in the soot and smoke.

The air swirling about shook the signboard posted on the roof with the name of Trindade branded into it. The passengers, surprised by the welcome, waved from the windows, in their eagerness to embrace friends who were scattered about in small towns all over the country.

"Look there, it's Caetana!" Diana's shrieks were thwarting Gioconda's plans, for she had been preaching discretion.

"Where is she that I don't see her?" Palmira, unable to contain her distress a moment longer, broke the ruler-straight formation, followed by Diana and Sebastiana. Gioconda, left behind, tried in vain to tug at Palmira's dress, to bring her back to the original rigid lineup.

Overcome by emotion, Sebastiana sought Virgílio's aid. He, however, wanting to have his arms free to embrace Caetana, to applaud her at the very moment she came down the steps as though stepping onto the stage of a theater in the capital, fled from Sebastiana without the least consideration.

Ernesto was unable to identify Caetana among the passengers.

"Where is she?" he asked Virgílio.

"How can I catch the first glimpse of her if I'm older than you are!"

He hurried off. Ernesto too wanted to rob him of the embrace that the actress had reserved especially for him.

Sebastiana sought out Gioconda's company amid the passengers getting off the train.

"What about the cake we left in the waiting room? Who stayed behind on guard so it wouldn't be stolen?"

To her amazement, Gioconda fled from her as well.

"Leave me in peace and try to find out yourself," she answered before rushing on ahead. In a conciliatory gesture, she immediately turned back. "Why are all these people determined to get off at Trindade if they're taking the train to a station farther on?"

The passengers, encountering the unexpected parade, were hurriedly trying to buy meat pies, sweets, newspapers, so as to break the monotony of the trip.

"Where are we?" one passenger asked. Polidoro paid no attention to him.

"What damned one-horse town is this?" the man persisted in a huff.

In his expectation of meeting up with Caetana, the tumult of voices seemed to give Polidoro an indication of exactly where along the platform the actress had just gotten off the train. Diana too, victim of the same illusion, ran past the cattle baron, colliding with the passengers. Her distress mounted as the train whistle announced the departure from the station and the passengers began to empty the platform to find their way back to their seats.

"There's Caetana!" Gioconda shouted, running toward a woman at the far end of the platform. But the actress didn't budge, despite her expectation of receiving a big hug. Gioconda didn't care. Each step was bringing her to Caetana, and that certainty filled her life. She went on, less and less able to see, her eyes dimmed by sweat and tears, and running the risk of stumbling and falling. A vague shape intercepted her mad dash, nearly knocking her off her feet. Furious at this cowardly act, she forced herself to identify her aggressor. Although the shape was headed off in Caetana's direction, Gioconda recognized Diana. That whore, with her arrogant selfish ways, was out to win the laurels of victory for herself alone.

Virgílio hadn't dropped out of the competition. Though he had managed to outdistance Gioconda, his footsteps were being dogged by Sebastiana, who was hindering him from making any headway.

"Let go of me, Sebastiana. Since when have we been twins?" he said, hoping his remark would send her back to the brothel. Especially since the shadow of Caetana, veiled by the roof, un-lighted in that remote corner of the station, was coming to meet him.

"Caetana, Caetana," Virgílio said, all agog.

Torn between the desire to remain in Trindade, the signs that the locomotive fireman was making to her as he started up the train, and the shouts of the anxious passengers, the actress seemed to hesitate as to what course she should follow. But once the train began to gather speed, the woman, on the point of missing it forever, jumped inside the very last car with unexpected agility. And when, from the door of the car, she waved to those who remained behind on the platform, with the nostalgic sadness of one who in the past has suffered the desperate loneliness of small towns, everyone could swear that it was not Caetana.

Diana, who had lost her voice from repeatedly shouting Cae-tana's name, begging her to leap off the moving train and straight into her arms, at the risk of hurting herself, thought that disillu-sionment was a motheaten coat. She sought comfort in Palmira and Sebastiana, not remembering that they had offended her just minutes before.

"If that wasn't Caetana, where's the real one?"

Nostalgic for the human warmth that at times he found next to Sebastiana's flesh, Virgílio joined the women. But Diana saw no reason to offer him refuge.

"Do you think I didn't see when you left us behind? Just so you could be the first one to embrace Caetana?"

Such selfishness wounded her sensibilities. She remembered that men, in the black periods of history, turned against the virtues that in earlier days had aroused their admiration. Virgílio preferred silence to stubborn defense, which might hurt Diana. They had all suffered far too much that afternoon. He especially pitied Gioconda, standing at the edge of the platform, seemingly about to fling herself onto the tracks like a modern Anna Karenina, unable to fathom the reasons that had led Caetana to miss the train or give up coming to Trindade.

Polidoro refused to leave the platform and come back inside the station, his attention concentrated on the newspaper that a thoughtless passenger had thrown out the window of the train. He nourished the hope of finding a note between those pages that the wind had begun to rip to pieces. Ernesto, sensing what was going through Polidoro's mind, leafed through the badly torn paper. He had no idea how to suggest to Polidoro with the necessary gentleness that Caetana, kept away by a case of the flu or the recent loss of someone close to her, had not been able to respond to his love. Or else, having accumulated so many treasures in her heart, she was afraid to confront them with reality. By failing to come to Trindade, she remained in possession of her destiny at least, stuffed into a bundle of clothes, whereas for Polidoro it had all been a dream that the grease of everyday life and the soot of the train had undertaken to make disappear forever. In the last analysis, dreaming was too great a burden for the ordinary mortal.

"Let's get out of here. A strong wind's begun to blow," Ernesto said.

In front of the passenger turnstile, through which he had decided to exit, Polidoro confronted Gioconda, who halted, expecting the rancher to step aside to let her go through first. He, however, chose to be discourteous: he took a step forward, leaving her behind. The rusty mechanism of the turnstile made a noise that gave him pains in his chest. They were signs that at the age of sixty he had no reason for celebration.

In the waiting room, once they were all together again, Gioconda was on her guard against Polidoro. She didn't want him to see in her retina, running about loose in the field, the hare that both of them dreamed of shooting with the same silver shotgun. She wanted to hurt him, even if her revenge was a bit late in coming.

"Don't fool yourself. Caetana never took that train. She didn't want to come back to Trindade. She's given us up forever."

Gioconda dissolved his dream in an implacable acid, after dissuading Caetana, by means of telepathic messages, from returning to the city. That whore, with the hard-won wisdom of her profession, was unable to accept a love story with a happy ending.

"What do you mean?" Polidoro stammered, barely getting the words out.

"Caetana pulled a fast one on us. She wanted us to be happy for at least four days."

Gioconda's arrogance resurfaced as she drove the knife in deeper.

"We're doomed to mourn her absence for the rest of our lives."

Without begging their pardon, Diana interrupted them. She was hungry and eager to go back to the house.

Gioconda looked at the clock. She was surprised at how hungry she was too. Her stomach positively refused to respect heartbreak. Virgílio joined the group. He was readier than ever to have some of the cake. His saliva had dried up, to the point where his words stuck in his throat. But, not wishing to make a suggestion, he had entrusted the task of expressing his feelings to Diana.

"I can't bear to take the cake back home. It's better to leave it here for the ants to eat," she said when it caught her eye. The three layers, like a pyramid in the desert, stood out starkly in the station.

Palmira too refused to carry the cake back. She argued in favor of its immediate consumption, demonstrating her practical side. If Caetana refused to reduce to crumbs against her palate the cake they had so joyously made with choice ingredients, it should be shared right there among everybody, as though she were present.

"It's her birthday, after all." And she lit the candles with trembling hands.

"Palmira's right. It's better to celebrate than to forget Caetana," Ernesto said, counting on Polidoro's support.

Rather than reveal his thoughts on the matter, the cattle rancher watched with curiosity as Sebastiana used Virgílio's handkerchief to wipe off the knife she'd taken out of her handbag. The group gathered around the cake had already begun the birthday celebration. Hence Narciso's voice, up to that point hidden in a tin box, could scarcely be heard, despite its obviously vituperative tone.

"Who's going to blow out the candles? To take over Caetana's role?"

Polidoro thanked him for the reminder with a slight wave of the hand. His attention was fixed on Gioconda. He did not want to lose sight of her, since she had suddenly usurped the memory of Caetana. Gioconda, for her part, on her guard, did not trust men. They would try, once again, to banish women from a party that existed only because of the joyful initiative of the Three Graces.

"Nobody's going to blow out the candles," Gioconda said, aware of the dangers. "They're going to melt all the way down while we stay here warming our souls, which are growing colder and colder."

After taking the knife out of Sebastiana's hand, she quickly cut the cake. She set aside the first slice for Polidoro, who was in need of a show of esteem. Gratefully, he took the first bite, but it gave him no visible pleasure. The crumbs fell on his shirt front without his caring in the least.

"The slices for the men are bigger than ours," Diana complained, seeing Gioconda satisfying male hunger with excessive generosity.

"It's simple. They're hungrier than we are."

The afternoon's emotions had drained Ernesto of his lunchtime proteins. He felt famished.

"Only a great pastry cook makes a cake like this," he said, to hymn its praises.

"Eat as much of it as you like. We've finished off the third layer, but there are still two left."

Gioconda sat down on the floor along with the others in complete silence. Flies buzzed as they tried to land on the spun-sugar doves. Palmira chased them away with her one free hand, smeared with icing.

"What time is it?" Virgílio was downing his second slice of cake as Polidoro, under pressure, accepted another. He still had his mouth stuffed full of the first piece.

"What a shame not to have brought cool *guaraná* or currant drinks." Palmira felt sorry for Polidoro, whose heart was slashed to bits, notwithstanding the voracity with which he was chewing away.

Relaxed because they were among brothers and sisters, the women let their legs sprawl apart gradually beneath the weight of that afternoon's exhaustion. Virgílio noted, by chance, the panties out of which there bounded, every so often, a tuft or two of curly black hair. He was worn out; all he wanted was to stretch out on his bed at home. Like the others, he felt bone-tired and shorn of all vanity. A beatific state, ideal for recounting to them the sad and stubbornly silent history of Brazil.

The stifling air threatened rain. Gioconda, fighting the heat, used the bouquet of flowers as a fan. At each motion, the magnolias shed petals. The minutes went by with unbearable slowness. Only a knock on the door brought back the life they had just been robbed of.

The interruption of his siesta woke Narciso with a start. He glued his ear to the door.

"Who's there?" he asked, neglecting to employ the usual clever wiles of police officers. Embarrassed by this public demonstration of his naïveté, he flung the door open, revolver in hand, ready to fire away.

Francisco came in, all out of breath.

"It's lucky for me that you're all here together. It spares me the trouble of going knocking from door to door."

He smiled with pride at the mission that had been assigned him. He turned to Polidoro.

"Guess who's arrived?" And he shifted the battered toothpick from one corner to the other of his mouth, out of which trickled a thin stream of saliva.

Polidoro did not move. Francisco's presence reminded him of family duties. It was time to go back home and take a cold bath.

"We haven't had any news, Francisco. But help yourself to some cake," he said indifferently.

The intimation that he was nothing but a scandalmonger obliged Francisco to refuse the slice of cake that Palmira had kindly held out to him. He looked at the woman with contempt, blaming her for the insult. He made as though to leave, but he did not head for the door; his eyes were riveted on Polidoro. The rancher, however, lying on the floor, seemed dead tired and not at all interested.

Very nearly overcome by the fear of not knowing what to do with the treasure that he was carrying about in his mouth, Francisco was tempted not to say one word, as a protest against this offense to his dignity. But in the end, his instinct as an informer took over completely.

"Come right away, Polidoro." His rasping voice took on an unexpected dramatic dimension.

"Where to?" Ernesto asked, having just emerged from his afternoon torpor.

"To the Palace Hotel. Caetana has just arrived with her troupe."

UNCLE VESPASIANO'S Victrola had traveled through nearly half of Brazil. Inside its venerable innards was the dust of the roads that cross the country. And even though Balinho had cleaned it with wads of cotton soaked in alcohol, Wagner's chords, heard in the Palace Hotel, never reached the desired volume.

Isolde's voice, proclaiming the uncertainties of life and death to an enraptured Tristan, was attenuated by the time it reached Caetana, who had shut herself up in the bedroom.

In the living room, keeping his ears open so he could change the record on the Victrola when the time came, Balinho was unpacking suitcases, scattering all over the floor musical scores, various rags and tatters, souvenirs of the trip. In his earnest attempt to decipher Caetana's secrets, his greatest pleasure was to oblige the woman to listen to a musical repertory compatible with her mood.

Certain arias could take Caetana a long way away. Projected on her retina was a landscape that only she could locate on a map. A journey that excluded Balinho, that did not take into consideration his desire to follow her. Refusing to resign himself to this sort of idyll, which left no room for anyone save herself, Balinho struggled to bring her back.

"Where is Trindade?" he had once asked her in distress.

"In the asshole of the world." Caetana held her breasts high as they heaved rapidly. "Where the gods lost their boots and didn't want to go back to get them. Even so, we'll get there. Only I don't know what day or what year." And she emitted sparks from her trembling nostrils.

Balinho turned up the volume of the Victrola. The heavy draperies in the living room, the antique furniture decorated with bibelots and recently restored flower vases still reeking of glue, bored him. Since their arrival in Trindade that afternoon, he had been in search of a listener who would pay attention to his stories.

In the end, Isolde's laments failed to move Caetana, secluded in the bedroom. The woman's indifference as the epilogue was taking place doomed Balinho to the exile of a gloomy living room. On his own initiative, he polished the "Vissi d'Arte" with a flannel cloth till not the slightest trace of dust remained on the record. In this way, Caetana would succumb to the pleas of Floria Tosca in defense of her lover, about to be put to death by the tyrant Scarpia. The mirror of Caetana's soul, sensitive to the perturbations that art gave rise to, would surely shatter into a thousand pieces, until her generous heart was laid bare. That heart that

Balinho did his best to suborn each day, as he searched for its shards on the floor.

The soprano's lament, totally absorbed in the intense exercise of compassion, sounded convincing on the rickety Victrola. Were he still alive, Uncle Vespasiano would have felt pity for such misery. Balinho rubbed his hands together, satisfied at an act surely classifiable as spiteful. He felt like a puppeteer from the fair at Caruaru, aware of the wretchedness of his status as a vagrant yet possessed of more than enough imagination to lead about, tied to his fingers, a Caetana who at times heaped on him insults, reprimands, and suspect perfumes.

The mirror of her soul, meanwhile, through some unfathomable mystery, and contrary to any sort of logic, refused to shatter to bits. Perhaps her arrival in Trindade had disturbed the sensibility of the actress, who was now allowing herself to be ruled exclusively by the sickly world of her own memories.

He waited for five minutes, attentively watching the hands of the clock. Receiving no answer, he knocked on the door. Caetana was wholly lacking in meanspiritedness. Only she could expect that in a city where they had once arrived as roving gypsies, their destinies packed inside one miserable piece of luggage, they had every chance of being put up at the Palace Hotel for a few days.

"Come in." Caetana's shout drowned out Tosca's heartsick plea.

The dim light of the bedroom, its one lampshade covered with a pink veil, did not allow Balinho to locate her. He felt his way along the walls to find her.

"Where else could I be except here?"

Sitting on the bench at the dressing table, in front of the mirror, Caetana was removing her makeup with a sponge. Her swift yet careful gestures revealed features that did not seem to be hers. Her ivory teeth could not be seen in that feeble light.

Caetana gave no sign of recognizing the dressing table as part of her past. It had been a common occurrence for Polidoro, sitting on the bed, to contemplate her, as she brushed her long black hair, totally dissociated from the desire that she aroused in him, to the point where he began shaking like a man suffocating to death or drowning, restraining his urge to fling himself on her body and pry her legs open so that the woman's agonizing, inhuman movements would mercilessly swallow his penis.

It had not been easy for Polidoro to reinstall the dressing table in the hotel. Gioconda swore that it was hers, a gift Caetana had offered her on the eve of her departure, even though it was part of the hotel's assets.

"You and the Three Graces planned to steal the dressing table. You acted without my knowledge. Kindly return it," Polidoro ordered.

Gioconda was stupefied. The long amorous summer had shrunk the last chunks of flesh that Caetana had left her as a remembrance.

"Don't you realize that it pained Caetana to leave behind, in a hotel of deluxe whores and travelers without the slightest scruple, a mirror in which her beauty remained forever imprinted?" Gioconda argued, even as she admitted defeat.

Balinho breathed in the fragrances of jasmine and lavender coming from the bed. Caetana still hadn't stretched out between the white sheets. She went on brushing her hair without the least sign of fatigue, stimulating her brain so as to refresh her ideas, till finally she flung the brush on the carpet in irritation.

"What's the use of fighting, Balinho? In the end, the gods are always victorious. They're shameless. They invented exile so we'd create the idea of a homeland, of health. They always knew, long before I did, that I'd stick my head back into this hole called Trindade, where the only thing people care about is cows and cow dung."

Balinho tried to calm her down. He suffered from her lack of self-control.

"Are you listening?" He meant the music that was playing. "It's Callas."

Music did transport her to a territory from which she returned with renewed strength, but now she went on vituperating those who ruled destiny.

"In the beginning, I worshiped all the gods. Even the greatest vagabonds among them. They, however, would have nothing to do with me. They were the ones who forgot people in the wretched cities of this fucked-up country. Why did they behave that way toward me? Just because in the mornings Uncle Vespasiano brought me, along with my mug of coffee, an unlimited quantity of dreams?"

So that he might hear her better, Balinho pushed the bench closer. In her private life, Caetana employed the same gestures she used onstage and in the circus ring, unfailingly grandiloquent, in contrast to the banal set speeches of her scripts, well suited to the tastes of her prudish audience.

"How am I going to allow them to introduce tragedy and failure into my life without my permission?" The effort made her throat dry. She eagerly drank the water Balinho offered her. And, with a melodramatic gesture, she tore off the cape protecting her. She motioned for Balinho to sit down on it. He carefully avoided looking at her nightgown, her breasts barely held in by the satin, so worn that it was splitting apart.

"The fucking gods are sharpening their fingernails on my flesh. But I'll have my revenge on them right here in Trindade."

She clutched Balinho's hand anxiously. Though he tried to free it from her grasp, she could not let go of him. In order to restrain her heart's extreme measures, Balinho counterattacked.

"Any day now, the Victrola is going to give out. It'll end up being buried underneath the fig tree where Judas hanged himself to attract the attention of Christians."

In the feeble light of the pink lampshade, he noted Caetana's intense interest in the story of Judas. Whenever she was attracted by the plots of Balinho's tales, she paid close attention to him, convinced that he could bring the outside world across her threshold. Enthralled, doubtless, by the skill with which he rebelled against trite plot developments.

Caetana's wrath persisted unabated. Life did not have the richness he forced himself to sow in it. With no authority to go on, Balinho began to speak, unhurriedly.

"I've read that Judas was the spy of a Roman senator who had been slighted by the emperor and therefore planned to destroy the empire. To this end, he gave Roman soldiers gold coins to hang that Christ of Judea on the cross. He sensed that the prophet was on the point of creating a powerful religion, in whose name slaves would sacrifice their lives. And so, when they killed Christ, they would be putting down a revolution born of desperate men, all of them eager to be swallowed up by lions in the arenas, in exchange for the kingdom of heaven. Such an unpredictable gesture that the Romans, masters of the world and of the powers of imagination, envied them their intense passion. They too wanted to take home with them the mantle of passion, to cloak themselves in it and protect themselves from the winter cold, and from despair. With that mantle on their shoulders, they were certain, all feelings would become possible. It was then that the senator summoned Judas."

Engrossed a few moments before, Caetana now returned to the reality of the room.

"But whatever in the world are you talking about, if what matters is the Victrola? Is it working or isn't it?" With an impatient gesture, she brushed away the story that Balinho had been telling her.

"For as long as it holds up. Any day now, it's going to be unable to take another one of Callas's sharp high notes."

The young midget had the gift of coming to her with lies every day, on the pretext that he was in search of reality. In return, she offered him unforgettable lessons.

"You don't know what you're saying, Balinho. That Victrola knows more about us than we do ourselves. It practically saw me being born, and is going to be at my side at the hour of my death. Uncle Vespasiano would never forgive me if I allowed it to fall silent forever."

The subject distressed her. She motioned for more light. She wanted to recognize objects, and herself in the mirror.

"We'll see if I can fight off these atrocious memories by means of light."

Caetana finally looked around the bedroom at Polidoro's arrangement.

"From the looks of things, he's older than I am. Whereas I confuse certain episodes, they remain fresh in his memory. The bedroom is just the same as it was in the past. He hasn't forgotten a single detail."

Even the dresser still showed the same spot of peroba oil that she had unintentionally spilled on it in her haste to get to the circus on time.

Balinho opened the drawers. As he unpacked the suitcases, he quickly separated the garments for everyday use from those meant to be worn onstage. He wanted to put the room in order.

"When will we be taking off on our travels again?" he asked as he folded the clothes.

Caetana studied the palm of her right hand. The guidelines of her destiny were engraved on it. The principal ones seemed to her to be blurred, and she had not inherited her uncle's skill in interpreting them. Vespasiano, however, being good-humored by nature, had always invented a destiny that was compatible with the dream of whoever had consulted him, just to make that person feel happy. Illusion, according to Vespasiano, ought to accompany the first light of day and the first swallow of coffee.

Convinced of such gems of thought, he would awaken his niece. Caetana resisted, having slept poorly.

"Don't you see, my girl, that day has already dawned? And that the sun is man's best friend? Unlike the moon, which is hostile and ambiguous."

On the alert against her inheriting the art of reading omens, which had been handed down from ancient Greece, he smiled, baring the few blackened teeth that he had left.

"I don't have the slightest idea how Brazilian girls are brought up. All I know is that I taught you to be free and to sleep very little. Where have you ever seen people like us, hoping that life will knock on the door? Let's get going. It's time to pack our bags. To clap the masks over our faces again. It'll be too bad for us when we no longer use those masks. We'll be ugly and banal. Or would you prefer being rich to being an actress? With banknotes in your trunks, but without charms to leave others spellbound?"

Heedless of material things, Vespasiano wore a length of rope for a belt so his trousers wouldn't fall down. His waist had expanded before Caetana's eyes from the beer he drank in the bars along the wayside; she had never left his side since she was a tiny girl. "I practically grabbed you out of the waters of the Nile, inside a little basket. I preferred to bring you up myself, rather than put you in one of those houses with a roof and poisoned walls. I didn't want you to learn how to embroider and cook. Was I wrong, my girl?"

He ran his fingers through her hair like a comb, to untangle it. Once she looked pretty, he forced her to run, to imitate statues, to train her laughter so that it could be heard from more than a hundred meters away.

"Never be idle. And never give up dreaming, my girl. That's the belief that saves us. With it alone on our faces we tread the boards. There are times when we're in the circus ring, which is misery for us, and at others the thin boards of the stage we're on have gone through the soles of our shoes. But some day you're going to end up in the Municipal Theater in Rio de Janeiro."

On that day, he had personally led her to the dressing room, so he could watch his niece cover her face with makeup capable of simulating modest blushes and passions. As a sign of his regard for her, gathering together all the money he'd saved, he would have a basket of wildflowers sent to her, to be brought onstage as she was acknowledging the audience's applause.

"Have you ever thought of stepping out some day on the same stage where Isadora Duncan and Sarah Bernhardt appeared? Did you know that the great French actress broke her leg at the Municipal, and that was why she had to have it amputated later?"

Balinho neglected his duties in order to listen to her. He forgot his assigned tasks. He had before him the spectacle that moved him the most. Caetana became restless, rose to her feet, sat down at the dressing table once again. She had put on weight, but her ample flesh had not undone the intricate knots of a fancy that Balinho had tied to his heart with powerful cords, which grew stronger with each passing day.

"Once the true story of the Brazilian theater is told, they won't be able to forget to include Uncle Vespasiano. Or men like him. I'm not referring to that shitty official history, which knows only how to milk the udders of those who come out on top, of those who only hop onto the stages of the theaters of the big cities, like human fleas. I'm talking about us, about us poor wretches who have gone all through the backlands, putting on shows in circus rings, on portable stages, without spotlights or even candlelight."

She toned down her violence to disentangle the necklaces that Balinho had taken out of a box, then sat down on the floor alongside him. She was entertained by the memories evoked by each object. Balinho smelled the odor of her armpits with tender affection. He came close to weeping, to prove to her how much he loved her.

Caetana pretended not to notice his emotions, which came pouring out like dung in a city peopled by cows and syphilitics.

"Don't be so worried about the lies that have to be invented," Caetana said, in an attempt to restrain his excessive sensibility. "If necessary, I myself will trot out the stories I have in my pocket. Don't forget that I was one of Vespasiano's listeners. And nobody was better than Uncle at revealing the real story of Brazil, at talking about the gaunt, resigned faces we saw on those highways and byways. The only people we met were doomed to oblivion. Who would tell them their own story or speak of them after they were dead? Is there any worse death than being forgotten, than never again being remembered? Or never knowing what it's like to be famous?"

She stood up impatiently. She did not want ever again to witness the misery that had jumped out of the suitcases like live frogs. The belongings strewn on the floor were swamp creatures.

"We carry misery about on our backs. Our fortune consists of trunks full of sand. If we were to sell everything that's inside, it wouldn't bring us enough to pay for a plateful of food. What a shitty life!"

She pointed out to Balinho the album of newspaper clippings next to the curtain. He made a move to hand it to her.

"I don't want to see it. What's this album worth, compared with my talent! An entire life that takes up only a few pages," she said dejectedly. She recovered, nonetheless, rummaging about among the objects.

"Hand me the picture of my uncle."

Vespasiano seemed to smile at her. Even inside the box, made of the cheapest wood and threatening to fall apart every time it rained, her uncle retained the arrogance of happiness. Nothing intimidated him—neither poverty nor being down on his luck.

"I now see that Uncle was a madman. He defied even the gods, through commonplace gestures. And he used to maintain that the best art was ordinary; he'd make a youngster and an old man smile at the same time. Could he have been right?"

Balinho showed her the photograph of a palace. The swans lending beauty to the lake gleamed like porcelain. They looked as though they had never flown.

"It's Itamarati," he said, to Caetana's surprise.

"And what's that to us? Don't you see that we make up a race of people condemned to live together forever? Who can separate us, Balinho? Who are we without each other? Have you ever thought of Prince Danilo without thinking of me? But, despite those palaces, we're the ones who go from all over Brazil, in the certainty that it exists and will neglect us in our old age. We who don't make enough to pay Social Security taxes."

Balinho folded the photograph. The palace of his fantasy had disappeared. The vision of a big house for an elegant, urbane young couple made him have a strange dream. But he would never leave Caetana. Nor would she ever stop telling him stories she'd come by for free. She was used to his ardor as she uttered scattered phrases to him, many of them taken from plays that she had acted in at Uncle Vespasiano's side since adolescence.

"And what other family do I have?" Balinho said, as though confirming to himself his intention of remaining with her.

Caetana stroked her stomach with concentric motions. Her mind elsewhere, she did not appear to have heard Balinho's veiled declaration of love.

"My stomach's protesting, but it's from hunger."

Balinho had brought a light lunch for them: milk, an apple, and a hard-boiled egg. Far too frugal after the trip in the cab of the truck, alongside a nanny goat that accompanied the driver everywhere. Its bleating blended with the country-music duets on the radio.

Caetana railed against the poverty that pursued them.

"Why are they trying to force this prison diet on me?"

Standing up in her long turquoise-colored nightgown, she beat her breast, blinking her eyes.

"Have I come so far down in the world that not even Polidoro pays any attention to me? Or has he perhaps ended up as a poor man?"

Balinho threw himself on his knees alongside the bench.

"Don't speak of coming down in the world, I beg you. There's not another actress like you in all Brazil. Tell me the name of a single one who's managed to leave the hearts of the people in tatters."

The scent of jasmine disappeared, only to be replaced by another that descended from Caetana's thighs. Depriving the woman of her intimacy all of a sudden, he felt as though he were in bondage to desire, unintentionally filled with the mysterious sap that, even when she was in a bitter mood, her body gave off. In order to fight against his imagination, which was inclined to bolt off like a filly, Balinho began to talk. By so doing, he was trying to forget that disconcerting intimacy.

It comforted Caetana to have Balinho on his knees at her feet, in an effort to reconcile her to a hostile reality that had never applauded her talent as an actress.

"At times I have the impression that I'm forgetting to say certain things onstage. I think my greatest fault has been putting on so much weight and dreaming useless dreams."

Balinho massaged the joints of her toes. She almost always wore sandals. On certain occasions she slipped rings onto her toes, like Gabriela Besanzoni, the Italian singer who out of love had lived for years in Brazil.

"If we owe this miserable lunch to Mágico, tell him that he's wrong about our rags and tatters. And that it's art that forces us to dress this way. Besides, who does he think we are, bankers? Well, give him to understand that what we really are is princes.

Because we're the ones who give names to the feelings and the famished faces of ugly Brazilians who persist in dreaming. Go straight to the kitchen. We're going to stuff ourselves with succulent dishes. I need to line my stomach with the fat that my dreams will consume. And have him send the bills to Polidoro Álves. He's the one who's going to pay them."

After the forcefulness of such a speech, Balinho had no reason to fear the future. Caetana had proved that the organization of the country had no need of their services. On the contrary: mere pawns of art such as they had been left with just one consolation: burning up the soles of their shoes on the road and dying.

After that Friday, Polidoro would smear them with honey. What reality had withheld from them in the past would now be given to them twice over.

"I'll bring back on the tray the seven fat years of Egypt," Balinho said, happy to have remembered this phrase from the Bible. Certain passages often came to him as a bonus, especially when he lacked bread. He then took pleasure, on such ash-gray afternoons, in inventing stories with a rapid tempo.

"I don't care if it's Egypt, Paris, or Cochin China, but bring some food," Caetana said with a laugh, forgetting her annoyance. Her face had grown younger in a fraction of a second. And she was radiant with a sensuality that excited her squire, already at the door, heading for the kitchen. As he opened it, however, he stepped back, leaving it ajar.

"What's the matter?" Caetana called out from the bedroom.

"I think it's him at the door. What shall I do?"

Caetana stopped short, forgetting her theatrical gestures. Her body was tense, and her muscles ached. Balinho came to her rescue. Once again the woman's odor permeated his every pore, along with her perfume. Suddenly, seized with a secret, nameless, vague ambition, he envied the man's lot. He felt defenseless.

When things became difficult, Caetana expressed strong feelings, relying on the peculiar dream that her uncle had passed on to her along with black beans, flour, and tropical fruits.

"What shall I do about the man? Isn't he the king of Trindade?" Balinho asked worriedly.

"Turn out the lights and let Polidoro in," Caetana commanded. Forgetting where she had left her cape, she began searching about on the carpet for it.

Balinho turned his back on her and went off without bidding her goodbye.

DANILO'S HEIGHT allowed him to reach up and get the gewgaws that Caetana was pitching on top of the armoires. The gesture, always a useful one, gave rise to an ironic smile on Balinho's part. It seemed to hint that nature had endowed Danilo with an excess of muscles to the detriment of his gray matter. His stubby, prominently veined hands would scarcely know how to encircle a woman's waist with the necessary delicacy of touch.

When questioned as to the title of prince attached to his name, Danilo retreated into a heavy silence as he eagerly polished the silver medals from the war with Paraguay that he carried about in his knapsack. He likewise avoided admitting his age. Faced with his friends' insistence, his green, hesitant eyes blinked repeatedly, at precisely the moment that his voice, suddenly turning rough, subtracted ten years from his life.

By lying so frequently, he had acquired the unshakable belief that he was telling the truth. And in his eagerness to demonstrate with effusion signs of his youth, Danilo was in the habit of bounding up and down entire flights of stairs, at the risk of tripping and falling.

Every so often, assailed by the feeling that he was on the decline, when a thousand drums echoed within his chest and the day took on unsuspected shadows, he drank heavily.

One night, lacking the courage to shut himself up in his room in the boarding house, he knocked on Caetana's door. She could smell the alcohol on his breath and feel the force of his sense of misfortune.

Danilo removed his beret, a present from a Catalan; she was surprised to spy his skull shaved to the bone with a razor.

"What have you done to your hair?"

That morning, as he had stood in front of the mirror, the glass had revealed to him how white his hair was and how excessively feminine his features were, in visible contrast to his abundant physical endowments. He had picked up the razor, motivated by the inescapable truth that he was going on fifty.

"I'm asking you only one favor, Caetana. Don't reveal my age to a single soul. I don't want people to discover that I've lied all my life. If it's necessary to keep the death certificate a secret, bury me as a nameless indigent. I have no excuses to offer the heavens for my misery." And he scratched his skull with fingernails chewed to the quick. He was prematurely suffering from the fact that his corpse would be greeted with cynical laughter. Death in itself was condemnation enough.

"Go get some sleep. By tomorrow this bender you've been on will be over." Caetana said, hastily urging him to go back to his room.

Danilo persisted. An artist like him deserved to be criticized only onstage. Balinho was right: offstage, his words came out all wrong, and his gestures were overly dramatic.

"They don't know what the passage of the years means to an actor! It's real torture for a person to tread the boards once he has begun dyeing his hair black."

Enveloped in the same crepuscular sensation, Caetana fell silent. She had taken to concealing her wrinkles beneath heavy makeup.

"May I stay just a few minutes?"

He settled himself comfortably on the floor, on the colored cushions from Caetana's bed. The fumes of alcohol on his breath gradually grew fainter, making it easier for him to speak as his drunkenness wore off.

"The only thing I've done in these last few years is to strum the strings of a guitar with the same tenderness with which I've played on the hardened heartstrings of others," he concluded, close to tears.

On the following day, Danilo returned to the subject of his death. Caetana, in the dressing room, was neatly setting out pots and tubes of makeup on top of the dressing table. In those months, having hitched up with the circus, they were awaiting better days, so they could resume their performances in the little theaters and movie houses in the backlands.

As was her habit, Caetana ate an orange before going into the circus ring. The wind outside made the much-mended canvases roar like an enraged lion.

"I've already told you I wouldn't be any good as a gravedigger. Why are you so obsessed about a ceremony where you'll be the only nonliving guest?"

Danilo offered her a caramel as a present and a token of good will.

"Isn't it true that, despite my uncouth appearance, I have lofty sentiments and a tender soul? Then why does everybody keep wanting to wound me to the quick? Isn't this miserable life we lead enough, dragging us from one end of Brazil to the other, with ticks, snakes, scorpions continually underfoot?"

At the concierge's desk in the Palace, on that Friday, Caetana put him on his guard. She did not want Danilo stumbling about in the hallways, knocking on the wrong doors, because he'd had too much to drink.

Prince Danilo was offended. It was not only his modest tee shirt, his satin trousers, and his decrepit boots, but his entire upbringing that had heretofore kept him from confronting well-bred people face to face. Only grave offenses made him react, breaking objects and knocking gentlemen over.

He found it odd, nonetheless, that the actress did not share his feelings with regard to social life. "I long ago gave up the glory and the wickedness of great capitals. On the other hand, I had asthma attacks every spring," he always said when he wanted to scourge with the lash of his innocence those who greedily coveted money and power.

Worn out from the trip to Trindade, Caetana asked them to hurry up with their luggage.

"Should we have come back at all? Or have we arrived in Trindade twenty years too late?" Danilo said, on the way up to the fifth floor.

Balinho entered the room with their valises and parcels. Caetana, standing in the doorway, was in no hurry to go inside the suite.

"We'll know in the next few hours." Indolence overcame her as she stood on the threshold. She seemed to be speaking with a stranger.

Allowed no place in the decisions of the group, Danilo felt offended, and thirsty.

"That Francisco fellow said that all the bills were to be footed by the cattle baron."

Caetana had dressed for the trip in a white tunic with a pattern of red cubes, now badly soiled. Her many-stranded pearl necklace weighed heavily on her neck. The train of the dress dragged on the floor, like a bride's. She kept putting her hands to her face to hide the dark bags under her eyes.

"It would appear that Polidoro has changed. He used to treat cows better than women," Caetana said.

She entered the living room, now filled with valises and boxes. This setting was familiar to her. Taken by surprise, she raised one hand to her breast, then immediately disguised the gesture.

"Ah, if only the rich knew that, during their last two minutes of life, it would be worth their while to burn *milreis* banknotes in the public square, they'd understand what a pleasure there is in crackbrained fantasy!"

She examined the furniture with a look of disbelief. Nothing had changed, she was certain.

Danilo came down by way of the stairs, not wanting to wait for the elevator. He was whistling "Recondita Armonia," which always came to his mind before he started drinking. He thought of Francisco. Caetana had warned him against the waiter, but she had surely been exaggerating. She had a mania for enhancing reality with strong colors, for she intended to present it exactly that way on the stage. Anything that did not fit these criteria merited her reproof. She trusted only those speeches that would lead to easy laughter or floods of tears.

In the lobby, the lighted candelabrum gleamed like those of lead crystal found in Europe, despite a number of burned-out bulbs that Mágico failed to replace, to save money.

Mágico pretended not to see Danilo. The actor's attire, bordering on the ridiculous, affronted the hotel guests who were reading the daily papers.

Danilo, aggrieved by these arrogant glances, went over to him.

"Aren't you ashamed to hide behind the counter and those dusty curtains, standing there shitting out rules of humanity? Do you think I didn't notice your look of contempt when you saw us arriving, half starved, our spirits broken? Have you ever traveled for five hours in the cab of a truck? Sitting on a wooden bench that anesthetizes your rear end to the point where you don't even feel that it's your own? Why do you treat us that way? Are you envious of our talent, of the gypsy life we lead, one you've never had the courage to live?" he said impulsively, unwilling to forgive Mágico's veiled reproach.

From the expression on Mágico's face, Danilo could see his mean and petty life by day and his masturbation by night.

"If you don't open your heart, your reward's going to be an ulcer, and a nosegay of hemorrhoids in your asshole," Danilo added emphatically, prepared to elaborate further.

Mágico was terrified. The actor, in harsh language, could read his frustrations like a book, rend his heart to pieces, in full view of everyone, failing only to put up for sale the envy and the loneliness that, contrary to his will, hid in secret places that he himself was forbidden to enter.

Mágico pointed to the sofa to indicate that Danilo should sit down on it. The latter's gleaming pate was attracting attention, as were, to an even greater degree, the well-developed biceps that popped out of the holes in his undershirt.

"Are you comfortable?" Mágico was referring to the leather sofa that had come from England.

On testing the springs, Danilo made a face. His unrefined appearance belied his sensibility.

Mágico approached politely, but he found himself unable to feign friendly feelings toward the actor.

"If you can divine so easily what people are thinking and suffering, why don't you read fortunetelling cards or play shell games instead of risking your life on the stage?"

Mágico was speaking in all seriousness. No other calling made men happier. Foretelling a person's fate promoted witch doctors to the rank of messengers of the gods.

Feeling trapped, faced with the prospect of abandoning the stage, Danilo answered back. "Who told you that I lack acting ability?" Confronted with such a threat, he drew himself up to his full height in indignation. "In that case, I can't accept your hospitality."

Danilo stood up to him valiantly. What did a man holed up in that hotel, so he couldn't see the ocean, the mountains, and God's creatures, know about life?

"Since when have I asked for your advice or owed you favors that give you the right to meddle in my life?"

Standing in the doorway on his way into the bar, Danilo made an obscene gesture.

"A banana," he said, and so as to be heard by the hotel guests present: "Shove it up your ass."

In the bar, Francisco pointed to the table next to Polidoro's.

"Have whatever you like to drink. As Polidoro's guest, all you have to do is open the bottles. We've been waiting twenty years for Caetana to arrive. The only reason we didn't write to her was that we didn't have her address. Where have the two of you been? Do tell: I'm all ears."

The first drink, poured with a heavy hand, was proof of the excellence of the ten-year-old whisky.

"I have other bottles set aside," he said, noting how much Danilo liked the drink. He sat down on another chair, taking advantage of the fact that the bar was empty.

"What other letter had they sent to Polidoro, besides the one that had arrived the previous Friday?" Francisco was careful not to arouse Danilo's suspicion. Trusting Francisco's sense of hospitality, Danilo felt protected. Caetana's insinuations had no basis in fact. Francisco, of noble extraction, knew how to open the gateways to pleasure.

"Caetana isn't at all fond of writing. That's why she's not a dramatist. On the other hand, she improvises onstage. She enjoys enriching the texts that have come from illustrious pens. One time she changed two sentences in a dialogue by the famous author Machado de Assis. And—can you imagine?—it was even better that way."

He rubbed his hands together. The drink brought on a feeling of great happiness. And he reached a state of bliss all the more rapidly, when regarded by a man such as Francisco as being worthy of pampering. If he were to have to pay for the drink himself, the few coins jingling in his pocket that he'd saved up wouldn't be enough.

"It's about time for Brazil to value its artists," Francisco said emphatically as he sat fawning over him.

His mind still focused on his favorite subject, Danilo paid no attention to him.

"Caetana respects other people's work. She makes changes in five or six sentences, and always for a good reason. As for writing letters, she never was a good correspondent. With the exception of the note she sent Polidoro when she left in such a rush, now is the only time she's ever written again, to announce her arrival in Trindade. She never wanted to be a writer—a profession, moreover, that holds few attractions. The one thing she's wanted, from the day she left the cradle, was to be a performer. She comes from a family of artists. Vespasiano, who brought her up, prided himself on never having had a fixed abode. He was a nomad. He carried his belongings about on his back, the way mollusks do, the way we do, often not knowing what backwoods in Brazil we've ended up in."

Francisco caused him to elevate his diction, speaking in long, carefully cadenced phrases. It was like seeing him acting onstage. In quick brush strokes Danilo brought him reality there inside the bar. Thanks to this gift, he enabled Francisco to participate in the adventures he had experienced, onstage and off. It had been a long time since Francisco had seen so loquacious a man, capable of supplying him with exciting news that he could spread immediately. He would have no trouble supplying additional details if necessary.

"Have another drink, Danilo. Don't hang back. The man who's picking up the tab can easily afford to buy the half of Trindade that doesn't yet belong to him," Francisco said insistently, refilling the ice bucket.

Prince Danilo drank avidly as he shot off verbal skyrockets.

"Did you manage to meet Uncle Vespasiano? He founded the theatrical troupe called Os Romeiros, The Pilgrims, which unfortunately no longer exists. The company was famous throughout Brazil."

Danilo returned to Caetana's past, which was also his own, moved in spite of himself by the suspicion that he was invading a barren region. Each time he approached it, certain new facts came out, which he adjusted to by dint of a precarious balancing act.

"It's hard to speak of those days, when we captivated all of Brazil. I have very little book-learning: I was a poor student. All I remember is scattered bits and pieces of stories. That's why I so often resort to untruths. I do what all artists do. Isn't it true we're all liars?"

Danilo drained the glass of whisky, a drink he wasn't accustomed to, as though it were cheap cane brandy. His heavy eyelids indicated that he had drunk too much.

"Woe betide us if it weren't for lying, Francisco. Thanks to falsehood, we believe in the memories that we'd doomed to oblivion. What would become of us without the affection of falsehoods, the bread of lies? It's the one warmth that fights off loneliness."

The look in Francisco's eyes, enticing not long before, now kept him from drinking too much.

"It's no use pretending, Francisco. You have the look of someone who never has a woman in his bed or hot food in the kitchen. Don't deny it. If things were different, you wouldn't hang around here for so many hours listening to me."

Francisco shielded himself behind an indulgent smile. He turned his gaze toward the bottle. Danilo brought him a feeling of solidarity, because of his weaknesses. Excesses pleased Francisco. He would not allow life to ensnare them, to set the two of them against each other.

Danilo closed his eyes, with the illusion that he was opening them beneath powerful spotlights, before an audience that was applauding him as he stood at center stage and demanding that he repeat a scene; but he needed to get to the epilogue.

"You're right. Every storyteller is a loner," Francisco admitted, feeling self-conscious, yet unwilling to give up Danilo's boisterousness, his dissonant shouts. Francisco had long since exhausted his stock of novelties. No longer beguiling the customers as he once had, he risked repeating himself, exhausting everyone. He had an urgent need, however, of news that took on an air of authenticity only beneath the aura of the poison of falsehood and slander.

Danilo melted. He had long been yearning for a sincere, firm friend, one capable of blushing.

"I'm going to serve you your whisky with an eyedropper, as a medicine. Does that satisfy you?" Danilo's guffaw burned his chest. His nipples, swollen with pleasure, poked through his cotton undershirt.

Francisco's sudden melancholy made him stop laughing. Danilo tried to cheer him up.

"What do people in Trindade do, besides shitting and fucking? Don't they read newspapers, don't they listen to 'The Brazil Hour' to find out what the military clique is getting ready to do in Brasília?"

Alcohol made him want to assume command, to bend Francisco to his will with stories that tended to become whoppers as he encountered the waiter's boundless credulity.

"Did you know Vespasiano or didn't you? Because, if you didn't, the story never gets past the halfway mark. Human imagination is really funny. It only accepts the miracles the world has to offer on the basis of what it knows about its own parish. We're simply headhunters, determined to shrink skulls."

Danilo smiled, showing teeth badly stained from nicotine. He was fulfilling his plan to seduce Francisco by persuading him to believe his legends, under the sway of an art that, developed on the stage, had always been the essence of theater. He had finally grown old in that profession, forming in the last few years a strange partnership with Caetana, despite their constant exchange of cruel and impatient looks. When the audience showed signs of getting tired of having just two performers onstage, they would alternate numbers. Caetana delivered exciting soliloquies, so natural that they appeared to be her own handiwork, while he, in addition to singing and playing the guitar, assumed the role of the lonely, outcast clown, always by way of grotesque gestures stemming from pitiless improvisation.

"I saw Vespasiano only once, in the circus ring," Francisco said.

At the time, people had sworn to him that Vespasiano's art was based on ambiguities. For, with the intention of turning the audience's emotions topsy-turvy and enveloping them in the diaphanous mantle of illusion, he wept in order to make them laugh, and then did the opposite by laughing to force them to shed tears.

In order to expose himself to ridicule and plunge a knife into his own heart, Vespasiano wore a pair of tights that particularly emphasized his imposing belly saturated with beer. The audience was thrilled at the sight of this big bulge exposed so aggressively. That was when he gave the signal for them to lower the bar of the trapeze for him. He would cling to the bar but stand with his two feet on terra firma, then pretend that he was in danger, having a close brush with death which was forcing him to run around the circus ring, fearing for his life. In a solemn voice he would proclaim: "Pray for me now." At these words, he ordered the safety net to be removed—the net that was in fact terra firma.

"I don't remember you," Francisco added.

"I was skinny in those days. I had long hair, and the pope still hadn't granted me my title of nobility."

Francisco got a whiff of the alcohol on his breath and immediately provided him with fried potatoes sprinkled with melted fat and salt.

"It's a papal dukedom, then?" Francisco was surprised at Danilo's having a title that, as far as he knew, existed only within the walls of the Vatican.

Danilo unhurriedly downed the potatoes, determined to pay attention to Francisco again only when the latter was bursting with curiosity. But his bold nature, which suffered when someone interrupted a story that he himself was telling, couldn't wait a moment longer.

"No, not a duke. I said a prince. Don't confuse the two. Any minute now, you're going to start calling me a baron. Have you ever heard of a more worthless title? It occupies the place furthest away from the throne. Don't you know that there's such a thing as a hierarchical ladder? The next-to-the-last step at the bottom is that of duke. The one above that is marquis. At the top of the pyramid is the prince. In other words, me," he said proudly.

"And is it as a prince that you're going to tell the story of Uncle Vespasiano?"

"Only Caetana has that privilege. Besides, in those years I traveled around a great deal. I managed to appear onstage in Europe, believe it or not." He scratched his skull with fingernails that looked more like hooves.

Afraid that he was failing to be convincing, he spoke even more emphatically. "On the last trip, I took Caetana with me. We went by boat. What a success she was! Brazil ought to bow before that woman."

Francisco feared Danilo wouldn't reach the universe that surpassed all his expectations.

"Does Polidoro know about these adventures?" he asked, on tenterhooks.

Danilo asked for a Partagas de Suerdieck. Holding the match flame a slight distance away from the cigar, he formed a ring of live embers at the end of it. After raising it to his mouth, he exhaled the smoke with satisfaction.

"Do you have any idea what it means to win over the entire audience of the Vienna Opera? I've never seen candelabra so dazzling. I felt as though I'd gone blind, like Saul on the road to Damascus. But let me tell you the whole story from the beginning. We were out on the terrace of that famous Sacher Hotel when a man in a cutaway coat came over to ask if there was an artist without a contract among us, roaming about Vienna. Although he didn't speak in our Christian tongue, Caetana, who'd listened to so much opera, asked in Italian why he was in such distress. After telling us that two of his singers had fallen ill that afternoon, he put us onstage as professionals capable of saving him from disaster."

Danilo was now downing his drink in exaggeratedly small sips, just to make sure that he was keeping Francisco caught fast in the web of his narrative. As an actor, he had learned to take full advantage of pauses; not only did they allow the performer a breathing space, they lent weight to the following scene.

Francisco suddenly felt at the mercy of an enemy who had taken control of his emotions, with no regard for his real feelings. "How did you know beforehand what character you'd be playing on such a demanding stage?" he objected, his mouth dry and his knuckles creaking.

Francisco's doubt, so trenchantly revealed, plunged Danilo into the dark and troubled world where words cracked to shards the moment they were uttered.

Francisco noted his uneasiness. He was afraid he'd put a stop to the prince's narrative flow. On his guard now, he would tone down the forcefulness of the story, thereby robbing it of the fresh-ness that it had so amply possessed up until that moment. Regret-ting the doubt that had undermined Danilo's confidence in him, Francisco tried to make amends.

"What difference does it make if it's Vienna, Rio de Janeiro, or Trindade? Performing artists, as a general rule, are masters of a repertory that can be used in any theater. No author knows his own text as well as you do."

As Danilo listened with relief to this remark, the vision of Francisco that he had on his retina went double. He held out his arm and fumbled about in the air in search of the man's real face, but Francisco's head disappeared before his very eyes. He leaned his elbows on the table to balance himself, resigned to being sociable with two faces, both of which were avidly devouring the news he was passing on.

"The director decorated Caetana's dressing room with so many flowers that she started sneezing. Solicitous and grateful as ever, he took the flowers so that they could be put in the lobby of the theater, to be handed out to the ladies who were coming in, attired in long dresses, their necks bending slightly beneath the weight of sapphire, emerald, and diamond necklaces and earrings. Charmed, they tucked the dewy carnations in the low necklines of their gowns. Some of them, however, because of their heavy breasts, asked for two carnations. So that the flowers would stand out amid all their other finery. The director informed us that we would be playing in *A Doll's House*, and that we were to speak Portuguese. Our role was to improvise the speeches in such a way that the actors could give another in answer. They, of course, would speak in German. Besides, the audience knew the play so well that it could easily follow the plot. That director had faith that art, above and beyond the obstacles of language, could thus find its own path of communication. Do you know what the mayor who came to see us did, as he sucked on peppermint drops? He hoisted the Brazilian flag, in a ceremony in which our national anthem was sung by Caetana, by me, and by the wardrobe master, an Austrian who had lived in Blumenau and spoke a Portuguese that kept going askew."

Fidgeting in his chair, Francisco feared interruptions. Or was afraid that Danilo, unable to proceed, would collapse on the table, or would simply lose the vivacity that made him move like a puppet on a string.

"And how did the audience react?" Danilo's voice, speaking now in falsetto, intrigued him.

"What elegant attire!" Danilo went on excitedly, paying no attention to him. "Some of it even had Belgian-lace trimmings, made by little old ladies. Then they opened the curtains. Before that, Caetana told me that she had seen *A Doll's House* in Rio de Janeiro. So, playing the role of Nora, she didn't miss a single entrance. Then, all of a sudden, she spoke of Vespasiano, her uncle who wasn't there with the two of them. At the end, the audience applauded wholeheartedly, appreciating above all our speaking in a tongue with Latin roots, a living proof that Europeans had been in the Americas. We too, down in the aisle, whirled round and round as joyfully as ballet dancers."

In an attempt to give wings to his memory, Danilo moved his body. The gesture threw him off balance, and he fell out of the chair. Francisco hastened to his aid, afraid of what would happen to Danilo if he went on drinking. He brought from the kitchen, right in the frying pan, corned beef with chopped onions and tomatoes as a salty tidbit to go with his drink.

"The salt will block the effects of the alcohol. And will give you time to tell me the rest."

Danilo was hungry. The salt and the fat soothed his stomach. He wiped up what was left in the frying pan with bread. Before searching his memory, he tested the strength of his biceps.

"When I was young, I would stay on top of women for hours without being a burden on their bellies. Holding my weight off them with my elbows and my gold rod." His raucous guffaws were directed toward the hotel lobby, where Mágico was.

"Where was I? Ah, yes, in Vienna. Caetana started to cry then. She was certain that we would never again appear on that stage. Her mascara ran, staining her face. The harder she cried, the more the audience clapped. When we came out the stage door, students pushed our car as though it were the old-fashioned carriage of Franz Josef and Sissi. Remember Sissi, from Romy Schneider's films?"

"What period are they from?"

"From well before '64, when the army banished the president of Brazil to Uruguay."

"What were those films like?" Francisco was moved by the mention of an empress who, from Europe, had awakened dreams on the silver screen of the Iris, still in business at the time.

"Better than reality," Danilo said emphatically. "Vienna doesn't hold a candle to the images of it on film. They'll show that series again some day."

Francisco, whose name was related to the emperor's, Franz Josef, couldn't resign himself to the fact that in Trindade no one knew anything about that great triumph. There wasn't a single newspaper clipping mentioning the city fundamental to Caetana's rise in the world.

"The Brazilian papers didn't have a word to say about it. That's how it is when you live in such a big country! If we were the size of Belgium, news would travel with the same speed whereby Montezuma's messengers, up there in Mexico, brought fresh fish to the emperor on the central altiplano, more than a thousand kilometers from the seacoast."

Mágico made a noisy entrance into the bar, interrupting their talk together.

"The hotel guests are complaining about the boisterous laughter of this actor, and also of the indifferent service they're getting in the bar," he said smugly.

"What guests do you mean? I don't see anyone here in the bar." Francisco was surprised at these complaints. He hadn't earned a single tip all day.

"Don't give another thought to this inquisitor. He only came here so he can hear our story." With visible scorn, Danilo scrutinized Mágico's faded cutaway coat, his frayed shirt cuffs.

"Nobody pays any attention to you. That's why you can't stand the lonely life you lead," Mágico said.

Danilo rose to his feet. Staggering, he made his hands into fists to confront him. Mágico kept his composure. He had no intention of having a fistfight with an individual in need of public charity.

"Besides being coarse and vulgar, you're a coward," Mágico added. At the risk of falling, Danilo tried to walk toward him. Clutching Danilo, Francisco did his best to persuade him to sit back down in his chair. He pleaded with Mágico to leave the bar.

"I'm a respectable man, with a name to protect," Mágico said, refusing to beat a retreat.

"And what am I, a pariah, who has nothing to lose except his poverty?" Leaning on Francisco, Danilo demanded that an illustrious gentleman be summoned to decide the question. He banged on the table with his fist. "Isn't there a real man in this part of the country? In that case, let's call Caetana. She never had the least fear of traveling all over Brazil, facing storms, deserts, and brigands. So why would she refuse to face the truth in this city full of shit and lies?"

With a jerk, he freed himself from Francisco and started off in Mágico's direction as the latter stepped back. His heavy boots made the floor shake. He did not see the stranger who had just come in.

"Where do you two think you are? In a cathouse or a soccer stadium?" The stern voice put a stop there and then to the violent scene.

Danilo did his best to identify the melancholy face, now at his side.

"Polidoro!" Francisco exclaimed in a terrified voice.

Polidoro's tight suspenders held his belly up. Danilo, his vision blurred, remembered Polidoro when he was much thinner, going down the hotel stairs with weary eyes with traces of fire in them nonetheless. And recalled how many times Polidoro had kept close guard at the door on the fifth floor so as to prevent Caetana from working at the circus. Vespasiano, ready for anything, used to go upstairs to yank her out of the bedroom himself. Polidoro confronted the man with loud exclamations to the effect that the woman belonged to him, and certainly not to an uncle who, using the stage as a pretext, was trying to keep her for himself alone. The fact that he had brought her up since she was a little girl, giving her bread, manioc porridge, and a bit of book learning did not give him the right to force her to try to fulfill dreams impossible to make come true.

"What kind of uncle is that, who instead of advising his niece to accept a house all set up for her in Trindade, where she would have an orchard with fruit trees, a poultry yard, fresh eggs every morning and money in the bank to buy whatever she might need, corrupted her mind with the intention of making her wander all over that Brazil out there, along with a band of gypsies doomed to a wretched life of illusions, and reduced to wearing clothes in rags? Where would she end up dying some day? Or why wouldn't he want Caetana to have peace and quiet in the last years of her life, at the side of a man who would close her eyes when she died and give her a dignified Christian burial? Enough of drama, Seu Vespasiano. Aren't you ashamed of ruining a life?" Polidoro said, in the days before the group suddenly left town.

Danilo held out his hand to him, but the cattle baron swept past him. From the balcony he could see the bar better. The scene disgusted him. He forbade any sort of scandal that might be attached to his name. He was running the risk of a good horseman's galloping out to the ranch to tell Dodô the news that her rival, the woman who wrenched sighs from Polidoro—even when he was still fucking his wife, in bygone days—had returned to Trindade with the intention of stealing her husband from her. After holding out for twenty years, the actress had come to tell Polidoro that she had decided to accept his rules of the game, once he built the house he had promised her long ago. As soon as she was settled in the house, he could visit her every day in his eagerness to make up for lost time in bed. Or have coffee with corn bread, on his way to the Palace.

"Be reasonable. You're both too old to behave like this. As for you, Prince Danilo, come with me. Go tell Caetana this minute that I've arrived. And that I'm not the one who's come twenty years late. *She* has, though, because she forgot to watch the clock."

Danilo lay on the floor like a log. He tried to regain the courage and the balance that drink had robbed him of, but he couldn't budge. Francisco then gave him the chair back. Polidoro dismissed Francisco with a wave of his hand. He headed toward the stairs all by himself, certain that he would find Caetana anxiously awaiting him.

THE KITCHEN was too small to hold all the people congregated there. After banishing the cook, Mágico begged everyone to keep cool. The hotel kitchen was no place for social gatherings, and even less a place for ridding themselves of the anxieties that the meeting of Polidoro and Caetana, on the fifth floor, had just brought on.

Sitting at a bench alongside the table, Virgílio leaned his elbows on the marble sink. He was still wearing the same suit, now badly wrinkled and full of cake stains, in which he had gone to the station. To relieve his concern, he was gnawing his fingernails. He had an urge to urinate. But, fearing that Ernesto would grab his seat, he decided not to go to the toilet. The pharmacist took great pleasure in squelching whatever he set out to do. He did not want Virgílio to be the first one to record the meeting of Polidoro and Caetana, which promised to be sensational.

"Thanks to Mágico, who owed me a few favors, I arrived at the Palace in daylight," Gioconda said.

"What sort of favors could they have been, if you had to come in through the back door?" Virgílio asked sarcastically, forgetting the tea she always offered him as a reward for his effort to recount to them the history of Brazil from the moment the first Portuguese vessel appeared off the shores of Bahia.

Gioconda's embittered smile bared her prominent set of gums. She did not deign to answer. A providential silence for Mágico, puffed up with pride at the thought that they suspected him of being subject to the torments of love. On being obliged to explain them, however, he left, his cheeks flushed with embarrassment.

The subject of eroticism impassioned Ernesto. How many times, in the Estação brothel, he had prudently taken one of the Three Graces upstairs, seduced by the vision of the naked back of a woman in the magazine he had been leafing through. In a fit of anxiety, he pressed Polidoro to describe in detail his feats in bed, which began from the moment that he nested his virile member between a woman's thighs.

"Give me a clearer explanation of how you fucked." He could worm confessions out of Polidoro, provided he never mentioned Caetana's name at such times.

Gioconda straightened her turban, which kept threatening to fall off her head. The gesture, observed by one and all, cleared the air.

"I saw a woman writer with a turban like mine in a photograph. I was left with the impression that, if I had it on my head, I too would travel, without even leaving Trindade," she said with pronounced sadness, accepting the chair that Mágico had brought.

"This whole scene seems like a party, except that we haven't invited Polidoro and Caetana," Francisco said, joyfully keeping his ears open for any information as to what was happening on the fifth floor.

"They'll be very busy tonight," Mágico retorted with unexpected cheekiness.

"What makes you think so?" Ernesto said edgily.

Mágico's insinuation made Gioconda feel even worse than she did already. She gave every appearance of being a long way away, until the pealing of the bells in the church tower, whose resounding echo carried with it the dream of eternity, brought her mind back to the kitchen.

"Enough of this nonsense," she said sternly.

"Since when is fucking nonsense?" Mágico shot back, suddenly encouraged by the widely held supposition that he was an ardent lover.

Francisco half-closed his eyes. The love of that heroic couple, who had come from a class at the bottom of the social ladder, had become a legend all over town. He looked at his watch; its hands moved at a snail's pace. Caetana and Polidoro must be so busy embracing that they hadn't had time to go to bed together. They were waiting for the light of day to fade—a light always unfavorable to lovers. At night, beneath the sheets, they could hide the liver spots on their skin, the wrinkles, the flabbiness of their bodies, their cellulitis, so as to give themselves over to the fantasies that had fascinated them for years.

"Have you ever thought of the force of that passion?" Francisco rubbed his hands together as though he were in their bedroom, seeing before his very eyes a series of scenes that he had never contemplated from close up, or ever imagined existed.

Virgílio moved closer to Gioconda. Pressed by the fateful nature of a love so far from there, on the fifth floor, heedless of the lot of each and every one of them, he pinned the woman in a close embrace, as if he were holding her tight underneath his now-aged body.

Who knows why Gioconda, in a generous impulse, pretended to feel for the professor a love that had long been gnawing at her vitals? Her body shook as though her very marrow were aching, there where she kept her soul hidden. Virgílio bowed his head, trying once and for all to give up his last dream of happiness.

"Of what use is love if nobody knows it exists? What sort of lover would tolerate fucking unless the traces of his passion remained engraved on his face, his body, for everyone to see?" Virgílio said with visible bitterness, in an attempt to convince himself that the task of testifying to the history of Brazil, the story of a collectivity or of even just one creature, was of far greater value than the profane love that any woman could offer him.

Determined not to lose sight of Polidoro and Caetana, Virgílio was prepared to remain on guard duty in the kitchen. He would stay there till the following morning. And in case Mágico kicked him out of the hotel and into the street to sleep in the open air, he would closely scrutinize any shadows coming from the fifth floor, reflected amid the lovers' sighs and moans.

"I agree," Ernesto said.

This was the first time he had admitted in public that Virgílio was right. As an example of his agreement with the professor, he recalled having read in a foreign magazine the story of a duchess served by three women who were ordered to sing softly, in the afternoons, vulgar, worldly songs that ladies in that era were not allowed to sing—on condition that the sounds, almost all of them disturbing, extracted from mournful throats, would be heard only by the four of them there in the room, where the noblewoman lived in strict solitude.

"Who can bear life without being able to count on a neighbor to bear witness? What fun is there in making people laugh or cry without an attentive audience?" Ernesto's sympathetic gaze encompassed both Virgílio and Francisco.

Gioconda wanted to leave them, uncomfortable amid the signs of passion that persistently spread from one end of the kitchen to the other. She also felt affronted by Ernesto's insinuation that she, like the chatelaine in the story, kept the Three Graces under lock and key. Ernesto begged her to stay. At that moment, Mágico brought a trayful of chicken pies.

"Where is Prince Danilo?" He broke a pie into bits, flinging the words on the floor along with the crumbs.

"He went to his room. He'd had too much to drink," Francisco explained.

"Yank him out of bed and have him keep his ear glued to the door of the suite as long as necessary. We can't bear this anxiety any longer."

Virgílio condemned such a despicable act. "When have we ever acted like sneak thieves, just to eavesdrop on the desperate confidences being shared by lovers who've been separated for twenty years?"

"Polidoro would have done the same thing. Besides, they might be in need of an injection to bring them back to life! Nothing is more exhausting than excesses of passion. How many men are there who have had a heart attack while screwing?"

At Francisco's suggestion, Virgílio looked at the clock. The daylight coming through the open shutters of the kitchen window was dim now. Mágico switched on the electric lights.

"Given what time it is, they've already begun tearing off their clothes. In the Orient, there are societies in which lovers take two hours to get undressed. One garment at a time, so as to intensify their mutual delight."

Ernesto had to leave then. Vivina served dinner at exactly six o'clock, without bothering to ask if he was hungry. But tonight he wouldn't manage to fall asleep at his wife's side without news of Polidoro—whether or not a sudden malaise had overtaken him as he mounted Caetana, who, for her part, had tried to free herself of the weight of this stud, whose good-sized appendage, through one of life's cunning artifices, had screwed itself between her thighs without giving any signs of coming loose.

"Neither of them is still only twenty years old. They've already gone round the Cape of Good Hope. At that age, a person has to take it easy. I only hope that Polidoro spends hours proposing to marry her, after he's divorced Dodô," Ernesto said.

Virgílio rose up in arms defending Polidoro's family. He respected Dona Dodô and the couple's five daughters. He had been a guest at their house countless times. At dinner, Dodô served him exquisite viands on a silver service, the table all decorated with flowers and fruit. He had a second helping of every dish, to Dodô's joy, since she deeply resented her husband's refusal to partake of her cooking, his preference for eating at the brothels and cheap coffee shops in Trindade and its outskirts.

"Polidoro also refuses to try other choice dishes available here at home," she would confess, not caring that Polidoro, sitting at the head of the table, could hear her. She meant for Virgílio, out of professional duty, to note that there existed in Trindade a woman who was about to die for lack of affection, the victim of her own husband.

Faced with these family ignominies laid out on the table, Polidoro eyed the very center of his plate, attracted by the vortex. But Dodô, all keyed up from the spicy seasoning in the food and the professor's abundant praise, did not let up on her attack.

"Here you have a husband and father who has gotten lost in the past. Twenty years have gone by, and the man still hasn't found the way back home. Ask Polidoro what year this is. He'll tell you that according to his calendar it's still August 1950. The very year that those damned mountebanks passed through Trindade just to blow the roof off our house and bring us terrible misfortune."

Francisco was burning with curiosity. Any sort of waiting wore him out. "Let's send a messenger boy up. That way we'll know if the two of them are still breathing."

They were all suffering from the irresistible temptation to lose themselves in the intricate labyrinths that Polidoro and Caetana were weaving within those four walls. The possibility of invading the bedroom brought still other impulses to life, particularly since it intoxicated them to exist on nothing but fleeting shadows and chicken pies.

Virgílio washed his hands in the dishwater. This gesture took on a special meaning for Ernesto. The professor had a mania for copying history. With this handwashing bit, Virgílio was reenacting Pilate's resignation.

"Do as you please, all of you," Virgílio said.

Ernesto could foresee the result. In his eagerness to come out the winner, and beneath his prudent outward manner, Virgílio went about things on the sly.

"Who's going to go up to the fifth floor?" Virgílio asked.

Francisco and Mágico exempted themselves. As employees of the hotel, they couldn't turn into spies. Besides the risk to their jobs, they had won the trust of Polidoro, who, as an heir of Bandeirante's, had half the business to run as he pleased.

The remaining half belonged to an heiress who now lived on the shore at Santos. Occupied by other business affairs, she never laid claim to her share of the property. She regarded the five-story building in Trindade as one of her uncle's wild fantasies. In his early years, Antunes had been a romantic sort, hence liable to fall head over heels in love with a city that could hardly be seen on the map of Brazil. The moment the will was opened, his niece telegraphed Polidoro, asking him, in his capacity as co-inheritor, to manage the property as he pleased. In return, he was to deposit the sum of money representing her share in her bank account.

"Don't forget Danilo. There's nobody better than an actor who's had stage experience when it comes to difficult situations."

In case Polidoro caught him loitering outside the door, he was to use as his excuse the need to go over certain speeches with Caetana which she had forgotten because of the exhausting journey. He did not want the repertory, built up with such great effort, to fade from her memory. Danilo would agree, with pleasure, to put to the test the dramatic aptitude of artists for revealing the secrets of life.

All of a sudden they heard a noise outside the door. Suspecting that it was an enemy eavesdropping, they grouped themselves around Gioconda. Ernesto, who had just accepted another pie— thereby ruining the appetite that up until then he had kept intact for the dinner Vivina would just be finishing preparing—choked on the crumbling crust. He made such a noise that Gioconda, fearing he was having difficulty breathing, gave him a series of thwacks on the back. In her clutches, Ernesto felt his life gradually draining away in an embarrassing situation. He could already imagine Vivina, summoned to the hotel, finding her husband clinging to Gioconda, the only one who had remained at his side as he breathed his last. The others, headed by Virgílio, would have disappeared, fearing that their reputations would be compromised. Gioconda, who held dead people in particular respect, would cross his hands on his breast, as soon as his death agonies ceased, intent on readying him for Christian burial, though she would regret the lack of a third party in the kitchen to help her tie the dead man's fingers together.

Accompanied by Dodô, who would have come from the Suspiro ranch for precisely that purpose, Vivina would cause a great scandal on coming face to face with Gioconda at the dead man's side, just for the pleasure of exposing the dead man and Gioconda to public opprobrium. Screaming at the top of her lungs, Vivina would condemn her husband, who was responsible for an orgy held amid pots and pans, dishes of mayonnaise, and bottles of wine belonging to the kitchen of the Palace, all of which, because of the excesses committed, had contributed to causing his death.

"Who can that be?" Virgílio said.

Mágico took the initiative. He ordered them to begin to work in earnest. He had a dinner to prepare that night. An urgent order given the hotel by the members of the Lions Club from São Fidélis, who were visiting Trindade.

"It's going to be a thirty-place banquet!"

Grabbing knives, forks, copper cooking pots, and aprons and toques left on the table by the chef and his helpers, they all got in one another's way. Virgílio lit the burners on the gas stove as Ernesto, as clumsy as ever, very nearly cut off his finger peeling a sweet cassava that looked to him like the phallus of a Mediterranean god. For her part, Gioconda was washing the dishes, singing lullabies with a calming effect. Since her attention was occupied by the water that was soaking her clothes, her turban came undone, revealing her hair fastened in place with bobby pins.

Satisfied with the preparations for the fictitious banquet, Mágico opened the door. It couldn't possibly be a thief. If it were, he'd come to the wrong door. The fortune was on the fifth floor, in the shadow of Caetana's opulent curves, so enticing that Polidoro often asked the Three Graces to imitate the actress's contortions in bed. When they failed to get them right despite the instructions they'd received, Polidoro fell into a rage.

Mágico was disconcerted by Balinho's presence.

"You again? Where have you been all this time, now that Polidoro's taken to living on the fifth floor?"

Balinho set a tray with dirty dishes and a meat platter down on the marble sink top, to make things easier for Gioconda, who was piling plates inside the sink, ready to wash them, a resigned look on her face.

"I didn't know the Palace Hotel had so many employees. And all of them without uniforms?" He feigned surprise.

"It has to do with a banquet that's being held to raise money for poor mothers in Trindade. Haven't you ever seen a bunch of citizens collaborating for the common good?" Ernesto said, blocking his path. Balinho went around him, looking for Mágico.

"Hand me some fruit and a pudding that's been made with at least two dozen egg yolks," he said in a trenchant voice.

"Who's going to eat a pudding that's really twenty-four eggnogs?"

Ernesto's sarcasm, noted by the group, saved Balinho from having to answer. The additional nourishment, capable of restoring the strength of a dead man, was proof that the lovemaking on the fifth floor had completely worn the two lovers out, though it had failed to make them stop. As soon as they shoveled down the pudding, they would go back to bed. Apparently, and contrary to the most idealistic predictions, they had begun to fuck before the church bells struck six. A love that, striving to lessen the bitter pangs of separation, had set itself no time limit.

The many voices all talking at once made it difficult for Francisco to recall events called into question by one of the members of the group: Gioconda insisted that Caetana and Polidoro had never engaged in subtle love games. She hid her distress by twisting Balinho's hair into little ringlets as he stood next to her at the sink.

"Isn't it true that Polidoro has been chain-smoking cigarettes ever since he went into the bedroom, and that he's downed an entire bottle of cane brandy all by himself?"

Gioconda's caress, proceeding down his head to the nape of his neck, grew more and more frenzied as it reached his skull, causing Balinho such a suffocating pleasure that, fearing the snares of sex, he pressed his body against the marble of the sink.

Ernesto went right on asking questions, paying no heed whatsoever to the signs that Gioconda was making that she wanted him to drop the subject.

"I don't know a thing about them. I've spent all my time between the second floor, where I'm staying, and the fifth. I've nearly broken my neck with all that running up and down stairs with trays and other things," Balinho said.

Ernesto was indignant. He had temporarily abandoned his home and fireside with the intention of participating in a story equivalent to a latter-day *Romeo and Juliet*. How disillusioned he'd been when confronted with the Brazilian version of the romantic pair, in which the two lovers, in an all-too-obvious demonstration of boredom and weariness, had slid between the sheets, anxious to get some rest. A sad ending for a love that had once been scandalous.

This time Joaquim, on the verge of death, would not need, according to the rumor making the rounds, to send the actress a bottle of poison as a sign of his intention to kill her should she rob him of his firstborn son, taking him far away, all through a

Brazil whose beginning and end no one could in good faith truly
locate.

"Those Portuguese brought us misfortune, giving us so much
land. I fear for my son, if he follows after that actress through parts
of the country full of snakes, swamps, rivers and unhealthy fevers,"
Joaquim commented; he knew all about the love affair between
Polidoro and Caetana, who had brought a circus to Trindade. An
ambitious woman who, unhappy in her gypsy's life, wanted to
settle down there forever. She had her eye on half the hectares of
land belonging to his son, and even those that Dodô had brought
as her dowry.

"Now that he doesn't care to talk to us any more, let him take
the pudding and be done with it," Ernesto said impatiently.

Balinho did not allow himself to be humiliated in public.
Brought up by Caetana since he was twelve years old, he had
learned the value of performing artists, the only beings through
whom reality could still be envisaged in new forms. Thanks to
the effects of art, words imprisoned in his brain were unleashed,
enabling him to invent stories.

"I'm an artist too. That's how I awaken her every morning,
telling stories that everybody experiences without even realizing
it. Thanks to me, for instance, Caetana hasn't forgotten the time
in Recife when Danilo, in his undershorts, was chased after by a
woman he'd bedded who'd sewn shut the openings of his two
trouser-legs while he was asleep so he wouldn't run away from her
house."

He smiled at the memory of Danilo trying to flee from the city,
terrified in the days that followed by the woman's threats to cut
his balls off.

Ernesto admired the boy's talent, using words sparingly, so as
to keep the most exciting part for the future, in case a friendship
developed between them.

"Have you ever thought of writing those stories down?
Mightn't you be a writer?" Virgílio said, fascinated by a cleverness
that, like his own, both unabashedly lied and told the truth.

"I've hardly ever gone to school. I've been with Caetana and
Os Romeiros since I was a little boy. The group broke up in

São Luís do Maranhão, amid glazed Portuguese tiles and French
rooftops. It's a story so long it takes two months to tell."

His body sagged beneath the weight of the tray. He finally set
it down on the floor, no longer able to contain, in the presence
of such a select audience, the phrases that he was assembling.

"To begin with, the boat that was taking us from Alcântara
to São Luís foundered at the entrance to the bay. Our trunks sank
before our eyes. In that hour of grief, Caetana, in the grip of a
strange spell, took to summoning up memories of Gonçalves Dias.
According to her, it had been there, almost in reach of demoniacal
breakers, that the poet had drowned, as he was returning home
after a long stay in Portugal. How sad to see our only fortune
carried off by the waves!"

"What happened to Os Romeiros?" Francisco was doing his
best to construct a coherent chronology that would allow him to
make future variations in the story without doing violence to its
essence.

"We found ourselves broke overnight."

Fortune had deprived them of their material belongings, but
it had allowed them to keep their talent intact. However, after
the tragic vision of death that had soaked them to the skin, the
actors were no longer the same. Poverty and fear had left the
imprint of a strange fury on their performance. Forgetting the
public, they had paid attention only to the other actors onstage.
Each of them wanted to outdo his or her rival, in a squabble that
grew more and more bitter with every performance. This rivalry
was the ruin of them all.

"You're a ham actor. How could you get more applause than
I did?" asked Balinho.

One night they traded blows onstage. At first the audience
thought that the fracas was part of the play. Vespasiano, usually
good-humored, was in despair. Caetana had a presentiment of the
end of Os Romeiros.

"The gravest misdeed of a real actor is to interfere with a
performance. Even after my mother's funeral, we still had to go
on with the show," she said sternly.

As she pleaded, Caetana's words seemed to be lubricated with the oil of the gods. Her blessing in public served to make the discord between them even worse.

That night, which Caetana called Saturnalian, chaos reigned. Balinho asked her to explain the complete disorder, but she, attuned to the harmonies of an intelligence that protected itself through mystery, flew into a temper.

On the following day, still drowsy, all of them noticed that half the actors had gone off with their respective rucksacks, without so much as leaving a farewell note. Uncle Vespasiano, a glass of beer in his hand, lined up for review those who had stayed. He read off their names in alphabetical order. And when he dismissed them, he struck from the list those who had left, blowing his nose with his handkerchief, as though he were attending their burial.

"And how did Caetana react?" Gioconda's nervousness yielded for a few moments to the spell that Balinho fell prey to as he told them the story of Os Romeiros.

"Caetana spoke with her uncle, who kept fleeing from her. On no account would he allow comments on the demise of a group that he had created, amid laughter, with desperate love.

"How many of us are left now, Uncle?"

In Brazil, with its mania for grandeur, there was no longer any place for them, modest actors with the courage to practice a calling that people would soon forget, leaving the little troupe with few coins in their pockets.

Vespasiano handed her the list of names. As she read it attentively, she felt destiny creeping up on them, switch in hand, tripping them up, flogging them for dreaming and hoping.

"There are so few of us now. We'd be better off if we'd been shipwrecked in the bay of São Luís. We wouldn't be alive to perceive such a sad fate," she said wistfully.

When she saw that her uncle was no longer smiling, despite the pleasure he took in drinking beer, Caetana rebelled. Her Greek tunic was whipped by the sea breeze.

"Our honor will be saved by those who have stayed. Even if there are only five or six of us, we're still performers."

She shut herself up in the dressing room that also served as her bedroom, a temporary bivouac that scarcely disguised her poverty. A week later, their baggage reduced to a minimum, they left Maranhão, never again to return.

"In what year did this tragedy take place?" Virgílio rummaged through his pockets in search of a pencil and paper.

"The rest can wait till tomorrow." Balinho was suddenly in a hurry to get going. Mágico opened the door for him. As he was leaving, he bumped into Polidoro. The cattle baron pried into every nook and corner of the kitchen. His rumpled hair accentuated his dejection.

"Where do you think you're going?" He had difficulty getting the words out.

"I'm about to take the pudding upstairs."

"There's no need for it now. Offer it to whoever wants it." And he pointed at Ernesto with a weary gesture.

The pharmacist refused it, and Balinho got rid of the tray, preparing to leave the kitchen once again.

"Caetana doesn't want to see anybody," they heard Polidoro's rude voice say.

Balinho was in a quandary. Caetana wouldn't go to bed without reviewing the day's rough spots with him first, both of them careful not to load their accounts down with events dependent on memory and the most vulgar chronology. "Where will I go?" Thoroughly bewildered, he felt like the orphan that he was.

"To hell," Polidoro roared, watching Balinho as he went out the door. He didn't seem to care that the youngster was heading for the stairway, determined to knock on the door on the fifth floor, to check at first hand whether Polidoro had in fact been lying, out of envy of his youth and his closeness to Caetana.

The smell of coffee, which Mágico was making, calmed everyone's spirits. Seated on the bench, Polidoro revived little by little, thanks to the strong black liquid.

"Didn't Caetana ask for me?" Gioconda didn't want to attract people's attention. She was protecting her feelings with an air of extreme reserve.

Brought back to reality by that voice, Polidoro scraped the sugar off the bottom of his coffee cup with his spoon.

"Only another artist can understand Caetana," said Gioconda.

She waited expectantly for Ernesto to comfort her. The pharmacist, however, thinking of his wife, who would be bringing platters full of food to the table, certain that her husband would not dare to be late for dinner, paid no attention to her.

Polidoro suspected that fate had reduced his circle of friends. Feeling disconsolate in the face of this realistic perspective, he was willing to let Virgílio, who was sitting next to him now, take advantage of Ernesto's distraction.

"There's nothing that perks up a man of fifty more than sallying forth into the world in search of the Holy Grail. Or, inspired by the sudden return of some lady, a Lancelot du Lac, or even a Roland, the nephew of Charlemagne, at the demand of a political party, be it the one in power or the opposition," the professor said, in an effort to resolve the mystery that Polidoro had brought downstairs with him from the fifth floor and was keeping to himself.

Virgílio's recipe for healing the ills of old age aroused interest, but Gioconda upbraided him for excluding women from the list of epic figures with names totally unknown to her.

"To you, all a woman is good for is to wriggle underneath your groin."

The insinuation that his perfidious cock blindly chased after women, without regard for their minds, forced Virgílio to defend himself. He would never insult the feminine condition in Polidoro's presence.

"I of all people, who have such great esteem for Caetana!"

"Why doesn't Polidoro come to the defense of women?" Gioconda challenged him with her chest puffed out.

"Polidoro is a typical Brazilian Don Quixote. That's why he's given rise to so many passions in these parts."

Virgílio's brazen self-assurance led him to wander from one country, era, and character to another, all of them beyond the limits of his dreams. As a consequence of these adventures, he was left with a sour petulance and a pronounced aftertaste of loneliness.

In his role as a protector, he made a weary circumnavigation

of the kitchen, in behalf of Francisco in particular, who was struggling to force coffee down Virgílio's throat, though the latter, in
his eagerness to speechify, resisted swallowing it.

"Caetana has never shared confidences with me concerning
Polidoro's aptitudes. But her face bore signs of the havoc wrought
by love. If she had experienced four more nights of love here in
Trindade, she would have given up her art forever. That was the
only reason she fled. Polidoro's passion overpowered her, robbed
her of her freedom."

Keeping his ears open for every word, Polidoro drank cup after
cup of coffee. He appeared to be witnessing thrilling scenes, on
an invisible screen in front of him. Even in his role as protagonist,
through trickery on the professor's part, he wasn't able to predict
events to come. From his seat he rooted for a happy ending for
the young boy who, a victim of his instinct for adventure, at times
shamelessly played the part of the villain.

"For a woman, freedom is an illusion. Especially when she has
in her bed a male such as Hector, the pure and undefiled Trojan
hero, before his defeat in hand-to-hand combat with Achilles."
On the other hand, Caetana had also become Polidoro's Achilles'
heel. She was the part of the hero's body that his mother, in her
eagerness to safeguard him, forgot to plunge in the tub full of water
prepared by the gods.

Ernesto put off leaving. All of a sudden life between those
kitchen walls aroused powerful sentiments in him. It offered him
strong-flavored seasonings like salt and pepper.

"Isn't it true that I'm part of this flock too, since I'm a childhood friend of Polidoro's?" Ernesto anxiously awaited the professor's reply.

Polidoro rose to his feet. Losing control, he dusted off the air
in front of him; it was as if he had been cheated out of seeing
sequences of a film indispensable for understanding it, though the
words THE END still hadn't flashed across the screen.

"Let me watch the film in peace!" Polidoro's outburst could
be heard out in the hallway.

Ernesto's interruption forced Virgílio to leave behind his past, in which, it so happened, he had been immersed since his youth. It behooved him to catch up with the present, which had not yet grown cold.

"Since Polidoro can't recount what happened on the fifth floor, I shall speak in his name."

He took a cautious look at the ranch owner, afraid of touching the very essence of someone else's emotion and being immediately punished. Seated on the stool once again, as in a saddle mounted on a horse trotting at a rhythmic gait that favored meditation, Polidoro too cooperated in interpreting the events of which he had been a victim.

Polidoro had found the door of the suite ajar, a sign that he was the master in his own house. The moment he came into the room, Caetana hid behind the screen. Besides being a circumspect woman, she was afraid that age would put an end to illusions that had fed on canary seed and crumbs of soft bread for twenty whole years.

Virgílio resolutely stepped forward into the field of deductions. When in doubt, he consulted the faces of his listeners so as to choose the version that could please everyone.

Filled with emotion, he went on: Polidoro, knowing how discreet Caetana was, knelt before the screen, like an Oriental recently admitted into the Forbidden City, after years of absence, to pay his respects to the last empress of China.

Luckily, the genuflection did no harm to his belly, saturated by liters of beer consumed during the past summer. His heart, however, a buffalo from the United States' Far West, beat fast, off on a mad dash across the prairies. The one trouble, in fact, with the epic sentiments that he was experiencing at that instant, was Caetana's stubborn refusal to come out from behind the screen. This delay, besides putting a damper on the cattle baron's emotions, made the uncomfortable position on his knees a sacrificial offering.

Frustrated by the failure of his gesture, Polidoro rose to his feet with the hope that his joints, drinking of the elixir of love that would draw from his body useless and rusted years, would not creak this time.

He heard a whistle. A signal from Caetana. Enveloped in an aura of light, she took the first steps toward him. The lingerie she was wearing allowed Polidoro to dream of her curves underneath. Her paleness, contrasted with her opulence, immediately made him regain certain illusions. In order to counter mutual examinations, Polidoro pressed her to his chest. The embrace allowed them to hide their respective faces. In that position, and in the heat radiating from their bodies, Polidoro persuaded her to make love, with the dimmed eyes of passion, to that brave knight. A love beneath the canopy of twilight.

They made love with an ardor equal to that of their very first time: at the circus, naked under a piece of canvas stretched out in the ring, after midnight, until the first light of day, without the filter of compassion, bathed their weary bodies.

Lancelot Álves put his arms about her, in the hotel now, forgetting that she was the king's wife, whom it was forbidden to him to desire. The only love-partner for whom he had waited for twenty years.

Virgílio paused. So that they would feel how love, once brought to fruition, also became paralyzing.

"What a fine story," Francisco said, bringing a bottle of wine. The narrative made them land in a country in which love, compressed by the gas of desire, emerged without hindrance, thanks to Lancelot.

"If that Lancelot fellow was really a chaste knight, he immediately lost his purity when he thrust his sword in the queen's scabbard," Ernesto said with a lascivious air, led on by the story, which aroused his lust.

Francisco filled their glasses with an elegance permeated by gestures indiscriminately inherited from customers, both drunk and sober, who were in the habit of dropping by the bar.

Virgílio took offense at Ernesto's idle chatter. He felt fed up with fighting against the immutable geography of the hotel, and with characters locked up in the dark bedroom of desire, strangers to the political limelight that was the driving force of Brazilian life. Still, he did not want to push Polidoro offstage without a convincing pretext.

"I won't go on with the story. Nobody can bear the sight of a love like that of Polidoro and Caetana without wanting to destroy it. Who among us can boast of being under the sway of passion?"

He stared at the pharmacist, thirsting for vengeance.

"Who makes your heart pound?"

On the brink of being judged by the group, Ernesto retreated as far as the refrigerator. He looked at his hands, still dirty from the soot of that afternoon's train. He too had a careless heart, which no one had ever mastered. He was not one to love in devastating, geometrical progression.

"I'm a married man, and I have a wife at home." He spoke louder, to drown out the sound of the motor of the refrigerator. "I have a table all set and hot food waiting for me this very minute. Who here is as greatly loved as I am?"

Though Virgílio's sudden shifts in the plot of his story made it easy for the group to flee from reality, Gioconda took even greater care to keep her secrets to herself. She was critical of Virgílio's boldness, which accomplished nothing, and the shamelessness with which he resorted to falsehoods in order to manipulate the fears of the little community.

Unfortunately, he lacked the cleverness to use fantasy as stuffing for his stories. He suffered from losses of memory, becoming incapable of filling the gaps with improvisations all his own.

"Nobody ever told me, in all these years, that the professor had the nose of a hunting dog! And I want him to know that I'm the one who has control over my own secrets. Nobody's going to steal a single one of them. It won't get him anywhere to come sniffing around in *my* burrow," Gioconda said.

She was aware that her sarcasm made her vulnerable to Virgílio's tactics for personally setting accounts, particularly since he now had Polidoro on his side again. Tempted, however, to flee from a homely logic, which had banished from her feelings the tasty fat that would perhaps have made them eloquent and creative, Gioconda decided to be a more active participant in the completely disorganized festivities, with no fixed hour and date for ending.

"Since when is Polidoro the only master and model of the passion that Virgílio keeps proclaiming?"

She smiled impetuously at Polidoro as, in open competition with Virgílio, she argued in favor of a love in the pay of fantasy and safeguarded by secrecy. "Fucking is a public act. All you have to do is go to the whorehouse. Love is a hog being fattened for slaughter in a dark room without a breath of air," Gioconda argued.

Her turban was shaking, accompanying the movements of her head. Relishing the effects of the strange festivities, she was beginning to feel from close up the destructive impulses that assail performing artists. Weren't they the ones who broke crystalware with disillusioned smiles?

"Bravo, Gioconda!" Ernesto said, forgetting all about his family. Vivina seemed to him a memory from the past. Out of habit, he looked at the clock. Vivina, at home at the dinner table, was helping herself to some guava preserves. She would have to wait for him. His most immediate concern was to see that the chrysalis embodied in Gioconda soared like a butterfly.

Polidoro accepted another glass of wine. With no heart for a fight, he beckoned to Gioconda. "After everything that's been said here, it remains to be seen whether or not I fulfill the request that Caetana made to me before the sun set."

"What was it she requested?" Francisco asked, high from all the tippling he'd been doing.

Wine had a soothing effect on Polidoro's temperament. "Gioconda's right. For the time being, the secret belongs to me alone."

Under the threat of a monotony that had made them old before their time, Virgílio went into action.

"Well, then. Let's fulfill Caetana's request," he said, offering to help.

Gioconda straightened her turban. Once she gave her fantasy free rein, she was the equal of the French woman writer from whom she had copied her headdress.

"Count me in too," she proclaimed excitedly. "I've just acquired a power of imagination I've always lacked."

Taking long strides, followed by Virgílio, she joined Polidoro.

Ernesto foresaw that his friendship with the cattle baron was in danger. Even already-crystallized sentiments could shatter to bits without warning. And, on noting that Mágico and Francisco had more initiative than he did, he grew indignant.

"Don't you know that whether in a democracy or in a dictatorship there's such a thing as natural law?"

Francisco refused to tolerate Ernesto's bringing up his popular background in an irreverent way. After all, revolutions were made with people of his sort. He waited for Gioconda's relentless defense. Intoxicated by the expectation of a future that would crown all of them with the thorns of illusion, nobody spoke up in his behalf, however.

This ostracism offended his conscious awareness. Any step backward in the social realm darkened his life. "Long live President Médici!" he shouted in distress.

"There's no need to exaggerate." Virgílio was embarrassed by the acclaiming of a dictatorship that in years to come would suffer the anathema of history.

Polidoro, a member of the party in power, smiled.

"Put your shoulders to the wheel, my good fellows. We've lots to do in the future. We have to make a go of it."

He was about to leave the kitchen when Francisco intercepted him, his mouth so tense he couldn't smile.

"One last toast."

"May I ask to whom?" Virgílio forced himself to abandon the sphere of dreams he had been immersed in.

"Who could it be besides Caetana!"

Francisco looked at Polidoro, hoping for a sign from him. The cattle rancher's mask refused to melt in the sun of his emotions. Without hesitation, Francisco raised his glass, accompanied by all the others.

"Long live Caetana," he said in a solemn voice.

Not a single voice was raised in opposition to the toast.

AT THE FIRST sign of a fit of laughter, Sebastiana hurriedly covered her mouth. She did not want people to notice that she was lacking three upper teeth, her one reason for not allowing anyone to kiss her on the mouth. She was afraid that, out of imprudent desire or curiosity, some stranger with an unsympathetic or lonely heart passing through town might run his tongue over each one of her teeth, so as to explore a set that had had gaps in it ever since she was a teen-ager.

Gioconda had recommended that she get a denture, but Sebastiana was reluctant to admit, even to the dentist, that she had three missing teeth.

Diana did not spare her feelings. With excessive frequency she mentioned classified ads placed by dentists in Rio de Janeiro who used drills and pliers with no concern for their patients.

"Those dentists pull teeth without asking permission. They'd make a fortune in Trindade. People around here are gap-toothed, or else they have a mouthful of decayed teeth and bad breath. I'm the only one in the house who doesn't." And, with satisfaction, she contemplated in the mirror her pronounced buck teeth.

Sebastiana got up from the table in tears, despite Gioconda's words of consolation as she accused Diana of committing the sin of disrespect for other people's feelings. "Some day soon you'll be sorry you've done that," Gioconda said to her, with the tone of voice appropriate for predicting the future.

Indifferent to the fate that awaited her, Diana kept stealing the potato from Palmira's plate. She was in the habit of serving herself small portions of rice, beans, and stew and wiping her plate clean with bread, claiming that that way there was more food for the others, who were putting on weight thanks to her sacrifice.

"In addition to stealing our food, Diana is also going to castrate us like hogs some day," Palmira retorted.

Diana pushed the tureen over to Palmira's plate, tempting her with the odor of bay leaves given off by the beans. Palmira fought against giving in to her overbearing ways. She mistrusted her gestures, devoid of grandeur. As proof that she was being cautious, she toyed with the ladle in the tureen but did not help herself.

Her resistance surprised Diana, who could see the hunger imprinted on Palmira's face.

"Since when do any of you have balls hanging down between your legs to be cut off?" Diana sat up straight in her chair. She took pleasure in using certain words, though she did so without affectation. The very use of them defied social conventions.

"I am unable to be crude, because I was born in a splendid cradle. I'm like Brazil," she said ironically.

Gioconda walked over to the window. She took a deep breath of the breeze that was coming in from the wide-open space outside. When she returned, she felt like setting the house to rights.

"The one thing you haven't said yet is that being a whore is an honorific function," she said, taking the wind out of Diana's sails. "And cut out that bad habit of pecking at other people's plates. Serve yourself and be done with it, or you'll catch a disease."

Friday had been an exhausting day. Especially for Gioconda, who had come back from the hotel late that night. Generally she avoided being out on the streets at night all by herself.

"How is Caetana?"

Palmira was waiting up for her with a plate of food all ready in the oven. Anxious for news, they had taken leave of their clients earlier.

"Bring the plate in here." Once settled in the easy chair, Gioconda flung her shoes far away from her and stretched out to relax her muscles. She avoided looking at the women.

"Does she still remember us?" Palmira handed her the plate, cold now.

Gioconda accepted the plateful of pork tenderloin with toasted manioc and rice and ate with gusto. In the hotel she had helped herself to two little chicken pies, the only food she had consumed since the frugal lunch at eleven that morning, except for the piece of cake she had eaten at the station as soon as the train had left.

Listening to the noises Gioconda made as she chewed, Sebastiana was eager for news, anxious to recharge her batteries of dreams through messages that Caetana might have sent her. Forgetting Diana's affronts, she knocked on her door and invited her to come downstairs. The three women, in a circle around the easy chair, kept Gioconda company as she ate with a will. Only as she took the fifth forkful did Gioconda look at them distractedly.

"I wasn't able to see Caetana. She didn't receive anybody. She had a lot of work to do."

Her heart was touched by the women's reaction. Only then did she realize that the Three Graces looked a little older every morning, with herself as the only observer. There was no member of the family, except Gioconda, to ease that burden for them. Only she told them how many wrinkles they had, making certain that she hadn't miscalculated. But she preferred to say nothing, to give them the illusion that they were still young.

The news had its effect on them. Each one of them reacted in accordance with her own character, intuited by Gioconda, as a general rule, long in advance. Diana, for example, given to violent reactions, inveighed against Caetana for refusing to see Gioconda, for not having broken into tears at the mention of their names. With nervous gestures she selected a few strands of her hair and twisted them into a fat curl that she then uncoiled and let fall down her shoulders. Palmira, in despair at human wretchedness, habitually let her head drop down onto her chest, like an Italian madonna, indifferent to the pains that the gesture caused her, perhaps because she was waiting for Sebastiana to intervene, ever ready to rescue her from an uncomfortable position. This time, though, the shock brought on by Gioconda's confession kept Sebastiana from taking practical measures.

"Is that good or bad?" was all she asked, faithful to a formula she invariably adopted when reality seemed to her to be forged from hard, intractable metals, liable to wound her heart.

Face to face with Sebastiana, Diana was on her guard, ready to spoil her happiness—an improper reaction at a time when they had been deliberately slighted.

"Why that mania of yours for asking whether something is

good or bad? As far as we're concerned, it's always bad. Wait and see if they let us into the Palace or invite us to a party for a wedding or a baptism. The only thing those males summon us for is to fuck, and they just do that as long as our bodies hold up."

Palmira tasted the dessert, rice pudding sprinkled with cinnamon, before passing the dish to Gioconda. Nobody said a word. Gioconda ate a second helping.

"I think Polidoro will come by tonight," she said in a casual tone of voice, not wanting to attract the attention of the Three Graces. It was time for bed. Sebastiana was yawning.

Almost the moment Gioconda had finished saying that, Polidoro's voice, right outside the window, startled the group.

"What if it's a robber?" Palmira tried to stop Diana, who was about to open the door.

In her eagerness, Diana shoved her away and flung herself into Polidoro's arms.

"It's a good thing you came. I couldn't put up with this mystery about Caetana for one minute more. Is it true that she's locked the door of the bedroom and refuses to see anybody?"

She treated him as though she were his hostess, eager to collect from her guest news that would warm the house.

"I didn't come as a customer," he said in a sharp tone of voice. "By tonight I was fed up with whores."

Though Gioconda did not join them, the Three Graces surrounded Polidoro, allowing him practically no room to move.

"Did you come to see us for our good or for our ill?" Sebastiana opened her eyes wide, to lend the question a transcendent dimension.

Gioconda offered him his usual easy chair and footstool. He looked dog-tired to her.

"Didn't you go home?" she said, to begin the conversation.

Polidoro loosened his belt, which was constricting his belly.

"I thought it better to drop in here. No matter where I went, I'd be loaded down with ghosts of the past," he said dejectedly.

Palmira served him some cane brandy, but Polidoro forgot once more to thank her for her kind gesture. He was habitually unaware of the presence of women.

"Caetana was always a woman who had her whims. We shouldn't be surprised," Gioconda said unhurriedly, pausing deliberately. Polidoro drained the glass of cane brandy in one swallow and held it out to her for a refill. He feared the loneliness of that night.

Gioconda had forgotten to remove her turban. But she would not wear it again. The spell would be broken once she undid the cloth topknot. Polidoro gave no sign of leaving, of going back to his own house without Dodô inside.

"Who's going to satisfy Caetana's whims?" Gioconda said, as though taking the first step toward sending him back to his own house.

As he downed the second glass, Polidoro went over the day's happenings in his mind. The trip to the station after lunch. The train arriving in Trindade not one minute behind schedule, while on the platform everyone was fighting for the honor of being the first to embrace Caetana. He too had made a dash toward the woman who looked like Caetana as he remembered her, an illusion that soon disappeared amid the general confusion, as he felt the pain in his chest that cut off the horizon of his life. Immediately thereafter, he sighed with relief: he no longer need bare his feelings in public or allow his friends to see in his face the bitter and desiccated flower of passion. A reason, perhaps, that had induced Caetana not to take the train. Though the actress, accustomed to the creaking of the boards of the stage with every step she took, adored dramatic scenes.

On the platform, he had struggled to free himself from Virgílio, the latter so eager to note down the first words exchanged with Caetana. The professor believed in the efficacy of stories in writing, though life had denied him a single valuable document.

On leaving the station, sitting behind the wheel of his car, Polidoro didn't know in what direction to go. But when Ernesto asked him for a lift, on the pretext of keeping him company on his way back to the hotel, he unfeelingly refused. Let them all go home on foot. He turned on the ignition, hoping to heat up the engine.

"Disperse the group," he said to Constable Narciso. "I don't want the people of the city to suspect that we were here. And to anyone who insists that he saw the train come through, say that it was a dream. Who among us didn't want a train when he was a kid?"

Ernesto forced his way into the car.

"If you all leave together, everyone will be convinced that the train went through Trindade," Narciso tried to reason with him.

The pharmacist upbraided Polidoro for his absurd argument. It was inevitable that the train had left evidence of its passage through Trindade.

"Whoever saw it will soon forget," interrupted the constable, who used to give orders to break into bedrooms in the middle of the night in order to catch some adulterous couple in the act. "Nobody here has any reason to believe in absurdities."

Nearing the main square, Polidoro spied the mango tree planted by his grandfather. In order not to arouse suspicion, he went through the gesture of a routine afternoon. On the way to the hotel, he imagined a situation wherein Mágico, having the wrong floor in mind, handed Caetana the keys to a room that she had no memory of. This gave the actress good reason to protest, unwilling as she was to revive the flames of an old love in a hearth where she had not previously burned the logs of her passion.

Then, for vengeance, Mágico stopped her just as she stepped into the decrepit elevator, simply to tell her, in solemn tones, dressed in his cutaway coat, that the hotel management made it a strict rule never to permit people from the theater to occupy quarters on the premises. There were no exceptions, not even for famous actresses like Caetana.

At these insulting words, Polidoro would spit in Mágico's face, grab his checkbook out of his pocket, and shout at the top of his lungs: "If that's how it is, Mr. Mágico, I'll buy the hotel; set a price and I'll sign the check here and now, in your presence."

Mágico was waiting for him at the door, certain that he'd drop by. He was the one who, sensing peaks of glory for the Palace Hotel, had sent Francisco to the station.

"I myself saw Dona Caetana to her suite," he said, in affected tones.

Polidoro paid no attention to him. At the door of the ancient elevator, he decided he'd rather climb the stairs. He was afraid that the contraption would break down between the third and fourth floors. As he went up the stairs, one step at a time, he chose the first phrase he would utter, and rehearsed it. A phrase that would express passion but at the same time be polite.

On the landing of the second floor, he remembered Caetana's smile, the first of a series that she had given him. In the beginning, he hadn't wanted to go to the circus; he had other business to take care of. But the poster with the woman's blurred face attracted his attention. He bought a ticket, intending to stay fifteen minutes at most. Art bored him. But the moment he saw her in the circus ring, along with her uncle, Danilo, and other actors, offering the audience words and gestures at once graceful and powerful, he was lost in a maelstrom of emotion. In order to dissipate the effects of the love springing in his breast, Polidoro clapped and clapped. With her hand on her heart, Caetana acknowledged the applause from an audience unaccustomed to the fatal thunderbolt of art, intermingled that afternoon with the black clouds in the sky.

As he extended his compliments to her backstage, he expressed his surprise at her name, a most unusual one in Brazil, not likely to have been given her at the baptismal font.

"What other name would you have preferred, if 'Caetana' is name enough for a woman like me? Would you rather that I'd been called Dulcinea de Toboso, she too being the victim of other people's hallucinations?"

Polidoro had never heard of Dulcinea. But Caetana wasn't surprised. She also couldn't explain how her nomad life had given her such an obscure and fallible education.

As she kept making expressive gestures, Polidoro was convinced that the woman could leave indelible marks on him. Her long nails, blood-red and filed to a sharp point, landed on exactly the right spot in his breast, like a sparrow balancing on the branch of a leafless tree.

In an attempt at a gallant gesture, he bowed his head so that she would feel the distress in his heart, which was beginning to tremble with love. But he lacked spontaneity. And he was immediately overcome by the worry that Dodô would suddenly appear in the dressing room, making a jealous scene, as he was taking the first step toward occupying a place in the actress's illusions. But his deepest fear had to do with the fact that Caetana was a foreigner, even though she was a Brazilian citizen. She was someone who, coming from very far away, showed herself to be immune to the influences of the new lands that she visited. No other soil would force her to give up any of her dreams.

"Give me thirty minutes' attention anyway." His pleading tone, against his principles, upset Polidoro.

Caetana consulted her watch. "Only a watch sets a limit on my heart. But my art frees me of the hands of timepieces. So, on the stage or in the circus ring, I am in command of the duration of every sentence I utter. There are sentences that can last more than a minute. Sometimes they even oblige me to skip the follow-ing one or they annoy the audience, which boos me in a fury. So what timepiece are you talking about?" Caetana dejectedly contemplated the faded canvas of the circus tent.

Polidoro was alarmed. The illusion of love, a poisoned arrow, had dealt him a fatal blow. She wanted to make a slave of him. He had seen that self-absorbed air in movie actresses. All of them with the same objective. Bondage.

"I'll stay as long as necessary. Nobody's going to banish me from my own property. Trindade is still my city. My cradle, do you hear!" he said, his pride as an owner of a large landed estate injured.

The interwoven white, black, and pink feathers that adorned Caetana's head trembled as a sign of her anger. Dressed as a demimondaine, in the role of a woman whom fate had already assigned a punishment that would satisfy society, Caetana attacked the man.

"What right do you have to show up and take the horsewhip of fate from the hands of God?"

Solemn and melodramatic, Caetana mixed together sentences expressing her own feelings with others belonging to the roles in her repertory. And she did so in such a way that he had difficulty telling the one sort from the other.

Polidoro grew more and more bewildered in her presence. Surely the woman was confusing him with an enemy she had left behind in the past, whom night thoughts, insomnia, and hunger had brought back without warning.

"Since when are you my lord and master?" Caetana went on in the same tone of voice, as though someone had rewound her.

This time the phrase, far from crushing Polidoro, elated him. His male instinct told him that the scene, played with rare boldness, promised to be prolonged beyond the dressing room and lead them toward the bed.

"Magnificent role!" He tried to feed the right lines back to the actress, as proof of his interest in an art that had never attracted him. "What play does that sentence, typical of the mistress of a sugar mill or the lady owner of a cattle ranch, come from?"

Caetana was surprised at his combination of naïveté and passion. His persevering gestures, his attempt to act out the scene with her, made her burst into laughter.

"What are you laughing at?" he asked mistrustfully. Might her laughter not erode the feeling that was palpitating between them?

"If I chose the stage, it was to embody strong heroines, with a taste for killing and dominating. Some day I'll be Cleopatra. When it comes time for her to commit suicide, I shall die like a queen. Despite the cruelties inflicted by the Romans and Antony's indifference."

Polidoro was on his guard. The actress promised him that she would be submissive in her love for him, seeing him in the person of that Antony, as she hinted at revenge against the politicians in power—the so-called colonels of Trindade, such as himself and his father. Quoting the queen, she warned him against the malevolent nature of passion, which could lead them to make their escape from the world, paying no heed to the perils of a journey that was self-centered and lacked a compass.

He looked at her in the mirror. Caetana adorned herself in fake jewels, giving them the same care required by real pieces of jewelry. Spread out on an improvised bench were souvenirs of her travels, of tours throughout Brazil, which had left the brand of nostalgia deeply imprinted in her uncle and her.

"I see that you, Caetana Toledo, are a difficult woman. You resemble the Portuguese women of old, who bade their husbands farewell at the piers of the port only so as to make certain that they were in fact setting out for America. And they showed no signs of suffering because their husbands were going to be away from home for more than ten years. Some of them would never come back. And not even then did those women dressed in black shed tears."

It consoled him to show off the things he knew about Portugal. He also wanted to pique her by confronting her with situations he'd learned about from books. He couldn't be humiliated by a circus-ring actress who thus far had still not attracted the attention of an impresario from the capital.

Caetana was getting ready for the second performance that Sunday. In a few minutes, she would go back into the circus ring. She was retouching her makeup to accentuate her eyes, which shone with such extraordinary brightness. She didn't seem to belong in the company of earthly creatures. In a manner of speaking, she had already taken her leave of him.

Vespasiano came into the dressing room. He called her by name, but she did not answer. Her uncle looked Polidoro over without surprise.

Polidoro was persistent.

"May I wait for you afterward?"

Confronted by Caetana's absorbed expression, which banished him to make room for a chimera of gas and smoke, Polidoro addressed Vespasiano, who was patiently waiting for his niece to say something.

"Why doesn't she answer me?"

"That's the way she always is before going onstage. Have you given any thought to how it's going to be on the day when she first steps onstage at the Municipal Theater up in Rio de Janeiro? That's our greatest dream. I'm certain that Caetana is going to make it come true. I only hope I'm still alive at that moment of glory."

Vespasiano headed out toward the ring. With a gesture, he

urged Polidoro to come with him. As they neared the big top, he clutched Polidoro's arm. "If you want my niece, you're going to have to come with us. Caetana's place is here. She'll never give up this world." He turned his back on Polidoro and proceeded to the entrance to the tent, then looked back. He was pleased to see that Polidoro had tagged along after him. "Don't make such a face! You won't be the first man to abandon family, money, an illustrious name, simply to follow an actress," he said in a gentle voice.

Though he put nothing in words, Vespasiano seemed to be hinting at certain precautions and precious information. His niece, under the aegis of art, attracted lovers to the stage, depriving them of the roof under which they had been born, only to devour them immediately with an insatiable appetite. Merely passing through her heart as an actress, they were then sentenced to exile. Confronted with such a picture, Polidoro took offense.

"Do you think I'm a clown?" he said, without thinking of the effect that such words would have in a circus.

"Why are you insulting clowns? They're the most tender-hearted and long-suffering performers of any show. I too am a clown sometimes—a clown who doesn't need dramatic phrases to plunge to the bottom of the well. Laughter is the only respectable universe in a land of fools and madmen. Don't you agree with me?"

His belly, betraying his emotions, shook underneath his loose tunic, which bore, just above his chest, a yellow heavenly constellation, spangled with white glass beads. His fake beard changed position on his face whenever he laughed heartily. It was as if he possessed two faces.

Though the preparations for going onstage bewildered Polidoro, he had toned down his crude manners in Vespasiano's company. He put his emotions through a selective filter. He didn't want Vespasiano to think of him as an obstreperous sort.

His attempt was watched closely by Vespasiano. As a reward, he explained to him the pleasures and the pains of the profession. The fact, for example, that to an actor feelings seemed to come over him all by themselves. They belonged more to the characters he portrayed than to the actor's own self. Without actors' noticing, desire grew from a single flame to a blaze, so that their profession went to bed with them with the aim of their dreaming together.

Vespasiano had entered the annals of the Brazilian theater only after the greatest of difficulties. Nobody could rob him of his fame now, which as it happened was highly deserved. A person had only to consult the book by Brício de Abreu to see Vespasiano's name in it as founder of the troupe known as Os Romeiros, itinerant actors who since 1930 had taken their talent, their knapsacks, their crates full of tattered velvet costumes, drop curtains, and folding chairs, all through the interior of Brazil. This record spurred him to go on. He showed the book, already falling apart, to anybody who cast doubt on the importance of the work that he and his company had accomplished.

"Our race wandered through the world without any fixed abode, since long before the Middle Ages, constantly persecuted by the clergy, by the nobility, by the cold, by poverty. Even here in Brazil, there was many a time when we lacked even the money to eat. In certain villages they paid us with vegetables, eggs, and poultry. One time we were giving a show on top of a stage when we heard the cackling of a hen that had been shut up in a wicker basket. It was quite a to-do. The poor creature laid an egg before our very eyes. We ended up holding our sides with laughter, grateful for the coins that dribbled into the hat we passed round as we left."

Polidoro sat down on a bench in the grandstand. The show would soon begin, but Caetana's uncle still had a few minutes to talk of the performers, who had nothing but scorn for houses, land, and other more or less permanent material possessions. Vespasiano was sweating despite the breeze coming in through the bottom of the tent. He wiped the sweat from his chest with the same piece of cloth he used to shine his boots.

"I brought Caetana up from the time she was a tot. My brother died of tuberculosis from all the binges he went on. The poor man spat blood, staining the bedclothes and his pajamas. He left no inheritance except a black cape from the University of Coimbra, a music box with a mother-of-pearl lid that a lady, whose name he never told me, had given him as a gift, and a few volumes of Greek works for the theater. There were certain plays my brother knew by heart. Even in the open countryside, amid cow dung, he would recite soliloquies as though he were onstage. On the eve of his death, he summoned me at midnight. I remember it well. I could hardly hear his voice; his lungs were full of holes, like certain kinds of old-fashioned cheese. It was then that he said . . ."

Vespasiano's heart was touched by the audience that clumsily climbed up and sat down in the grandstand. Most of them had come to see a public performer for the first time. It was a very small audience. He gave no sign of being concerned. Wishing to prove his detachment, he turned his trouser pocket inside out to show how broke he was.

"Did your brother know he was going to die?" Polidoro was worried about intruding on Caetana's family circle, just as he had been when he heard the story of Dodô's family before marrying her.

"He always knew. Ever since he was a kid, he used to say that life was short but worth squandering gloriously before it was too late. His greatest concern, before putting his soul in the hands of God, was his daughter. He wanted Caetana—whose illustrious name comes from the house of the dukes of Alba, a lineage with ties to the sublime Goya—to be an actress, like all the rest of the family. No one knew anyone from their bloodline who had fled from that destiny. It was necessary to prepare her to face adversity, without giving up the profession for that reason. He spoke of failure as naturally as other people spoke of fame.

"I took Caetana by the hand and bought her a dress to replace the old one she was wearing. But I bought the wrong size, and it turned out to be too short. The solution was to make a hem with material left over from the costume of a play. To my vast surprise, Caetana protested. She didn't want to be treated like an orphan, a cat on the hearth. I made her see that she was being unjust, for I would even give up eating for her sake. It was quite true that life was hard on the sort of people we were. We never earned enough money to rest our itinerant artists' carcasses in any theater in Rio de Janeiro. Maybe we would have lived a more comfortable life then, without having to keep moving all the time over roads of beaten earth, which in those days we used to travel up and down on in a wagon. How often we used to get stuck in the mud for days. Teams of oxen would come to pull us out. And in the dry season, the gravel thrown up by the wheels nearly blinded us. In those days, in her free hours, Caetana would train her voice in front of the mirror, after sucking on a paste made of sugar and lemon. And she would say to me, dreamily, that if she were rich she would leave us behind and go to the city of Milan."

Vespasiano held on to his memories, tracing designs in the air with his pudgy hands, which lacked agility—a bad habit from his stage performances that had stayed with him. He obviously mistrusted the spoken word unless it came accompanied by a flurry of gestures.

"Why Milan, may I ask?"

She insolently defied her uncle, as though she wanted to punish him for the many hard years, for her much-mended clothes.

"I'm going to be a prima donna," she had said to him. "I want to perform in opera, which is sung theater, in case you didn't know."

"Don't you see that being performing artists is already costing us our lives?" Vespasiano would exclaim. "And yet you want to cross the Atlantic, to live in a country that isn't ours, just so you can be unhappy in a foreign language? Isn't Brazil enough for you, a country so vast and so lovely that we'll never live long enough to get to know the whole of it?"

Polidoro clung to Vespasiano's every word. He was afraid to hear the end of the story—the revelation of a secret that would wreak harm on the future. The smell Vespasiano gave off, coming from his armpits, entered Polidoro's nostrils. He felt nauseated. He couldn't bear physical contact with another man.

Imprisoned in the circle of memory, Vespasiano didn't notice Polidoro's distaste. Once again he identified wholly with the wanderings of the past, the countless times they'd fled from cheap boarding houses during the night for lack of money to pay for the room. In Pirenópolis, however, Caetana calmed down when they proved to be a success.

"They offered us a lunch with fifteen desserts. Caetana was next to me at the head of the table. She had a hairdo embellished with a rhinestone tiara, wanting to look older and richer. Perhaps that was why, beneath that crown of dreams and gleaming stones, she asked to address the gathering.

" 'Nobody's ever going to give me orders.'

"Words such as that, though from a girl only fifteen years old, in fact came forth from a mare with a shiny, wild mane. The lobes of her ears were almost the size of the pearl earrings that she was wearing. I wondered, regretfully, whether there was anyone in the world who would ever touch her heart with unlimited tenderness. For she had tough skin, a snake's skin. She claimed that I was the only person she respected. As proof of her love, she once kissed me on the forehead. And that was only when she saw me being flung onto the bed, and was afraid I was about to die. She wept, feverishly babbling nonsense at me.

" 'Ah, Uncle, what will become of me if I need you all of a sudden? What's the use of my winning a triumph some day if you're not there to see me?'

"She fixed her black eyes on me with so much anguish, as though she wanted to perceive, once and for all, the mystery that she bore within her soul, as short-lived as a flower.

"The loving devotion of my niece raised my spirits. I had reason to be thankful for a feeling that had been kept so well guarded and that came to the surface only in her hour of grief. So I lent her the Victrola, which was used exclusively for our performances. She wanted to hear her favorite arias all by herself in her room, or beneath the stars whenever we camped out between cities to avoid paying for lodgings."

Polidoro listened to him as though the show had already begun. He closely followed the family drama revealed by Vespasiano, amid excessive gestures, laughter, tears, and sighs, his life laid bare for a paying customer like Polidoro.

"Do you mean to say that Caetana has the theater in her blood? Is it a family affliction?"

Polidoro feared he had inadvertently offended Vespasiano yet again, with these words so tactlessly spoken.

Vespasiano smiled. He appreciated such frankness, which was only to be found in stables or else on the stage, through hidden and tangential expressions, employing art as a pretext. Moreover, he nursed the hope that, having succumbed to the delights of the theater, Polidoro would end up funding a production worthy of a theater in the Cinelândia district in Rio.

"She has it in her blood and in her heart. It's a passion that's going to hurt anyone who loves her."

The look in his eyes, for the first time a roguish one, belonged to a vaudeville scene in which it was hinted that Polidoro might turn out to be his niece's favorite, thanks to gold coins.

Polidoro took heart. He felt compensated for having inhaled the smell of Vespasiano's sweat, the latter being quite unaccustomed to products that deodorize the body. Caetana's uncle's assent to Polidoro's passionate attraction to his niece came at just the right time. With the help of allies, he would convince the actress to extend the thirty minutes that Polidoro had asked her for.

Vespasiano rose to his feet. Seeing his niece at the other entrance to the circus ring, he bade Polidoro farewell. He would go into action later, but at the moment he had orders to pass on. He invited Polidoro to make himself comfortable in the one dressing room. Polidoro thanked him: he would accept the invitation another night.

"Well, we'll leave it at that, my friend," Vespasiano said, taking his leave.

Polidoro hid in the empty lot in front of the circus. He kept looking at his watch, but he couldn't tell how many hours went by. Darkness had already fallen. Finally, the applause died away as the audience left the tent. He went around to the dressing room in the back of the tent.

"I've come to fulfill my part of the bargain. Now you fill yours," he said, in his starched linen suit and with his hair disheveled.

Caetana, still in her dressing gown, began to peel several garlic cloves. She rubbed them vigorously on her right hand, raising the cloves to her nostrils every so often. She avidly inhaled the intense odor, which also reached Polidoro, throwing his instincts completely off balance, whetting his desire to throw her to the floor beneath his body.

From her tabouret, Caetana held out the same hand, which reeked of garlic even from a distance, for him to kiss. This social practice, not a part of his upbringing, intimidated Polidoro, who drew back, not knowing where to hide. The gesture that Caetana was demanding had actually been a frequent daydream of his mother's. Magnólia had spent many a December dreaming of a cavalier who would kiss her hand some day, so vividly she came to believe that, despite the boorish males of Trindade, such gallantry had managed to survive for centuries till finally it reached her. Destiny decreed that Magnólia was to die without overcoming her husband's resistance, his refusal to perform in public, with his own wife, so simple a gesture—the only one that would have erased from her memory the figure of a man, well known to everyone, who had even had lunch at her house, a man whose languid gaze, long curly locks, well-trimmed mustache, riding habit appeared on the horizon of her dreams with a frequency that made her tremble. "If you want to make love to me, take the garlic test. Come on, kiss my hand."

Polidoro could feel his distended testicles, the fierce torrent of desire mounting his thighs, impotently taking root in his flustered genitals. Overcome with fury, he sniffed her hand, her arm, breathing hard. He licked her fingers with the tip of his tongue, the woman's skin tasting like roasted meat. Impelled by a twofold hunger, he stuffed the entire length of her fingers into his mouth. Their moving joints blocked his palate, almost making him vomit. He felt he was devouring the woman's vulva, moist and cavernous.

Caetana yielded parts of her body, Polidoro's oppressive tongue smearing her arm with saliva and garlic, without his being able to predict its next movements. Finally, exhausted perhaps from excavating that skin, having gone down nearly to the bone, he raised his inordinately large mouth, reeking of garlic, close to hers and breathed whiffs of liberated passion at her.

"Are you pleased at the way I smell?" he asked, avenging himself for the love to which he had succumbed amid a disaster that had no name.

Caetana rose to her feet, violently pushing him away. Polidoro persisted, his body bent over her. Caetana shoved him away once again and returned to her dressing table.

"Is that the way you treat me?" He tried to embrace her from behind, to press his outsized genitals against her ribs.

In the mirror, she reproved him for his gesture. The scene, taken in by both of them in the glass, made Polidoro feel ashamed.

"You've passed the first test. We'll see each other later."

With a wave of the hand that still retained the smell of both of them, Caetana dismissed him. Polidoro disappeared into the darkness, avoiding being caught by Vespasiano.

In the house at Estação, Palmira, tapping him insistently on his back with a bottle, erased his memories.

"Shall I pour you another drink?"

Polidoro irritatedly answered her question. Palmira lacked the sensitivity needed to console a man wounded to the quick. She had not acquired refinement in her dealings with human feelings, in spite of the number of men who had passed by way of her bed.

"Is it no longer possible to get a little rest in this house?" he upbraided her, holding Gioconda responsible.

"This house isn't one to sleep in. If you want to immerse yourself in memories, go back home, under your own roof."

Gioconda faced up to him, indifferent to his disparagement and to the fact that he'd seen her with her hair held down by bobby pins, with the turban lying on the floor alongside the easy chair.

The woman's frowsiness touched Polidoro's heart. Like himself, Gioconda was a victim of the tyranny of the years, which chose its hapless victims from among the innocent.

"I'm on my way. Today was a tiring day."

"Please don't go. Tell us about Caetana," Diana said, blocking his way to the door. "You're the only one who can assure us that she still loves us."

In her eagerness to persuade him to keep them company through the endless night, Diana spattered him with saliva mixed with the *guaraná* juice she'd just finished drinking.

Fatigue accentuated Polidoro's loneliness. He lacked the courage to open the door of his own house and find the living room with all the lights turned out. He looked at Diana. Freed of the duty of taking any one of the Three Graces to bed, he gave in to her plea, wiping his face resignedly.

He felt obliged to show in public a happiness dating back to bygone days, to review the anxiety-filled trajectory of his passion. On seeing Diana's face, which served him as a compass, his spirits revived enough for him to tell just about any story that had Caetana and himself as main characters.

Diana settled herself comfortably on the floor, like a greyhound at its master's feet. Grateful for the attention that Polidoro was paying her at Gioconda's expense, she began to untie, in a gesture that was unthinkable coming from her, the laces of Polidoro's shoes, before slipping them off his feet. Overcoming her aversion to the smell of grimy socks, she gently massaged the man's feet, doing everything short of wiping his sweat away with her long hair, like Mary Magdalene.

Diana's attitude, aimed at undermining Gioconda's prestige in the latter's own house, displeased Palmira. Faced, however, with the prospect of missing out on what Polidoro was about to say, she remained within Diana's orbit, sitting down next to her on the floor.

Polidoro sat up straight, despite the slight titillation Diana's by now nervous caresses caused him.

"I don't know how to explain. But when I reached the third floor, I was suddenly afraid that I'd lack the strength to climb the remaining flights of stairs. And, mind you, I'm used to walking, to riding on horseback for hours, not to mention my having continually mounted the best women in this town." His tone of voice, gentle and devoid of pride, might have been speaking of someone else. "There I was, weary and hobbling, and all on account of a woman! Luckily, Vespasiano had warned me the very first day I met him. But what's to be done about those illusions that people insist on carrying around hidden inside their hearts, since otherwise their bosoms grow chilled from sadness?"

As he spoke, with emphatic pauses, he was careful to remain faithful to the truth of events. He wanted to satisfy the expectations of the Three Graces, especially since Gioconda, at the other end of the parlor, wasn't paying any attention to him.

Sebastiana had her handkerchief at the ready. Tears came easily to her at such times. Through the look in her eye she had sworn, nonetheless, not to interrupt the flow of his narrative. Whatever story he told would be regarded by all of them as a true one. And so it was that Diana, in order to warm his ankle bones, went on stroking his feet. In this way, he would go on with ardor, far removed from the vortex of the story that he was telling, a man's passion.

Slowly, Polidoro poured out his emotions in the presence of these ladies, who granted him the indulgence to invent. These women, so sensitive, could easily imagine how his heart shook in his chest as he went up the stairs. Each step was a bead in an imaginary rosary. A prayer that devoured timid and faltering words, addressed to a nameless being.

Resting on the landing of the fourth floor, he was searching for an argument that would convince him of his love for Caetana, despite her long absence. If, in all those years, she had made no use of the mails, when there were post offices throughout the nation, to dissolve the ties of passion by letter, he had reason to believe that the words of love of long ago, uttered amid the rustle of the sheets, were still intact.

Possessed of this certainty, he sucked in his belly, tightened his suspenders, tried to button his jacket, at the door of the suite. His effort to make himself look more handsome was useless, an imaginary mirror with a cruel and vengeful tendency seemed to say to him.

He could not back down. He had come a long way, and the feeling foremost in his mind was that he had worn out the soles of his last pair of shoes and his feet hurt. At the door he said: "I have always been a male whom women lust after." The sentence, when repeated, sounded convincing. Thus spurred on, he knocked. Caetana was already waiting for him.

"Was it Caetana herself who opened the door?" Diana said, interrupting his reverie even though Gioconda, who had come closer to the group, condemned such an attitude.

Gioconda never trusted Polidoro's character. Accustomed as he was to fighting bulls, to treading ground undermined by snakes, spiders, and scorpions, it was hard for him to cultivate courteous gestures or poetic phrases. He looked nervous, trying to pull his feet from Diana, who was holding them by force. In that struggle, Polidoro painfully recalled the world that he had left behind and handed over to Dodô. The return to the reality that centered on his wife, his daughters, his sons-in-law, and his grandchildren brought on facial tics, anxiety, a nervous outburst.

"You fucking whore!" he shouted, putting an end to the alliance established with Diana. "How dare you disrespect me? As though I were pouring out shit instead of the pearls of my feelings. Since when have I been a liar and a coward? Am I not telling what happened, the way I promised to do from the start? Do you think I'm inventing details so as to escape from a painful truth? Is that what that interruption means? Or would it suit you better if Caetana had died, since you can't bear knowing that she's still alive, in all her splendor, and nobody here can dispute her royal dignity and authority?"

Polidoro got up out of the easy chair. He wasn't going to stay one minute more in a house where an anxious whore had offended him. He had no intention of giving in to Gioconda's pleas, as she picked up the shoes he had kicked a good way away in his indignation—a kick so well aimed that it had hit Sebastiana and Palmira, sitting innocently on the floor, the target of his violent temper. But they were surely not so harmless as they led people to believe. For they had allied themselves with Diana, a vicious hag who could hardly rein in her perverse instincts, the consequence of the thousand penises that had passed through her vagina.

"Calm down, Polidoro, it's not worth making such a fuss about. It wasn't meant as an insult." Gioconda tried to dissuade him from storming off. He was too old to work himself up.

At the door, calmer now, he inhaled the smell of the parlor with disgust.

"I prefer to suffer beneath my own roof, even if I'm pursued by the phantoms that Dodô left in the house on purpose, just to keep an eye on me. She thinks I don't know that she feeds those shades on choice delicacies to keep them satisfied and attentive. She's a dangerous woman. The one thing she wants is to banish me, to stay behind with everything I own."

The sentence served to drive the clouds from his face. There was the trace of a smile on it. His chest was heaving under his shirt, slightly stained with sweat after the long day.

"Aren't you going to tell the end of the story?" Gioconda asked, serving as a shield for Diana, who had lost her courage.

"I'll tell it some day. Stories are like day-old bread. The longer they stay in the drawer or in a person's memory, the better they seem afterward."

He opened the door. The night air made him sneeze. He hurried out to the street, longing to climb into bed, between the sheets.

Gioconda felt Diana's arm linked in hers. She shook her whole body in her impatience to free herself from it and headed toward the kitchen to brew coffee.

"Can Polidoro have caught cold?" Sebastiana sighed, wanting some coffee.

Gioconda considered the effects of spring on delicate beings. It was a season that brought restlessness, hope, acne to people's faces, and green back to the trees. On the other hand, the pollen that was loosed on the air left people's hearts violent and helpless.

"It's the sign of spring," she said distractedly, putting water on the fire to boil.

"Spring in the middle of winter?" Diana corrected her, having recovered from Polidoro's rudeness.

"Anything's possible in Trindade. We live so far from civilization. But maybe Caetana will come to visit us tomorrow. And tell us the end of the story herself," Gioconda said, in an attempt to put an end to the day's unexpected incidents.

AT NIGHT Polidoro managed to empty out his memory. All he had left was a deep well, with muddy waters that nobody was able to drink. A pleasant state that gave rise to the firm conviction that he would remember Caetana's name the following day without daring to repeat it to himself.

In the hope of going straight to bed, he put the doorkey in the lock. He took a look at the furniture in the living room, which he'd dropped in on like a visitor. Dodô had good grounds for reprimanding him. He had never wanted to fall prisoner to a house that, in point of fact, he had never regarded as his. In the midst of such thoughts, he was starting to unbutton his shirt when he heard Virgílio's strident voice outside.

"At this hour?" He did not conceal his distress. His downcast brow was a sign of his dejection.

"I'll only stay long enough to learn the truth. All Trindade now knows about your meeting Caetana except me. The friend you're fondest of, despite Ernesto's vying for my place."

Virgílio sat down at the head of the dining-room table, next to the fruit bowl. Since he was thirsty, he peeled a tangerine with nervous gestures. The peeled section spurted juice on Polidoro.

"Is this accursed Friday never going to end?"

He sat down next to Virgílio, visibly despondent. Surely Caetana's presence in Trindade was responsible for all the turmoil. Virgílio himself, who for more than thirty years had turned out his bedroom light before nine to go to sleep, had eyes that were burning as brightly as a beacon.

"If I tell you, do you promise to leave the minute I swear I don't have any more to say?"

Virgílio's mouth was half full of tangerine. He was having trouble chewing. With his hand upraised, he gave his word.

Polidoro reconciled himself to repeating secretly, to himself, the story he had been brooding on. With an attentive listener like Virgílio, perhaps he could now test the authenticity of the facts and discover the mistakes in his tale.

Ever since the news of Caetana's arrival came that Friday morning, he had been searching for a logic that, applied to everyday life, would bring practical results, while at the same time taking care not to impair, with excessive flights of rapture or tireless ambition, the love that the actress had devoted to him over the years, with irreproachable fidelity. Hence, before Caetana opened the door on the fifth floor, Polidoro had a moment to regret the campaigns in which his heart had long been wounding itself by way of a whole series of contretemps. And time too to reproach himself for his rudeness, since he had not thought of bringing Caetana a birthday present. He ought at least to have brought what was left of the flowers that Gioconda had left behind on the bench of the train station, before the group disbanded after Francisco's announcement.

As he knocked on the door, he heard voices. Taken by surprise, he suspected the presence of some enemy who, intending to give him a pair of cuckold's horns, would forcibly embrace Caetana before his very eyes, and then proclaim in the bar of the Palace Hotel that he had gotten the better of Polidoro, despite the latter's fortune and love for Caetana.

All upset, he scratched his chest. His fingernails, which he had forgotten to trim, aroused in his flesh the bitter sensation of jealousy. Panting, he foresaw the danger of dying at the entrance to paradise. He hastened to do some breathing exercises. When the door opened, a beardless youth subjected him to long and careful scrutiny, and did not invite him to come in.

"Who might you be?" the boy murmured in a low voice, so as not to be overheard by someone who might be in the living room. His arrogant manner of speaking was different from that of Mágico, whose insolence concealed servility.

"Polidoro Álves," he answered, hoping that his name would open the door once and for all.

The young man ordered him to wait there. Through the half-open door, Polidoro saw part of the inside of the living room that he himself, despite being pressed for time, had reconstituted. At the sight of the pieces of furniture and objects, now contaminated by Caetana's heat, he was tempted to dash home and send a note to Dodô at the ranch, urging her to come back: her husband was wasting away with fever. He leaned on the doorjamb. He had eaten almost nothing all day. The only thing in his stomach was his breakfast, buttressed by the birthday cake.

"Please come in," Balinho said. However, on catching him unawares, leaning against the door, pale, listening, Balinho smiled. "We left our secrets on the road."

Accused of eavesdropping, Polidoro lacked the strength to defend himself. With clumsy gestures, he sat down in an easy chair upholstered in an almost completely faded green fabric. He had hoped to find Caetana in the living room, prepared to throw herself into his arms—a scene that, being a crowd-pleaser, was naturally part of the actress's repertory. Onstage, Caetana acted as though a fever were smothering her to death. With the vigor of a peasant lass, she was better than anyone else at embracing any man. And also, depending on the circumstances, at behaving like a lady with a weary backside seated on the sofa.

The living room, plunged into darkness, would camouflage the signs that the ever-insidious years had imprinted on sensitive faces like hers. Balinho approached, with foppish elegance offering him coffee.

"Sugar?"

Polidoro said no. Balinho loaded his coffee cup with sugar, paying no attention to his preference.

"It will do you good. It's recommended for strong emotions."

Polidoro's hands trembled as he held the cup. He drank the coffee, grimacing the while. And when he looked around for Balinho, the boy had disappeared. Perhaps he had gone to fetch Caetana. He would return to the living room only at the head of a retinue made up of miserable wretches, raggle-taggle performing artists. And would then announce, like a herald, the entrance of the actress.

Balinho came back into the room. He went directly to the Victrola, which had to be handled carefully. Polidoro identified the phonograph even in the dark. Callas's voice, in "Casta Diva," portended austere times for himself and Caetana.

"A fine song," he commented. "I haven't heard music of that sort since Caetana left."

Balinho withdrew to the bedroom amid the shadows, Another shadow promptly took his place in the living room. The body stole into the room with impressively silent footsteps. It was carrying a lighted candle that illuminated its face. Caetana was like someone walking in her sleep, her eyes half closed. She stopped in the middle of the living room, certain that Polidoro was watching her.

He rose to his feet with difficulty, regretting not having chosen the chair with the hard seat instead of the easy chair, with its slack springs, which put his agility to the test.

Caetana was clutching to her bosom a bundle that shyly nestled there. Polidoro strained his eyes to make out what it was: a cat whose eyes gleamed in the dark like burning coals.

The candle flame, flaring up in the breeze coming from the open window, allowed him to contemplate the woman. Her hair drawn up to the crown of her head in a topknot. She had put on weight. And her negligee, of a light fabric, did not hide her abundant curves.

Polidoro smiled with pleasure, foreseeing the moment when he would squeeze that flesh, which so lavishly displayed contours exactly suited to his tastes. He had known her entire body, fingered every last bit of its surface. From certain recesses he had gathered perspiration with his tongue, to quench his thirst. Her breasts, willful as ever, heaved freely in the darkness. As round as a soft pillow. Accompanied by the purring of the kitten, the woman's bosom let out generous exhalations, as though she were panting for breath.

Polidoro strained to inhale deeply, in an effort to recover Caetana's odors, which had lingered in his mind all those years. She was bringing him a body saturated with the memory of its scents. Above all of a night when he had unrelentingly sniffed her flesh with the keen flair of a wild animal. He had parted her hairy pubis and asked her, scarcely breathing, to place her intimate, powerful odors in a pocket flask. He wanted to have her fragrance close at hand whenever he wished to bring back certain memories.

"How are you, Polidoro?" Her attention occupied by the cat, she did not hold her hand out to him.

Her voice sounded crystalline. The years had not spoiled its harsh, rasping timbre. Like the taste of Portuguese wine, he had told her one night, causing her to burst into relaxed laughter.

"A little codfish and oil, and I'll become a genuine masterpiece of Portuguese cuisine."

Caetana came closer.

"You know me. But you don't know him."

She pointed at the cat. The light from the candle, on the sideboard now, helped Polidoro familiarize himself with the creature's contours.

"His name is Riche. He's been with me for seven years now. He's fierce, and a tough critic. Whenever he scolds me or warns me of dangers, he uses some seventy expressions. He's also going to survive me. Cats never die."

She slowly smoothed his fluff. Riche reacted drowsily, purring. His long ash-colored tail moved sinuously, stretching out, brushing her pubis.

Polidoro's eyes did not leave the cat's. The feline stuck his tail up, hard and straight, in an obscene movement. The only thing he didn't do was penetrate Caetana's vulva. The coordination of the gestures exchanged between the woman and the cat, in complete connivance, disconcerted Polidoro. His member, tumescent and imprisoned in his undershorts, was as velvety and dark as the tail of the cat, the guardian of the temple that he was eager to desecrate as soon as possible.

Ashamed, he hid how flustered he was.

"Welcome to Trindade." His thundering tone of voice frightened the animal, who, with one bound, leapt out of Caetana's arms to the floor. She tried to pick him up again, but the cat hid between her feet.

"Calm down, Riche," Caetana murmured, oblivious of Polidoro.

Polidoro was resentful at not being the object of such rapturous attention. He did not want to protest, nevertheless.

"I didn't greet you at the bus station because I thought you were coming by train. We were all at the station."

Accustomed to the semidarkness now, he was gradually becoming able to make out her expressions.

"I didn't come by bus, but in the cab of a truck that didn't charge us anything. As you're well aware, artists in this country are practically beggars. Art doesn't pay. Particularly for actors like us, who rebel against an inhumane market." Every one of her words came from an aching heart. She looked tired.

"You'll be safe here," Polidoro said, holding out his hand. For a woman it was always easier to cling to a man who had kept the remains of a love rooted in his heart for so many years.

Caetana did not notice that he was approaching with his hand outstretched, in a gesture offering her stability and a future. Seeing the woman's body shrink from his, Polidoro suspected that the emotion of their meeting once again had blinded both of them. He nonetheless remained with his arm extended, in case she needed it. He was cheered by the memory of having offered in the past to remain at her side. He had repeatedly proposed to provide her a house with a back yard, table settings, bedclothes, a full larder, everything to make her forget the hardships of life in the theater.

Once she returned to Trindade, she would have no reason to worry about the future. He intended to give her the same care he extended to his own family. All because of the strength of the love that he still professed for her, even today fiery hot and extravagant each morning as he shaved.

Caetana gave no sign that she had understood his message. Followed by Riche, with his rare talent for gliding along at her side without getting coiled around her legs, she moved here and there in the living room.

Fascinated by the cat's movements, which combined harmoniously with Caetana's, Polidoro allowed his arm to fall to his side, upbraiding himself for going too far in his demonstration of an appetite that didn't consider Caetana's embarrassment and the presence of a sly and treacherous feline, and that could only be appeased if he got her into bed with him.

It gave him pleasure to realize that Caetana, despite Riche's vigilance, was treating him with the intimacy that women ordinarily accorded their husbands, failing only to open her valise and give him back the pair of pajamas and the slippers that, in her hurry to leave, she had packed in with her luggage, in order always to be accompanied, as she slept in other beds, outside Brazil, by the memory of a love as enduring as it was ardent.

Now, however, Caetana's love for him, having become more prudent, did not express itself through gestures reminiscent of her former passion. As though she had allowed the memories of a past that had grown as old as the two of them to become yellow with age.

"Did you know that I was a failure?" she said mercilessly as she removed the hairpins from her hair, which fell over her shoulders.

Polidoro trembled. That was the sign that Caetana wanted him in bed—or on the carpet, in case they didn't have enough time and serenity to get as far as the mattress.

At the sight of her hair let down, he rushed toward her with his arms wide open, shouting, "Caetana, Caetana," though at the same time he paid close attention to the cat, to avoid getting entangled between its legs. He had nearly reached her side when, suddenly reacting, she frightened at the same moment both Polidoro and Riche, who kept mewing without a letup.

"Don't touch me, Polidoro."

Not heeding her warning, he came at her in a furious rush. His arms enfolded her; he tried to press her lips shut with a kiss.

"Give in to your passion, Caetana. Or can you already have forgotten me?"

She protected her mouth by turning her head this way and that, at the risk of twisting her neck painfully. Finally, overcome by Polidoro's brute force, she let him kiss her.

"I'm not your slave." The castigating phrase was uttered coldly.

The timbre of her voice pierced Polidoro's illusions like a dagger thrust. It had a paralyzing effect on him. He suspected that the woman had come back to take her revenge for some misdeed he felt himself to be innocent of. She was humiliating him to pay him back for an act that had wounded her to the quick in the past.

"What did I do that made you stop loving me? What was the use of waiting twenty years for this love if you now refuse me and turn me into a man without a country and without a future!"

Worn to a frazzle, he scratched his chest—a habitual gesture whenever fate had tormented him throughout the years marked by Caetana's absence.

"Don't be tragic, Polidoro. Since when have you wanted to take over my role? I'm the one here who puts on stage performances. I'm the one who has the right to burst into tears at any moment. Not you, the man who buys more cows and land every day, and on top of everything else has a rich wife."

Though Caetana's tongue-lashing was meant to restore his good sense, Polidoro ignored it. He took pleasure in behaving as if he were onstage, living the part of a character doomed to commit any imaginable sort of madness.

"If you didn't come back out of love, what are you doing here at my side, now that I'm a corpse?" Using the intonations of high tragedy, Polidoro was in fact taking over the role that belonged to Caetana, the only actress present in the room.

Insensitive to the outpouring of the man's feelings, Caetana asked him to sit down. She would have liked to tie him to the chair with ropes. He obeyed, suspecting that she intended to sever this vein of inspiration that he had just discovered. Playing a role, his intuition told him, was a new source of pleasure for him.

"You act as though you were at a country fair, selling me zebus or a fringe of fertile land," he said diffidently.

Caetana did not always prove herself capable of correctly interpreting Polidoro's sentences, some of them full of rural metaphors. For this reason, they had had their differences in the past, although Polidoro always hastened to make light of their disagreements, since once they were in bed together passion cemented their mutual understanding. His memory, after twenty years, had turned generous. He found himself unable to recall a single spat between them. Better, then, to settle down comfortably in bed now for the frolicking that their bodies and their unmistakable lust were past masters of.

"I'll give you five minutes to get in bed with me. You didn't come all this way just to chat with me. I'm still as much of a man as ever, and full of appetites," he said in his theatrical tone. He was finding it difficult to abandon, perhaps because it afforded him the only access he had to this woman's imagination.

Caetana's stubborn silence impelled him to pace back and forth in the living room, at the risk of bumping into the furniture in the darkness.

"If you needed a check, instead of love, you had only to send me a telegram or phone long distance. I would have made a bank transfer within a few hours. You didn't need to cross so many Brazilian states in the cab of a truck," he said, giving vent to his feelings but avoiding her gaze.

He finally halted in front of her. His voice quavered. "Pretend at least that you love me," he implored.

Mindful of the scene they were staging, Caetana sat down to make room for him to move around in the living room. She crossed her legs, arranging her negligee across her knees with broad gestures. The light from the candle on the sideboard, at the entrance to the room, did not facilitate their scrutiny of each other.

Polidoro was annoyed.

"We're going to see each other, and that's all there is to it. What difference does it make if we're twenty years older?" Determinedly, he fumbled for the light switch.

The sudden brightness interrupted Caetana's ramblings, which had taken her on a long flight of memory. Reluctant to allow her face to be seen, she hung her head down toward her stomach. She murmured something, her voice barely audible. As Polidoro approached, she spoke more loudly.

"If I was going to end up a failure, why didn't Uncle Vespasiano shatter my dream from the very beginning, when my father gave me to him to take care of? Why didn't he warn me every morning that in Brazil there existed a multitude of toothless actors and actresses, doomed never to tread the boards of the Municipal Theater in Rio, that he was one of them, and that I would share that fate with him?"

She raised her head contritely. She had aged. The bags under her eyes gave her the physiognomy of a Buddha transported to America with the aim of revealing new ways of life. She shook her hair, which seemed to weigh heavily on her shoulders. It was thick and black. Her hands, intertwined at the level of her breasts, went through a series of movements measurable in fractions of a second, which brought back to life in Polidoro the memory of powerful gestures of days gone by.

He knelt at her side without touching her.

"What failure are you talking about, Caetana, if you visited the humblest hamlets in Brazil just to bring fantasy to the very door of simple people's hearts? Who else did that except you and Os Romeiros?"

His own vehemence came as a pleasant surprise to him. Discovering in himself a verbal sensibility that was manifesting itself for the first time, he was afraid of losing this unexpected gift for lofty oratory even before taking Caetana to bed with him.

Polidoro—under the aegis of the Holy Spirit, whom he had called upon—accused television performers of clinging to the shoreline like crabs, insensitive to the loneliness of towns with fewer than a thousand inhabitants, far different from the down-and-out itinerant companies of players who ate with their bread the dust of the roads. As he spoke, Caetana seemed to see before her eyes, brought back to life, her own Uncle Vespasiano, eating cheap fried sausage as he stubbornly defended theater for the poor, a tradition that had come down to them from medieval fairs.

"Thanks to all of you, Caetana, those wretched country people know what theater is. That magical thing that made me cry when I wanted to laugh!"

Caetana resisted. It was hard to tempt her into the fatal kiss. He mustn't give up his desire, though it was weaker now, because of the effort he'd made to express his feelings—which grew more intense in the intervals in which he searched for words capable of making a woman smile. Polidoro hoped to collect, in the next few minutes, the proof of his victory, directly from Caetana's parted thighs.

In the expectation of devouring her genitals, of getting inside them like a base and cunning serpent, he went on with unusual enthusiasm, now and then chasing Riche away with the tip of his shoe, without Caetana's noticing.

"If I saw you performing now, I'm certain I'd ask you never to give up the stage, not even to live in the house I've always wanted to offer you in Trindade. Even at the risk of losing you, I prefer to revere your art," he said, disguising this whopper by repeatedly blinking his eyes.

"How does it happen that an actress is going to give up her work just to stay with me in a city with so few inhabitants?"

After this tribute, Polidoro leapt to her side on the sofa. He had the right to share with her the odors, the vapors, the sighs, the moans that they would exchange as they waited for their love to assume concrete form. Ready to make them come like eager and relentless chargers.

Riche, however, imitated Polidoro and jumped up onto the sofa, placing himself between them. Polidoro contained his rage, his desire to throw the cat out the window. There was visible antipathy between the animal and the man. Riche's purring, quiet before, now sounded like that of a tiger. And, not satisfied with having such a weapon at his disposal, he curvetted, shedding hair the way a molting canary sheds feathers.

Taking no notice of the drifting hairs, Caetana soothed the cat along its restless back. Unlike Polidoro, who was acutely aware of the ash-colored enemy hairs attacking his bronchial tubes. Allergic by nature, he began to sneeze. And his sneezes kept him from remaining near Caetana.

Caetana felt sorry for Polidoro, who had capitulated to the fine-textured fur of a cat. She looked at Riche, trying to guess his intentions. Polidoro, for his part, stifled his sneezes with his handkerchief.

"Talk to me, Caetana. Don't remain silent, please," he begged, still attached to the verbal world that was already starting to escape him.

"Ah, what right did I have to be a Maria Callas when I never even learned to sing? Or to be Ângela Maria, who has the screeching, ruined voice of the Brazilian people? Or even a Dulcina de Moraes, whom I saw in São Paulo, and who made me weep with grief? Once, when I was just a little girl, I left Itaboraí and went to Rio de Janeiro to try my luck on the radio, on Ari Barroso's program. But do you know what he did, with that sarcastic, cruel laugh of his? Without the slightest pity, he had them sound the gong. I went downstairs in the elevator of the radio station half-dead with shame. I didn't want them to see me wiping my eyes with my crumpled handkerchief."

Polidoro was torn between the duty of praising her virtues and the desire to snuff out her dream of glory. He suspected that those words were part of a farce in which Caetana had invested the best of her talent. In her fifties, what was doubtless lacking in her vast repertory was a role that would make her soul glow as she approached her twilight years.

"Until I came to Trindade, I had hopes of going back to Rio some day. Afterward, however, I followed my uncle till the day he died. When we buried him there—in Goiás Velho, a place I've never gone back to—I chose those ugly little towns as my only stage."

The confession did not appear to be a painful one for Caetana, who recited it as though she had rehearsed it. She opened a wooden box and took out a cigarette, then tapped the end on the table, to fit it into her sandalwood cigarette-holder, a gift from the mayor of Palmeiras in Alagôas. Her eyes followed the smoke dejectedly.

"Do you know where we'd come from? From Recife, where we were unable to put on a show. The sea breeze and the ghosts of Dutchmen, who still wander about the canals, drove us out of there. We went to perform on the speaker's platform of a union hall, in a working-class district on the outskirts of the city. The leader of the labor union is a Frenchman, a former priest who's a metallurgist today, married to a woman who'd been a Brazilian nun. The two of them insisted on showing me a new society that has nothing at all to do with your cows and your country estates. It's just that I'm too old for that sort of dream. It's quite enough to belch and vomit my own up every day."

She paused, as though to catch her breath before really letting herself go.

"Isn't it true that performing artists contend with the gods for the right to act out the stories of humankind? And that they want to usurp by force the throne of those divine beings? Ah, accursed profession that left me poor and lacking a roof over my head," she said in a fury, not remembering Polidoro's presence at her side.

Digressions of this sort bored him. Ever since he'd been a youngster, he'd preferred concrete subjects, things that one could reach out and touch. The soul merely exhausted him. It thwarted the passion of his body, which ran to fat and faithlessness.

"What a mania for mixing God and art together! He has nothing to do with it." Irritated, Polidoro rose to his feet. The smoke that Caetana exhaled was reaching his eyes. "It's your Uncle Vespasiano who's to blame. You could have become a rich estate-owner a long time ago!" he said, having already forgotten his strategy for seducing her.

Polidoro's stubbornness had not become any less intense as the years went by. Even today he wanted to shut her up in a harem, to fit her with a chastity belt to keep her from making her morning ablutions. His way was that of a despot, preoccupied with his power over his ranches and zebus.

"I don't even know why I'm telling you these things," she said. "Perhaps because I need courage to ask you for a favor you owe me."

Her negligee, which reached down to the floor, surrounded her with a mystery that, in the middle of the argument, intensified Polidoro's desire to put his hands between her legs, to experience the taste of the juices from her vagina, where in other days he had bathed his member with wanton frequency. Like an unbroken horse, he had discharged the sperm that effortlessly spurted out of him on the woman's lilies of the field, those Biblical flowers so rare in Brazil.

"What favor do I owe you that I haven't yet paid you back for? Why haven't you ever once protested before in all these years?"

Furious, he immediately contained himself. He had chosen to be magnanimous. In the final analysis, Caetana had been his wife, in bed and in his heart, in a way that Dodô had never managed to be in more than thirty years.

Taking advantage of Riche's drowsiness, he took Caetana's hand above the cat's body.

She was frightened by the insistence with which he struggled for her joints, her hardened veins, her weariness, her disillusionment. For a few moments, she allowed herself to be stroked.

Caetana's passivity seemed to him to be a rare virtue. He greatly appreciated evidences of reserve in a woman, as long as they were soon abandoned in bed in favor of passion. Caetana, for example, was extremely careful to keep her dignity, a quality that suited his taste. She had not been born, as the Three Graces had, to be a whore. Deeply touched by the certainty that she had kept herself for him all through those many years, Polidoro stroked her arms, more robust now, in a combative mood. Then, immediately thereafter, her breasts, despite the distance from her imposed by the presence of Riche.

Bruised from his caresses, Caetana pushed him away. She was absorbed for the moment in gestures belonging to a role that she had played many years before—to be precise, that of a widow who, finding herself besieged by the enemy out to impugn her honor, got up from the sofa and headed for the chest of drawers in the living room.

Caetana, like that character, opened the drawer, from which she took the box inherited from her father and left in the safekeeping of Uncle Vespasiano, convinced that any proof it might contain would testify in her favor as she confronted the enemy.

In the play, the widow, dressed in black, pointed out to the mercenary satyr the jewelry in the bottom of the velvet-lined box as she vehemently proclaimed:

"Take from me the gem that is worth a fortune. But leave me my honor, which is my sole treasure!"

That lady, preferring poverty to public contempt, touched the heart of her enemy, who was tempted to return to her the fortune already in his hands. His hesitation did not escape the widow, whose eyes, swollen from the tears she had shed for her recently deceased husband, beamed at the possibility of keeping both her honor and the jewel.

The role fit Caetana's situation. She revived it with visible pleasure, playing to Polidoro as her costar. Except that, despite being possessed of talent equal to his, she had taken from inside the box not a jewel but a manila envelope.

Polidoro intuited that Caetana was bringing the envelope to him beneath the beam of a yellow spotlight, as the boards of the stage of a little theater in the backlands creaked and the audience was taken by surprise. She had brought to life, before his eyes, a character so disturbing and so fascinating that it would be difficult for her to abandon the role. He, however, with no training as an actor, found it hard to evaluate her intentions and figure out how to give the role even more depth.

Caetana, her face tense, handed him the envelope, which was closed with sealing wax.

"Here is the debt you owe me. My one reason for coming to Trindade was to settle accounts with you."

Polidoro, inside the skin of a stranger, accepted this responsibility reluctantly. He was doing as she wished because he was a gentleman. Certain that her request would be granted immediately, he was behaving like the romantic leading men of his youth. He too felt tempted to experience adventures he had seen on the screen. Above all to relive the movie in which the honorable lady placed in the envelope, along with the message, a bit of cotton impregnated with an Oriental fragrance kept carefully stoppered in a crystal flacon for decades, the obvious aim of which was to arouse in the English colonizer, who lived in India and to whom the message was addressed, a passion that he, finding himself so far distant from London, was in need of.

"May I break the seal?" Convinced that he would impress her with his elegant manners, Polidoro awaited the results of his wiles.

Standing before her adversary, Caetana bowed her head like

an icon of the Orthodox Church. One simple gesture, out of keeping with her way of holding her body.

"I trust your honor as a gentleman," she dared to avow, as her role demanded.

Polidoro trembled with emotion. Caetana was on the point of giving in to his effort to seduce her. Once he had broken the seal of the envelope, he would have his hands free to embrace her.

Without betraying his eagerness to possess the woman who had remained faithful to his memory, he broke the bright-red seal.

"Let's see what there is inside," he said calmly, ready to reap his victory.

The moment he had uttered those words, some object hurtled at him with such violence that he lost his balance and fell to his knees.

"What's the matter?" He hurriedly regained his composure, without concealing his disappointment. The spell of the rare instant had been broken.

"Behave yourself, Riche."

Caetana was trying to coax the cat into her lap. But Riche, hidden in the curtains, paid no attention, fearful, doubtless, of the punishment he would receive from his mistress for his mischievous trick of leaping on Polidoro in one bound and knocking him down.

"Is that any way to act, Riche?" Avoiding the cat's eyes, she tried to console Polidoro.

"I'm so sorry. Riche sometimes behaves like a jealous tiger. I can't suppress that strange instinct in him."

She turned her attention back to Riche, delighted at the agility of an animal who with one well-aimed leap had toppled over a man of Polidoro's size.

Polidoro bent down in search of the envelope that had flown out of his hands. With his eyes fixed on the floor, he did not notice Caetana's indifference to his lot.

With her attention divided between the man and the cat, Caetana asked Polidoro please to hurry up, and leaned down to help him look for the envelope. In their haste, their hands touched, and Polidoro grabbed her fingers.

She wrenched her hand away.

"Look right now and see what's inside."

When he opened the envelope, he could not immediately identify the card. Though Caetana hadn't offered him any clue, there inside was the proof of her surrender.

"The queen of spades!" he said finally, examining the card closely.

Riche came when Caetana called him. Clinging to her feet, he rubbed his presumptuous muzzle on the carpet.

"What does this card mean?"

"If you don't remember, it's because you don't want to pay your debt," she said, in a forceful, surprised voice. She had always regarded him as an honorable man, more likely than not to pay debts contracted at the gaming table, even if there were no witnesses to his folly.

"Give me back the queen of spades! I release you from your debt." Tugging at the card, she prevented Polidoro from making the next move.

With a flurry of gestures, she went over to the Victrola. From among the records she chose "Vissi d'Arte." With that aria she intended to bid farewell to Trindade and any sort of wild fantasy. Like Tosca, she too was swallowing her last dream, bitter with gall, in the presence of a man as insensitive as Polidoro, who had doubtless thrown her over for a twenty-year-old virgin.

As Tosca bade farewell to art and love, Polidoro put his arms about her from behind, pinning her body firmly against his. It had been a long time since he had seen her looking so beautiful and so determined, her hair disheveled, her upraised hands leading the orchestra, her most deeply hidden aspirations thwarted.

"Ah, Caetana, how happy you make me!"

The woman's buttocks yielded to the force of his member, which, plunged into such an abundance of flesh, immediately grew in size. For a fraction of a second, she yielded to the impulse of love, as though she found pleasure in recovering, if only for a moment, the body of the man whose contours she could feel as he desperately pressed her to him.

Polidoro was kissing her neck, his tongue extracting its salt, its smell, his nostrils at last plunging into her hair rinsed in lavender water, with everything just as in bygone days, when with a sudden jerk Caetana extricated herself from that death grip.

"There's a matter we still haven't settled. What have you decided?"

Left by himself in the middle of the living room, Polidoro shamefacedly lowered his arms, covering his member. His conspicuous demonstrations of passion had turned his cheeks beet-red. To relieve himself of his discomposure, he looked for the queen of spades, crushed between his fingers. He forced himself to recall his memories having to do with that noble lady. Cards had always had a predominant role in his amorous frolics. The two of them delighted in playing a game that consisted of throwing the cards at a predetermined target. The one who came closer to the coveted objective would be declared the winner, and was then supposed to demand a forfeit, varying from a kiss to a bite on a toe, the demands becoming more audacious as the game went on. Most of the forfeits consisted of Polidoro's penetrating Caetana, on condition that he remain inside her for a long time, till he fell back on the bed, admitting defeat, his penis shriveled and exhausted.

"Of course I remember." At the thought that they would soon be repeating the same games, Polidoro waxed enthusiastic. "The cleverest of games. Better than card games, roulette, baccarat."

"And doesn't that queen remind you of anything else in particular?" she gravely persisted.

"That lady was a pledge that I would keep my word. The promise that I would. Whatever you might ask for, I would give it to you the moment you presented that card. Even if you were to demand a ranch of a hundred and fifty hectares and a hundred head of cattle from me."

Twenty years before, after the card had been handed over, Polidoro had offered her a furnished house in exchange for coming to live in Trindade. And he had also guaranteed her a life annuity. He for his part demanded that her love be put to the test each day. It was not enough for him to feel it to believe in it. Especially after learning from a Polish whore that a woman could tell if a male was really passionately in love when he was prepared to sacrifice part of what belonged to him. He had to empty his trouser pockets to make his beloved believe in the force of his ecstasy.

At the time, the Polish harlot had offended his sensibilities. Up until then, in his eyes, love was paid for with kisses and flowers. Only over the years did he learn that love could also assume the concrete form of land and money.

Overwhelmed by passion and by the money he had heaped up on top of the night table, Caetana had had her doubts and turned a deaf ear. Meanwhile, she carefully tucked the queen of spades away in her handbag. Perhaps keeping it for the future.

"If I pledged my honor, I'll keep my word. Not that I'll be leaving my family poverty-stricken," Polidoro said. He fell to his knees as he gave vent to his hurt feelings. By such eloquence, he hoped to touch Caetana's heart. Provided she wasn't one to take unfair advantage of a man's word, pledged in the madness of passion, which pays no attention to financial matters. For he was not prepared to give up his fortune and be plunged into poverty.

"Don't be afraid, Polidoro. I'm not about to cheat the Álves family out of their money. I just have one request to make."

Polidoro noted her sarcastic tone of voice, her disapproval of the courtliness that had caused him to kneel before her. Born in the wings of a circus tent, Caetana had drained her life to the last drop amid canvas swelled by the wind and downpours, and stages whose boards creaked at each performance. She had long since ceased to move in the best society. In recent years, above all, far distant from him, she had fallen into the habit of keeping company not only with performing artists, but with loan sharks and hooligans as well. She had forgotten how to judge reputable men such as himself.

Proud at having at last paid homage to Caetana in a way that would have pleased his mother, Polidoro rose to his feet. Life held such an opportunity in store for very few men in Trindade. Even though Caetana was not worthy of the gesture.

"Whatever you please, Caetana. All you need to do now is say what it is you want." In his effort to imitate a military posture, his belly popped out of his trousers.

"I want to be Callas at least once in my life!" She felt relieved at this public avowal of the dream that, until that moment, had been her heart's inviolable secret.

"Callas? Who is she?"

"She's a damned Greek who hasn't let me sleep for years. I'm consumed with envy of her. While she's performing certain tragedies on the stage, I suffer inside and fall into helpless rages."

"What do you expect me to do so that you can be that Greek woman?"

Riche entwined himself around Polidoro's legs, keeping him from walking. Perhaps the cat envied him his human nature, experiencing piquant and imperishable sentiments.

"I'll be the star of a performance we'll put on. Don't ask me for instructions. You'll know soon enough," she said impatiently, wanting to hurry him out of the living room.

Polidoro would not accede to that. In his capacity as impresario, he demanded a minimum of security.

"You're out of your mind, Caetana! What performance are you talking about? There's not a single theater in Trindade!"

"The rest will be at my expense," was all she said.

Polidoro stretched out on the sofa, indifferent to the fact that Riche was frisking about on his chest. He distractedly stroked the cat's head, as the animal purred at this sign of affection. Polidoro thought he'd made a friend. Laboring under that illusion, he gave Riche even more intense caresses, some of them meant for Caetana. Riche drew himself up, rounding his fluffy back, kneading his paws on the sofa. And, before jumping down onto the carpet, he scratched Polidoro with his sharp claws.

Noting Polidoro's shocked surprise, Caetana reassured him.

"Never trust Riche. He double-crosses everybody except me."

Polidoro waited for her to make a move to come to his aid. The years weighed heavily on him, and he felt unable to assimilate so many emotions in a single day.

"Go home, Polidoro. We'll talk tomorrow."

She feared for his health. Both of them had gone too far, but they would not share the same bed that night. She opened the door leading from the bedroom.

"You can come in now, Balinho."

The young man felt acutely the effects of the bright light in the living room.

"I hope you haven't had your ear glued to the keyhole listening to what we were saying." She took pleasure in chiding him in front of Polidoro.

Balinho placed the phonograph needle at the beginning of the record, which was already on the turntable. Again the voice of Callas.

"Have something to eat before you leave."

Polidoro did not respond to her polite invitation. He had grown used to his thankless lot and the depression it caused him. Also, he was afraid to face his friends, who would see him empty-handed, his body tense with frustration.

"Bring us a pudding that's been made with at least two dozen egg yolks," Caetana said to Balinho. She gave Polidoro a smile of consolation. "Just one serving of that pudding brings a dead man back to life."

"What will we do with our lives after the pudding?" he said disconsolately, knowing beforehand that no sort of answer would help him keep alive a dream nourished on twenty years of expectation.

"Nothing, absolutely nothing. At least I'll have been Callas for twenty-four hours."

Caetana went over to the sofa, where Polidoro lay stretched out, exhausted. She raised her hand to his head. Slowly she began rumpling his hair, as though this could affect his thoughts. It was the only affectionate gesture she had made toward him during all those hours as darkness fell.

THAT MORNING, Venieris the Greek did not suspect that fate was pounding on his door to force him out of his routine, which was always inside out when it came to furnishing him with reasons for being happy. Not once since his arrival in Trindade had he taken the interurban bus, or thumbed a ride in a car, to leave the city where for fifteen years now he had felt sad and hemmed in, a long way away from his beloved Aegean Sea.

The neighbor's rooster had awakened him as usual at seven o'clock. He was looking forward eagerly to the coffee that he himself fixed soon after his feet hit the floor. Resolutely, he crushed two bananas on a plate with honey and raisins and did light exercises with his arms, well worth his frequent care. Half an hour later, he opened his shop, in the rear of which he lived like a hermit, with no need to go about the city on foot.

In the shop, it gave him pleasure to breathe in with a certain rapture the smell of naphthalene bought by the kilo, scattered about among the carefully piled-up lengths of fabric, which he personally dusted. He was afraid that silverfish would eat the finest silks. Only when his dusting was done did he open the shop, to customers who, in general, brought him great expectations and news of the world.

In his eagerness to live once again amid human beings after the long, lonely "white nights" such as the Russians suffered from, scantily peopled by dreams, he began to ask questions as to their respective families. Such an interest was incapable of wounding anyone's feelings. Everybody in the neighborhood knew that this was the Greek's way of compensating for the lack of a family of his own.

Only by means of this expedient, to which he had constant recourse during the day, did Venieris manage to leave his loneliness behind. And he deliberately entertained the illusion that he was married, with the duty of feeding a hungry brood, all of them the offspring of his own blood.

"Wouldn't you like to take home a length of silk? Nothing can compare with its delicate softness." His eyes bulging slightly, he enticed the lady customers in the shop.

Every dress not yet made merited his attention. From the amount of fabric needed to the pattern, Venieris exhaustively discussed details regarded as relevant. When asked to suggest a fabric, he opted for colored prints, preferably bright ones, flower or leaf designs the opposite of conventional patterns, that suited his asymmetrical imagination.

Only then did he embark upon the most painful step. Certain of the ritual to be fulfilled, he spread the dust-free bolt of cloth on the counter. Like a nearsighted person, he brought the shears up close to his eyes. This examination slowed down the rhythm of his breathing.

"I can't make a mistake when I cut it."

His air of anxiety infected the customer, victim of the tension created by Venieris for the express purpose of enhancing the value of his rare talent at cutting a length of fabric without the aid of a measuring stick.

"Three meters are enough for that dress." He consulted the model in the magazine. "Not a single centimeter more or less."

His penetrating eyes studied the place where he should begin cutting, so as to narrow the margin for error. With pious respect, he picked up the shears, breathed deeply, plunged to the bottom of the well of his fear.

"Why don't you use the measuring stick and be done with it?" Virgílio asked one time when he was buying a length of cloth for Sebastiana as a Christmas present. "That way you'd spare us all so much anxiety. Have you ever thought of what would happen if you were to make a mistake and cut too little?"

He followed each of Venieris's maneuvers with curiosity. At times, overcome by doubt, the latter took many long minutes deciding where in the length of cloth he should start cutting.

"When I cut too big a piece, it's not important. I give it to the customer as a gift. Though remnants might well have served as the basis of my professional pride," he said, in perpetual doubt, not taking his eyes off the cloth. "The worst thing is when it's two centimeters short. In cases like that, I take responsibility for the loss, and I try again, at the risk of making a mistake a few more times on the same day. And so, to avoid financial losses, I need to get eight hours' sleep, so as to have steady hands."

Certain female customers with sensitive characters begged him to use the measuring stick. They suffered from the Greek's self-imposed obligation to be right on the mark. Yet out of gratitude, he never shirked his obligation to practice to perfection a craft for which he had been trained back in Smyrna, long before deciding that Trindade would become his residence and his calvary for the rest of his days.

"When I reach seventy, I'll resort to using the measuring stick. I'll no longer have the eye of a lynx—a characteristic of my people—nor the taste for taking risks, which is part of doing business. Even though I'm a tradesman who fancies himself an artist."

In order to lay to rest his conversational partner's suspicion that he did his work by using the wiles of a magician whereas life was a matter of much simpler acts, hinting that he was lending mystery to a craft that had used traditional methods for centuries, he came to his own defense.

"You can take the remnants left over from my mistake home with you. They're good for wiping away tears of joy."

His resignation to life's hardships convinced no one. The dark circles under his eyes were an indication that, all alone in his house, he spent his Sundays weeping. On Mondays, he proclaimed his disapproval of other people's selfishness. Nobody had so much as brought soup to his door. Nor had anyone inquired whether he was alive.

However, at the sight of the headlines in the newspapers confirming the world's violence, he felt ashamed of cursing the gods dear to his heart. They were ever-present in his memory, because of a collective unconscious that had come down through centuries to supply him with memories that could shed light on his Greek origins. In the face of proofs that the gods staged criminal assaults against human destiny, Venieris laid aside his pair of shears, attracting his customers' attention.

"How to give praise to those gods and esteem them if they brought us tragedy—and did so only out of envy! They didn't want us to be happy. Especially Zeus, who was cruel and authoritarian."

Nobody in Trindade could enlighten him, unless Virgílio was present. But Venieris got upset all over again, even when people managed to understand him.

"I don't worry too much about my happiness. I was fated to be born a Greek. I know that tragedy lurks about our house. At any time, the gods may stick their noses in places where they shouldn't," he confessed to Polidoro after they had had a few drinks together at the Palace bar.

"What is this mania of yours that makes you want to be un-happy?" Polidoro was weary of a Greek who persisted in being unhappy in the name of his homeland.

"How can I be happy if I don't have a country, a wife, and children?"

"A wife is easy to come by," Ernesto said to cheer him up. "What's hard is to get rid of her later on."

As Venieris did his best to awaken their compassion, his two friends tried to drag out of him by force his reasons for being so sad, to deliver him from exile.

Venieris, having made up his mind to rely on their sympathy, seized upon the very last resource he had that might touch the heart of Polidoro, whose soul opened like a flower when confronted with certain arguments.

"I don't even have a language to speak in. For whom would I recite a single verse from that poet of the days of old?" He immedi-ately regretted having mentioned the poet, whose name escaped his memory.

"Casimiro de Abreu," Polidoro hastily interrupted in his eager-ness to be helpful.

"What poet are you referring to, a Greek one or a Brazilian?" Ernesto asked, more prudent than Polidoro and much less of a success with women. Unintentionally, he lowered his eyes to Polidoro's trousers, in an attempt to see, through Polidoro's white Panama hat, how big his testicles were. Fearful, however, that they would catch him in the act of sizing up Polidoro's balls, he averted his flushed face.

Venieris looked annoyed. He couldn't believe that so eminent a pharmacist didn't know the name of a poet of such great magnitude.

"I'm referring to the Greek. The guy who wrote a long story full of heroes and battles. One of the heroes never got killed because his mother had immersed him in a tub of water blessed by the gods."

"I know: Homer!" Ernesto exclaimed, his culture compensating him for his modest-sized testicles; Polidoro's were much heftier, though Ernesto had never weighed them, the way Sicilian mothers used to do in the old days, pointing to the pendulum of the scale as a reason to demand a bigger dowry for their son. He had never seen his friend's member in its adult phase. Except for one night at Gioconda's, when he had gone into a bedroom on the second floor without knocking. In the bed, alongside Palmira, Polidoro was startled, and leapt to his feet, his penis erect by way of greeting. Ernesto then saw his bull-sized genitals and understood the pride he took in them.

"That's the one. He was a confrere of Virgílio's, whose name our historian received at the baptismal font."

Venieris prided himself on an erudition that had come down to him by way of songs and stories his grandfather had told as the family sat at the table, scared stiff that the Turks would break into the house to rob them of their last few belongings.

Venieris was not ashamed to express his trials and tribulations. Such venting of feelings in front of everyone appealed to Polidoro. He decided to help the Greek before he decided to leave Trindade.

"I'll lighten the burden of your exile in return for your promise to go at least once a week to Gioconda's place. Who ever saw a man who's happy without a woman in his bed? Or can it be that Greeks don't like women?"

Ernesto, whose ambition was to appear to be a dominating male, let out a resounding guffaw. Then, to tone down his laugh, which revealed even more of his teeth than already stuck out naturally, he draped his arm across the nape of Venieris's neck, as though he were a woman.

"Don't be angry. We know what he-men Greeks are, as brutish in bed as Turks. Even though certain famous Greeks in the past had delicate tastes. Isn't it true that they had a yen for ephebi of rare beauty?"

Ernesto's unbridled libido made him engage in cruel and inelegant acts. Demonstrating his displeasure, Polidoro put his arm around Venieris's neck from the other side.

"That isn't the case with any of us. We don't go in for such things here. With so many desirable women around, who's going to think about teen-age boys who have balls as big as ours?"

Venieris was not particularly aware of the verbal vibrations between the two men. His mind was on how a rich landowner could help out a lonely Greek. With money perhaps? Polidoro didn't make loans. When people came to him to ask for one, he would point to the local branch of the Bank of Brazil.

"What can you do for me?" Venieris asked timidly, without hiding the tremor in his right hand, the fingers of which were gripping the shears.

To Polidoro's displeasure, he kept asking the same question over and over. Like certain compositions he heard over the radio, repeating the same musical phrase some ten times to stress, with unbearable monotony, the main theme, which kept emphasizing the same notes put together to form a single melody.

Three days later, on the pretext of having come to pay bills left by Dodô and the girls, Polidoro returned to the shop.

"From today on, I'll come once a week, just to make you speak Greek with me. It'll do you good," he said, pleased to have entered into such an agreement.

He sat down on the high stool in front of the counter. On the other side of it, Venieris was practicing wielding his shears on a remnant of linen suitable for the purpose.

His heart, without a master, which no one came to claim at any hour of the day, unburdened itself easily, even before strangers. Nevertheless, instead of manifesting joy, Venieris cringed. Poli-

doro did not approve either of whining or of vain overexcite-
ment—except for the kind that stemmed from love.

Venieris feigned incredulousness at first, and then, immediately thereafter, antipathy toward such an absurd proposal. "Since
when do you understand Greek, Polidoro? Don't you know it's
practically a dead language, like Latin? It lost its mystery many
centuries ago, and there is no longer any prestige in speaking it in
social circles. Especially since the Turkish invasions."

Venieris protested vehemently as he brought him, from the
back of the shop, a pot of lemon verbena tea, perfect for calming
a person's nerves. He took pleasure in offering a kind of hospitality
characteristic of Levantines, a race he swore he did not belong to,
but certain of whose habits he had assimilated—in particular that
of bestowing gifts, even modest ones, on his friends, the moment
they set foot on his doorsill.

Before Polidoro had a chance to react, Venieris hastened to
admit his rudeness in refusing the favor he'd asked. Of late, he
had been allowing unpardonable gestures, ones that wounded his
fellows, to escape him. This behavior was justified by the fact that
for years now he had gradually been losing command of his native
tongue, which was the spoken portrait of his soul, without having
gained another, equally vigorous and effective one to offset this
loss.

"My Portuguese is ugly. It's no good for expressing a feeling
with a beginning, a middle, and an end. I always have the impression that words despoil my emotions. That's why I began to paint.
Through pictures, I hold on to my belief in reality," he mused, as
if he were no longer in the midst of a conversation with Polidoro.
He appeared to be sailing a long way away, through the green seas
of his forebears.

His distraction and his propensity for shedding tears were well
known. Here was the proof. Any trivial thing gave him a good
excuse for weeping. Overcome with emotion, Venieris turned his
back on Polidoro. At the entrance to the shop, he tried to balance
on a pile of odds and ends of cloth a placard announcing the sale,
at ridiculous prices, of remnants of printed fabrics suitable for
summer, hailed in the loftiest of panegyrics.

Polidoro slowly drank the herb tea. He suspected that Venieris had resorted to the unpalatable beverage simply to wreak vengeance on him, just because Polidoro spoke Portuguese with the perfection of the native speaker. He forbore, however, to protest. Accepting an invitation to have lunch at Venieris's house was worse than having to drink his tea. Polidoro couldn't abide grape leaves, which Venieris ordered from Rio de Janeiro, stuffed with lamb or mutton, a typical dish in his country.

"I don't understand Greek, but I have a good ear for languages. I can manage to understand a few words of Italian because I've heard a little opera."

Polidoro went over to the cash register, which lay half open. The money in plain sight inside it did not arouse his cupidity. Leaning on the counter, alongside the register, was a painting that was drying, a still life that Venieris had just finished. A black shadow came over Polidoro's face. To flee from his memories, he went to the other end of the counter and finished his tea, sipping loudly.

"I'm even able to smile if I choose the most beautiful words of your language," Polidoro said, fighting his anxiety. "Isn't it a musical and bellicose language, which resisted the Turks for centuries, not allowing them to drown it out with their shouts, which had come from the desert? Aren't the Turks Bedouins who live on the backs of camels?"

With Venieris, Polidoro was not afraid of letting his ignorance show. Besides being uneducated, the Greek was still floundering as he tried to assimilate the reality of Brazil, even though he had gotten off the boat in Rio sometime in the 1940s.

"If you don't practice Greek with me, who is there that I can speak it with? In another year, you'll have forgotten your language. Have you ever thought of what it means to lug around the corpse of a language inside of you? To drag all over the four corners of the earth the mortal remains of an unburied tongue?"

His arguments appeared to overcome Venieris's resistance. He served Polidoro another cup of tea, still warm in the pot.

Distracted by the plea he was making, Polidoro accepted the tea. He wanted everybody in Trindade, including Dodô, to know about his altruism, his intention of going to Venieris's shop, squeezed in between the bakery and the grocery store facing the square, merely to hear him mumble in a language that was all awry, that nobody spoke. Just so that the merchant's sad illusions wouldn't fade away altogether.

"How will you be able to go on living in Trindade if you don't give vent to your feelings and unburden yourself of your secrets at least once a week? With me, you can say whatever you want to. Without any danger. I'm not disloyal, nor will I betray your confidences. Furthermore, who can I give away your secrets to if I don't understand one word of Greek?"

Venieris was persuaded. He had to pour out his grief into Polidoro's ears, a tomb in which he would place flowers, his cares, his news, his frustrations. With each passing week the size of his debt to him would grow.

He was so enthusiastic about the weekly practice, in which he improved his Greek with Polidoro—who, for his part, all engrossed, recovered in those hours the memories that Dodô tried to destroy at breakfast—that Venieris begged the cattle baron to come to the shop twice a week. On the first visit, he would occupy himself with subjects having to do with Trindade and Brazil, which he was now trying to come to know better. On the second, he would explore the area of feelings, those sparks that set the barn full of hay on fire, with the cruel and violent flames licking the shed and leaving the scorched earth bare, its secrets destroyed.

"Do you think I'm an idler with nothing else to do?" Polidoro asked gruffly.

Venieris gave him another painting as a present—a porcelain vase full of bright-red carnations.

"Who knows whether you'll come twice a week in the future? I have the time, and I'm a stoic Greek."

On that Saturday, Venieris lowered the shutter over the door, indifferent to the creaking of the iron gear-teeth, ready to withdraw into the long loneliness of Sunday, which had begun to torment him since early that evening, when he said goodbye to his last customer. He was not expecting a visitor. Certainly not Polidoro, who invaded the shop without a by-your-leave.

"Because you pay so much attention to your shears, you keep forgetting to oil the joints of that accursed shutter. The damned thing groans more than a whore in bed pretending she's coming," Polidoro said, sitting down beside the counter.

Surprised to see him when it had already begun to grow dark, Venieris bade him welcome in Greek.

Polidoro put a stop to his touching torrent of words with an impatient gesture. He seemed apprehensive.

"I came for different reasons today. Don't talk to me in Greek."

Polidoro had left the Palace Hotel and come directly to the shop. He had no one except Venieris to appeal to. Caetana had let him in on part of her plans. He didn't have much time left to go into action. The rest of the information would be coming along later.

Grateful for the interruption, Venieris lowered the shutter halfway over the door. He headed for the back of the shop to offer Polidoro a cup of tea, as he did every week.

Polidoro had dressed with care, as though he were going to a party. He had recently been afflicted with facial tics. He kept looking repeatedly at his watch.

"Who is it you're expecting, Virgílio or Ernesto?" Venieris asked insistently, guessing his intentions. When he came with Virgílio, Polidoro resorted to elliptical sentences so that it would take them a while to understand him. But when he came all by himself, his language was precise and direct.

The moment he asked him the question, Virgílio appeared at the door. He doubled over so as to get in. The effort brought a constrained smile to his lips.

Venieris sensed how important this meeting was. The two men had a momentous secret weighing on their chests.

"I'm at your service. Your wish is my command," he proclaimed immediately, to reciprocate the honor being paid him, and at the same time discharge the debt he owed Polidoro.

"Very well, I accept," Polidoro hastened to say, fearing that the Greek might regret his decision.

Venieris pounded on his chest three times, a sign that he would fulfill the mission assigned him. He regretted that his talents were limited to wielding a pair of shears, tubes of paint and brushes—a modest sphere of activity. He would never be a hired killer, or a cunning courtier who would drop into the wine poison hidden inside his ring.

"What was the last painting you did?"

The question left Venieris and Virgílio speechless with amazement. Both of them had been prepared to hear a secret that would have a profound effect on their lives.

"The last oil painting?" He paused. He was afraid of being imprudent, of finding a disaster awaiting him. "I gave it to Dona Mariquinhas, who was left a widow last week, as a gift. I presented her with the still life after the seventh-day Mass for her departed husband. In return, she insisted that I stay for dinner. I just had to taste the suckling pig with coconut, which came from her very own kitchen. As a matter of fact, the piglet was a bit scorched. We were downright boisterous at the table. And although we hadn't once mentioned the name of the deceased, Pedro seemed to be present nonetheless, applauding the repast being offered in his memory."

"Your most recent painting," Polidoro broke in. These abundant details annoyed him, as though Venieris were hinting that, after dinner, following the suckling pig with coconut, or as an appetizer, he had also eaten Dona Mariquinhas's private parts. Not even he, with his weakness for women, had ever given a thought to that respectable matron. Perhaps he ought to reconsider his opinion, to concede that, despite her present sorrows, she was a choice morsel for a dreary Sunday. Especially if she were stretched out lazily on the crocheted bedspread that she herself had made with her own chaste hands.

Polidoro examined the shop, which had never been redone in all those years, and Venieris's face. Perhaps, with the description of the sumptuous dinner, Venieris had wanted to hint, in Portuguese, how eager he was to insert his member in protected preserves, to be used only for the procreation of a family, as was the case where Dona Mariquinhas was concerned. This was all the more likely, since Venieris rarely frequented Gioconda's place.

The vision of a Greek rod, timid up until then, trembling with a pleasure that was unknown to him, tormented Polidoro.

"I locked my paintbrushes up in the drawer. I'll return to them now only if I feel inspired." Venieris felt out the space between him and the two men with carefully delineated gestures. He appeared to be painting on an imaginary wall in front of him.

Polidoro effaced the disturbing images. He went farther inside the shop. Like a despot, he invaded Venieris's modest living quarters in the back. In the front room, he recognized the pieces of Chippendale furniture that Dodô, overcome with tender affection for the Greek and not knowing how to get rid of them, had decided to send to him, without even consulting him.

"Is this where you paint?" The empty easel in the corner of the living room was the proof of Venieris's abandonment of the craft.

"I'll take heart again some day. I'm a slave to inspiration. Without it, my hand gets scared and I can't even mix the colors."

Venieris explained with pleasure that his artistic aptitude was based above all on the fact that he was Greek, and on his having turned his back on a native land that from his earliest years had scarcely belonged to him. He had always felt that the Turks had usurped that land without even conferring the sensibilities of the conqueror upon that macabre deed, which would have done the Greeks good: they might have become—who could tell?—more Greek than even the classical Greeks. They would not be the first ones in history to have followed such a path. It was said that there had been conquerors who, seduced by the virtues of their slaves, had wisely absorbed their cultures, in many ways superior to the conquerors' own.

"Let's leave such subjects for later," Polidoro interrupted him, to pick up, with swift motions, a white canvas lying forgotten next to the chest of drawers and place it on the easel. "Inspiration, my friend, is a luxury of the gods. From today on, put aside your shears and the women who invade the shop and get to work."

Polidoro's great strides brushed against the walls. His eagerness ranged beyond the limits of the living room.

Virgílio had vowed to himself not to intervene in this clash of wills. In general, Polidoro complained of his meddling in other people's affairs. However, since Polidoro had hinted at a mystery, without in turn providing the necessary clues, he felt justified in claiming his rightful share in any secret. He did not want to be a mere spectator without an active voice, especially since Polidoro owed him a debt. He had not been told in reliable detail what had happened after Polidoro had left Caetana's bedroom the night before with his hair all rumpled.

Now, instead of passing on pleasurable revelations to Virgílio, an eternal aficionado of the history of Brazil who confused the adventures of the cattle rancher with those of Pedro I, that Portuguese cat who had burned its paws and its tail in the live coals of the women of Rio de Janeiro, there Polidoro was, urging Venieris to chain himself to his easel and paint with the fury that came naturally to great painters. As though the Greek's artistic passion, temporarily affected by a lack of desire or the absence of the muse, needed in fact to be recovered for the good of Trindade.

"Why did you send for me?"

Virgílio could scarcely conceal his jealousy. At Polidoro's insistence, he had left his house in a rush, at the very moment that he was writing down, in persuasive sentences, his impressions that ran counter to the current ruling thesis—in itself deliberately misleading, since it affected the character of the Brazilian male, emphasizing his improvised style of confronting reality—that the Portuguese had discovered Brazil by pure chance. "Was it so that I could serve as a witness to your admiration of the Greek?"

For the first time in the history of their friendship, Virgílio, thrusting out his chest, rebelled against Polidoro, making clear his status as a professor, albeit a retired one, the practitioner of a profession without which human society would have been plunged into the blackest depression.

Concentrating on the easel, Polidoro paid no attention to him. It was urgent to go ahead with Caetana's plans, to take the steps that she had demanded of him on the fifth floor of the hotel. He could not fail. He was prepared to put up any amount of money to make her dreams come true.

"Isn't it true that I'm the ideal companion for Caetana?" he asked all of a sudden. "The perfect male for her?"

Venieris's attention was focused on keeping the lid of the teapot on as he filled the cups. The heat of the infusion brought a homey feeling to his cheeks. Polidoro thanked him for his kind attentions with surprisingly well-mannered gestures. He was intent on charming both the other two.

"Caetana came from Recife for just one reason: to make me a declaration of love. She wants to be certain that she has not chosen the wrong man as the great love of her life. The challenge she's laying down for me now is one meant only for a real man such as myself."

"What challenge is that?" Virgílio was lapping up his every word.

"I am to meet the seven challenges of Mercury," Polidoro blustered, sweating energy. Standing ramrod-straight, his belly sucked in, he looked like a Russian character from the nineteenth century whose chest was covered with medals.

Revived by the tea, which burned his mouth, Venieris bobbed his head up and down in approval. He sided with Polidoro. He too lacked dreams that could be eaten with sugar, cinnamon, and honey. Hence his loyalty was boundless. Polidoro had saved him from losing a language that, even though riddled with Turkish sighs, was nonetheless preserving an immeasurable cultural heritage. Moreover, impelled by the sense of grandeur communicated to him by his friend, he felt capable of plunging into that golden utopia.

Despite the Greek's surprising euphoria, Virgílio did not voice an opinion. Excluded from that sort of conquest, whose target was the American continent, he felt that a cantankerous god had shot at him, beneath the red casing of jealousy, darts poisoned by human enigmas.

On seeing that he had been dethroned by the Greek, who, with the art of a painter, had invaded the cattle baron's heart, Virgílio's breast heaved. It would be of no use now to speak of Brazil as a new, powerful country, with wild fantasies, onto which Polidoro would set foot some day for the one purpose of being happy. Whatever he said to him, he would find Polidoro's attention occupied by the Greek. Despite his stricken lung cavities, which made it hard for him to breathe, he felt like a hero with dark circles under his sleepless eyes, having given up taking his revenge on the two men.

"You were wrong, my dear Polidoro. Those challenges were not met by Mercury," he said, clearing his throat with elegant nonchalance. "It was Hercules who was responsible for such exploits. Even today he continues to astonish the world by his deeds, which defy belief. If you wish, I'll describe each episode separately. And though your memory may get the details all mixed up, I will complete the entire cycle."

He adjusted his hat, which he almost never took off, especially not on solemn occasions. His gestures, usually so restrained, were as agitated as though he had wings and were flying as swiftly as the god he had mentioned. Before the heedless eyes of the other two, he continued to pour out the troubled waters welling forth from colder regions of his heart, struggling the while to disguise the feelings that made him feel ashamed.

Polidoro was making rapid calculations on his fingers, adding and subtracting numbers at random. He finally concluded that Virgílio was five years older than he was, as could easily be seen from his face. It was plausible that, if Virgílio were to die first, it would be up to Polidoro to pay for the coffin, since Virgílio's parents were dead.

"Hercules or Mercury—it all comes down to the same thing."

In his wrath, Polidoro went on painting Virgílio's portrait with merciless brush strokes. As Virgílio stood before him, a cold, lonely stream of sweat trickled underneath his shirt. He took a good look at Virgílio's hair, dyed a mahogany red. The white roots looked pitiful. And, despite the care that this minor civil servant took of them, his clothes had the same outworn look as he did. The swift, free radiance of the laughter of his youth no longer set anyone's heart afire.

Heedless of Polidoro's hurt feelings, Virgílio smiled.

"If I was able to discover Caetana's mattress, why wouldn't I embark now in that Portuguese caravel, with you as the helmsman?

I want to follow the stars with the astrolabe in my heart. And I won't forget to bring along a sextant to contemplate the stars we don't recognize."

Virgílio was relieved. He finally felt freed of the jealousy that had strangled him with iron claws, had nailed him to the Roman cross, and had wound a rosary around his neck, keeping him from speaking or giving free rein to his fantasies, in the old days always shared with the cattle baron.

Polidoro raised his cup.

"To victory," he said as a toast, with Venieris's approval, since he was obviously opposed to wastefulness of any sort. He would not have allowed a bottle of wine to be opened when there was still some tea in the pot.

"You two are going to act like Boyars privy to a conspiracy," he said, wiping his mouth with the back of his hand. "Am I right this time?" And with the enthusiasm of an ally, he looked at Virgílio and smiled.

The professor was unable to hide his bewilderment. How had Polidoro, lost in the sticks in Trindade, learned about the masters of the steppes?

"Even I couldn't have put it better. Those Boyars were more than conspirators. They resembled our friends in Brasília. They dethroned kings and princes. It was necessary for Peter the Great to strip them of their prestige and create a new class."

Virgílio, who threatened to go on recounting the entire history of Russia, was interrupted by Polidoro on the pretext that his own verbal talent needed an outlet. He felt as if a lamp lit with oil from a whale harpooned in the Indian Ocean were inside him, illuminating the inner workings of his brain. Even the impulses of his heart, which had made him extol to excess the world of feelings, had been reined in, to the advantage of his intelligence, now in Caetana's service.

He pointed again to the easel.

"Starting today, you're going to paint a stage set representing an ordinary-sized theater. Several huge panels that will create the illusion that a real theater exists in Trindade. A theater with an opulent entryway. It's through that entrance that we're going to go inside, as soon as the panels are set up in front of the old Iris, which is closed now."

Virgílio couldn't figure out the purpose of this commission. A theater based on an illusion!

"Who is it we're trying to fool with a fake theater?" Venieris's curiosity broke the pact established among the three of them.

Polidoro excused him. There was no malice in Venieris's innocent gaze. It gave him pleasure to specify the dimensions of the panels. Of the size of a real theater, but without a dome on top. A modest roof would do. This would save Venieris the exhausting labor of going up and down stairs countless times. Since he was no longer a youngster, they were sparing him a task that would be too much for him.

"Unfortunately, I can't commission a theater for dwarfs just to make your work easier. I need to transform the old, cramped Iris movie house into an imposing theater—the theater that, to our shame, we neglected to build in Trindade. The truth is that the powers that be always turned us down," Polidoro said, forgetting that he had invariably belonged to whatever party was in power in the state.

"What is there going to be inside the Iris after this surgery?" Virgílio asked, looking ahead. "It's a building with cracked walls, and it smells of mildew," he said in the Greek's defense. He saw Venieris's life in danger, trapped beneath the ruins of the Iris.

"What poppycock, Virgílio! The Iris is more solid than we are. We'll be dead and buried before its walls collapse. Besides, Venieris's mission is to give us the illusion that we're attending a performance in a real theater."

"I need to know who's going to be present onstage," Venieris said.

The Greek had abandoned his modest demeanor for the flamboyant temperament of a diva. With his thin fingers he smoothed his hair down, eager to convince the others of the extent to which his recent artistic life had subjected him to dramatic pressures. Here was a man pursued by the dawning light of ideas, making his first demands, completely convinced of his role as a great artist.

The Greek's insensibility, together with Virgílio's impertinence, annoyed Polidoro. Had the pair of them, overcome by vanity, perhaps forgotten that Trindade, before Caetana came, had been soil where not a single seed of art had ever been sown?

"Well, I'd like you to know that in Trindade there is a place for only one great performing artist. And that artist's name is Caetana."

He had the impulse to accuse them of pettiness. These souls had withdrawn into a daily life with so narrow a perspective that they attacked the values upheld by culture and sensitivity. It was necessary to do battle with them, before arrogance settled forever in the face of the Greek, now standing rooted to the spot alongside his easel, his convictions apparently reinforced by the strength emanating from its iron framework.

Refusing to take part in the dispute, Virgílio sought refuge in the kitchen. On the stove, the teakettle gave signs that the water inside had reached the boiling point. A braid of garlic, hanging on the wall, awakened the memory of Caetana. A Caetana who he knew was determined to bring them her art after a delay of twenty years, though with no intention of telling where she had gone during that exile. She had surely crossed Brazil countless times. In strange little towns she had not given up the seeds of her illusions. Yet no dream of hers had been powerful enough to put her on the stages of Rio de Janeiro. Throughout her many tours, Caetana had bidden farewell to cramped stages, to shaking canvas, ever in search of the ultimate fantasy. Perhaps Trindade had been the one place on earth that kept the memory of her stardom alive, nurtured by Polidoro's love each time the sun set.

Virgílio shivered at the sight of the dirty pots and pans and an agateware mug on top of the sink, signs of the Greek's loneliness. It seemed to him that Caetana had returned only to resuscitate the dead, superstitions, collective fantasies, everything that they, inveterate idlers that they were, had allowed to fall into oblivion.

"So did I neglect my grandfather and fail to inherit from him everything he knew? Or did he purposely rob me of the best part of his story? In that case, what was the point of my grandfather's life, aside from fornicating and filling his belly with cracklings?" Virgílio said, his mind wandering from the details of the kitchen.

Polidoro cupped his hand around his mouth and called Virgílio. He felt he'd been insulted by the professor. "Did you hear what I said to you about Caetana's art?"

Virgílio obeyed his summons. The effluvia of the kitchen distorted reality.

"How many hours of my life I've spent at the Iris! I saved up my pennies just to exchange them for the dreams that movies offered me. They were so exciting I forgot about the fleas that were biting my backside."

Polidoro had brought on that reverie by means of a quick embrace. In return for the gesture, Virgílio was to provide him with assistance that would justify his undertaking, independently of Caetana's wishes.

Virgílio suspected what Polidoro's intention was. Proud of his capacity to establish analogies between present reality and a different one that had ruled the past, he adopted his usual professional pose.

"You're going to equal the story of Count Potemkin, the favorite of Catherine the Great of Russia. His passion for gambling led him to ask the tsarina for a fortune, on the pretext of rebuilding, near the city called Petrograd at the time, certain villages that needed public upkeep. The empress, madly in love with Count Potemkin, gave him the money, which was immediately squandered at the gaming tables. And when she wanted to take a close look at how the people were living, the count did not hesitate. Confident of the empress's love, he had a number of stage sets painted, with houses and well-defined streets, and placed them in front of the peasants' huts, thereby concealing the misery of her subjects. And so, from her carriage drawn by horses who had wild manes and were bathed in sweat, Catherine appeared to be well pleased with that setting so cleverly simulated."

"And did she see through the deception?" Polidoro asked anxiously.

"Love is a tyrant; it blinds lovers and stifles ideas. Catherine lived her life immersed in the illusion of grandeur and eroticism. Why should she be disturbed by the follies of her lover, as long as he did not rob her of her place in history, which was in fact the only thing she craved? Her ambition was to leave definite marks on the history of her country, and the rest be damned."

He paused. He was thirsty and wanted to retain their attention. He too, settled in the easy chair, was intrigued by a plot that he was gradually drawing from the hodgepodge that he had in his imagination.

"The Nazis were worse than the count. They built in front of Treblinka a façade that was an exact copy of a train station, so as to camouflage the horrors they committed behind this stage decor."

He was walking around the living room now, so tiny that it allowed him only the smallest of steps, proud of having showed off his culture that had grown richer, above all after he had been freed of his apathetic students.

"Such antecedents confirm that we are easy prey for illusion. Any falsehood is convincing, from the moment that it is presented to us beneath a pleasing outer covering." He eyed Polidoro, as though he had made use of these examples in order to establish a moral position.

Polidoro was persuaded that Caetana was right. It was necessary to follow the classic examples cited by Virgílio.

"From now on we're going to weld Venieris's hands to his paintbrushes and his palette. He'll provide us with the illusion we're lacking."

Polidoro's enthusiasm found no place of refuge in the immigrant. Accustomed to solitude, Venieris had lost the habit of strong feelings that are shared in bed or at table.

"But all I know how to paint is flowers, greenery, and vases!" he broke in, nervous in the face of such a responsibility. "I've never painted a single house in my whole life! Not even when Dona Dodô wanted a painting with a little dollhouse where people could be happy without a great deal of effort."

"Dodô has never learned how to deal with reality. She's always gone to the wrong people. Since when were you born to make tiny dollhouses? It's even better that you lack experience. There's a need for innocence in art," Polidoro pontificated. And he went on:

"Tell us the truth. Haven't you ever hankered after a house, with a wife, children, and a fireside? Well, what you're going to do is something similar. Don't forget, though, to give the theater a red roof, whitewashed walls, and blue doors."

Venieris nervously rubbed his hands together.

"How could I get married if I never had the courage to buy the first bricks with which to build a two-story house?"

Visibly downcast, and beneath Virgílio's reproving gaze, Venieris used a crumpled handkerchief to wipe his face, which was streaming with sweat. It humiliated him to be a bachelor, prey to sorrow and suspicion. Especially not being able to enjoy the warmth of a woman in the middle of the night—one who, when he fell ill, would bring him bowls of hot soup and soothing compresses.

"Since fate has bestowed on you the privilege of now doing what you've never been able to do in your entire life, we haven't a minute to lose. To work, your lordship, painter of Trindade!"

Glowing words exhausted Polidoro. He hurriedly left the shop. And, unlike Orpheus, a poet who, according to Caetana, had lost his muse by looking back, he went on, certain that Virgílio was following close behind. In the last few hours, Caetana had united them forever.

GIOCONDA put the key in the door with determination. Her state of mind counseled a rhetoric suitable for a new order of things.

"Follow me through the streets of Trindade! Should they wish to flog us, we will fight back with the fatal stinger of queen bees. That's how we'll devour those hypocritical males and their fat old females."

Trailing along behind her were the Three Graces, each of them in a different mood.

Palmira fingered the empty purse she had crocheted herself on Sunday mornings. Clutching it to her dried-up bosom, she felt against her own flesh, soaked with unexpected sweat, the damage done by closing the house on Saturday night, of all times. On no other day did they attract so many rough customers, whose appetites, repressed during the week, surfaced with visible fury in the beds of the women at Estação.

Gioconda noted the gesture. For a long time she had been trying to correct Palmira's love of money, an unpardonable vice. Despite her hurry, Gioconda halted at the front entrance. The garden was growing greener and greener after all the rain.

"Aren't you ashamed of being so close-fisted, Palmira? Don't you want to be a queen at least once in your life?" she said, exacting from Diana and Sebastiana their adherence to a cause that in her opinion was of a political nature. Ultimately, the strange art of organizing reality that went by the name of politics was also indispensable to whores such as themselves.

Under the pressure of a gaze that always ruled her life, to the point where Gioconda even salted her food, Sebastiana gave in. As a proof of her good will, she placed amid the dyed locks of her hair a magnolia, whose petals, dramatically luxuriant, still had drops of fresh-fallen dew on them. She was confident that her peroxided strands of hair would water the flower and not let it wither. The gesture allowed her to dream of the happiness coming from an unplanned Saturday with the sun beaming and a dusty road threatening to take her a long way. Though her life was obsessed by her lack of incisors, which made her face ugly and had aged her in just a few years, she finally smiled—a smile that appeared so unexpectedly that it moved the other women to pity. None of them dared to tell her that the flower, of a vibrant yellow, clashed with her face, which had a tendency to accumulate wrinkles and a sadness inherited from her dead mother.

Gioconda had gone back home just before dawn. In a feverish state, she had tried to mask her feelings by making gestures that hid her bright eyes. Blindly, she kept bumping into the walls, paying no attention to the noise that echoed all through the house. Though Diana demanded apologies by resorting to illicit means, in which she was a specialist, Gioconda parried her offensive with alternate grunts and sighs.

With rare grammatical correctness, she had manifested her desire to be left in peace. Early on Saturday morning, she had realized that there fell to the lot of every individual one and only one instant of grandeur in an entire lifetime. It behooved a person, therefore, to be cautious. This just might be the day of redemption.

"Why all this prattle if we're never going to live a single moment of grandeur?" Diana needled her.

"That day is going to come knocking on our door very soon now," Gioconda said with an air of mystery. She tried to simulate a vitality that her voice, broken and hoarse, did not show when she was nearly overcome with rage. But she altered her ill-feeling against Diana. She looked at the women, generalizing the admonition.

Gioconda's conciliatory mood was a fleeting one. Diana was to take advantage of these fractions of a second to attack her. In recent years, she had displayed traces of intractable skepticism. Unknowingly, she appeared to ally herself with a school of philosophers convinced of the scant value of human life. She cultivated this feeling with pleasure, to show how different it was from Sebastiana's naïveté.

"Even if we were to save a child from a flood, who would pin a medal of merit on the chest of a whore?" She came at Gioconda with circumspection, prepared to use unfair weapons.

Gioconda returned her attack with serenity. She was out to garner sympathy.

"There are many forms of grandeur, my sweet Diana. What do you have to say to me about pride and dignity?"

As she massaged Diana's neck with movements from bottom to top, she convinced herself that she was transmitting a masterful lesson, which the Three Graces would never forget.

Anticipating success, Gioconda paused. The silence in the

parlor allowed her to ascertain the state that the furniture was in after so many years' use. None of the Three Graces, however, voiced an opinion. The pupils of their eyes seemed to inhabit a world where there predominated only those values measured by money and violence lying latent in the hearts of Trindade. In an attempt to console herself for the apathy of the Three Graces, Gioconda made a rapid trial balance of her riches. Thanks to her repertory, replete with practical principles, she had become the owner of Estação. Whereas they—pessimistic, toothless—were mere employees, with no guarantee of a job in the years to come. Soon enough, age would banish them from their beds in the brothel and from the profession at the same time.

Sebastiana, whose sensibility was a consequence of her long series of childhood ailments, noted the tension between the two women. In the delirium of battle, both yielded chunks of their respective flesh in defense of the human condition, so helpless a prey to the tedious nights of Trindade. She feared an unfavorable outcome, just at the moment when the hope of moving about the city like real ladies was beginning to dawn.

"On this very Saturday, we will obtain our certificate of manumission. It's as though Princess Isabel, she who freed the slaves, were here with us."

In recent months, Sebastiana had been giving evidence that she had assimilated the lessons Virgílio gave her in bed, for lack of others in which she had never been outstanding, either for her mastery of them or simply in her aptitude for them.

To her surprise, Diana rebelled. Unwilling to go along with any libertarian undertaking that was not accompanied by riches, Diana put no store in the efficacy of any such freedom. To her, gold, rubies, and emeralds were now the only symbols of the right to come and go wherever one pleased on the face of the earth.

At times Gioconda recognized that Diana had better credentials for confronting reality. She decided, nonetheless, to take precautions against any excesses of optimism.

"Stop being so dramatic, Sebastiana! I don't want to be accused some day of not knowing how to manage your dreams. Or of not living up to your fantasies. I can't put up with such a great responsibility any longer."

These words got to Diana. Feeling herself slighted in the scale of Gioconda's affections, she defied her, with her hands at her waist, as her flashing eyes distributed whiplashings to the others.

She would remain in the house as an active member of the group known as the Three Graces only for the money she received. She now gave no sign of being fond of them.

Moreover, she had reason to complain. Since the early-morning hours when Gioconda had come back from the Palace Hotel, the latter had acted as though Caetana, in the suite on the fifth floor, were under her exclusive guardianship, and she had no intention of sharing her with anyone.

In the morning, Gioconda had given all of them just fifteen minutes to get dressed, vowing that she would leave behind any of them who took longer. Heedless of the past that had kept them beneath the same roof, she did not offer them a single affectionate gesture.

"Today we're going to sit in the wicker chairs of the bar at the Palace. Nobody is going to keep us from frequenting that accursed hotel," Gioconda vowed bitterly.

Even though she had reasons to ally herself with Gioconda, Diana was opposed.

"We're running a risk by going into that bar. We'll end up being stoned to death, like Saint Stephen."

None of the women came out in defense of Gioconda. The silence put an end to her aspirations to climb the social ladder. It would be better, then, to give up the role of guardian of the three thankless women. She threatened to leave them.

Palmira insisted that Gioconda come along with them, show-ing Diana the inside of her purse, where she had already placed her lipstick, rice powder, sponge, and comb. She felt happy. For the first time in all those years, relieved of her worries about poverty, she could hear for once the sound of loose coins inside the purse, a sure sign of her prosperity. Franciscan poverty, which she sensed she was fated to experience in the future, did not frighten her. It had the merit of relieving her, all of a sudden, of the responsibilities of a false affluence.

Her ardent words touched the heart of Gioconda, who had long been lacking proofs of affection. She found it hard to bear the solitude that her forceful character gave rise to.

Aware of the good that she was doing Gioconda, Palmira went on in emphatic tones: "This stroll through Trindade is going to cost us dearly. We'll be poorer still. On the other hand, all I really want in my savings passbook is fame," she said with a smile, practically dancing with Sebastiana, who was walking alongside her. She joyously imagined the men in the Palace bar rising to their feet to welcome them.

Sebastiana noticed that Palmira, carried away by her euphoria, was reserving the triumph of that Saturday for herself alone. Feeling the threat of being left behind as they walked, she asked for a turn to speak, beneath the afternoon sun beating down on them, having forgotten to protect her skin beneath the little yellow parasol, with a few crooked ribs now, that had come from Rio de Janeiro.

"I would rather be stoned to death like a saint than stay on in a whorehouse. I can't put up with the sweat and the gunk of those men on top of me for one minute more," she said, falling in step alongside Gioconda to give public proof of her obedience.

Sebastiana's support reassured Gioconda, despite Diana hiding the corrosive poison of envy in the secret compartment of her heart. Gioconda looked at her watch. The hands zealously marked the time, while not forgetting their obligation to age the women. She decided, once and for all, that she would not be a victim of the appetite of the three whores again, even if they stayed together in the same house in the years to come. She had devoted her life to them as long as they shared a single touching thread of youthfulness. Thanks to that, she had allowed them to convey to her their personal plans. They, however, the voracious harpies, had begun to demand that she make all their dreams come true, from marriage to a rich man to the purchase, by Sebastiana, of the little yellow parasol that she had seen on TV on a certain afternoon in midsummer, when the torrid noonday sun beat down on the corrugated-tin roof of the back porch.

That behavior, which in the beginning Gioconda had accepted with delight, ended up by exempting the Three Graces from experiencing the bitter taste of any sort of personal failure. They began to delegate to her nothing less than the task of existing in their place. In the domain of fantasy, it was as if they had appointed Gioconda, before a public scribe, the one and only heiress of the years yet to come.

The obligation of looking after the three women weighed heavily on Gioconda. How often she had thought of knocking on the door of their rooms to give back the power of attorney they had granted her; she did not do so only out of fear of the emptiness in her heart the moment she gave up her responsibility for them.

"Enough of that now," she said firmly. "I'll tell you later on of my meeting with Caetana."

The Three Graces, by common accord, and urged on by the vision of a human cornucopia that would shower them with words and illusions, stepped up the pace so that Gioconda, left behind, would be forced to run after them, to ask for a truce, panting for breath beneath the shade of the next mango tree.

The maneuver to defeat her did not escape Gioconda. She decided to fight it out with them. The sound of the loud beating of her heart nearly came out through her mouth, and her joints ached. But in this match the one who gave in would be acknowledging the domination of another. It was necessary to defeat Diana, the leader of the rebellion.

Palmira and Sebastiana lost the rhythm. The one kept stumbling over the other, even though Diana was pulling them along by the arms. Palmira, extricating herself from Diana's pair of tongs, leaned against a *jequitibá* tree along the edge of the road. Its crown shed a shadow generous enough to shelter a countless number of enemies, without forcing them to come into intimate contact with one another.

"I can't stand it any more. I give up," Gioconda said with relief. Sebastiana massaged the aching muscles in her legs. Used to going around the house in slippers, she flung her high-heeled shoes a long way away, indifferent to the disappointed look she got from Diana, who blamed the others for her defeat.

"Didn't you all notice what you've done?"

Sebastiana searched her memory. On the slightest pretext, she used phrases that Virgílio had passed on to her. They were of help to her in the most disparate circumstances.

"Truth is always dangerous," she declared, eager to drive Diana out of the shade of the tree. Her instinct told her that she had chosen exactly the right phrase this time. Virgílio himself had assured her that, in the theological order, the explanation of which was difficult for her to understand, truth, with its scepter of glory, could reach individuals only through a thousand mirrors that reflected a series of distorted images. It was those glimpses that furnished people with excuses for confronting one another in fatal disputes. As for wise men, the victims of a search with no practical result, they were the first to drain the contents of truth to the last drop.

Seeing the women's dejection, Gioconda proclaimed that there was no victor. As a sign of her good faith, she decided to recount, there and then, in the open air, her encounter with Caetana as day was breaking, after the three women had shut themselves up in their respective rooms. She herself, in her night-gown, was about to slip between the sheets, when a strange call vibrated so forcefully in her bosom that she immediately got dressed, went downstairs, closed the front door of the house, and without stopping to think about the dangers, walked to the hotel in the middle of the night.

Mágico opened the door and let her in. "What is it you want?" He was so surprised at her visit that all trace of cordiality was erased from his face.

"To give Caetana a hug."

It was almost daylight. He, however, did not want to disregard a request that would disrupt the peace and quiet of the hotel. Between yawns, he took her up to the room. The creaking of the elevator, half stuck, made him feel ashamed. He feared for the guests with sensitive ears.

Gioconda trod the hall carpet cautiously. She could scarcely appreciate the engravings on the wall, purchased by Bandeirante at a public auction in São Paulo.

"And where does Danilo sleep?"

On the previous afternoon, at the station, Gioconda had suspected that Caetana, along with her baggage, would bring a well-built man, passing him off as her lover.

"On the second floor. That way it's easier for him to climb the stairs when he's plastered, since the elevator doesn't always work."

The moralistic reflection annoyed her. On the rare occasions on which he had gone to Gioconda's place, Mágico had taken all sorts of petty precautions. Before getting into bed, he had made certain of the whiteness of the sheets, and whether he was the first to use them, failing only to ask whether the women scrubbed their cunts with the same thoroughness that he applied to the washing of his own member.

At the door, Gioconda panicked. All through those long years, she had never received a single word of hope from Caetana. She had trouble breathing.

"Are you all right?" Mágico asked.

Gioconda leaned against the door.

"When she took the train that Friday, she forgot to say goodbye to us. We always knew that Caetana would be back. That was why we embraced one another on Fridays when it rained," she murmured before knocking on the door.

Balinho answered it, still dressed in the suit he'd arrived in, full of grease stains from the chicken he'd eaten at dinner.

"You may come in, Gioconda," he said in a firm tone of voice. He dismissed Mágico with a wave of his hand. "It's a good thing you came. Caetana's been waiting for you for more than four hours."

In the living room, in her nightgown, Caetana held her in her arms as though she didn't want to let her go. Riche kept Caetana from moving her feet, as the actress's heartfelt sobs emerged from her diaphragm.

Beneath the shelter of her ample breasts, Gioconda felt her

forceful, tireless breathing, a skill owed, perhaps, to a technique she'd learned from some magazine.

"So here's the friend I baptized in the font of life," Caetana said, all excited.

Caetana's arms were like mechanical tongs that robbed Gioconda of the emotion of the meeting. On the other hand, the prolonged embrace allowed both of them to recover—in the long minute, as the heat of their bodies warmed their dreams—a past almost without traces and definite dates. The world of days gone by, whose memory had apparently been completely destroyed, stirred in the confused and fetid swamp of the emotions of the two women, whom the years had pitilessly constrained. Only by conquering that zone of shadows and suspect odors would they succeed in bringing back to life, as in a dark mirror, scenes of a magnitude that would redeem their lives.

When she began to sense that Gioconda was outdoing her in the ardor of their embrace, Caetana drew away. Human warmth now exhausted her. She no longer felt nostalgia for the magic charms emanating from another's body.

Gioconda was offended.

"The name you gave me was of no use to me. I was still the same whore as always. The difference is that now I'm the owner of the brothel. I go to bed with someone when I feel like it."

Caetana was not misled. Besides piercing her heart with sharp darts, giving rise to strange sentiments within her, Gioconda had come to the room, in the wee hours of the morning, to beg for dreams of glory. She had hoped that Caetana would not have admitted to her own failure, that despite the harsh truths she had been forced to face, she had not stifled certain illusions. And it was precisely those illusions that Gioconda had come to ask her for.

"You still haven't forgiven me for the hopes I aroused in your heart." Arrogantly, Caetana impressed upon her the fact that she would never have stayed with her. She would not make such a sacrifice for anyone. After a long recitation, involving Riche, urging her on without a letup, she added ruefully:

"You're an ingrate. Have you forgotten that I offered you the chance to be a performing artist?"

Speaking practically to herself, she confessed that art, as she had been taught by her Uncle Vespasiano, had the property of devouring the vitals of humans in exchange for offering them a passionate vision. There was no other way for the artist to invent his own dream except to commit acts of sorcery and wickedness.

"I gave you the name of Gioconda to create other names in the shadow of that first one, so that you could believe in the deception that frames our poor lives."

Regretting her scorn of a past that fought against the mediocre verisimilitude of everyday life, Gioconda sought shelter in Caetana's arms. The folds of Caetana's body seemed to be solid and throbbed gently.

"Forgive me, Caetana. Will I still have time to dream again?"

She was about to burst into tears when Caetana stroked her hair, which smelled of coconut-oil soap.

"There is one chance left." She tried to stop the convulsions of Gioconda's body, nestled next to hers. "All of us who have failed are fated to meet in Trindade. Some of us already live here, and others are arriving by train and by bus, at the same hour. Only the spirit of vengeance incites us against destiny."

Gioconda's breath, which in the beginning smelled of citron, now gave forth the strong odor of the gall of passion. She bore her bleeding heart in the palm of her hand. Caetana pushed her away. She wanted to climb into bed between clean sheets, to forget the dissensions, common to mortals, that love gave rise to.

Life, in those years, had reached Caetana devoid of intense feelings. Her last lover, in Belém, had left on her skin the odor of overripe fruit. Her senses had grown cold. She lacked the instinct to accept blindly the body of another. That same instinct, when alerted, reflected back onto the passion of the other person, who was aiming to climb into her bed, signs of an avaricious and parsimonious emotional frugality. She could no longer anoint herself as she once had, with the oil of youth, which an amphora, lost in a shipwreck along with immemorial ships, had in former days spilled out on the sand of the coast of Brazil.

She poured herself some of the cognac sent up by Francisco, whom she hadn't thought of thanking. All alone in the world since the death of Uncle Vespasiano, she no longer had any reason to keep up appearances with amorphous and mendacious courtesies. Her gestures had long since lost their utopian meaning.

She drank the cognac down in a single swallow, like Russian vodka. "We don't have much time left. Dawn will soon be here. As of tomorrow, people who are failures will turn into artists. Would you care to join us?"

It pained Gioconda to show in public, at the counter of a bar, her life slashed to pieces. As the owner of a so-called boarding house, which was nothing but a brothel, she enjoyed the intelligence of men and of the Three Graces, women doomed to grow old together. In the future, they would collect in a saucer, to be passed among all of them, their teeth, which would keep falling out.

She watched Caetana, who was walking about amid the furniture in the living room, unable to follow anyone else's sentences if these went on and on in endless subordinate clauses. It had always been like that. With rude gestures, she was in the habit of demanding that verbal expression be brief. The world could well be contained in a single sentence. People lacked the ability to synthesize.

Sometimes she was accused of being inconsistent, since she acted out onstage the texts of long-winded dramatists, but she vehemently defended the melodramatic situations these represented.

"Any author needs a minimum of five sentences in order to be faithful to the life of a fellow human being. It's those monotonous sentences that justify the character. Only in that way does he or she cease to be a caricature."

The three moles near Caetana's chin gave her face vivacity. Gioconda went back over to her, seduced by the mystery that emanated from the actress.

"I admit I failed. What shall I do now?"

Caetana sank into the easy chair, visibly weary. She looked at Balinho, sleeping on the sofa.

"I've come here to change my life. That's all I know."

Caetana's world, permeated with symbols, upset Gioconda. That complex scheme of enigmas was of no use to a courtesan with a practical sense of existence. To her, when it came time to see to the management of what she possessed, there existed in everyday life a dramatic modernity that was far superior to the attitude of a dreamer. As she portioned out the food in the blue-tiled kitchen, she easily rid herself of fortuitous images that gave no promise of bringing affluence to the house. In this she was very different from Caetana, who had devoted herself to the work of clothing reality in the colors of the rainbow once again. A chromatic virtue that, by strengthening her social role as an actress, had endowed her with the language of creators, odd individuals who from atop their trapeze had the perspective of the world of an acrobat on the point of executing a triple somersault without a net.

"What are you proposing? That we live in a dream? That we give up our status as whores and become performing artists?"

Gioconda examined the proposal coolly, setting aside her feelings for Caetana. She had a house and a family to protect. She was responsible for putting beans and rice on the table. If she were to choose a path carpeted with prickly heather and thorns, she would have the rest of her life to regret it.

Caetana could not bear Gioconda's long-standing habit of mixing together the data of reality and beans and rice, her difficulty in suddenly taking up an occupation aimed at grandeur. In fact, no one had been brought up since childhood to dream of fame, but how many millions of human beings were there who would not be prepared to shorten their lives in return for the fulfillment resulting from fame?

"I came to put on a performance. Do you agree to be my actress? To be applauded in the middle of a scene here in Trindade?"

Caetana stroked Gioconda's face with her index finger, a lingering, delicate caress.

Isolated from the world of affection, Gioconda succumbed to

Caetana's beseeching. Once she returned to reality, she would never again be the same.

"So that was the reason that during these years all my muscles ached and my head sometimes seemed to explode?"

Her voice was leisurely, unhurried. She was convincing both Caetana and herself.

"Very well. The Three Graces and I agree to be actresses. Can it be that we were born for the stage and didn't know it? What's more, it's better to be an actress than a harlot."

She straightened her hair in front of an imaginary mirror, in a gesture copied from television actresses, her mind seemingly elsewhere. The calculated motion repaired her makeup, ruined by the tears that the director had demanded of the woman brought face to face with her dying lover. Behind the cameras, he thus demonstrated how the theater could be a perfect den for haughty and sensitive lions, some of which had been brought from the very heart of Africa. In this arena, human beings, beneath strong spotlights, gave free expression to outraged and troubled feelings with the naturalness of an art full of masterfully performed tricks.

Caetana rebelled against such vanity. Not even she, a professional accustomed to wringing tears from the most gullible spectators, acted with such shamelessness.

"Please don't assume your role before the proper time comes!"

She kneaded her belly, wanting to rid herself of certain irksome gases. She needed, once and for all, to find an outlet for a talent to which Brazil had never paid tribute.

The admonishment was good for Gioconda, who, deeply touched, recognized Caetana's mastery of her art.

"When do we begin to rehearse?" The emotion in Gioconda's voice made it reach such a high pitch that it awoke Balinho and Riche the cat.

"What's the matter?" Balinho asked in bewilderment. "Do you want me to tell you another story?"

He rubbed his eyes, not knowing what city he was in. He was always afraid, each morning when he woke, that some day Caetana would decide to do without his skill in transforming the first fifteen minutes of any narrative into two or three hours of sheer escape from reality.

Bright rays of sunlight were coming in through the window.

"Bring us coffee, Balinho." Caetana had suddenly turned extremely polite. "And how are the Three Graces?" she asked Gioconda, yawning.

"As old as we are. But they'll immediately grow young again when they hear the news I'm bringing them. Isn't it true that art is rejuvenating?" Her eagerness was making it impossible for her to leave.

"Tradition has it that artists are the oldest creatures on earth. Sometimes they rejuvenate amid a storm of emotions and drama."

Her impersonal tone excluded her from the hardships of the profession. Like Riche, who was clawing the back of the easy chair, she too was using her talons, sinking them in human tissues. Polidoro himself, plunged into despair, had sucked her convex nails in days gone by, accusing her of storing underneath them, at their very roots, poison and rare spices. A hiding place for amorous pleasures of the senses.

"How fat Polidoro's gotten!" Caetana remarked all of a sudden. "Just as I have. Except that I go on being an actress despite the weight I've put on. The stage rids one of heartbreak and excess fat."

She smiled for the first time. Her eyes, narrowed to slits, barely allowed her to see Gioconda.

"I often deceive myself into thinking I'm young. And when it's necessary I feel I'm the empress of China. Take a look at my fingernails. Don't they resemble a mandarin's?"

The city, seen through the window, seemed to consist of just a few houses. Beyond the dusty pane, Caetana contemplated the distant, faded buildings. She had no desire to take a stroll through Trindade, hemmed in on every hand by pitiless stares.

Balinho opened the door of the bedroom so that Caetana could go to bed. It was the moment when he transformed music and poetry into the only language that compensated for the affronts she had endured.

Caetana made a move to say goodbye to Gioconda. She stroked

her face, as if claiming as her due a world that had been extorted from her. The sad, empty gesture touched Gioconda. She had made every effort to inculcate in the Three Graces the happiness for which she used Caetana as her model.

In the middle of the main square now, near the bust of Polidoro's grandfather, the famous Eusébio, having arrived there after their long walk, Diana showed signs of her dissatisfaction.

"What else did Caetana tell you?"

In the grip of a wave of strong emotion, Gioconda did not have the energy to go on.

Palmira and Sebastiana, paying her back for her kindness, practically slobbered her face with kisses, hiding the landscape from her eyes.

In her eagerness to free herself from the two women, Gioconda grabbed her handkerchief out of her pocket. After wiping off all that saliva, her face lit up.

"Now that we're actresses, let's go to the bar of the Palace!"

Outside the pharmacy, they ran into Ernesto, on his way to bring medicine to Seu Joaquim. He held out against joining the parade of women out of fear of Vivina. He still bore on his chest the marks of the times when she had raked his flesh in her jealousy. At the height of the crisis, eager to discover the source of certain scents and stains, she forced him to hand over his undershorts. Subjected to this inspection, he had found himself obliged to confess that in the last few months he had fallen into the habit of giving in to a recent compulsive weakness. He had, in a word, taken to ejaculating, even in the pharmacy. At the peak of the summer season especially, perhaps because of the effects of the heat.

"I'll talk with you some other time." He walked away without looking back or asking where the women were going.

Gioconda felt sorry for Joaquim, who was perhaps on the point of receiving extreme unction.

"That's a lie Ernesto made up," Diana said. "He didn't want to be seen in our company."

"If that were so, Polidoro would have sent us word not to leave the house. Or to come visit the Palace bar."

"Who told Polidoro we were going to the Palace?" Diana broke in.

"From the moment we became actresses, every right has become ours," Gioconda answered, refusing to argue.

"Ernesto is a coward not only out in the street but in bed as well," Palmira said with the scornful self-assuredness of a city lady. "He doesn't allow the least emotion. He sometimes even forbids me to come."

Gioconda admired Palmira's talent for dramatizing facts. "None of us will play our parts as well as you," she said as a compliment.

At the door of the Palace, Mágico was busy watching the hustle and bustle in the street. They stepped up the pace, each wanting to get there first.

Mágico didn't recognize them: his memory readily blanked out when it came to names and faces. However, in order not to reveal that he was getting old, he let the four of them in, unwittingly giving them the illusion that the Palace and the world belonged to them.

"Allow me to show you in, ladies," he said solemnly.

They followed him through the lobby, which was all lit up even though it was a bright sunny day. The chandelier impressed Sebastiana. The light pouring down from its crystal pendants forced her to close her eyes.

"Who invented that marvel?" she said, not knowing what to call it.

Eager to show off their wealth, the Three Graces wore satin dresses of a glaring pink and green. The garish colors attracted the attention of the hotel guests. Mágico absent-mindedly led the women into the bar. Francisco, behind the counter, hurried over when he saw them at the door.

"A table for four," Gioconda spoke up, her voice betraying dreams of Paris, and especially of the Eiffel Tower. She intuited that Francisco would consult the reservation chart to place them at a table befitting their importance.

As Gioconda practiced her new habits, the Three Graces, in their eagerness to be noticed, whirled about in a provocative dance. In a word, a number of the customers had been waiting their whole lives for that visit.

Diana in particular strove to show them that she had been born in a silver cradle. As proof of her background, instead of laughing, she came out with trills. She smiled now at Gioconda, who, clutching Francisco's arm, paid no attention to her. Diana resigned herself. She was beginning to understand the progressive-minded spirit of Gioconda, who was responsible for their presence in the Palace bar.

Diana had long resented living in the seraglio that the house at Estação had become, as the women in Gioconda's harem exchanged among themselves, from dawn to dark, sighs and time-worn words, in an intimacy now sad, now ardent. They lacked the virtue of giving subtle shadings to everyday life, impelled countless times a day by volcanic feelings and random eruptions whose source they were unable to identify.

They had finally gotten a close look at the bar described by their customers, usually in bed. Caught up in trivial particulars that were not always understandable, each of the women pictured the bar as being completely different.

Francisco held himself ramrod-stiff, prepared to stand in the way of any misbehavior by the four women. He lingered for some time talking with them, however, shifting the little toothpick, nearly chewed to pieces, from one corner of his mouth to the other. Ill-at-ease, he hooked his fingers in his vest pockets. The colorless fabric of the garment matched the paleness of his face.

"How long are you going to make us four ladies of Trindade wait?" Gioconda felt she belonged to a class that, having taken just one step up the social ladder, was already confident that it had acquired inviolable rights.

Francisco bit his tongue. He was discovering the complexity of his mission.

"Why don't you speak with them?" he said to Mágico.

It was only then that Mágico recognized the women. But, contrary to what was expected of him, he turned his back. The time-honored prejudices of an establishment that was opposed to progress did not concern him.

"Either you tell us which table is ours or we'll choose it ourselves." Gioconda threatened to come farther into the room.

In retaliation for such treatment, Diana erased with the tip of her shoe the invisible line that Francisco had drawn at the door to stop them.

"We don't need this beanpole to show us our table."

Attempting to restrain Diana's impulsiveness, Gioconda did not see Palmira and Sebastiana jostling Francisco.

"Get out of our way, you pansy!"

They marched resolutely into the bar. Gioconda, who did not have the authority to proceed with the negotiations, acknowledged that Francisco, from that moment on, lacked the social standing to be of any moral support for the social changes taking place in the city.

In their high heels, and with little triangular steel plates on the tips of their shoe soles, the Three Graces scratched the floorboards of the room. Close behind them came Gioconda and Francisco.

"Wait! Where do you think you're going?" In his distress, Francisco's voice came out sounding feminine and strident, like that of a castrato.

At the head of the procession, Diana made the rounds of the tables. None of them suited her.

"No, not this one. It's much too close to the window."

Sebastiana relinquished the leadership, which Diana took over without hesitating.

"How about this one?" Palmira consulted her.

Diana clacked her full lips in disapproval. Circumspectly, she assumed the heavy responsibility of arriving at a decision. Of answering for Trindade's crazy goings-on.

"This one's noisy; it's very close to the bar. We wouldn't be able to talk or exchange secrets."

Standing a short distance away from the group, Gioconda noted how nonchalant Diana was, after having ruthlessly taken over in her stead. Palmira and Sebastiana, as though she were dead and buried, were resigned to awaiting the laws of succession.

In the face of this cruel revelation, Gioconda felt her body on fire from head to foot. Especially since she did not see them in deep mourning, or weeping. The fault was hers, however. Out of ingenuousness, she had refused to see Diana's effort to strip her of the leadership that came naturally to her, moving as always to the sweet strains of a flute, with the subtleties of a hooded cobra from the Orient.

Undiscouraged, she began fighting back. She had everything in her favor, beginning with Estação, the house that belonged to her. With her index finger upraised, she stepped forward to confront Diana.

"You whore!" Gioconda shouted, forgetting that she had sought out that public place as ideal for displaying their status as ladies.

Diana, who had just approved of a table, entered the lists against her.

"You're the one who's a whore!"

"You're the one who didn't wait for me to be buried before taking my place. You're nothing but an ingrate. Tell me who it was who saved you from syphilis, from gonorrhea, from the tick that didn't want to let go of your back till I put a piece of bacon on your skin and lured the wretched creature out? Or perhaps you've forgotten?"

She was about to recount other instances when Diana, reinvigorated by the juices of memory that Gioconda had injected in her, cut her off.

"You've forgotten to mention the erysipelas! And the dandruff that came close to destroying my entire head of hair! I was cured only because you rubbed mashed bananas into my scalp every day. And when you saw that I was upset about my future baldness, you calmed me down by saying that a person could lose a minimum of forty hairs a day without going bald. One afternoon, you remember, you said in a cheerful tone of voice: 'We're going to count the hairs that have fallen onto the floor or are caught in the comb.' It wasn't an easy job. The hairs flew about, wandering off from the bed. Since they were peroxide-blond ones, they were hard to tell from the yellow sheet till Sebastiana brought a blue towel to serve as a contrasting background. Thanks to what you did, I persuaded myself that I wouldn't go bald. How can you forget now to recount those facts among the others?"

Diana upbraided her in a gentle tone of voice. Enjoying whiling the time away, they seemed to be back in the kitchen of the whorehouse, waiting for the water to boil so they could make coffee.

"Sit down, Gioconda." Palmira offered her the high-backed chair. The gesture restored to Gioconda the authority that had nearly been usurped.

Francisco, a stranger to the reconciliation taking place among the women, tried to separate them, his arm still raised.

"Please, ladies." Even though he felt uncomfortable about the way he was treating them, he screwed up his courage to go on. "Calm down—none of this quarreling. There's only one enemy present here, and that's me. Set-tos of the sort you're having end up weakening you."

In his effort to settle this row as Mágico looked on, he had failed to notice that Gioconda and Diana, who had already made up, were looking all around at the tables, trying their best to memorize the details of the bar.

"Are you enjoying yourself, Palmira?" Gioconda put a hand on top of hers to share the warmth of her ambition.

Francisco floated about in a private sphere, which offered him sensations he had never experienced before. Like Polidoro, he felt he had the power to interfere in other people's lives.

"Make peace with each other, ladies."

Smiling, he kept running his hands over his chest, where his ribs stuck out. From the mammary region of it came discharges that enabled him to keep company with the souls of these women, detecting their oddities and mysteries.

"Have you thought about the future? Each of you living all alone in the basement of a house, without a single friend to bring a bowl of soup or to weep at your side, as your teeth fall out on account of that confounded pyorrhea?"

Nobody was listening to him. For Sebastiana, in a state of grace, the bar made it easy to fall into dreams of memorable amorous exploits.

"What a beautiful room! Nobody here would get into a scrap when it came time to divide an inheritance."

Such candor touched Gioconda's heart. To encourage her, she promised that they'd come again. The future could be as beautiful as the decor of the bar. As she made Sebastiana this promise, she saw Francisco, glued to the table, proposing an armistice.

"To whom are you referring, Francisco?" Gioconda asked.

In his role as peacemaker, Francisco had no time to answer her question. He had duties to fulfill. As she spoke, Diana became interested in the passionate discussion at the next table concerning the Brazilian team, on the eve of their playing in the semifinal match in Mexico City for the world soccer championship. To attract their attention, Diana tucked in a loose lock of her hairdo here and there.

"Isn't it true that Pelé is going to bring us the World Cup?" Her raised voice turned metallic.

Francisco, still going on with his spiel about harmony, slowly moved toward the next table.

"Where do you think you're going?" In an attempt to bring him back, Diana pulled on his jacket, offended at how little attention was paid her by men whom she addressed who, as it happened, were also her long-standing bed partners.

Just then, at the same time as the other women, Francisco noticed that Gioconda and Palmira were holding hands. The intimate, sisterly scene brought tears to his eyes. During the following week, he would have more than enough to tell his customers, especially in view of the abundance of details involved in that theatrical performance. What was more, he had kept a drama from tumbling down on top of two of the most renowned courtesans of the region.

"Luckily, you gave in to my pleas!" His nostrils dilated with pleasure as Palmira leaned over to embrace him.

"There's no need to thank me. It's enough for me to see that you've made up. Who knows the meaning of loneliness better than I do! Not being able to count on the affection of anybody in the world. Coming home and not finding anyone to bare one's heart to in the middle of the night!"

Touched by the human drama of which he was a part, he did not notice until later that Palmira, far from showing her gratitude, had leaned over closer to him merely to reach for the ashtray on another table.

Francisco's oratory—modeled on the style of Virgílio's long phrases, which was attracting a following in Trindade—annoyed Diana. His obvious aim was to paralyze his listeners and dominate their will. "Bring us a drink right away. A whisky, perhaps," she ordered harshly, without regard for the waiter's feelings. He was an ingrate who went by bus to neighboring cities just to get himself women more exciting than they were.

"Where do you think you are? This isn't a whorehouse. It's the most elegant bar in Trindade," he retorted, offended.

Sebastiana paled, her face contracting into a grimace of pain. The figure of her stepfather, revived by the shouting, was driving her from home once again, as her mother, in silence, heard the man suggest to her daughter that a brothel was the right home for her. Where would a young girl find better shelter? For females disinherited by fate, it was the equivalent of convent walls.

Gioconda couldn't bear to see any of the Three Graces left defenseless. Even Diana—who would at times spatter Gioconda's dress with grease merely to wound her vanity—deserved her compassion.

"Don't cry, Sebastiana. Things aren't going to stay this way for long."

Sebastiana's tears fell all the faster. Her charge's venting of her feelings gave Gioconda the strength to fight back. Obstinately, she placed herself alongside Francisco, measuring his height. In her high heels she was several centimeters taller than he was.

"Even if we were nothing but ordinary whores, we'd be proud of such a humane and tolerant profession, which makes no distinction between the rich man and the poor one, the handsome man and the ugly one. Except that you were wrong. We're now actresses about to become famous."

The men at the nearby tables, attracted by her arrogance, applauded her passionate speech. This masculine support filled Gioconda with pride. Out of gratitude, she made a bow. In this position, she felt something strike her shoulder very lightly. With no idea of what it might have been, she saw on the floor a red rose missing some of its petals, thrown by a stranger. Touched, she looked around. Sebastiana, crossing her path, rushed toward Virgílio, who was just coming in the door.

Blushing at this display of affection, the professor passively accepted the envy of his lot demonstrated by the men present.

"Calm down, Sebastiana. We still have a lot to do before the final victory," he admonished her, on his guard against her assault, protecting the bouquet he was carrying in his hand.

In this way he made it clear that he had come in order to defend them. That was why he had thrown the flower, which he had intended to land in Gioconda's lap, though he had missed his target.

"This time you're going to have me to deal with." Virgílio challenged Francisco boldly, forgetting the lessons of the teaching profession, which recommended moderation. "Beg these ladies' pardon," he said.

"Since when am I obliged to humiliate myself in front of whores?" Francisco's unexpected bravery surprised them as well. With unrestrained gestures, he stood up to Virgílio, at the risk of swallowing what remained of his toothpick.

Virgílio set the bouquet down on the table. He was worried about the outcome of the affair. The waiter's reaction made him feel embarrassed. He looked at his watch, expecting that Polidoro, faithful to a punctuality inherited from Virgílio himself, would appear in the bar. It was two minutes to five, so he had a little time to kill. In his anxiety, he could feel his bladder burning. It was the same urge to urinate that came over him when reality weighed upon the lightness of dreams or illusions.

"I'm going to pee, but I'll be right back. I'll give you five minutes to apologize to the ladies. If you don't, I'll make sure I throw you out of the bar." And he solemnly headed for the lavatory.

Every minute that went by made Francisco feel fatter, as though he had ingested a mixture of barley, wheat, and mashed bananas. The last two minutes were almost up when Virgílio, still buttoning his fly, came back into the room and headed straight for a table far away from the women. He sat there, reading with great interest a letter of apparent urgency. He interrupted this reading only to glance quickly around the room.

"How about my whisky, Francisco?" he asked, in a cordial tone of voice now.

Sebastiana suddenly felt the burden of the years. She discovered she was discontent, the orphan of a love that until just a short time before had seemed about to offer her a name and riches.

"And what about us, Virgílio?" she remarked discreetly, certain that she could make him see reason. The professor went on reading, as though he didn't know her. "What happened to the five minutes you gave Francisco?" she inquired.

Francisco, who was serving the professor his whisky, called his attention to the woman. Sebastiana's pleading gaze convinced Virgílio that they indeed knew each other. With an offhanded gesture, Virgílio shook his jacket and took up the scene at the point where he had left it.

"I'm not a man to forget my promises. I have never been neglectful of a lady's honor."

He rose to his feet with exasperating slowness, offering his arthritis as an excuse. Aches and pains hindered his movements, forcing upon him a rhythm that did not accord with his ambition to live.

He looked at his watch once again. That idiot Polidoro, who zealously kept an eye on the hands of a timepiece as he had never paid careful attention to his prostate, worn out from age and inordinate passions, was leaving him all alone at the mercy of his enemies.

"Very well, Francisco, fate has favored you with eight minutes instead of five. The one consolation you have left is to behave like a gentleman."

His eyes blinked in the expectation that Francisco, as a sign of gratitude for all his patience and kindness, would present his apologies.

Francisco, who was always being accused of servility, decided for the first time to take his revenge for the mistreatment that life at the bar had inflicted on him. No traces of the toothpick were left in his mouth.

"I agree with every word you say, Professor. And I'd like to see who's man enough to throw me out of here."

The men present, excited by the possibility of bloodshed, demanded war, while Gioconda and the Three Graces formed a circle around the professor to defend him, a move that definitely wrenched Virgílio out of his apathy. It touched him that the women were thanking him in that way for the affection that he had always deposited in their beds.

"I prefer to act like Leonidas and his three hundred Spartans at Thermopylae, who chose to die when confronted by a superior army rather than live in an occupied country. I am determined to resist this man in front of us, a worthy representative of the forces of obscurantism."

Virgílio dragged out his speech, to give Polidoro time to arrive. It would not be appropriate for him to be one more minute late.

Francisco cut short this braggadocio with a peal of laughter. To his satisfaction, he had won the sympathy of half of those present. Especially of those to whom he had served double-sized drinks for the price of a usual one.

"I've always been a he-man, except that nobody ever allowed me to prove it," he proclaimed at the top of his lungs, so that those words would become public knowledge all through Trindade, independently of his own effort to spread them far and wide.

Facing such peril, the professor closed his eyes, trying to plunge into a state of oblivion, the semblance of sleep. Immersed once again in semiwakefulness, he heard a baritone voice burst forth in the room.

"What's all this racket?"

Held spellbound by that familiar sound, which made the room fall silent, he opened his eyes. Polidoro, at his side, was expressing regrets at being ten minutes late and lamenting the havoc that the altercation appeared to have wrought.

"We have too many he-men in this country," Polidoro said in stern reproval.

The waiter pretended not to see him. Blindly, he groped

around the tables where he was sweeping, eager to locate the tray he had dropped at the sight of the flock of whores invading the redoubt.

Their minds now put at ease, the men offered a toast to Brazil, about to win the Jules Rimet Cup. Francisco, bustling from table to table, poured drinks with a lavish hand.

Polidoro went through the bar without deciding on a table, annoyed at the presence of the women—a discomposure that Gioconda noticed. He belonged to a society that reduced women like them to poverty without ever thanking them for the favors they did for it.

"It's a lucky thing you've come, Polidoro," Gioconda said.

She pointed to a chair, between Palmira and Sebastiana, in order to ease the heavy breathing coming forth from Polidoro's hairy nostrils.

"May I ask why?" Polidoro refused the seat offered him.

"It's time to announce that we're actresses now." Supported by her tribe, aware of her recent privileges, Gioconda defiantly tucked back the curls in her hair that were out of place. Standing up and followed by her claque, Diana applauded Gioconda. The gesture, imitated by the other tables, turned into a general uproar.

Polidoro wiped his face with his hand. His five o'clock shadow made him look older. He lacked the courage to confront Gioconda. He feared the bitter generosity of her whore's heart, in which vengeance was making its appearance just because Caetana had arrived twenty years too late for both of them.

"Are we actresses or not?" she persisted, her hands on her hips.

Polidoro cleared his throat. His voice sounded harsh at times.

"Serve the ladies, Francisco," he ordered.

His eyes measured their approval. But Gioconda, immersed in a universe that contained herself and the Three Graces, defied him.

"They're great actresses, in fact. They're going to make their stage debut shortly."

She paused. Solicitously, he attempted to reduce his debt toward her:

"Anything else?" His eyes took on the dark shadings of secret wrath.

"This will do for the time being." She consulted the wine list.

Polidoro installed himself at a table farther away. The women's petty sniggers reached his ears as an affront. Drooping in his chair, he could not hide his fatigue and the feeling that he had fallen into disrepute. He looked around the room for Virgílio. Leaning on the counter, the professor didn't know which way to turn.

Out of pity, Polidoro invited Virgílio to join him. On that Saturday of oscillating lights, he was in need of constant care; meanwhile, he sipped the whisky that Francisco had begun serving again.

AS HE LEAPT out of the jeep parked in front of the Palace Hotel, Constable Narciso's undershorts threatened to fall down. His abrupt braking to a stop had attracted the attention of Mágico, who kept a sharp eye on the movement in the street.

Narciso scrutinized the terrain before advancing. The *jequitibá* tree in the immediate vicinity was a good place for an ambush. As he busied himself tightening the belt around his belly, more and more distended by malt beer, he cursed his occupation, which forced him to make frequent forays into an ugly, scorching-hot district of town. Dying trees all about, and cows left loose to graze, with ticks visible to the eye. The fruit on the ground made him melancholy: nobody was gathering it in a basket.

He had awakened in a bad mood. His unshaven beard bore witness to his state of mind. His family, in Rio, settled in the working-class district of Méier, sucked away his salary and his sweat. Affection, brief and slight, came his way only from Gioconda's whores. And so at the drop of a hat he gave vent to his trials and tribulations to the barflies at the Palace.

Mágico's voice on the phone, intermingled with sobs, had been incisive. He was clamoring for an authority capable of restoring order in the hotel, which Caetana's excesses were theatening to turn topsy-turvy.

Narciso's reticence, motivated by the burning sensation in his stomach after his greasy meal, inspired in Mágico his first heroic words. "And aren't you paid regally for doing your duty?"

He had been reluctant to call Polidoro, who was taking a siesta. He was afraid of Dodô, who he knew was back in Trindade, asking questions, guided by the keen sense of smell of a pointer.

"Welcome, officer." He held out his hand in reconciliation, in a gesture of ridiculously exaggerated cordiality.

"You'd better have a good reason for dragging me out of my lair," Narciso muttered half to himself, ignoring Mágico's overly effusive greeting.

Mágico ran after him.

"The problem, officer, is that, whereas certain men waste their lives on women, my perdition is this hotel." And he pointed to the façade, which was beginning to turn green. The mold went all the way up to the fifth floor.

"Just look at the state of the walls! Nobody wants to save this architectural masterpiece."

Indifferent to the fate of the building, Narciso went in through the central archway, disdaining the revolving door, which squeaked each time it went around. Determined to inspire fear, the constable moved about arrogantly, despite his potbelly, which was his prow. He kept adjusting the brim of his felt hat, in an effort to conceal in its shadow his hooked nose, with a Semitic look about it, inherited from his grandfather.

Out of respect for the hotel guests, he had put his revolver in its holster. This was contrary to his habit of slipping it between the waistband of his undershorts and his sailor's leather belt, which his eldest son had sent him as a Christmas present.

Narciso halted, unable to believe his eyes. In front of him, in symmetrical rows, a number of sheets, hanging up on improvised clotheslines, were making it difficult for the hotel guests to find their way to the lounge.

The light from the chandelier fell on Balinho, who was feverishly wringing out the newly washed sheets. His gestures brought to Narciso's mind the corral of his uncle's ranch, where he had learned to milk cows. Water dripped into the three tubs haphazardly set out along the floor.

The spectacle depressed Mágico. But since he was convinced that in the next few minutes Balinho would be dragged off to police headquarters, his spirits rose. "Didn't I tell you, officer?" He prided himself on making a diagnosis that identified in a few seconds a situation bordering on chaos.

In his function as a police officer, Narciso at times created the illusion of multiplying objects in front of him, by means of a series of contractions of his eyes. By so doing, he seemed to be reproducing reality from a distorted angle. Once he'd downed a dish of macaroni, however, he became more demanding. He stubbornly insisted on concrete proofs, acting against his exacerbated imagination. He therefore tested the fabric of the sheets with his fingertips. Made of pure cotton, painted with landscapes, they revealed crude darns. The fibers, about to fall apart, gave forth a fresh smell of coconut-oil soap.

"They were so dirty. Luckily, they hadn't lost their original colors. I very nearly rubbed them with pumice stone," Balinho exclaimed as he went on working.

Narciso was sensitive to any sign of disrespect. The scales of justice, which he represented, were gradually breaking his back. Here was a presumptuous young man who, after invading someone else's property, wriggled out of making a sincere and remorseful statement to the authority present.

"Don't you see the representative of the law standing before you?" The constable's voice echoed through the passageways formed by the sheets stretched out on the lines, as he toyed with his revolver.

Peering over the shoulders of Narciso, who was blocking his view, Balinho looked through the door at the weather outside. It was threatening to rain. The accumulated humidity would make it harder to dry the things hanging on the line. Caetana's temperament rebelled against having to wait. He wrung out the sheets once again, more slowly this time.

Mágico feared that the constable would shoot and the bullet would lodge in the bevel-edged mirror, the only one from a series of eight still left in the lobby. Balinho, however, indifferent to the revolver, which Narciso returned to its holster, went on with his work.

Narciso's trousers had lost the neat press they had acquired that morning from the old-fashioned iron. Nervously, he stroked the butt of the revolver. He faced his adversary, a young man without resources yet with a propensity for passions carried to an extreme, an abyss that made him reduce his daily sleep to four hours so he could extend his radiant stories beyond the hours decreed by convention.

Narciso evaluated the moral weight of the witnesses present. He was counting on them to judge the incident, once the guests of the Palace, bothered by the difficulty of getting past the wet sheets to reach the street, had retreated to their rooms, waiting for the sheets to dry.

"Who is responsible for this violation of the law?" he asked in a conciliatory tone.

Balinho took a break. He felt dog-tired. Caetana had driven him out of the suite at an early hour, giving him express orders.

"I want the sheets with me onstage. I can't forget them on the day of my triumph," she said, deeply moved.

The lengths of cloth, yellowed by the years, were, along with Uncle Vespasiano's Victrola, all that was left of bitter days. They had crossed Brazil on the backs of mules, in trains pulled by old-fashioned locomotives called "smokers," in coaches whose shaky wheels produced a music that made it easier for them to sleep amid the laments of the cattle drovers they met on the road.

"Ah, Balinho, this country no longer exists! It disappeared when progress came its way. It's the extract of an opened bottle of perfume. We don't even have the bottle left to stick our noses into and sniff the memories it has retained."

Caetana opened the drawer. Inside it were musical scores, letters from admirers, and a deck of cards for poker and *bisca*. She looked through the drawer carefully.

"Take this gypsy blouse to be washed as well. Remember the fortuneteller who read my fate in the cards?" Balinho brought back the desolation that Caetana had felt, shut up there in the room. She bade farewell to the bundle of clothes as though it were her soul that was about to be washed, to be robbed of its last memories.

"I'm the one responsible, officer. What did you want me to do? Hang the clothes outside on the line, at the risk of having a petty thief take them home? People like that are insensitive to history. They can't tell the difference between ordinary sheets and those that were once in the circus rings and on the stages of Brazil, soaked in sweat, being used as scenery! We always lacked money to paint reality on heavy cardboard flats, of the sort that never fly all around the stage but stay in place, and cost a bundle. These sheets here can be carried away by the sea breeze or a gentle mountain wind. They seem like passionate ghosts."

Balinho's argument became more impenetrable. Narciso had trouble following it. His eyes begged help from Mágico. Because of his worldly occupation, the manager would be more sensitive to descriptions of an artistic nature, with their tendency to employ symbols in which Narciso did not know how to anchor the vessel of his sensibility.

"Brazilian performing artists who make money and have an easy life are rare. The majority wander about the outskirts of cities without ever setting foot in a famous theater or having their names displayed in neon lights on a façade. Caetana, for example, never sold out. She preferred art to money. She did not want to go to Rio de Janeiro and run the risk of becoming a prostitute, kept under guard by pimps."

Balinho was threatening to go on and on; Mágico, fearing a journey conducted by way of hostile, dangerous emotions capable of setting men's hearts on fire, decided to cool everyone down.

Ceremoniously, he plunged his hands in the tub. And, with his hands cupped in the form of a drinking gourd, he offered Balinho the water wrung from the sheets, to drink. Balinho accepted it; his throat was dry.

"Hurry up, Balinho. There's not a drop left," Mágico said edgily.

Balinho licked Mágico's fingers. The taste of salt from the man's sweat made him even thirstier.

Narciso became impatient. Nobody paid any attention to his needs. His own family only telephoned to confront him with problems. And Mágico, as his host, had not even offered him a cup of coffee.

"Let's get to the subject that concerns us. How many hours before the sheets dry?" he inquired, his authority restored.

"I'll take down all the clothes before I go to sleep, so that there's no danger of their getting mildewed," Balinho answered.

Mágico noted the capitulation of the constable, who had become the malefactor's accomplice.

"And what about the hotel guests? Many of them are refusing to leave their rooms as a sign of protest." He appealed to Narciso's civic spirit.

"To hell with all of them. What do they expect me to do, throw them out the window? I'm not a fireman, but a police official!" Mágico's jacket, with gold stripes on the shoulders and sleeves, and a collar visibly worn threadbare, irritated Narciso exceedingly.

"Do me the favor, then, of unblocking this elevator crammed full of valises. I don't know how many trips Caetana's baggage has made from one floor of the hotel to another," Mágico said, in a tone of voice half exasperating and half resigned.

The afternoon had in store for the constable events outside his usual routine. He was able to see at close hand how ordinary reality underwent havoc far beyond Polidoro's influence. At the same time, he experienced the unexpected pleasure of enjoying, as an officer of the law, the right to invade houses, to mistreat vagrants and suspicious individuals. And even to put Polidoro and those of his sort in jail.

Narciso breathed in the benign gas of power, freed of that other, lethal one, which came from Polidoro, to whose avarice he owed the gift of money, always a scarce commodity in his case, so that he was open to endless bribery. Polidoro never sent gold nuggets his way, to help buy an apartment in Copacabana for his ambitious family. But the loose change that Polidoro gave him compromised his honor and his future, He woke up every morning covered with rashes, stiff in his legs, his veins choked with fat and disgust.

Narciso inflated his chest with the black smoke of cheap tobacco. Life took on a somber aspect. His lungs breathed out the excess of nicotine. In recent weeks, the human condition seemed to him to be a lead weight that pulled his clothes out of shape and made him even clumsier.

"In that case, I'm taking Caetana to jail instead of you. She's the one responsible for violating the law," he said dejectedly.

He thought of his wife. When he went to bed with her, a habit that had become less and less frequent, she raked his back with her fingernails, never to keep him inside of her, but with the intention, albeit disguised, of making him return to Trindade as soon as possible. Unable to remember that she had once been married to a high-spirited man given to rash gestures, who, until the night before their wedding, had thrown flowers from the street up to the balcony of her house in the suburbs as she waved a white handkerchief.

"Caetana is like a songbird. Isn't that what you're about to say, Balinho?"

He tried his best to understand the race of artists, who carried about on their backs, like a snail, a house consisting of valises crammed full of a shabby, motley wardrobe, and also, as stage scenery and props, pots without handles, bottles of gypsum, stumps of trees that served as benches. Already the sheets, despite the faded paint, gave wings to people's imagination. They transported the spectators to cold countries, where sleighs and wooly reindeers simulated the swiftness of dreams.

"Nobody locks an artist up behind bars," Narciso said ruefully. He suspected that art, even when it made use of a decrepit, nearly blind artist, had the gift of enslaving the memory of others, without ever again freeing it.

Mágico had his doubts about Narciso's sudden delicate sensitivity. No brute such as the constable could have suddenly invaded the world of mirrors, of death pangs, and of a certain type of tears, after putting to flight with a pickax the most genuine emotions.

But if Mágico was surprised, Narciso himself was startled by the tremors of his nipples underneath his shirt. He heard strange noises in his chest, different from those that emerged after he'd eaten too much pork-and-bean stew.

For the first time, he was invading a sphere composed of ingredients that he couldn't give a name to. The very act of speaking about art made everything affect his nerves. Even the joints of his lower limbs became lubricated, permitting him almost juvenile movements. He ran the risk of discovering that in fact he had not been born to be a constable. How could the possessor of a soul now so transparent go back to fighting with brutes, ruffians, ruthless murderers?

Standing in front of the innocent sheets, he thought up more and more imperative reasons to leave Trindade—a city that doomed to apathy a man who, if he were beneath the rule of law, would struggle to guarantee Caetana the right to realize her dreams.

Narciso gave Balinho an intimate clap on the back. He saw in him the courage to promote national artists while remaining immune to sordid traffic in money.

"How about promoting Caetana's art in Trindade? If you like, I can arrange a place for her. This lounge, for example, would do for a performance. With the sheets hung up and the tubs, we'd create a fine effect. It would be like a lake of swans. I'm going to have a talk with Caetana."

Balinho dissuaded him from searching out the actress. After years of tireless travel all over Brazil, she was resting. Every trip exposed her to rigorous tests. She, however, had never resigned herself to defeat.

"Men are petty, and they've made her suffer. But never the

art that she bears within her, right in the solar plexus. Geniuses climb onto the trapeze without a safety net," Balinho emphasized, to cool the constable's enthusiasm.

Narciso sensed Balinho's intentions. He was inviting him, by means of metaphors, to become part of his fantasy. To wear tights that, despite their pitiless revealing of the contours of his body, would help him fly through a space of which he would be the sole owner. Though he was flattered, he wasn't cut out for the role of a trapeze artist. He would fall short of Balinho's fantasies. He lacked style and an attraction for the abyss. It was becoming more and more painful for him to get through each week. Especially in Trindade, where on Sundays life grew dark before clouds warned that a storm was about to break.

"Tell Caetana of my visit." Narciso hitched up his undershorts, his mind made up. Balinho had orders to stop any intruder who appeared on the fifth floor. Caetana's independence was now overwhelming, above all because no one else could steal from her the bread and soup that Polidoro would provide. After all, she had offered the cattle baron the treasure of her private parts. With no other woman had his member shriveled, only to become erect again, ever willful, so many times in a row. Moreover, in her artist's heart, anxiety and resentment amalgamated like a noble metal.

"Caetana appreciates being worshiped from a distance. She is modest and blushes easily. The more deeply moved she is, the more she devotes herself to the chores of art. And art, officer, seeks out secret paths. It filters through walls like water. Mold appears on the surface in less than a month."

Thanks to Balinho, Narciso shivered with an unprecedented emotion. The illusion that made him into an artist having dawned, in a few minutes he would go up to the fifth floor. Nothing would stop him.

"I want to kiss Caetana's hand before my saliva dries up. Unselfish kisses, with no evil intentions," he said contritely.

Banished from human passion, Mágico was indignant. The constable was betraying him without the least consideration. And, for the first time in his life, Narciso was passing up money. He was allowing himself to be bribed in return for the ecstasies that Caetana's art promised. Mágico swore to take vengeance. Discreetly, he hid behind the counter and dialed a phone number. Fortune smiled on him: Polidoro answered.

"What is it?"

He should come immediately to the Palace to control the lecherous impulses inspired in Narciso by Caetana, who was totally innocent, up in her suite.

Polidoro was furious that another male would vie with him for his woman. Caetana had kept herself inviolate for him all through those long years. In his memory, he hung her on the wall alongside the niche of Our Lady of Aparecida, the patron saint of Brazil. He had never imagined that any member bloated with salt and desire would throw open Caetana's secret doors, washing them clean of lust and rain.

"I'm going to saddle my horse this minute and mark his face with my spurs."

But even if he rode at a gallop, he would not get there in time to wreak punishment on Narciso. He had better go by car.

Narciso and Balinho consolidated their new friendship, exchanging secrets and hopes. The witchcraft of words brought with it a burden of inertia. Narciso made no move to take out of the elevator the suitcases ready to be transferred to the Iris, even though he did not want to go up to the fifth floor via the stairway. Caetana shouldn't see him panting for breath, unable to get a single word out.

The constable struggled between sluggishness and the craving to embrace Caetana. Set in motion finally by the whirlwind of adventure pointing toward the road to happiness, he drew himself up proudly.

"I'm going to take the suitcases out of the elevator."

He dried the sweat from his face and resolutely adjusted his testicles inside his undershorts. Once his fly was closed again, he felt confident.

"Where shall I put the suitcases?"

He smiled politely. Those suitcases had traveled much farther than he had. Not only throughout Brazil, a country seen through the green glass bottom of a bottle, but also from different floors of the Palace Hotel. The rusted catches of the suitcases offered no security, and only strips of cloth held them closed.

"Put them by the stair rail."

Balinho forced Narciso to tire himself out, crossing the lobby countless times, but he obeyed. When he'd finished lugging them away, he was out of breath.

"Why not visit Caetana tomorrow? You'll be more rested."

He couldn't pay tribute to a lady when he was gasping for breath, his lungs furnishing him just enough air to say three words at most.

Balinho's suggestion did not favor Mágico's interests. It suited *his* purposes to have Polidoro surprise the constable on the fifth floor, deep in conversation with Caetana.

"Never put off until tomorrow what you can do today, my grandfather used to say," Mágico commented.

Narciso disregarded the advice. At the moment, he valued the voice of youth. He had to heed a suggestion made with detachment. At the same time, beneath the yoke of the vices inherent in the position he held, which early in his career had taught him as a fundamental principle to believe in others' bad faith, he mistrusted Balinho.

"Are you talking as a friend, or are you trying to humiliate me?"

Had the young man perhaps raised doubts as to his virility, his advice amounting to a hint that Narciso was impotent? So advanced a case that not even the most diligent of women would restore life to his instrument, which had reached the end of its melancholy trajectory?

Annoyed by the suspicion, he lowered his eyes toward his undershorts. His testicles in repose gave him a scare. Besides being out of breath, he could no longer count on the imprudence of youth, or on the dreams that came in its wake.

"Why don't you go get some rest at police headquarters?"

Wanting to get him out of the hotel, Balinho spoke in a harsh voice.

Narciso leaned on the stair rail. He could not lose heart. The actress was waiting for him. It was her duty to sow illusions along with the grains of wheat of her art. Already Caetana was blowing from afar gentle warm breezes in the direction of his chest, which longed nostalgically for youth.

The result was instantaneous. Free of the shadow of old age that had been enveloping him, Narciso again began breathing regularly. He even felt in good enough shape to dispense with the elevator. He leapt over the first step. He would run up the five flights of stairs in one go.

Balinho foresaw the constable's arrival at Caetana's door.

"Caetana's biggest weakness is her temper. She starts shouting for no reason at all. Above all, she doesn't forgive people for having prevented her from being the most beloved actress in Brazil."

Remorsefully, he intertwined his hands and held them against his breast with a harsh and distorted eloquence.

Narciso didn't know which to listen to: Balinho's subterfuges or his own heart, which preached in the desert of his chest a palpitating sermon as sweet as a fortified wine, making him believe that felicity was necessarily to be sought in a miserable, cruel Finisterre, where schooners and sloops fought it out against the turbulent waves of the waters off the cape.

"Don't leave us, officer. I insist on serving you a cup of coffee." Mágico was hiding his nervousness.

"If I knew at least that Caetana wanted to see me!" Narciso said, adjusting his hat brim in an effort to get his ideas straight. His thoughts kept wandering to Méier and then back to Trindade, with the result that he did not hear the squeak of the revolving door behind him.

"I thought you were never coming," Mágico whispered so the others wouldn't find out about his phone call. Good luck was on his side; he couldn't let it change to that of his enemies.

Polidoro disregarded Mágico's gelatinous hand. He was in a hurry to demand explanations.

"What business do you have bothering my friends?" he roared like a tiger.

"Who told you that lie? I came to protect your guests. To save Caetana from this prejudiced manager, who detests people who perform behind footlights."

Polidoro looked Narciso up and down sternly. The time had come to keep the actress from being besieged by a man who lived at his expense. Narciso was sweating, something that repelled him. As a seducer, the constable had everything possible against him. The Three Graces received him with scorn, foisting off on one another the duty of tolerating him in bed.

"I won't accept your apologies. Go back to police headquarters, which is where you belong. There are lots of thieves on the loose who require your attention."

Narciso was brought low by the weight of this public humiliation. He couldn't bear it that Balinho was witnessing the scene, just as they were beginning to be friends. During his stay at the hotel, he had suffered shifting but enjoyable emotions. Some of them came from the inappropriate illusions about the actress that he entertained, since he knew her only from descriptions and from a photo of her which Virgílio kept at his house. The picture, taken in the main square alongside the bust of Eusébio Álves, coincided with the lightning visit that President Getúlio Vargas had made to Trindade just after the 1950 elections.

The photo had served only to accentuate his uncertainties. It scarcely showed her breasts, which had the reputation of being superb. Ever since he'd been a little boy, in the working-class suburbs of Rio, he'd gotten all excited over the curves that swelled women's chests, the equilibrium of a strange anatomy entirely oriented toward perturbation and passion. According to what Virgílio claimed, Caetana's breasts, carved with the inspiration of Phryne herself, had the form of a generous wine cup, a milky color.

For a long time, Narciso had admitted in the Palace bar his aversion to women's cunts, a seismic region, sheltered between the thighs, through which he sometimes passed. Like a mere transient without the right to caresses, he forgave himself for bringing his face up close to a hairy patch of woods, smelling of certain wild animals that never chewed on a flower to improve their disposition.

He could not understand the French. As far as he knew, they cheered themselves up by ensconcing their tongues in the hidden recesses of a woman's genitals and taking deep breaths of them, possessed of a canal like the one their own mothers had, where he himself had been obliged to stroke hard with his arms to realize his intention of coming into the world.

Polidoro put off deciding what Narciso's fate should be. Abandoning his friendly manner, Balinho was making signs that the officer ought to be punished for the abuse of his confidence. In Caetana's defense, he was tearing up the pact of friendship he had recently signed with the constable.

Such support, far from unleashing Polidoro's thirst for blood, inclined him toward clemency for a man who had been his faithful servant in the past. The constable noted his hesitation. His destiny lay in the hands of the cattle baron, who could easily have him transferred to hell. A police headquarters that he could leave only for sporadic visits to his family, so that his children would get married without his being there and he would not even be able to wear his brand-new suit, hanging in the closet protected by mothballs, that had been made especially for such solemn occasions.

It disturbed him to think that the family would not suffer from the prolonged separation. When he went to Rio, they exchanged the briefest of greetings, their kisses soon turning into vinegar. In a few hours, he felt like a stranger. His children forgot to take a close look at him, and above all to check up on his feelings. When he asked for coffee, expecting that it would come to the table freshly made, served in a fragile, elegant cup, his wife suggested that he serve himself lukewarm, oversweetened coffee from the thermos.

Whenever he found himself in situations like this, Polidoro hesitated, his weakness of will showing immediately on his face. Dodô often accused him of being a coward for not punishing those who had offended him. But he was always moved to compassion and broke into humble tears.

"To order someone killed is to prove one's power. And it's best to order the whole family killed, so that there's no spirit of vengeance left. The same thing holds true for life and for memory. Watch your step, Polidoro; it wouldn't take much for there to be nothing left of you inside me. Maybe I'm already living with a corpse and don't know it," Dodô had said before getting into the car that was to take her out to the country estate, not suspecting that Caetana was arriving.

Mágico brought them coffee in agateware mugs, contrary to Narciso's dreams of grandeur. No one thanked Mágico for this gesture.

"More sugar?" he said ingratiatingly, hoping that the drama would envelop him in the folds of its splendid drapery.

Polidoro was seeking a triumphant exit that would be forever framed in the memory of those country bumpkins, so little acquainted with epic poses. He was on the point of creating such an effect when Narciso grabbed him by the arm.

Polidoro reacted instantly.

"Since when do you dare apprehend me? Where are the handcuffs?"

The theatrical tone was inspired by Caetana, who was guiding him masterfully from up on the fifth floor. In this act requiring great concentration, he knitted his thick eyebrows, to show that he would soon be using his machete against his enemies.

Incredulous, Narciso could hardly believe that he had grabbed the cattle baron's arm rather roughly, a presumption that he himself would be the first to condemn. To make amends for the gesture and conceal his feelings, he assumed once again a submissive expression altogether familiar to Polidoro.

"What other police officer has been as faithful to you?"

Blinking his eyes rapidly, Narciso displayed a friendliness that Polidoro ought not to have accepted. The brute seemed sincere, however. Polidoro felt disconcerted under the pressure of such pendulumlike feelings.

Balinho noticed in Polidoro's face the sort of contraction preceding remorse, close to compassion. He would not turn a deaf ear to Narciso's act of contrition. The constable's humiliation was imminent.

"I am very sorry, Dr. Narciso, but the place for a police officer is in jail, checking up on prisoners, not on artists such as ourselves."

With overweening pride, Balinho buried the last remaining ties of friendship that had flourished between the two in the shadow of the sheets hung up to dry.

Laboring under this burden, Polidoro turned heartless once again. Clad in the purple mantle of vengeance, he could not disappoint the audience. And, secondly, he had always envied the well-aimed blows that slowly wore away men's weary hearts.

"Leave Caetana alone, once and for all. It's my honor that's at stake." In order not to give up this unusual sentiment, he concluded: "Clear out of here this minute, Narciso."

As he pointed the way out to the street, he forbade Narciso to set foot in the hotel during the coming week. And likewise to frequent the Palace bar, between whose walls, stained with tobacco, wine, tears, and blasphemies, his confidences found refuge.

Balinho was delighted. Polidoro's speech was a perfect model of masculine gallantry. A pity it had been so short. He had simply forgotten to set forth in detail the life of the actress, casting light on artistic incidents unknown to Trindade and to Brazil.

Polidoro jumped over the first stair, borne by the hope of reaching the fifth floor safe and sound. As he went upstairs, lulled by the illusion of victory, a tremor in his legs forced him to lean on the banister. The memory of Narciso's face reminded him of a martyr in a holy picture. He feared that he had gone too far, throwing him out of the hotel with the aid of a phalanx of wicked angels. He thought about making amends for what he had done, but he was certain that Narciso would take improper advantage of him again. It was not reasonable to trust a male who had been proved to carry about such extreme covetousness between his legs.

The sudden blow that Polidoro had dealt the police officer had hit him below the belt. Betrayed by everyone, Narciso had had an impulse to take out his gun and wreak his vengeance. All of a sudden, however, there appeared before him his wife's face, in the house in Méier, as she was getting ready to visit him in prison. On Thursdays, she would bring with her a kilo of pears, bills to pay, and urgent notes from his children. This family constituted the sordid patrimony he had garnered down through the years.

At the vision of a disheveled wife who read him the riot act for being behind bars, his hatred began to die away. At the same time, it cheered him to think that Polidoro, once his troubles were over, would go on throwing the same coins on the table.

"Didn't you hear?" Balinho said, impatient at Narciso's delay in leaving the hotel. He was about to escort him out the door when Mágico stopped him.

"It is I who will see Officer Narciso to his vehicle." The elegance of the sentence restored the strength he had expended that afternoon.

Narciso recalled the Christians sacrificed in Roman arenas. He felt that he was one of them now. Mágico's outstretched hand, inviting him to lean on him, was suggestive of evangelical charity.

He very nearly clung fast to him. They would leave the hotel lobby like husband and wife, enveloped in the same cloak knitted with the dramatic needles of conjugal love.

But he resisted Mágico's display of pity. He slowly took his pack of cigarettes out of his pocket and removed one without passing the pack to the others. He kneaded the cigarette between his fingers so that his torturers would breathe in the smell of tobacco, then scratched the match on the side of the box and raised his collar as though he were wearing a trenchcoat. He felt like a gangster in a Humphrey Bogart film. He inhaled the smoke with avid determination. Only when his lungs gave signs of giving out did he exhale a deep breath in the face of the two men.

Immediately thereafter, he took his revolver out of its holster and stuck it in his belt, between his undershorts and his belly. Dismissing his retinue of myrmidons and henchmen with his right hand, adorned with a death's-head ring, he left the hotel at a martial pace.

THE PROTESTS arrived one after another at the suite on the fifth floor, in the form of notes slipped under the door, with Mágico's acquiescence. Some of them, those that were too forceful, were incinerated by Balinho in a sort of improvised pyre.

From beneath the pink eiderdown, Caetana breathed in the smell of burning paper and was worried. Balinho, calming her down, assured her that the odor was coming from the street. The June fires were celebrating, ahead of time, Brazil's participation in the World Cup in Mexico City—a fact that doubtless threatened to set fire to the soul of Brazil.

Balinho appraised the dissatisfaction of the writers of the notes. They had to be placated. Those creatures, having boarded Caetana's dream, were simply requesting new magic potions that would allow them to continue with a transatlantic voyage aboard a ship that threatened never to take off from terra firma.

"How about having a few friends in for tea?" Balinho's authority became visible principally at sunset, when Caetana listened to him with particular attention.

"Don't force me to receive enemies. Just those whom I can seduce into embracing art. I don't want to abandon the back yard of memory and show business," she said, in boundless fidelity to her illusions.

Since her arrival, she had shut herself up on the fifth floor, despite Polidoro's warning about the perils of hiding herself away so she was forgotten by the city. Her first week in Trindade having already passed, she had not yet worked up the courage to be seen in the main square or in the streets. No eye had been able to count how many more wrinkles she had when she arrived at the Palace.

Confident that Polidoro was taking the proper steps at the Iris to carry out her orders, Caetana's mind was at ease. As a performing artist, she had one task: to define the ever-changing paths of art that for decades now had been crisscrossing her bosom.

Balinho pressed his point, convinced of the need for her to attract friends. "A quick afternoon snack and an exchange of a few brief words. In thirty minutes, they'll all be back home."

Caetana was afraid to meet with guests again. If she, who had crossed Brazil from north to south, had failed, what had happened to them, simple cactus flowers of Trindade? Perhaps their general disillusionment had weakened their spirit and dimmed the sparkle in their eyes.

"Who is there left after all these years?"

Her dark tunic made her words even gloomier. She was doing her hair up in the form of a topknot. As she put the hairpins in place, she went over to the window. The view bored her.

Balinho knew she needed the stage in order to feel alive. Holed up in the hotel, she would not tolerate this prison much longer. She was acutely aware of the absence of a country that always came to her mind by way of miserable little towns. Their names, though she did not remember them, became the only familiar faces to laugh and cry when she and Prince Danilo invented monologues that didn't even exist in the texts of writers whose names she had also forgotten.

Balinho curled up at her feet. It was a sign that both would light a fire on the hearth of memory on which to roast remembrances, like succulent potatoes baked in their skins.

"Do you remember the story of the twelve peers of France, which I told you before we went up the Saõ Francisco River? And that I told to you again in Pirenópolis, the very city where you and Uncle Vespasiano were on the day you turned fifteen? Just after the holiday riding contest, when Seu Pedro served us twenty-eight different dishes in his restaurant? We were just finishing when that prospector with a scar in the form of a cross on his chest showed us, in the midst of a handful of gravel, some little stones as dazzling as diamonds, though his eyes gleamed even more brightly than the stones, to the point of scaring us."

In those days, in Trindade, Caetana couldn't bear interminable plots. She liked only stories that didn't take long to tell and had predictable endings.

"Deliver me from those confounded Frenchmen. The one

thing I want to hear is my own story, told by someone who remembers the details I've already forgotten. Tell me what I did in the past to have so many black marks in my heart."

She was amusing herself by sharing these little confidences when they heard someone hammering on the door. Balinho tensed, ready to defend Caetana. On drawing back the latch, he discovered a tame donkey in the hallway, its head hanging down, all decorated with colored ribbons and crepe paper. Tied to the door handle so that it wouldn't run away, it was in a panic and struggling to get loose.

"We were speaking of the twelve peers of France, and just look what we have here," Balinho said, suspicious of an animal that had doubtless witnessed events tied together by a Gordian knot, and was part of the legend told by the blind wandering troubadours of the Northeast, who falsified the life of the Emperor Charlemagne in hopes of incorporating Brazil and their own dreams into it.

Caetana stroked its back. Humility shut the animal's mouth. Its short mane gave off a peculiar odor. She sniffed its coat, which reeked of cheap cologne.

"The people of Trindade never learn. Instead of flowers, they send the saddest of creatures in the eyes of an artist. Like Northeasterners, the donkey is in exile in Brazil."

Riche took one sniff of the donkey's legs. He did not appear to recognize in the species any superiority to his own. With great hauteur, he curled about Caetana's legs once again, making it difficult for her to move. He did not want her to go anywhere near the animal.

"I agree to receive my friends and find out who sent me the donkey with the intention of driving me out of the Palace Hotel, since there isn't room for all of us in this one suite."

The news spread in just a few minutes. Polidoro, urged not to put in an appearance, feared that the euphoria of the party would create conjugal problems for him. There was the risk that Dodô, on learning of the event, would hurry back home to accuse him of polluting the marriage bed, deserted for so many years now, through a brazen love affair with that whore who called herself an actress.

It was best, then, for Caetana to cancel the party. Balinho, however, was opposed. For the first time, he and Caetana would receive friends, on a Thursday afternoon. They planned to offer the guests maracock juice, manioc-flour tea cakes, and fancy pastry, already ordered, and, above all, interminable stories. Balinho was young and deserved to have a good time.

Venieris accepted the invitation, on condition that he be allowed to bring with him the apelike painter, his clothes spattered with different colors, who was now helping him make the stage sets. He had given up his shop in order to devote all his time to the Iris. Meeting Caetana, however, would renew his inspiration. He was no doubt bringing into being a work of art that transcended the narrow confines of Trindade.

Virgílio too, in his eagerness to chronicle historic events, promised to come, even though this would displease Polidoro, who swore that he would post himself at the entrance to the hotel just to see who brought him.

At the door of the hotel, Gioconda greeted Polidoro, bringing with her the Three Graces, thereby overtly disobeying him. Promoted to the status of actresses, they were practically never at Estaçõ. They spent their days in the streets and at the Iris movie house. Whenever they happened by a mirror, they would try out typically theatrical gestures. And if they hesitated as to the most suitable physical pose, they went for help to Gioconda, in whom they recognized a talent for directing.

Diana, more docile now, requested a role at once dramatic and tyrannical.

"When is Caetana going to visit us at the Iris?" she asked anxiously. "Only she can assign the roles, tell us what play we're going to perform."

"Why do we need somebody to order us around if art is free and uncontrolled?" Sebastiana said.

Refined by her recent intense social life, she had acquired a courage that enabled her to be seen with her mouth wide open and not feel the anguish she had once suffered. In any event, old age would end up robbing her of her remaining teeth.

"I was the first of the Three Graces to lose some of my teeth. That means I'll have a long life, since I'll start feeding myself on pap and dreams."

Firmly planted next to the revolving door, Polidoro did not desert his post.

"If Dodô finds out, we'll be running a risk. We might even have to cancel the performance at the Iris."

Scorned by Gioconda, he thought of asking Narciso for help, though his feeling of offense at the wrong that Narciso had done him was as intense as ever. Under no circumstances did he want Narciso to go up to the fifth floor. "That police officer abused my trust," he kept saying.

"Why don't you join us, and we'll have an afternoon snack together?" Gioconda suggested inside the elevator. Since Polidoro did not answer immediately, she pressed the button for the fifth floor, to the applause of the Three Graces.

Caetana received them at the door. Her red dress contrasted with the gray afternoon, which threatened rain. The Three Graces, stealing a march on Gioconda, threw themselves into her arms. Caetana did not know whom to pay attention to first. Each of them was fighting for the privilege of receiving the warmth of her bounteous breasts. Diana finally leaned her head on Caetana's bosom. Suddenly she gave a cry that frightened the others.

"What's the matter?" Sebastiana asked.

Diana didn't say a word. She would rather suffer pain than annoy Caetana. The actress, who had allowed herself to be kissed by Diana without answering her effusions in kind, pushed her head away.

"This brooch must have hurt Diana's scalp." She pointed to the jewel, pinned to the very bottom of the V of her low-cut dress. "It was a gift from an Italian woman who had driven in a jeep over the dunes of Fortaleza. She came to my dressing room just to confess that she'd never imagined she'd come across a talent such as mine in a country like Brazil. Especially in a poverty-stricken itinerant troupe, without scenery, that had never heard of Pirandello. Uncle Vespasiano went so far as to weep with emotion. He gathered us together immediately for an extra performance and offered the Italian woman a handful of scenes, all of them from the Brazilian repertory of days long gone, of which he felt himself to be the depositary. One time, when he'd put quite a few drinks under his belt, he confessed to me: 'I carry around with me a strange seabag of provisions. Instead of cheese, salami, and bread to satisfy my hunger, it contains the last remains of the words uttered by actors who are already dead. I'm the last Brazilian performing artist who still combines the circus and the theater. Do you know what it was called in the old days? The big top.' "

In these reminiscences, Caetana skipped from one year to another without observing any sort of strict chronology. It was easy for her to forget the modern age and its creatures. In a way, each word that her memory disclosed excluded the Three Graces since none of them managed to get a word in edgewise when she recalled Vespasiano.

"To better explain that combination, Uncle used to talk of an account by Arthur Azevedo, who had been fascinated by that splicing together of comedy and drama in the circus ring in a way that no one had ever seen before."

Gioconda was uneasy. Besides the fact that Caetana was neglecting the arriving visitors—Venieris in particular, who had been relegated to the background next to the faded curtains—Caetana's personal performance, played to the hilt, gave the other actresses, the Three Graces and herself, no opportunity to develop their respective talents.

Diana, who in recent days had acquired a refined sensitivity, intuited Gioconda's misgivings. Above all her envy, now lodged in her breast like a thorn driven deep into her flesh. Feeling at one with her, Diana took a step forward to separate herself from the other guests. She noted Caetana's disapproval. Her attention was focused on the story she had not yet finished, and she thought she was being made fun of.

"Tell me, when all is said and done, what is the meaning of friendship? What becomes of gratitude?" Caetana protested. Her hair, amid her sweeping gestures, rustled like dry leaves. The pendants that dangled from her delicate earlobes tinkled.

Her language, deliberately in code, was a reaction to wounds inflicted in her own suite. Balinho, from some distance away, was also the victim of her disapproval. He had invented a festive gathering during which everyone was fighting over the same treasure.

Virgílio was annoyed by the competitive nature of the women. Perfidiously, they fought among themselves for the men's favor, without the discretion that the circumspect nature of their sex called for. Wishing, nonetheless, to put his virtues as a moderator into practice, he went over to Diana. "I regret not having known Vespasiano more intimately. No one would have explained Brazil to us better than he," he said with self-satisfaction.

In order to hear what she was saying, Venieris, followed by some others, sat down on the floor around Caetana. The narrow circle restricted her performance. But how many times had she gone onstage with a fever, in costumes full of mends and patches, with burned-out footlights that made it difficult for the audience to see her facial contortions?

"Uncle Vespasiano began his career in the Politeama, in São Paulo, a large shed made of wood with a corrugated-zinc roof near the Old Market, frequented at the time by cattle dealers who had just come to the city. He ate out of a tin plate, but soon he was allowed to eat at the actors' table. When he first began to play onstage, people threw potatoes and rotten eggs at him. Not to mention the jeers and catcalls. One night they even hurled a crown woven of grass at him."

Ernesto was all excited. It struck him as odd that art could be rebuked by the same means used against Christ, methods that the Church had deigned to choose as a symbol of the suffering of the Saviour, who, through such cruel treatment, had redeemed humankind.

"The audience may have been right, in fact," Ernesto reflected aloud in a fearless voice. "If they chose a crown of thorns for Christ, why not send your uncle, as a warning, one made of grass, which is cattle fodder?"

Caetana pretended not to hear Ernesto's interruption. She was certain that her audience, held together by the yoke of her narrative, would not allow itself to be carried away by intricacies of the plot, which had nothing to do with the verbal circus that she was personally endeavoring to put on in front of them with canvases of sighs, ropes of joy, and tiers of seats of sudden surprises.

"As I was saying . . ." she went on, thinking of the care that her uncle had taken to transmit this story to her. He had been convinced the story threatened to vanish from the national memory if she did not pay close attention to the details that Vespasiano, in his zeal, persisted in passing down to her. "Circuses moved about by muleback or in carts drawn by oxen, until gradually railroads arrived, to the misfortune of rural people. Some of the circuses were mud huts covered with old pieces of cloth. And so it was easy to take them down and put them up again in other locations, not far from the one before. Thus there was constructed at the same time a circle of hell and of illusion. The troupe at times consisted of twenty miserable wretches who proclaimed how happy they were in the circus ring. In return, all they asked was for people to laugh and weep."

"We produce the same effect," Sebastiana broke in, having finally understood the nature of the battle joined between the women from the whorehouse and Caetana the actress, who was denying them the right to shine onstage.

Prince Danilo discreetly entered the room. He had difficulty seating his corpulent body on the floor. His thighs, as massive as blocks of stone, jostled Ernesto and Gioconda, and they shoved back each time he moved. He had arrived just in time to hear the observations of those pretentious amateurs.

"It's entirely different," Danilo said, cutting Sebastiana off short. "Have you ladies ever put on *Othello*, *The Crystal Princess*, *The Gambling Brothers*, or even *Blackfriar*? Or has the thin wood partition of your place ever torn in half in a windstorm, as happened to our backdrop? We had to mend it as fast as we could, using needles, heavy thread, and bits of melted rubber that we got from the tire of an old Chevrolet truck."

He waxed enthusiastic as he reviewed the hardships they had

lived through in the course of those years—giving proof of a love that society, depraved by the scorn it felt for art, did not have the ability to appreciate.

"Who is there who wouldn't trade a fortune for a flash of genius?" he insisted, his gaze obstinate and revengeful.

"How about taking a string of onions and making out of it a crown for your glory, instead of a crown of grass?" Ernesto said ironically, more outspoken when Polidoro wasn't present.

Caetana stayed on the sidelines of the argument. With slow gestures she undid the hairpins that held her topknot up. With her hair spread loose over her shoulders, her appearance was even more striking.

"Do you know what Procópio, the great Brazilian actor, said about a certain type of people? They're the hangers-on of fame. It was only out of camaraderie that he didn't charge them for riding in the same streetcar he took," Caetana said with obvious ill-humor.

Her cruel words made the audience feel uneasy. Balinho, who up until then had done his best to be discreet, foresaw the failure of his ideal of gathering together around Caetana those who had been enraptured supporters of the spectacle now being mounted at the Iris.

"Let's all have tea." He clapped his hands together energetically to undo the misunderstanding. "It is being offered in honor of all you ladies and gentlemen. Caetana herself received the cook in this very room to examine his capabilities. Only then did she approve the shrimp patties."

Smiles appeared on everyone's face. All of them were susceptible to such charms, whose effect was immediate. Balinho himself, aided by Francisco—who, in his eagerness to watch for signs from Caetana, kept stumbling over the guests—was passing the trays around the room. Each of the guests, by tacit agreement and in a spirit of farsightedness, grabbed two patties.

"I don't remember having had any lunch," Sebastiana said to justify herself, ashamed of her appetite.

Palmira, for lack of a plate, set her extra patty down on the floor, on top of her napkin. She didn't take her eyes off Riche, who was purring at her side.

"It's better to latch on to two than just to one. I'm always afraid things will run out," she said, not expecting anyone to overhear her amid the louder voices.

Caetana, whose ear caught sounds in registers imperceptible to others, was touched by that pale woman with pretensions to stardom. Palmira had grown ugly, and the years had done away with her body's conspicuous contours. Whereas Caetana had become fatter through overindulgence in the contradictory cuisine of her native land, Palmira had lost weight.

"Growing old is sad," Caetana said vivaciously, not intending to make an offensive remark about anything but her own age, a splendid monster lavishly squandering death and wrinkles. "That was Uncle Vespasiano's favorite motto in his last year of life. He talked that way just as twilight was falling, overcome by a strange anguish. He defended the proposition that no human beings suffer as much from old age as actors and actresses. Every time they come onstage, they desperately need to fool themselves into being certain that they're still young. Facial wrinkles have the power to destroy their talent, which craves to fight it out with what is enduring and eternal."

With the collaboration of Danilo, who furnished her with details to enrich her narrative, Caetana remembered her uncle's bottle-green cutaway coat, and even his white vest. And the way he smiled with merriment when they called him "baron."

"Coffee baron, regale us with your wealth of talent!" he himself would retort.

Even at the end of his life, in his dirty, frayed cutaway coat missing several gilt buttons, Vespasiano stood proudly erect, like the owner of a sugar mill or a vast coffee plantation. He had begun to mix up the speeches of his repertory, which had dissolved at the whim of the years. And though Danilo corrected him, he did not notice his mistakes. Caetana, for her part, reproved Danilo. He must never again call attention to the errors made by an artist of such magnitude, who now deserved only rest and respect.

Anyone who bore in his memory an existence as thick as porridge had won, once and for all, the right to forget life and everything else that came in its wake.

"What difference does it make if lines from *Othello* are jumbled together with ones from Joracy Camargo?" With those words, she brought such arguments to an end.

Vespasiano seemed to appreciate the bitter dispute. It moved him that his niece, whom he had brought up, would die for his honor.

"Did you two know that Mirandinha, a clown as full of life as the dawn, died spitting up blood in the lobby of the Carlos Gomes Theater?" Vespasiano said, rummaging around in his memory damaged by drink, by pork fat, and, above all, by the effort to survive, forced to cross a swamp in order to reach the dubious flower of illusion on the other shore.

At such moments, with rare tenderness, Caetana led him about by the hand like a blind man. She sat him down on the high stool. "Do you remember that description in the old almanac? 'Alongside the veranda where they had exchanged confidences slightly shaded by the leaves of the climbing vine.' "

The reward for such a reminiscence had been Vespasiano's broad smile.

"And what about the Victrola, my girl? It's my legacy, don't forget. I don't have anything else to leave behind. My entire life is in the music that I've heard on it."

Virgílio proposed that they bring their confidences to an end. It was a holiday, and they were on the point of bursting into tears beneath the spell of Caetana's words. Seeing that they were captivated by the charms of the afternoon, which in the next few minutes would leave them forever, he proposed that they all give their hosts an ovation, as though they were at the theater. "Isn't it true that we have just witnessed two performers improvising a brilliant text onstage? What is more theatrical than life in the raw, like a live ox split open? Isn't it true that we were happy too?"

On his feet, free of the bodies jammed together against him as they sat on the floor, Venieris stood up as the applause echoed down the hallways of the hotel. A mere spectator, he had had the illusion that he had gone back to his homeland. To Epidaurus, to be exact, where he could throw a coin from the last row of the amphitheater and hear the echo produced by the perfect acoustics. All in harmony with the human tragedy that had unfolded within sight of everyone.

His vigorous applause put a damper on the enthusiasm of the other guests. Caetana noted the Greek's vanity, trying to impose upon them a tradition of five thousand years, without taking into consideration the fact that Brazil was not yet even five centuries old. The weight of the culture represented by Venieris suffocated the members of that circumspect society.

"Sit down, Venieris," Diana ordered imperiously, as though she had read Caetana's heartfelt wish. "Here comes another round of patties. I only hope they're more of the shrimp ones."

Instead of being grateful for the gesture, Caetana felt that Diana was drawing her bow to launch an arrow soaked in poison as well as in devouring displays of affection. The fear that her wings would be clipped in the name of love was immediately evident in the actress's face, attracting Balinho's attention. Readying himself to smooth rough edges, he moved around the living room, stopping in front of Diana, Ernesto, and Virgílio, who required attention. He made the same trip countless times. His youth was in his favor as he visited those souls, along with the comfort of knowing that, whenever he wanted, he could find his way to the door that led outside. Yet, in fact, the one place he loved to linger was next to the hearth of Caetana's breast.

Caetana did her best to bring to an end the party, paid for out of her own pocket filled with Polidoro's money. Those people, crowded together on the floor and needing bibs, soiled their clothes and the floor with crumbs from the pies. Anyone walking through the room, as Balinho was doing, dirtied the soles of his shoes. Uncle Vespasiano, who had appreciated good manners, would have been the first to chase them away with a broomstick, disapproving of the noise they made as they sipped their tea and their maracock juice.

"The party is almost over," Balinho said, foreseeing uncontrollable situations. "Caetana has fond hopes that you ladies and gentlemen, when it comes time to go to bed, will take with you to your pillows the assurance of the happiness that we have shared here. Caetana thanks you for having come."

In the role of ventriloquist, Balinho assumed affected gestures, imitating Caetana. Nonetheless, his decorum and affability made them forget the actress's intolerance.

Danilo did not approve of the honors accorded Balinho. As an actor, who ran the risk of living the life of others in addition to his own, he did not deserve to be assigned a lesser role in public. He was searching for the best way to protest when Gioconda stepped forward.

"When we arrived, Caetana asked us to tell the story of friendship. Neither she nor the rest of us gave the right answer. Now that we're saying goodbye to each other, I wish to state that the only story worth telling is the one about lies." She stood there motionless, awaiting the reaction of the group.

The disapproval of such a doctrine spread through the room. Caetana, accustomed to the reverse side of words, stared at Gioconda, seemingly not knowing who she was. It was not Gioconda's notions that repelled her in and of themselves, but, rather, the rivalry that was established between them from that moment on.

"You're learning fast, Gioconda. As a matter of fact, falsehood is the only truth that interests us. The rest is crude and barbarous. For the very reason that reality is always in the service of the illusion of the poor and the shrewdness of the rich. That's why you women and I are *de trop* in Trindade, or in any other city," Caetana said, exchanging indecipherable signs with Gioconda.

Ernesto asked the women for protection. Those enigmatic phrases had for him a high fat content. They were harmful to his perception of the world. As for Venieris, having recently become a part of the art world, he was coming out with all sorts of dubious wisdom, capable of disturbing the gentle and contemplative nature of his painting.

In his occupation as a student of history, Virgílio felt the need to lend the moment the last solemn remarks that the party still had the patience to tolerate. "Contrary to what has been suggested here, I do not always find it honorable to invent. It is a false prerogative of which artists ought rightly to be accused. In my opinion, and with no intention of offending anyone, artists have no scruples whatsoever."

"What are you doing here among us, then? Aren't we all artists? Even the Three Graces are struggling to be recognized as such," Caetana said, giving vent to her resentment.

"I don't know why I'm here either," he candidly admitted.

The impasse created by Virgílio prevented them from leaving the living room to go back to the Iris. Nobody was prepared to mend the wounds that had been inflicted after the delicious shrimp patties.

"Of course you know," said Sebastiana's wee voice, in a timid but spontaneous show of independence.

Virgílio, who had always chosen her as his favorite, felt that his authority as a master—doubly confirmed, in bed and in his academic chair—had been threatened. He motioned to her not to say anything more.

Sebastiana, however, in torment paid no heed to these hints. "Our talent is reserved for the stage. Wouldn't it be better to leave here and go directly to the Iris to rehearse? I can no longer bear to live without art!"

The woman's sighs spurred the historian on, eager as he was to enjoy the same sort of emotion as had been instilled in his favorite Grace.

"We're a band of filthy men and women happy with the illusion of art," Diana broke in, proud of her speech.

Ernesto no longer recognized the city where he had been born. The imposition of new habits perturbed him.

"What society are all of you talking about anyway?"

"We all have Renaissance souls, but were born in Brazil. And therein lies our misfortune," Virgílio said.

Such pessimism roused the pharmacist's spirits to fever pitch once again. "And what about Pedro I's battle cry of Ipiranga? Was that meaningless?" Ernesto shot back with patriotic vigor.

"The Tietê River, the scene of that great glory, is full of shit and progressive-minded illusions today. What else could we expect after presidents like Juscelino Kubitschek, Jânio Quadros, and now Médici?" Fearing the consequences of these harsh words, he hastened to amend his statement: "It's a good thing history has remembered their names and will have mercy on them."

Balinho held the door wide open in his hurry to see the last of them. Exhausted, the guests formed a line. Some of them kissed Caetana's cheek, others her hands. Although she did not shun these tokens of affection, the actress did not return them.

"And don't I get my kiss?" Gioconda said slyly.

Caetana ran her hands through her hair. She felt warm, despite the breeze that had invaded the living room as darkness fell.

"This kiss is a quick one. The other, more lingering ones will be at the Iris, when we put on the performance."

She leaned down toward Gioconda, who was shorter than she was. In that position, her mouth rested on Gioconda's right cheek, near the corner of her lips. It stayed there, for a few fractions of a second before it was pushed away by Gioconda, who, on feeling an uncontrollable ardor, fled out the door.

"When will Caetana come to visit us at the Iris?" the Greek asked.

Venieris hastened to take Gioconda's place. He was sailing, absent-mindedly, the waters of the Aegean, not believing in passions, even when they overflowed in his presence.

Caetana extended her hand to him. Her rings weighed heavily on her fingers. She had worn too many adornments, just to impress Gioconda and the Three Graces. The Greek, like a gentleman, held her hand aloft just long enough to perceive the small dark patches spotting her skin as an unmistakable sign of the years.

THE VAST expanse of the Retiro estate extended as far as Espírito Santo. Dodô returned from this enormous country property with a different accent. She admitted with pride that she was an inhabitant of the states of Rio de Janeiro and of Espírito Santo at one and the same time, and after so declaring awaited the laurels owed her for her brilliant culture—which, it so happened, people generally refused to grant her.

To Polidoro's joy, Dodô had twice postponed her return to Trindade. Since her departure, she had transferred the thankless task of keeping a close eye on Polidoro to her eldest daughter, who heard rumors that Caetana, lodged in the Palace Hotel, threatened to lure him into her fold.

Using the unveiling of the bust of her paternal grandfather as an excuse, the daughter persuaded her mother to come back home immediately. She could not fail to turn up at a ceremony that rendered homage to the Álves family, including every single member, even the dissidents, who had grown up in the wake of old Joaquim's fame.

Dodô demanded a new dress. She did not want to wear the luxurious rags and tatters hanging in a row in the closet. The mirror made it hard for her to take pleasure in her figure. It was better to resort to means that gave promise of lending beauty to women who lacked it.

"If, as a matter of fact, I have green eyes, the best thing to do is to make the most of them," Dodô said as she inspected the house.

Having every confidence in her dressmaker, who had agreed to deliver the dress promptly on the following day, an hour before the ceremony, she sought out Venieris's shop. He would no doubt suggest a silk fabric to make her body look less bulky and enable her to enjoy the feeling of lightness she had lacked for so long.

"Preferably with a yellow background. Besides bringing gold one's way, it brings good luck as well. And that's all I want," Dodô said cheerfully, as she went up the rua Nova accompanied by her daughter, exchanging greetings with friends she met.

Finding the shop closed surprised both of them.

"Where did that Greek go? Don't tell me he went back to Turkey!" Her hands on her hips, she was the picture of indignation. At that point in life, it was quite enough to be frustrated by her husband's total absence in bed.

Francisco, who was passing by, couldn't resist offering his help.

"I'm from the Palace Hotel. If you're looking for Venieris, you can stop. He's gone off to be an artist. Didn't you know?"

Dodô read a secret meaning in the waiter's shifty eyes.

"Where has he hidden himself, if I may ask?"

Francisco pretended he had no idea.

"This city swallows up even foreigners," he answered, feigning perplexity.

Irritated, Dodô turned her back on him. Her daughter, fearing her fits of temper, dragged her off. In the main square, near the screen that still shielded the bust of Joaquim from profane eyes, her daughter consoled her: "You've no lack of dresses in your closet. Anyway, it's not proper to have a conversation with that flunky," her daughter assured her.

Dodô paid her no heed. According to what the man had asserted, he worked at the Palace. In the kitchen surely, since he reeked of onions. Polidoro had forbidden her to visit the place. He had sworn he'd leave home for good if she ever disobeyed that order. Despite the battle joined between them, she had preferred to give ground on this point.

Once they were back home, they let dinner get cold without their really counting on Polidoro to join them. The daughters murmured slight protests, so as to please Dodô. They finally concluded that, with their father gone, they would have a few hours of peace and quiet.

The following morning, Dodô hesitated between a dress that was dark but somber, and a pumpkin-colored one that matched her distant ideal.

"And what's happened to Polidoro?" she asked her daughter, who had come downstairs to have breakfast with her.

Dodô ordered that the sheets be examined. If they were wrinkled in the morning, it meant that her husband had spent the night at home, and had gone on to the public square very early, impelled by his sense of responsibility. He didn't trust Mayor Pentecostes. Vanity made Pentecostes forget the appropriateness of dignified public deportment. In his eagerness to please the local administration, he resorted to base flattery and trite cant.

In the doorway, ready to go out, Dodô insisted that they hurry up.

"What it comes down to is: did my husband sleep at home or not?"

Looking at her watch, she noted the time.

"Let's go. Heaven only knows what he's doing. Maybe it's better if I don't discover the truth."

In the square, she would force Polidoro to confess. Perhaps, indifferent to her pain, he might turn her to salt with one look.

Pentecostes came to meet her. At a gesture from him, they brought her a parasol. And in a most courtly way he touched her lightly on her elbow, crooked to hold her purse, and led her to the bronze bust, now covered with the national flag.

"We still have ten minutes to go, right?" Dodô didn't know what to say to the mayor when she noticed that Polidoro wasn't there.

"Time waits for no man, Dona Dodô. On the other hand, it's an honor for us to await the arrival of Seu Joaquim."

In accordance with his wishes, Joaquim's old Cadillac stopped with an ostentatious roar not far from the place where the ceremony was to take place.

Ernesto helped Joaquim out of the car. Other hands were hurriedly thrust forward with the same intention.

"I came for the celebration, not for my funeral," he said, waving them away with his cane.

As soon as Joaquim had gotten out of the car, and at a signal from the mayor, the group of schoolchildren began waving the same little flags that had been used every year in the Seventh of

September parade. Pentecostes had ordered that cookies and a cold drink of *guaraná* be distributed among them before they lined up in the square.

"Who hasn't shown up yet so we can get this thingamajig started?" Joaquim asked.

Surrounded by Dodô, his children, his grandchildren, and the rest of the family, he could barely stand up. He had great misgivings about the face that the sculptor he'd thrown out of his house had given him. Enemies were never credited with decorous and elegant gestures. He had reason to expect, however, that the sculptor had aged him by ten years at least, above all ridding him of his eternal mustache, just to hint that even his private parts were bald.

The town councilmen vied with the family for a more prominent place. They all wanted to be in the photographs. Dodô, put out with Polidoro for being late, and with the mayor, who had put her to the left of Joaquim when in her opinion she deserved to be on his right, a place now occupied by Pentecostes himself, made her face a blank, lacking only the black veil of widowhood.

"What's this, daughter?" Joaquim rapped on his shoe with his cane. "With a face like that, you're going to age quickly."

His remark upset her even more. The males of the Álves family were essentially crude. They practically ate with their hands. "On the other hand, we brought you a fortune," Polidoro used to say to his wife when she backed him into a corner.

Pentecostes looked at his watch. Because of the delay, half of those assembled for the ceremony had disappeared. The children came and went, pissing behind the trees. Dodô did not calm down. Her husband was placing the black border of shame around her face. As though it were a death announcement. They must all feel aggrieved at her disgrace. Perhaps he was rolling on some other woman's mattress. There was no lack of whores and eager cunts about, she thought in indignation.

"Ladies and gentlemen." With a gesture, the mayor asked for silence. Everything was in an uproar. Forgetting the man whom they were honoring, those awaiting the ceremony were chatting together. The one subject of conversation was the world soccer championship. Some of them would be off to Mexico City the following day, in the hope of arriving for the very last match.

"And what if Brazil is eliminated?"

"Don't even think such a thought. Médici is a president who has luck on his side. Everything he touches turns out exactly right."

"He even deserves it. He's very likable. And we're getting rich under his baton."

Without hiding his nervousness, Pentecostes decided to begin the ceremony, which threatened to turn into a failure.

"Unfortunately, in spite of the lateness of the hour, we'll wait just one minute more. Time enough for the church bell to peal for those who are, happily, still alive, summoning them to lunch." And he gave a smile, forcing the others to appreciate his good humor. "The illustrious Polidoro Álves will be along soon. There is no one better than he at stimulating the cultural life of our hardworking community. Moreover, he is a man inspired by filial love, which impels him to make any sacrifice for his distinguished progenitor, of whom we shall now speak."

The minute the mayor took the pages of his speech out of his pocket, Joaquim stopped him with his cane, which he appeared to use instead of his hands. He trusted only those gestures forthcoming from his wooden cane.

"With this shepherd's crook I herd any lamb that has strayed. You'll see," he said to Dodô, after Pentecostes had stopped searching for his glasses in the pockets of his suit jacket.

"Is there something you wanted, Seu Joaquim?" the mayor said, surprised at the interruption.

"The fact is, I'm an old man, Seu Pentecostes. I'm going on ninety. So I don't have any time to waste. I'm itching to get back home. It's best to start the ceremony straightaway. Show me the bust. That way I can check and see if it's me or if it's the face of my neighbor."

Joaquim's voice, drowning out the mayor's, could be heard by the children in the group from the schools. It was hard to believe that an old man, on the eve of his death, should have such a full, majestic diapason.

"And my speech?" Pentecostes was so bewildered he didn't know what to do.

Joaquim shrugged, indifferent to the mayor's political ambitions. And, to the astonishment of those present, the children shouted out, beneath the protection of the little Brazilian flags, their total support for the man being honored.

"As you can see, Pente," Joaquim said ironically, "even Brazil is in a hurry. It's tired of official speeches."

Her mind far away from these events, Dodô was thinking of Polidoro, the author of so many acts of sheer folly. Something serious was happening. She had inklings of the imminent shipwreck of the family, which was about to founder even though people threw them cork floats, lifebuoys, and flotation jackets. Any attempt would come too late.

"When has anyone ever seen your father fail to show up?" she whispered into the ear of her daughter, who pulled on the sleeve of her mother's dress, forcing her to be quiet.

She could not share the anguish she felt. Even her daughter, though an interested party and a victim, seemed to be apathetic toward the fate of that branch of the Álves family. She had to arouse their awareness, sharpen their weapons. She turned to her daughter.

"I know you don't care. Your one concern is your husband. But some day he too will leave the marriage bed, the way your father has done. If I don't keep a close eye"—overtaken by a sudden hoarseness, she lowered her voice—"on our fortune, we'll be lost. In a word, our patrimony will evaporate like perfume, leaving only a memory. I'm making you heiresses of poverty. Paupers! I, of all people, who brought all of you girls up with the illusion that you were rich!"

Dodô broke off her verbal outpouring. The last words had emerged from a throat lent force by anguish. Her chest ached. She felt enveloped in a strange vapor that blurred her vision.

"Control yourself, Mama," her daughter said. "Don't you see the scandal that Grandfather is causing?"

Dodô returned to life with the same rush of energy that came over her after drinking carrot-and-orange juice in the mornings.

Forgetting Polidoro, she now directed her attention toward banal events, to which she had the rare capacity to add salt and sugar when she felt that they were lacking.

She noted the mayor's embarrassment. Sharing however, the feelings of the absent Polidoro, who did not hold Pentecostes in high esteem, she rejoiced at the unhappiness that, visible to all, drifted across the official's face.

"Why haven't we unveiled the bust yet?" she said in irritation, addressing the mayor, the pages of whose speech, still folded, trembled in his hands. "You made such a fine speech! It nearly brought tears to my eyes."

The Álves family stepped forward in a body, followed by Ernesto, who was acting in Polidoro's stead, though without his authorization. Now, joining together around the bust, they prepared to respectfully withdraw the Brazilian flag hiding the bronze statue from public view.

"Just a minute—wait for me."

Virgílio hurried across the square from the far side. Taking higher bounds than usual, he was not forgetting that Roman legions, with their renowned infantry, ruled the world thanks to the swiftness with which they reached the farthest corners of their domains. This rapidity came from the energy of elite troops, and also from the discovery of taking leaping bounds forward, which freed the foot soldier for speedy travel. In a few seconds, he reached the group.

"It's a good thing I got here in time. As Polidoro's representative, I want to see the bust at the same time as the rest of you do. He didn't come in person, but he's here in spirit."

Dodô refused to put up with this outrage. "Where is your authorization?"

In an attempt to restrain her rebelliousness, her daughters surrounded Dodô. "I beg you, Professor, remain at our grandfather's side. It's an honor to have you here," one of the Álveses spoke up and led him over to Joaquim, who didn't so much as glance at him.

"Having climbed a splendid marble staircase that brought us all to this pinnacle of glory, I ask the distinguished Dona Dodô, along with our notable Joaquim Álves, to unveil the bust and, naturally, the plaque that goes with it," Pentecostes said.

The eldest daughter, in her role as her mother's guardian, pushed her forward. Dodô drew herself up to her full height, in her capacity as proprietress of a fief so vast that she herself did not know what its boundaries were. The mayor pointed to the green-and-yellow ribbon affixed to the flag.

"One, two, three." The professor set the rhythm in a nervous euphoria. Pentecostes, meanwhile, urged her to adopt a slow, solemn pace.

"We're in no hurry, Dona Dodô. Take all the time you think necessary."

"Don't pay any attention, Dodô. Finish this whole business as soon as you can," Joaquim said impatiently. With the tip of his cane he began to raise the edge of the cloth. He was proceeding with this when Dodô yanked off the national flag, unintentionally allowing it to fall on the ground.

Urged to voice aloud his appreciation of the work of art, Joaquim refused. On seeing himself thus perpetuated in bronze, with a total absence of modesty, he recalled one by one those who had died before him. The presence of a mustache on the bust, notwithstanding the spitefulness of the sculptor, brought back to him the memory of the tiny, lively features of Bandeirante's face. He had disappeared from Trindade without leaving Joaquim so much as a farewell note, thus proving his lack of interest in a city that had been incapable of appreciating the luxury of the Palace Hotel. It was only many years later, when Joaquim had practically forgotten him, that the news of his death on the coast of São Paulo, amid a pack of wolves fighting over his fortune, had reached him. And because Polidoro had always retained an unlimited admiration for the explorer of new territory who hailed from São Paulo, his recompense had come in the form of an inheritance. Joaquim's son had been bequeathed fifty-one percent of the ownership of the hotel, with the right to impose any decision he pleased on the other partner.

"Bandeirante would have appreciated this square," Joaquim said, having isolated himself from the rest of the family. He felt himself to be the accomplice of a past that he was part of only through a vague and fleeting power of memory. The present, with its infernal ostentation, emerged disguised in a deliberately overdone fairylike lighting effect, suitable for a festivity to which he would never be invited.

"How do you feel on being confronted with your own fame?" Ernesto commented, determined to utter the formal words that would have been forthcoming from Polidoro, had he been present.

The bugle corps awaited a signal from the mayor to enliven the square. Pentecostes, however, disappointed by the course of the solemn ceremony, which had not even managed to attract Polidoro or arouse Joaquim's enthusiasm, absent-mindedly forgot to call for the music as a way of bringing the city back to life.

Joaquim moved around the column that supported the bust. Forgetting that he was the one being honored, he felt pity for the loneliness of that man. In just a few minutes, he would be abandoned forever. After his death, his name would be confused with that of any other passer-by. He felt an urge to piss on the statue, to leave a human trace on that repellent face, sullied by the years.

Suddenly the sound of a solitary accordion burst forth.

"I haven't given orders yet," Pentecostes protested in defense of his authority. He was permanently distrustful of his subordinates. Any servile attitude of theirs always concealed some act meant to cheat him out of his power.

The accordion player went on without missing a measure, paying no attention to Pentecostes's protests. Joy, which in the beginning had been something specially ordered, was now entirely his own creation. The accordion player felt as though he were in the countryside, the stalks of Indian corn stirred by the breeze from the southwest.

Virgílio asked to put in a word.

"I forgot to announce to all of you that I am not the one who is here before you. It was Polidoro, who named me his representative, who spoke." Virgílio forgot that he had already offered this explanation.

"He's far more sclerotic than my father-in-law," Dodô said to her daughter in a low voice.

"Very well, play a farewell song now," Pentecostes said, letting the bugle corps go to it, to drown out the sounds of the accordion amid the other instruments. In keeping with his obsessive nature, as the music dragged on, he asked Joaquim to express to the guests his feelings on seeing the bronze bust. "It's not every day that a person becomes a statue," he added pretentiously.

Joaquim walked around the pedestal, scratching the surface of the metal with his cane, leaving Egyptian inscriptions that would never be read.

"The day is not far off when pigeons will come to shit on my face. It's sad but true. May God's will be done."

He was already leaving when Virgílio stopped him. "Please, Seu Joaquim, say a few words for our guest book." And, pantomiming swearing on an imaginary Bible, he indulged his pride in his profession as a historian.

Leaning on his cane, Joaquim bent over in a reflexive posture, ready at last to assume the glory that Trindade was forcing upon him.

Pentecostes cast a glance at the musicians. Obediently, they stopped playing their instruments. Virgílio took his pen and notepad out of his pocket. The tremor in his hands of late days made it hard to write by hand.

"You may begin. We're ready," he said, to set at ease the man to whom homage was being paid.

Joaquim, however, threatened to leave.

"Well, then, Seu Joaquim?" the mayor implored, crumpling up the pages of the speech he hadn't read.

The old man eyed those present. His flock and his bitter fellows, all coveting his fortune, hoping he'd die shortly.

"Now, with your permission, I'm going home to piss, because in matters like this glory is very remiss. If I don't take care of my bladder, I'll burst before my time."

Indifferent to the reaction he had aroused, he took the first step. Standing tall and straight, he headed for his car.

THE GLAD tidings during that week warmed the heart of President Médici, whose surname, shared with a Renaissance prince, flooded the country with the splendor of gold and blood.

"They say that torture exists in Brazil. They give people electric shocks and insert whole bottles up their asses."

Ernesto's admonition was immediately ignored. Since he had no proof of the things he said, they couldn't believe him. Sheer intrigue by communists on the loose. Brazil was experiencing a golden age in the economic realm and in sports.

"He who is not with me is against me," Narciso interrupted, with renewed vigor after the fracas in the Palace Hotel.

Facing the public square, on the same corner as usual, they were waiting for Polidoro to come by, around five.

"Have you seen Polidoro since the incident?"

The constable dissembled. His hands thrust into his trousers, he feigned indifference. What reason would he have to fear Polidoro? He looked at his watch.

"I must go. I'm chasing down a bandit. This time he's going to pay me."

Polidoro appeared a few minutes later, speeding along on foot, as swiftly as a meteor. He signaled to Ernesto to follow him. He had urgent business to attend to at the Iris.

In the hotel, Caetana was on pins and needles, not having received any news. She had begun to mistrust the administrative ability of her longtime friend. His slowness in making preparations to put on a show whose prime virtue was its simplicity was public knowledge. Unless his ill-will stemmed from the difficulty of admitting the talent of the woman who, in the name of art, had refused his cows and his vast estates.

Seeing the state of nerves she was in, Prince Danilo encouraged Caetana to leave Trindade in the dead of night. Or demand that Polidoro get rid of the band of incompetents to whom he owed the chorus of praise that accompanied his every move. Otherwise they wouldn't manage to be ready for opening night.

"Besides, he never showed any artistic sensibility. How can he be expected to mend his ways now?" Danilo said, aggrieved. Polidoro had set aside the back room on the second floor as the actor's quarters, and cast sullen and indifferent looks his way.

Balinho burst into the room. His forwardness, which Danilo had never managed to imitate, even onstage, displeased the prince. Balinho was more of an actor than he was.

"Trindade is divided into two groups," Balinho blurted out. "The first defends Caetana and is readying its clothes, its jewels, and its emotions for the performance. The other one is of recent formation. It's pulling for Dona Dodô and is sharpening its fingernails with pumice stone. This lady, you see, was informed by her own daughter, after the unveiling of the bust of Seu Joaquim, that Caetana was back in town and installed in the Palace. It was a hard job getting the woman to contain her anger. She wanted to camp on the doorstep of the hotel that very minute, since she had sworn to Polidoro that she would never enter the Palace. In order to avoid the scandal of seeing Dodô screaming at the door, her son-in-law convinced her that, if she took into account the distance between the street and the fifth floor, Caetana might well believe her insults were a love serenade."

Balinho took on an even healthier color every time he managed to make life intriguing for Caetana. He wanted to keep her nerves as tense as the strings of a wet, lonely violin. When the fruits of the actress's soul proved to be bitter, he hurriedly plunged them into a tubful of scalding-hot water, to force them to ripen. As a reward, Caetana warned him against the cunning of others, whose aim was to cheat artists.

At the same time, she condemned Danilo's vengeful impulses toward Balinho, whose origin lay in a daily routine that fed on the escape that his art afforded him. But if the truth were told, her vanity as an actress was nurtured by the quarrels between the two of them, both seeking to win her heart.

"We'd better shut ourselves up here on the fifth floor till the end of that squabble. Have you ever thought what would happen if Dona Dodô decided to imitate that foreign woman?" Balinho hesitated but couldn't manage to hit on her name. "The one that rode through the whole town on a horse, without a stitch of clothes on, and only her long hair covering her privates. Polidoro might even accuse us of causing that scandal."

Caetana was not intimidated. Her circle of petty enemies strengthened her will. She foresaw with complete conviction a brilliant performance at the Iris, with Dodô in the audience, in despair at the public's appreciation, her own husband with his eyes shining, seduced by Caetana's art.

"An actress like Caetana doesn't deserve to suffer the burden of such iniquities," Balinho concluded.

Danilo was hungry, and always went for his meals to the coffee shop on the corner, where Polidoro had left orders that he didn't have to pay the check. But as they were about to leave the living room, he halted in his tracks.

"That youngster doesn't understand anything about life," he retorted.

Busy cleaning her fingernails, Caetana took in Danilo's contradictory impulses, wanting on the one hand to satisfy his hunger, and on the other to indulge in oratory.

He went on and on. His melancholy voice heightened the effect of his threadbare clothes.

"The only thing that fritters life away is time, the accursed passage of the days. What difference does it make if we stay indoors or out? No matter what we do, we're doomed to grow older."

Showing unexpected independence, he refused the glass of beer brought by Balinho.

Her mind apparently far removed from the dispute, Caetana withdrew to the easy chair. This unfriendly nucleus was all the family she had left now. On the one hand, Balinho, screening her eyes. On the other, Danilo, the prince in rags, whose unhappy temperament Uncle Vespasiano had condemned.

"All I know is that art is a sorceress who installs herself inside the mouth of a singer or an actress," Caetana finally said.

She contemplated one of the photographs of Callas on the wall, which she had pinned to a board varnished by Balinho so as to assure the diva the homage she deserved. To him, the Greek woman was a witch—the only one left from the Middle Ages, and the only one that the Church and its following of fat bourgeois had not managed to burn at the stake in the public square. But if she lived in Trindade, within Dodô's reach, she would surely be sacrificed. Brazil was not ready to be moved by Callas.

"Sometimes I wonder whether it wouldn't be worthwhile to shut oneself up in a convent on the day Callas stops singing."

She had always heard it said that machines were worth owning for their immediate usefulness and for the ability possessed by many of them to shorten the process of reasoning. She, however, was seeking not an elaborate system of logic, but simply the illusion that certain townspeople of Trindade would give her a stamp of approval equal to her fame.

The entire wall next to the chest of drawers was covered with photographs of Callas. By accumulating so many frustrations, which increased as she stood before the photos, she continued each day to dissolve any nodule of love that might arise out of her anguished female nature.

Balinho closed the door behind Danilo. Alone with Caetana, he was afraid he would never drive away the black clouds that hovered over her. Especially when, with her long-standing habit of cutting other people's phrases short, the actress demanded that he be brief. Sentiments could well be sliced right through the middle without anybody's noticing that they were missing.

When she fell into a fury, the three moles on Caetana's neck took on a noticeable color. Three points of light in a probable constellation extending down to her pubis. Balinho had chanced to glimpse Polidoro's embarrassment as the latter was contemplating the signs emerging from the woman's low-cut negligee. Enveloped in that sphere of desire, he longed to change places with Polidoro, and from that precious angle recall the kisses that the cattle baron had surely bestowed on the mysterious chestnut-colored moles.

Her heart touched once again by the youth, Caetana forgot Callas's perfection.

"Some day you're going to bury me in this country. Unless you escape first, carried away by a lecherous passion. In that case, I'll forgive you. It's always indecent to deprive oneself of certain experiences. It's better to open the floodgate of instinct once and for all, and drain it of the water of an accursed love, rather than continue to idealize the lover's dung."

Her feelings very often oscillated from one extreme to the other. They alternately made the room stifling hot and freezing cold, a sign that he should leave it. Balinho was just going out when Caetana stopped him.

"Do you know what I want at my funeral? For people to say that I didn't deserve to die. How will a show go on without the actress? How does one get one's money back for a performance that still isn't over?"

Kneeling by the Victrola, Balinho chose a single aria from *La Bohème* to raise her spirits.

"Unlike Mimi's, these hands of mine are never cold." Caetana stroked them, without any sign of emotion. "Just my heart."

They heard a noise at the door—an intruder who disturbed an almost conjugal equilibrium between Caetana and Balinho.

"If it's Polidoro, let him in."

Quickly choosing a rhinestone brooch that clashed with the overall Oriental effect, she hurriedly closed the low-cut neckline of her negligee.

The cattle baron gave her hand a deliberately lingering kiss. His lips nearly licked the joints of her fingers. The illusion of perfume from the Far East intoxicated him. He no longer knew what course to follow.

Caetana withdrew her hand, the object of his insane desire. With an impulsive gesture, she shut her body up inside an imaginary ark, depriving Polidoro of sensations that he alone fed on. She rejected his languid look. She would not be a partner to a bacchanal brought on by overworking a memory reduced to tatters. At each visit, Polidoro showed less fear of opening the veins of his love, from which he allowed to flow the black and execrable slaver that smeared their bodies.

Before Polidoro could launch other overtures that teetered on the edge of the abyss, Caetana made as if to speak. Her theatrical gestures seemed to add several inches to her height.

"Since yesterday, I've been trying to tell you that a single night of success redeems the failure of a lifetime." Following this declaration, her fiery nostrils scorched the earth and her slightly red skin. Her black negligee, despite its threadbare neckline, had just above the heart, as a sign of luxury, on ideogram whose calligraphy made it seem as though there had suddenly appeared in the living room a dragon locked in the embrace of a strange hydra. When she had bought the negligee—in Caruaru, in the state of Pernambuco—the Chinese at the open-air market, who had strayed from his tribe into that backland, had translated the elegant graphic sign: "I now live with bliss."

Disillusioned yet again, since he craved only to drag Caetana to bed with him, Polidoro discovered that he was part of a conspiracy that already involved half of Trindade. A political movement was taking place among the townspeople that had managed to bring together those who up until then had dreamed in vain, and who, overcome by charitable hope, were allowing any sort of dream to prosper. These dauntless sun worshipers paraded jauntily through the streets as though they were wearing suits and uniforms embroidered with silver threads.

The iron spring poking out of the easy chair hurt Polidoro's backside. From that vantage he observed the whiteness and the opulence of Caetana's breasts, which in the past, when they leapt from his hands in one harmonious bound, were the most beautiful ones in Brazil. This distinction had never been taken away from her. In Latin America, perhaps only Cuban women, about whom he had heard favorable reports, might contend for the same honor.

As he was sixty, he no longer hoped that his penis, brought to erection by the temptation of secrecy and forbidden loves, would behave magnificently. But, just as Caetana was staking her life on a night of glory, he was wagering his on a single fuck that would offer him the same storms and earthquakes as nature. Surely, approaching the gods and fornicating under their inspiration would bring forgiveness for part of the failure that was approaching. He was already leaking sperm with an inexpressive odor. In short, in its distress, his member would struggle like an octopus at the height of summer on the sands of the Brazilian shore, to which it had been transported against its will.

Beneath Polidoro's gaze, Caetana was opening and closing drawers. In an impulse to put things in order, she meanwhile concentrated on the off-key flats and wild falsettos coming out of Uncle Vespasiano's Victrola. Reality, faced with the apparent threat of a plague of locusts, seemed to dissolve at the sound of the music. Docility succeeded displeasure. She seemed completely engrossed, fascinated by the spell of the voices recorded on the single disk.

The volume of the music aroused Polidoro. His hand brushed his trouser fly. He seemed ready to pull out his stiff member and brandish it, proclaiming: Have you perhaps forgotten that we broke apart at least two beds together?

"Aren't you going to offer me a cognac?" His lugubrious voice was a substitute for the acts of his imagination gone mad.

Caetana's hips undulated slightly. The heat and the fullness of that flesh reached him. Excited by the backside that once upon a time had earned enraptured demonstrations of his passion, he crossed his legs, in an effort to get the better of his desire. Caetana would reject impulsive attitudes. She stubbornly ignored the fact that for more than three thousand years a band of desperadoes had longed for potions that would regenerate their genitals, which had been drained dry, and would prolong the urgings of sexual pleasure. In search of these aphrodisiacs, they dug underneath roots, without the least fear of snakes, scorpions, lizards, and other dismal swamp-dwelling creatures. In anticipation of the swift courser of sensuous pleasure, they sprinkled their soup and their goblets of red wine with sparkling minerals. All with the aim of attaining a spasm that, born along with man, occupied his dreams until the very last moment before death. Illusions of love for which they all fought, striving to reproduce in their hearts thousands of times the cloudy crystal of desire.

He drank down the cognac in one swallow, wanting to erase the turbulent vision of Caetana and himself in bed when they first knew each other. Self-conscious, their bodies naked, dramatically embarrassed. Polidoro held out his glass to her for another drink. Those beings, deeply distressed back then, had dreamed of the successful maneuvers that would assure love's ecstasy. Above all the erect rod, a sordid obelisk in the service of the glories of war.

"The rest is dried sperm, Virgílio. It goes straight into your undershorts and the washtub," he had confessed to the professor in the Palace bar—an outpouring of feeling made in the hope that Virgílio, shocked by his crudeness, would swiftly produce a more lyrical version of the purpose of sex.

Caetana's negligee reminded him of a Japanese, at one time a day laborer in Trindade and now a tradesman in the Liberdade quarter of Saõ Paulo. Some two years before, he had sent Polidoro a pomade that had had a surprising effect. It was made of ginseng root, blue Spanish fly, tiger balm, the testicle of a monkey, and the sex organs of Tartar stud horses. He had had it brought by boat to the port of Santos, and forwarded it to Polidoro with the promise that it would bring a dying man back to life.

Caetana reproved him for drinking. It was only a few days now before the performance. With all his follies he wasn't going to be the one to rob them of their illusion of glory.

"I've suffered the torment of failure during all these years. My one passion now is success, even if it lasts only five minutes."

"Do you mean to say you've lost your sexual desire? You don't want even me?"

It was hard to believe that Caetana, so ardent in the old days, had turned into a sculpture, insensitive to the tongue that, on licking her hidden recesses, had introduced her to love.

"I don't owe you any explanations, Polidoro." As she stood there her breasts quivered with indignation. She threatened to leave him all by himself in the living room.

Polidoro trembled before the primordial source of his desire. He enveloped her in a daring embrace. Attuned to a chaotic musical scale, his feelings gasped for breath.

"Control yourself or I'll call Balinho," she said, dismissing his overture in a determined voice.

"Damned guttersnipe. Why doesn't he shine my shoes instead of blackening my nightmares?" Polidoro was busy heaping insults on the youth when he noted Caetana's cold, rigid bearing, a warning that he had not penetrated her heart. She had put a padlock and a key on it.

"Cognac doesn't agree with me," he tried to temporize. "I'm worn out. The preparations for the performance take all my time. I even missed the unveiling of my father's statue. He must be furious with me. I feel old age knocking at my door. I'm afraid my body is going to die before my heart does. And what need will I have then to resort to those confounded mandrake-root pastes, dried-tumblebug infusions, or dung-beetle tea?"

Polidoro's pleas, piled up in front of her, were an attempt to revive the passion that in the past had left residues, hairs, saliva, and other juices on the mattress that Virgílio had brought back up to the fifth floor.

Caetana's gaze was a relief to him. Since they were partners in the adventure of reviving the past, she had avoided offending him. Now that her arrogance had given way to a gentle smile, she disarmed Polidoro, who considered that he had been pardoned. To dissuade him, nonetheless, from entertaining any hopes, she contemplated the gallery of photos of Callas. Hammering the nails in, Balinho had damaged two frames around the photographs and the newspaper clippings.

One of the pictures in particular entranced her. Overcome by a rare sadness, the diva seemed to be reconciling herself to art at the cost of her own life. If she wished to join the ranks of the gods of her Greek race and become one of them, they demanded of her the sacrifice of happiness. There before Caetana then was the bitter and lonely legend. Callas's hair was caught up in a topknot, a coiffure that Caetana sometimes imitated, and from her neck hung a gold necklace loaded with gewgaws difficult to make out in detail, aside from the cross of the Orthodox Church.

With the universe to which she had never had access facing her, Caetana forgot the harsh life that fate and Uncle Vespasiano had forced on her, obliging her to drag herself all over Brazil, without the reward of ever stepping out onto a stage such as that of the Municipal Theater in Rio de Janeiro, which, as it happened, she had never even been inside.

Suddenly, her mind having wandered far afield from Polidoro, she had the illusion that life could still be changed for the better. It was possible for her to feel glory in the palm of her hand, the skin of which, like an apple, she would polish on the worn velvet bodice of a European peasant lass. Beneath the spell of this fantasy, she rubbed her hands together. She would soon be making her debut in Trindade and be twenty years old once more.

Polidoro recovered his critical acumen. As for Caetana, instead of throwing herself into his arms, after his vehement defense of the human body, she applied her dream to foreigners, who had always exploited the riches of Brazil.

"Who was that Callas you've enthroned on your wall like a saint?"

Polidoro's barbed remark poisoned her mind. Impelled by a collectivist spirit, Caetana extricated herself from the sphere of art to confront the capitalist for whom money was the one parameter.

"Hold your tongue, Polidoro. Whenever you speak of Callas, use liturgical language, as though you were in church."

At her brusque gesture, the brooch fastening the neckline of her negligee gave way. She did not notice the cleft between her breasts, exposed to Polidoro's cupidity. She went on, more furious than ever.

"She was the only one permitted by the gods to visit their temples without a veil and wearing high-heeled shoes. She could have been a priestess and still not owed them any favors. There has never been another voice like hers. Or could it be that you wish to prove me wrong?"

Fascinated by the view before his eyes, which included Caetana's breasts and the embroidered ideogram, Polidoro forgot what the argument was about. The brushstrokes spread across her bosom were proof that the woman was right. They granted him permission to advance through the front gates, which would lead to her pink nipples.

Overcome by these enchantments, he tried to bribe her. To

touch the heartstring that would make her so sensitive she would allow him to share the intimacies of her body. His memory was studded with irremovable delights.

"When will the great gala performance be?"

Unlike Dodô, who wore house slippers firmly attached to her feet in the comfort of her own home, Caetana's silver-coated sandals seemed to come loose at each pace that, visibly nervous, she took in the living room.

She halted in front of the window, paying no attention to Riche's meows and Polidoro's effort to seduce her. Through the dusty windowpane, life was dim when it reached her. Her mind seemed far away, ready to board the train that would take her to some distant place. Another city, which would automatically erase Trindade from her memory.

"Have you forgotten I'm here?" he shouted disapprovingly.

Caetana came away from the window. She looked around the living room. Balinho had promised to bring a fruit salad.

"What is it you want?"

Polidoro tried to thrust his pelvis at her, the aggressive, protuberant area that set his body and soul on fire, his flesh seasoned with salt and sugar in excessive quantities. Nobody in fact knew how to administer doses of the two in well-balanced proportions and thereby awaken the compassion of others, in his case Caetana's especially.

"On exactly what day will the triumph take place?" he asked gently, despite the woman's disconcerting silence.

"On Saturday, June 20."

Polidoro's sudden starts of surprise did not impress her. In her eyes, the human body no longer deserved the same pity. And desire, which in the past had scourged her flesh with its whiplash, seemed like the stub of a candle with a wet wick.

"On the eve of Brazil's victory. This time we'll bring the Cup home," she said dreamily.

She was confident of a victory that people would begin celebrating the night before. Brazilian memory, steeped in cane brandy, semen, and blood would show that it was also inclined to pity. Benevolent and vulnerable, it would help the men of Trindade to remember that Caetana, twenty years earlier, had given them the gift of hope and the power of desire.

"What do you expect from those loutish he-men?" Polidoro broke in, irritated.

"Men are no longer of any use to me. All I ask of them is applause and oblivion."

The words did not ease his pain. Yet to his surprise, today's jealousies did not set the powder magazine of his strange feelings on fire. It was as though love had made his emotions few and far between. Even if she wanted him in bed, they would be quick visits. For years he had borne in his body, like a sign of punishment, the marks of the suffering he had experienced. The fever of passion, which had made him imagine himself in swamps where life was perpetuated through the outcries of his panicked chest, no longer attacked him. Death had become his mistress. He shared with her the enraptured delirium of love and fear.

He toned down his pessimism, trusting that there existed some corner free of guilt and persecution, far from Dodô, who burst into his life slamming doors, shattering others' eardrums.

"I'll give you five minutes to confess to your feelings. Then we'll go to bed together," he said.

Caetana spent a long time deciding, as though it would take her a whole lifetime. Trapped by a desire commingled with injured pride and the pleasure of reprisals, Polidoro turned his back on her, to put a damper on the fervor of his emotions. He suspected that love was also symphonic material, lending itself to capturing and reproducing any and every sort of sound.

"Speak up, Caetana!" Not knowing what else to say, he pointed to the sofa, chosen all of a sudden as the scene for repeating their long-ago love bouts.

Caetana's eyes followed his. She had sometimes sat her posterior down on the faded blue upholstery of the sofa. Yet it had never been the setting of fiascos or ecstasies. She had always abhorred making love outside of bed, away from the rustle of clean sheets.

Caetana gave no sign of remembering the cries of love that they had exchanged in the bed in the adjoining room.

"Haven't you noticed yet that it's the same bed? Only the sheets have been changed."

The woman's gelatinous gaze annoyed him. Her resoluteness, on the other hand, forced him to admit that he in turn had forgotten essential details of Caetana's anatomy. Though he tried desperately, certain attributes indispensable to the understanding of a body escaped him. He still retained a vivid memory—that much was certain—of the fever concentrated in his lower belly, which upset him—a heat that consumed him as he stroked her with his callused hands.

Riche's instinct could foretell Caetana's torment. The little warm snow-white creature prowled around the woman, displaying the sensuality of his contortionist species.

Caetana paced up and down the living room. She had before her a fat and expectant adversary. Every time she changed direction, under the illusion that she was performing onstage, she caught up the train of her negligee a second before the curtain opened and the audience burst into applause.

"Perhaps you've forgotten the honor card in the spade suit, your pledged word? Do you think you're through with me fair and square just because of the Iris Theater?" she said, draining to the last drop the minutes she had granted him.

Polidoro pushed the glass away. He did not want to overstep any bounds. The jealousy that prowls about tormented souls weakens them in the end.

"For twenty years, I've had my ears stopped up with cotton. No siren has seduced me with her song. But don't get the idea that lots of them haven't tried."

His strategy was aimed at threatening her with the loss of him, drowning her soul in a sense of insecurity. He was feeling cheered at the prospect of reeling off a list of his amorous exploits when the door opened. Without offering his apologies, Balinho came in, twirling the keys in his fingers.

"Who can equal Caetana?" he proceeded to say, in his daily role of relieving her of her resentment.

Polidoro cursed him under his breath. Every time he'd tried to chase Balinho out of the room, he'd failed miserably. He asked him for wine, to send him a long way away, down to the hotel kitchen, but Balinho brought the bottle and the corkscrew out of the liquor cabinet right there in the living room. "If Brazil prized its artists, it would give Caetana a standing ovation." His solemn tone made him seem older. He stroked the first wisps of beard that had appeared on his face.

Polidoro couldn't stand sycophants. He preferred to take his leave.

"Tonight, at midnight, we'll be waiting for you at the Iris. As Cinderella hurriedly descends the staircase of the palace, I promise that she'll be welcomed with flowers, *guaraná* juice, and appetizers. Can we count on you?" Polidoro asked.

Caetana accompanied him to the door. In a swift attack of vertigo, she dreamed that she had signed a contract in gold lettering, each clause of which guaranteed her fame and illusion in close embrace.

"I'll come this time. It's only a few days till opening night," she answered.

With a nod of her head she approved Polidoro's professional rectitude. At the moment, she had nothing to criticize him for.

CAETANA was right. The performance at the Iris Theater that marked her return to Trindade should be on the night before the Sunday afternoon when the Brazilian soccer team would become, in Mexico City, the third-time winner of the world championship.

Polidoro put Virgílio in charge. Because they lacked a director, he would assume that function, whose objective is to lend life to theatrical spectacles.

Venieris, in a senseless gesture, rebelled against the professor. He did not regard Virgílio as qualified for a job that demanded artistic talent. His knowledge of dates and of the names of kings in strict chronological order did not give him the skills to take charge of the imaginary world of actors.

"We're like sparrows, Polidoro. We come and go with summertime. Winter freezes our wings," Venieris said as he was painting various scenes, especially doors and a staircase, on cloth panels set up for that purpose. The façade of the Iris, overlooking a vacant lot, would be adorned with these panels. The spectators in front of them would believe in the realism of the world of illusions, despite the breeze that might occasionally blow the panels about.

"Where shall I paint the main door?"

Venieris's question, apparently addressed to everyone, was in fact directed to Virgílio, so that he'd come to his rescue.

The professor had been the first to tell him of a European aesthetic movement that was enthusiastic about pastiche as a way of furthering the inventive vein of artists who were unsure of themselves, who found themselves incapable of opening up original paths in art on their own.

"The more such artists add to what already exists, the more people there will be who identify with their art. Invention isn't the right way. It comes to be a danger," Virgílio said emphatically. "Look at Van Gogh, for instance. In a fit of delirium, he cut off his own ear in front of a broken mirror!"

In the face of Virgílio's refusal to help him, so as not to lend his backing to what might turn out to be an artistic disaster, Venieris resorted to the memory of his ancestors. "I'll decorate the Iris with those Greek ghosts. After all, a high content of sugar and hope flows in my blood."

"Very well," Virgílio said hastily. "Now that you've asked, I'm prepared to help you. I'm still a professor."

He took a close look at the panels, which seemed solid and blended in with the wall. They did not move with the breeze coming in through the swinging doors, which were permanently rusted open.

"An entrance should always be imposing. As though it were the gate of paradise. Everything here is false, but of good quality. We must encourage dreams and banish unbelievers, who refuse to see beyond what we are going to show the audience," Virgílio said with satisfaction.

Gioconda flitted about excitedly, threatening to crash into the windowpane like an insect.

"Be careful!" Virgílio grabbed her by the arm. "The paint isn't dry yet."

Gioconda's instinct was out of control. With the Three Graces at her heels, she kept bumping into things. The accumulation of so many disasters gave her the feeling of already living some dramatic role that Caetana had not yet assigned her.

"What are we doing here, shut up in the Iris, sleeping, eating, doing gymnastics? All for the sake of art? But who is it I'm going to bring to life?" she complained in a loud voice.

By common accord, they had agreed to close the doors of Estação so that they could focus all their efforts on the artistic vigil at the Iris. As a result of this decision, Gioconda had trouble sleeping, communicating her insomnia to the Three Graces, although they remained unbending when it came to the customers who demanded their return to the brothel, whoever promised to pay them double for their services if they would come back.

"No fucking. We're living in the service of art now. Isn't it true that artists sacrifice even their very last drop of blood just to redeem human grandeur? Go to hell!" Diana pontificated on behalf of the others.

Palmira was waiting for a role to be assigned her, making patient notes in a schoolchild's composition book, which she shut whenever a snooper approached. "They're aphorisms of no importance, for my own edification. I've never felt so deeply moved. I now understand why artists are absent-minded and forget to pay their debts."

Gioconda asked them to be humble. She herself took charge of sweeping out the movie house converted into a theater. Diligently, she eliminated the dust accumulated underneath the seats. This aim of perfect cleanliness made it easier for her to concentrate on some unforeseeable character, of the sort fated to awaken impossible dreams in that character's interpreter.

"How hard it is to be an actress!" she protested, finding it hard to bear up under the weight of so much responsibility.

Her outburst attracted the attention of the others. Surrounded by the group, Gioconda apologized. She had always been a distinguished unknown. She needed to learn how to undertake the task of being famous. Above all, to erase from her memory her career as a whore, to suppress the gesture of lifting, before strangers, her hand to the breast, where a heart lay in tatters.

The sleepless nights spent in the Iris exhausted them. Gioconda demanded a leader. The presence, in short, of Caetana, who never showed her face, while Polidoro, with all his comings and goings between the theater, his own house, and the Palace Hotel, wore out the soles of his shoes.

Gioconda's criticisms immediately fell on fertile soil. Virgílio feared that the flock would scatter, at the risk of never getting back together. "Did you want an easy life? Well, I'd like you to know that nobody here is permitted to disrespect the other artists, to sow discord, merely because he or she has a delicate soul."

With conviction, the professor assured them that the structures of art rested on a boundless fidelity to any reality that the artist might choose to defend. Hence, some doubts inherent in the text itself served to enrich it, but never to narrow the margin of dreams or reduce the correlation with reality.

The idleness fostered debates, rallied the group around an ardent ideal. Venieris was an example, carefully cleaning his brushes. He went from one color to another with uncertainty in his heart. When he tried to mix the pigments to produce a dark brown, meant for the rotunda of a church, a color he had decided on that very day, the hue came out a sunny yellow, the exact opposite of the somber tone he was after. Absorbed in this task, he failed to notice that the hairs of his heavy paintbrush were falling out, as from a scalp suffering from the effects of seborrhea.

"I object whenever I want to," Gioconda said to the historian, protesting against his despotism. "Don't think you're an artist, with the right to order me around. Though you've had the name of a poet all your life, you've never composed a sonnet."

Her long skirt made her look like a gypsy. She twirled round and round so that they could see her charms, almost invisible in the badly lighted theater.

"Yet the priest who baptized me was opposed to my being given the name of the poet. He asked the family to give up the idea, but my father stood his ground," Virgílio replied.

His father had been an elementary-school instructor too, hoping that his son, the bearer of a name such as that, would go to Paris to study some day.

"And he ended up in Trindade," Sebastiana broke in with unpremeditated aggressiveness. She was forgetting that when Virgílio frequented her bed he left with her his semen and fragments of history, particularly that of Pedro I, the violator of Brazilian sexual mores.

"Thanks to Trindade, I met you," he gallantly replied, expecting to make her feel remorseful: Sebastiana was an easy prey to sentiments engendered in the dark or by candlelight. "Homer's blindness was worse than being a poet of my sort. Instead of seeing life beneath the sun's benedictions, that poor Greek lived amid shadows. He never handled a document the way I have. That's why he invented falsehoods in return for a mess of pottage."

Ashamed of having hurt the feelings of her best customer, Sebastiana remembered what he had done for her. He had always paid her the money she asked him for without protest, even when his virile member failed him. Instead of weeping like the others, Virgílio gave her presents the following week. So many that a line of little elephants formed on the shelf of her room, with their backsides toward the door for good luck. All acquired for the same reason.

Palmira, whose heart was touched by Sebastiana's catastrophes and her missing teeth, lowered her voice. "May I bring you some coffee? Or anything else you might need?" she said to Sebastiana in an almost amorous whisper.

Virgílio thrust out his chest, For the first time, he felt the pleasure of having a woman submit to his will in front of everyone. His body was warmed by an abundant thermic reflex. He understood the brutality practiced by certain men on women, as a means of attaining that sort of pleasure. His mouth had never filled with saliva in bed, with the woman underneath his body subject to his designs on her, only because up until now he had lacked the certainty that such a sexual practice could also become an implacable instrument of power.

By a stroke of luck, and thanks to Sebastiana, light had been shed on that obscure feeling. Prepared to reward her for the discovery, he exempted her from domestic duties. "Save your strength for the show, Sebastiana. In your capacity as an actress, you are now destined for noble tasks."

Paying no attention to the tiff between the lovers, Gioconda was keeping watch at the door. Polidoro had promised to bring her news of Caetana. The actress could not allow such an indefinite situation to drag on any longer. Nobody even knew the title of the play, or whether they would have to sing, dance, or just play-act.

Diana too rebelled against the fact that time was running out, arousing in her a feeling of uselessness, the insecurity of not knowing if the following day would be rewarded by an empty theater.

"What am I doing here at this hour of the night? I'm getting poorer by the day. Who's going to pay my bills?"

Her dejection led Diana to trace broad movements in space. As she walked across the stage, the boards creaked, as though the floor had never been reinforced with solid-headed nails.

Virgílio came up onto the stage, determined to head in the right direction this tribe on the point of succumbing to discouragement.

"Up until now, I've been discreet. I didn't want to brag in front of all of you. But I can't hold back the truth any longer. Just look where I've been sleeping for the last few nights."

He spread out on the stage a filthy tarpaulin he'd been using as a bed. The dust he raised made him sneeze.

The melodramatic gesture not only thrilled the small audience, but had the effect of placating everyone. They were all able to understand the reasons that obliged Polidoro to be away from the theater. Given his eagerness to be young again, to recover the same frame of mind as in the days of his love for Caetana, it was only right that he should leave them by themselves, in a universe devoid of hot food and affection.

Diana lit a cigarette, exhaling the smoke in Venieris's direction; she felt strangely attracted to the Greek. He had boarded the boat in Piraeus, a port famous for the whores who, with the sea as the horizon before them, did not resign themselves to the limits of terra firma.

Far from exciting him, vulgarity annoyed Venieris. But, appeased by his artistic concerns, he did not react. He would not permit himself to fall back into his old habits. The truth was that the tiny shop that had previously been his home had become too small for his present perspectives. On the other hand, when he looked at Diana, he felt his lack of the comfort of a woman's body. On winter nights, it gave more warmth than a bowl of thick soup or a cup of steaming-hot tea.

"Do any of you want to suggest something for me to paint?" the Greek asked, sensing that the invitation, in fact addressed to Diana, risked arousing an amorous expectation that would become confused with the demands of creation.

Elusive overtures, capable of giving rise to general misunderstandings, always attracted Diana. She abhorred a man with a restless penis, in a hurry to enter her vagina merely out of the fear of losing his erection. In those days in particular, she was gradually learning the value of ambiguity, which consisted in attributing to one's fellow human what was vaguely located in one's own heart.

Bewildered by events, nonetheless, she emphatically proclaimed in Venieris's presence her status as an artist. As proof of her statement, she began to tap-dance, even though her body had difficulty keeping step, and notes in the wrong rhythm emerged from her chest.

"I need to lose weight," she remarked bitterly.

"We'll never get as far as the performance if we go on like this," Gioconda warned, fearing that so many protests would stifle the unusual amorous feeling that had now spread through her whole body.

Diana's personality, continually overshadowed by Gioconda, reacted with hauteur, balking against being shut up in the corral toward which she had been prodded since she had been a little girl. Her face took on an unexpected freshness. "Before they step out onstage, singers too invoke the saints. Because I had my doubts, I gargled with lemon juice, salt, and hot water. Salt is miraculous; it even cures a voice as cracked as a kingfisher's. The best cure, though, comes from talent and luck."

The happy atmosphere that had suddenly settled over the Iris threatened to dissipate the effects engendered by art. It was a well-known fact that it is not possible to be happy and to conjugate the verb "create" at the same time. Such a prediction frightened Diana. Her body felt torn in two. The blood of one part irrigated illusion; the other distilled the lonely taste of gall.

"What use is it to have a clear soprano voice if we don't know how to sing! We don't have scores, musical instruments, or texts to read. We can just barely count on having a theater," Diana perorated, placing herself at the forefront of a recently initiated rebellion.

Concentrating on Diana's pessimistic speech, which brought them back to reality, they had not seen Polidoro come in, accompanied by Ernesto.

"That's enough of all this wailing. It sounds like what goes on at that wall in Jerusalem," he said, and called them together immediately for the habitual inspection. "What's happened in my absence?"

He had designated Ernesto for the task of supervising the harmonious cast that he had left behind when he went off to the Palace.

Ernesto was ill-at-ease. He was against humiliating artists at the height of their creative powers, or passing judgment on acts of insubordination. Nothing managed to divert him from his occupation as a pharmacist.

"It's better for Caetana to criticize these people. Or tell them that they have neither talent nor discipline." He voiced his opinion warily, not wanting to offend Polidoro.

Gioconda invaded the stage, beside herself. She almost tripped on the stairway. Her hair was disheveled.

"When is Caetana coming?"

"She'll come one minute before or one minute after midnight."

Polidoro examined the objects that Virgílio had brought from his house to be used to decorate the pieces of furniture that made up the stage set. They were suitable for drama—tragedy or comedy, depending on what Caetana wished to represent. Life, heated up in the theater, served the artistic ideals of the collectivity.

Amid a flurry of intent gestures, Polidoro displayed a certain indifference. Loving as he did an unapproachable woman, he might lose her, because of a feeling of resignation that he had failed to experience in the past.

He left the stage. It was just a few minutes before midnight. Caetana was about to arrive.

"Why didn't you tell us sooner?" Gioconda fretted. She could not manage to control herself in the actress's presence. Twenty years before, Caetana had filled her heart with a substance that resisted being rusted away by time.

All on edge, Gioconda resorted to the Byzantine mirror. The Three Graces accompanied her, vying with one another to see the reflection of their respective faces on the surface of the glass.

"How ugly I am!" Sebastiana concluded, devastated.

"It's too late to complain," Diana put in. "The best thing to do is to make a style out of one's ugliness. Change character. That way, everybody will end up thinking you're good-looking."

"Do you realize what you're saying, Diana?" Venieris asked, as he tried to locate his own face in a corner of the mirror not yet occupied by anyone. "It's what goes by the name of aesthetics. Isn't that so, Virgílio? Enjoying what one invents without knowing the reason why?"

His attention concentrated on the clock, Virgílio did not answer. It would soon strike midnight.

"Through what door will Caetana enter?" Virgílio asked Polidoro.

"There aren't all that many doors," Polidoro answered gruffly.

Ernesto was passing around the appetizers that had been on

the table. The bottles of *guaraná*, in a bucket filled with chunks of ice wrapped in newspaper, were staying nicely chilled.

"What we've no lack of here is doors. We even have fake ones," Venieris protested. He had devoted all his powers of invention to the art of visual deception—making others believe in the existence of whole cities planned in detail by the imagination. Moreover, in order to confirm his thesis of illusion and strengthen it at the same time, he had brought from home the previously mentioned Byzantine mirror and a screen that had four panels, all of them pasted over with old posters on remote Greek themes.

"And what if Caetana doesn't come, just to make us suffer?" Gioconda fretted.

She contemplated herself in the mirror, afraid of losing hope, of returning to the brothel with a wounded soul that would also have an effect on the Three Graces, who were fatter now from having eaten so many sandwiches.

"What loneliness! God help us," she said in a low whisper so they wouldn't hear her.

Diana enveloped her in an unexpected embrace, hugging Gioconda so tightly it was as if she were trying to keep her from seeing the triumphal entry of Caetana into the Iris.

The loving gesture, so many years in coming, moved Gioconda. Perhaps there would still be time in the future to enjoy a game full of caresses and warm puffs of breath.

On hearing noises from the outside, Gioconda pushed Diana away. Diana, however, pulled her back to her tiny breasts, smiling at the vainglorious humanity that had rushed toward Caetana, who had just come in.

The perfume that engulfed everyone's nostrils seemed to be of animal origin, a beast of exotic beauty, the apocalyptic vision of each member of the group.

"Silence!" Virgílio exclaimed, taking careful note of the scene.

Wrenched from his very guts, the historian's outcry impelled Diana to open her arms. Almost suffocated, her gaze blurred, Gioconda could only half see. Diana hid Caetana, escorted by Balinho and Prince Danilo, from her view.

Balinho bore a lighted torch in his hand. Listening closely for

Caetana's first words, he looked like a sort of Nebuchadnezzar who, in stupefaction, watched the anonymous, ownerless hand engraving the scale and other signs on the wall of his life.

It was past midnight. Danilo and Balinho did not bother to apologize. Art did not require good manners. Besides, they would not allow themselves to be ruled by the petty reality of Trindade, a backwoods town of unsophisticated rural habits. Polidoro himself realized that all of them lacked urbanity. He often sighed at Dodô's customary way of settling herself in a chair on the sidewalk just to watch the people passing by.

"Don't disgrace me, Dodô! Take that chair off the sidewalk!"

Her answer was always the same: "Since when do I need to act as though Trindade were a big city? The only thing I see from here are old jalopies, toothless halfbreed farmhands and dung from cows that are left to wander about on the loose. Incidentally, a lot of those cows belong to us."

Polidoro offered Caetana his arm. She refused to take it, concentrating on keeping her balance atop her buskins, which she had kept in reserve for this night. She felt she was bringing to life a character whose name now escaped her. Nor did she want to imitate Callas, with those black platform shoes that looked as if they had come from Greece—from Mycenae or from Agamemnon's fiery memory! Fat and regal, she had stolen from Callas, it was true, Tosca's bright-red cape. As for her tiara, perched on her topknot, it gleamed with rhinestones.

"May I escort you to the stage?" Virgílio stepped forward, disregarding Polidoro. He acted like a dauntless impresario who had engaged Caetana despite her capricious temperament.

Caetana leaned on him for support without hesitating. The thought came to her for a moment that the human arm, like a marble pillar, could withstand any calamity. Virgílio, for his part, accustomed to struggle with documents, letters, pages of books, and a Sebastiana who did not subject him to excessively agile and merciless acts, could not bear up under the actress's weight. Threatened with the prospect of falling on the floor at any moment, he looked around for a man near him to take his place.

Ernesto, putting down the tray of appetizers in alarm, came to his rescue. Noticing the swift substitution of a new partner, Caetana looked at them scornfully.

"Either there are no real men left in Trindade, or there are none left anywhere in the world!" She headed for the stage by herself. "My fan," she requested.

Danilo opened the pouch of accessories. Inside it were loudly jingling trinkets.

"How hot it is in here!" she said. "It's the scorching heat of hell I needed."

Her technique for fanning herself was excellent. Each movement of the fan swiftly revealed the courtly figures painted on it. The rapid motions kept her public from fully appreciating the Goya-like motifs.

Palmira, who had acquired in the last week a boldness that everyone had noticed, approached Caetana, fascinated by her hands. "I've always wanted to have a fan like that one. I never thought I'd see one so close up. Exotic foreign products never come to Trindade."

Caetana stopped fanning herself. With pleasure she showed Palmira the caparisoned horses painted on the fan. "It was inspired by Goya, the Spanish painter. I have a fair knowledge of the subject, since the name Caetana was given to me by the woman whose portrait he painted, first nude, then clothed. A *maja* seen from two angles. An aristocratic member of the family of the dukes of Alba, incidentally."

Venieris, bowing several times in succession, interrupted the conversation between the two of them.

"My art is at your service, my lady."

Jealous, Polidoro sent him back to his work with an incisive wave of his arm. Then he came over to Caetana. His breath enveloped the woman.

"Let's begin all over again. Otherwise we'll become the slaves of illusion."

Faced with four steps separating her from the stage, Caetana was wary. Her buskins made it difficult for her to mount them.

She was afraid she'd fall, and the grotesque was scarcely compatible with art. Seen from close up, without the magic of lighting effects, the ridiculous turned into a vulgar joke, something to be jeered at.

Virgílio urged her to go up the stairs. "Are there any of us who aren't ridiculous?" he said, as though he'd guessed what she was thinking.

She pointed to the stage, where Gioconda was walking across the creaking boards. She wished his mind would wander elsewhere. "I'm the star of the show, and I'll receive my helpers down here. It's still too early to share the stage with them."

Gioconda left the stage. She no longer recognized her friend. Like an archer, Caetana loosed arrows capable of killing other people's illusions. Gioconda was already going down the stairs when Caetana stopped her. A sudden tenderness had come over her.

"Don't feel humiliated or condemn me. The whole thing is a farce. A thorn that everyone has buried at the bottom of the garden of his or her soul."

An intense intimacy emanated from her. Her gaze guaranteed that she would still open to Gioconda, amid the ruins of the Iris, the depths of her heart.

Venieris approached the two women, who immediately fell silent. Impassioned by his own art, he showed no signs of being attracted to Caetana.

"Can anyone tell me whether metal beams existed in the last century?"

The interruption annoyed Caetana. And, as if the Greek's attitude were not enough, Virgílio himself, ever the patronizing gentleman, fought not to be outshone. "Certainly. They had everything in the last century," he said proudly.

Despite her eagerness to climb the last stairs separating her from the stage, Caetana preferred to stop and do battle with the arrogant historian.

"The drama of the twentieth century lies in its having been overdecorated. It looks like a wedding cake with too much icing and too many doves. Not to mention that boobs and braggarts proliferate at every turn. They come in bunches, like bananas. And none of them puts a stop to this business."

Virgílio was overcome with sadness. Caetana, the proud performing artist, pained him by not knowing that for years on end he had dressed in rags and known poverty, all because he had loved documents gnawed away by silverfish.

"I would like to have the floor for a few moments," he said circumspectly, seeking to get around the impasse.

"No more of that. You've already spoken up a deal during these years. You've taken unfair advantage of words in the classroom," Diana said, silencing him with clenched hands. "I'm the one who's going to speak up now. I want to know what we're going to put on. Where's the text? Where are the instruments? Outside of the performing artists—us, that is—everything we need is missing!"

Her protests did not shake Caetana's convictions.

"For the time being, we don't need anything. Perhaps the one thing I do need is a diamond solitaire, whose brilliance can be seen from a great distance."

Polidoro was indignant. "When we tread the boards, what genre will we be bringing to life? Opera, a drama, a ballet? Or will we simply stand there in silence?"

"It's going to be an opera."

"And what is an opera?" Gioconda was upset about the responsibility that was an integral part of her new job.

"A mystery. At least till the performance." Caetana drew closer to the stairway, attracted by the empty stage.

"Who's going to play the instruments?"

"Who's going to sing?"

The strident voices tumbled over each other. Standing on the first step of the stairway, Caetana was unaware of them, entirely absorbed in the notes coming from the Victrola.

"They're the cherubim and the voice of God!"

Balinho offered her his hand. He had noticed how tense her voice was. Leaning on him for support, she mounted the remaining steps. On the stage, it pleased her to be looking at them from above.

"Don't worry. We still have a few days left." Uncle Vespasiano had taken care of everything, from heaven or from hell.

Everyone crowded onto the stairway, wanting to mount the stage as quickly as possible. Nobody was willing to give up art, especially the audience's applause.

Polidoro tried to stop them. "Stay where you are. I'm the one who's going onstage. I need a pulpit."

His attitude had changed: he was in open competition with Caetana now, and no longer wanted to be a bit player with two or three lines to speak. If the illusions stemming from art had immunized Caetana's heart, preventing her from suffering the trials and tribulations of love, he too sought the same protection.

"We'll begin rehearsing tomorrow," Polidoro shouted. And, turning toward Caetana: "I'll be the prompter, and Virgílio the director. If there's no audience on the opening night, I'll fill this theater with cow dung. It's something I've got plenty of in my pastures. My soul is nothing but a zebu brought from India."

Balinho screwed up his courage. He went up onto the stage determined to confront Polidoro, who was fencing with the foil of betrayal against Caetana to make her pay for her having failed his amorous hopes.

"Where do you think you're going, you rascal?" Polidoro grabbed Balinho by the arm.

Polidoro's despotism exasperated Gioconda. "We won't put up with any more of your madness," she protested, standing close to the footlights.

The Three Graces, in stubborn defense of their respective positions, made their way ahead of the others. The tumult spread.

"You're a dictator, sir," Balinho protested, free of Polidoro's tenacious grip.

"What harm is there in being a dictator in a country that stands in need of order?"

"You're the very opposite of the gods, who preached disorder." Boldly, paying no heed to the appeals for peace and harmony being made to him by the Three Graces, Balinho challenged Polidoro.

Virgílio clung to Polidoro, as though the pair of them were lovers. He was taking shelter from the imminent storm. "Please, ladies and gentlemen. In the name of art, I propose a truce."

He paused. Paying close attention to Virgílio's speech, Polidoro made himself comfortable in the warmth of the historian's body.

"Why are we squabbling, if we live for art and art bestows its blessings on us? Furthermore, why are we cursing dictators? Getúlio Vargas was one, and the people loved him. Médici himself is applauded today, everywhere he goes. From soccer stadiums to the Jockey Club in Rio."

Virgílio held out his hand, which Balinho examined. It was delicate, and oddly hairy. In fact, Sebastiana, in the middle of their caresses, sometimes pulling on his hair, called him "my little monkey."

Suddenly, in a friendly mood, Balinho grasped Virgílio's hand firmly. He rid himself of the frog in his throat that beset him whenever something moved him.

"Don't forget that Caetana is the only artist in this house. It's thanks to her that we're treading these boards and posing as actors. People like us don't appear on the stage without the help of real performing artists. Without them, there's no show. And nothing is more dismal than an empty stage."

He offered Polidoro, at his side, a face with a lackluster expression, without emotion. He looked appreciably older.

"You may understand a great deal about cattle and land, but you don't know anything about the theater. As for Professor Virgílio, who looks after dead people and papers eaten away by silverfish, he risks going astray. The only one fated to be right on the mark is the artist. And even Virgílio couldn't say why."

"Bravo!" Diana interrupted, elated by Balinho's gift for words. "How lucky Caetana is to be assisted by this young man. Are you happy, Caetana?"

The mystery of happiness, discussed in public, revived Polidoro's spirits. Perhaps Caetana, who had made the stage an outlet for her emotions, would finally confess, before this select audience, her love for him, kept a deep secret out of modesty or even out of vengeance. The time had come to rid himself of feelings that weighed on him as though he were carrying a dead man.

"If she isn't happy, I'm here to serve her," Polidoro said, deeply moved.

His recent entry into the world of the theater had loosed him from the bonds of secrecy. Public confession, far from making him blush, brought him serenity. Life seemed more bearable to him now that all of them were sharing their anxieties and uncertainties.

Caetana behaved with deliberate solemnity. The revelation of one's feelings, without the resources of art, struck her as intolerable. Only phrases that were the handiwork of others had the ring of truth on her lips. They were in accord with the one reality that she knew. She never doubted the emotions that dead authors put in her mouth. It was through this fountain that life poured forth. On no account would she give up her art.

Scowling, Caetana fixed her gaze on the false horizon. She began to drag herself slowly across the stage on the imposing buskins. The sound of her footsteps echoed in the ears and in the dreams of the anxious flock. Balinho and Prince Danilo, as though following instructions, joined the procession, which lacked only a canopy, rosaries, and candles. The Three Graces could not hold back. Joining the others, they deprived them of the sense of spectacle they claimed as their own exclusive property. They were all following an invisible baton that was orchestrating their movements, and under all the tension they ran the risk of wilting.

"And what about happiness?" Polidoro pleaded.

His languid eyes grew blurred in the heat, whose source was Caetana. The woman's dampness, which he attributed to desire, forcefully took up lodging in his own body as well. He stepped up the pace and touched her shoulders. Caetana responded to his caress. The sequins on Tosca's cape quivered. Her distress accentuated the pearliness of her skin. Unable to bear so many discomforts at the same time, she removed her tiara. The abrupt gesture made her hair fall over her shoulders. It had a brightness that was missing in her eyes.

"Never put your hair up again," Polidoro whispered in her ear. Growing more and more daring, he opened the veins of his love before the eyes of everyone and finally allowed the black and accursed sap to flow, to refresh his hidden desire, repressed for years within his body, amid sighs, incense, and thuribles lit in honor of the martyred saints.

At these words, Gioconda's lower belly suffered a direct blow. She could not fathom what sort of sentiment it was that so precisely made her insides churn with jealousy. Especially since she did not know who was to blame, or against whom to launch her ladylike protest.

"Answer, Caetana," Gioconda said, close beside Polidoro.

Surrounded by adversaries, Caetana whirled around, waving her fan in the face of both creatures in her eagerness to cool the atmosphere and free it of passions. If they took over, the group would not reach the day of the performance alive.

"God made me of clay as a sign that I was fated to be human."

Leaving the last word hanging in the air, she ordered Balinho to bring the screen up onto the stage.

"I want boundaries between us. Since Uncle Vespasiano died, I'm a solitary performing artist."

Balinho pushed the screen onstage with Venieris's help.

"Be careful. It's a very valuable piece. I always go back to my homeland when I look at those landscapes," the latter said.

Caetana took refuge behind the screen. Out of sight of everyone, she draped the red cape over one of the wooden borders, in a slow gesture that made Polidoro tremble. She was practically stripping naked in public as part of a general rehearsal.

"Do you need any help?" Palmira asked, eager to go around to the other side.

Caetana emerged from behind the screen. Free of the cape, with the dress clinging to her body and nearly half her breasts exposed, she looked reinvigorated. She loosened the dress, a bit too tight around the waist. Only then did she turn her attention to the audience.

"Despite my hurry to be famous, it was a long time before I

became a success. Life took me far from capital cities. Even so, I'm not going to let any of you puncture me like a party balloon. I'm the one who's going to decide how I'll die."

Her dramatic voice aroused emotion.

"You're our only star," Diana said, leading the ovation.

"You have no rivals in Trindade and its neighboring cities," Sebastiana said, seconded by Palmira.

Only Gioconda, the prisoner of ambiguous feelings, abstained from celebrating the actress's triumph. Standing next to Polidoro, with whom she was vying for Caetana's attention, she was linked to him by bad luck. Caetana shed no light on what their respective hearts were demanding.

To thank them, Caetana made repeated little bows in their direction. The festive atmosphere prompted Ernesto to pass around the appetizers again, as Venieris hammered the blocks of ice to bits for the glasses of *guaraná*.

As they were deep in conversation, a loud noise attracted their attention. It was Narciso, beating the butt of his revolver against a chair.

"We're going to put a stop to this carousal!"

His voice echoing throughout the theater was proof of the effectiveness of the acoustics. He put the revolver back in its holster and, to keep his hands occupied, pulled on his suspender straps. The gesture, copied from Chicago gangsters, made him feel secure.

Polidoro went down the stairs as nimbly as Riche.

"Where do you think you are?"

In a rage, he wanted to kick Narciso out of the Iris. He could not forgive the constable his insubordination and his boorish manners.

Perceived at close hand, the police officer's arrogance alarmed Polidoro. Narciso had assumed that expression with the intention of warning him. Having accumulated so many humiliations and so many coins, Narciso was eager to take his revenge, to empty the cylinder of his revolver as he aimed it at his adversary.

"I came to do my duty," he said with unshakable determination.

"Since when do you give me orders? Or don't you want to stay in Trindade any longer? Would you rather go up into the mountains, even farther away from Rio?" All he had to do was telephone the governor and Narciso would be transferred to the worst district in the state.

Narciso trembled. He tried to stall for time, to go over events in his mind.

"I've been ordered to close the theater. It's rebuilt precariously and violates municipal ordinances."

"Who decided on this inspection?" Polidoro's incredulity went hand in hand with his wrath.

"What do you think I am? A shitty underhanded policeman? Well, I'd like you to know that the only thing I obey is the law!"

His voice betrayed that he was lying. He was advancing across a field strewn with land mines, ready to blow his body to bits. He had doubtless carried his arrogance too far.

"Does Pentecostes know about this inspection?" Polidoro demanded details.

"The mayor took the car and disappeared as soon as the complaint reached him."

"How does it happen that he and the public building inspector decided to challenge me?" The cattle baron couldn't get over the scare they'd given him.

"I'm just following orders," Narciso said, acting tough again, to humiliate him publicly.

"You traitor, tell me the truth this minute! Since when do you dare cross me? Me, of all people, the one who's paid for your services and still does? And pays dearly!"

"Are you accusing me of corruption and of accepting bribes?" Narciso let go of his suspenders. His gesticulations of protest whipped through the air like slaps in the face.

"I accuse you of being a thief and a toady. Now, then, tell me who's behind you?"

Narciso came at Polidoro, who held the constable's arms in the air. They pitted their strength against each other as everyone ran over to separate them. Only Caetana remained onstage.

"Bastards! Just because you have money, you're trying to corrupt people like me, when I'm having such a hard time putting up with so many frustrated dreams all by myself!"

"Speak up once and for all, or you're going to regret it. I swear I'll send you to the end of nowhere."

Gioconda stepped between them.

"I'm tired of machos. I've wasted my life in bed with them."

Narciso calmed down, clinging to the hope of staying in Trindade.

"Dona Dodô. She was the one who made the formal complaint."

Polidoro ran his fingers through his hair. Overcome with anxiety, he was afraid that Caetana would bid Trindade farewell, isolating herself in a modest Brazilian boarding house, on a street without a name in a town not even on the map. He would never smell her skin again. Borne far away from him, it would take on a deep tan perhaps, beneath the implacable sun of the Northeast.

"Dona Dodô already knows about the Iris, then? And about the performance we're going to stage?" he inquired in a panic.

"When she made a formal complaint, the official responsible for public buildings was obliged to proceed to inspect the theater and to forbid its being used. The building is in terrible shape, even though the spider webs and the grime have been swept out, and Venieris the Greek was intending to construct a fake façade. It stinks inside here, despite the cheap perfume that Diana sprayed all through the auditorium."

"If Dodô knows, she's going to do everything possible to boycott us," Polidoro said to Virgílio. The professor, following the instinct of the born chronicler, decided to dig deeper into the subject.

"What led Dona Dodô to do such a thing?" he asked the constable with an amiable smile.

"She learned that her daughters and her sons-in-law backed her. And apparently Seu Joaquim did too. They accuse Polidoro of wasting money hand over fist."

Narciso headed for the stage. He tried to get a good look at Caetana. No longer in the light, her figure was surrounded by

shadows. Narciso sighed. He had no time for dreaming. He stroked
his belly, already tasting his vengeance.

"And of squandering the family fortune on a third-rate
actress."

Polidoro lunged at the constable in a fury. He was on the point
of attacking him when a grave voice echoed through the Iris.

"I don't need an intercessor, Polidoro."

Caetana's chest heaved, nearly pushing her breasts out of her
dress.

"All I need is enemies. Like the ones I've had up until today."

She crossed the stage to the stairway in her buskins. She made
a move to go down it, then halted and from there scrutinized
Narciso and the empty seats of the movie theater.

"I've lived my life under the ever-present threat of catastrophe.
When my uncle pointed out to me the highways and byways of
Brazil, dusty and dismal, I went down them without fear of snakes
or men. Money and arms have never stopped the advance of art,
even in the most wretched of hearts. Though others would like to
exterminate us, people of our sort multiply even in impossible
conditions. So let the entire Polidoro Álves family come to crucify
me. I'll be here waiting, in this Iris Theater; it's so ugly, but it's
the only one we have."

Sebastiana burst into tears. If they were driven out of the Iris,
she saw herself back at the brothel, saw the four women together
again in the kitchen, in a melancholy mood, anxious to make a
pot of fresh coffee. Every so often, one of them would go up to
the second floor with a john, and the others, sitting there amid
the cold tiles of the kitchen, would hear the mattress creaking in
the dead of night.

"Calm down, Sebastiana," Caetana, on the last step of the
stairway leading to the stage, consoled her. "Don't you know that
there has to be an enemy lurking if the performance is to succeed
in imitating life? Let's not change our destiny as artists just on
account of those nosy overseers. From now on, we'll stay in the
Iris, as though it were a city besieged by enemies who've refused
to let food and water through."

Balinho sat down on the step below Caetana's. From there he felt like one of the twelve peers of France.

"The only thing they want is for us to fail," Balinho said, suggesting a subject to her.

Caetana thrust her chest out so she could be heard from the last row of the theater. "Who are they to defeat us, if life itself has already taken over that task! We've had failure on our chests for a long time, like a blanket in winter."

Caetana's figure had taken on the same imposing appearance as that of Callas tackling the role of the priestess Norma. Balinho touched her arm, urging her to go on, so as not to allow Narciso to speak.

"I bid our enemies welcome! Including Constable Narciso. As long as art exists, this house belongs to everyone."

Because she was paying too little attention to the execution of her high notes, Caetana's voice came out in a falsetto register. This did not keep her from unleashing a general catharsis. All of them embraced one another as though they had routed out the enemy after a painful siege.

"More appetizers?" Ernesto was passing the tray yet again, insisting that they have something to eat. The emotions of the last few minutes had weakened the artists' constitutions.

"We need wine for a toast," Diana said, moving distractedly in circles around Narciso. Forgotten by everyone, Narciso no longer had any idea what to do. He cleared his throat in the hope of attracting the attention of even one friend that he might have left. Nobody seemed to hear him, nor did the sound of his boots as he started to leave appear to matter to anyone.

Just as he was about to reach the door, he looked back. Maybe Polidoro at least would demand that he be present. And want him back onstage just to punish him, swearing that he would get him thrown out of Trindade the next day.

Overcome by an indefinable feeling, Narciso went on out the door. The cool early-morning air made the pain he felt in his chest even more intense.

DODÔ ASKED her father-in-law for advice. With so many dangers in view, she could not be too careful. In a few weeks, they would have lost half their fortune. She had long suspected that on his trips to Rio, now less and less frequent, Polidoro had been buying foreign currency and stowing it away in some secret cave, or sending it to a numbered bank account in Switzerland.

As soon as the actress discovered the key to the strongbox or the cave where Dodô's husband went at night to pray to God and the devil, they could consider their fortune lost. Because of his long-standing feeling for her, Polidoro would not resist her siege. Especially since, for lack of another passion in recent days that would cast him into the fires of hell, there to scorch his desire, he had painted his old love in fresh and deceptively intense colors, bearing no relationship to reality.

"Everyone betrayed me, Seu Joaquim. That tramp has been in Trindade for weeks, living at my expense, and nobody alerted me to the dangers. Thanks to my eldest daughter, I'm no longer a woman betrayed. Isn't it true that conjugal betrayal ends when one tumbles to what's been going on?"

Joaquim noisily stirred the sugar into his coffee with his spoon. He wanted to put a stop to the woman's complaints. He had pleaded his habitual drowsiness after lunch, and his advanced age, to avoid her visit. But Dodô, at the door, had demanded that she be heard out. When it came to honor, she took priority over the other members of the family, always boldly demanding gifts of money and loans, though rarely advice, from the old man, as she was now doing.

"Who do you think I am, Dodô? An expert in affairs of the heart? A physician who attends the soul?" he grumbled, to get rid of her.

She persisted. She had pushed her straight-backed chair closer to his easy chair with the aim of keeping his attention. She would not let him sleep.

"It's not Polidoro's body that matters to me, Seu Joaquim. I'll lend the man's carcass to that decadent actress, who came to Trindade in search of financial resources. Poor woman, she doesn't even have a house to live in. But if that's so, why didn't he tell me? I'd be pleased to send her some money through the mail every month; there was no need for her to starve to death. We have plenty of cattle and hay, enabling us to have funds to alleviate human miseries such as that. But coming to my door with the aim of stealing what belongs to my daughters—that I won't permit. She'll have to walk over my dead body."

In her hurry to get dressed, Dodô had taken out of her closet a dress that fit her too tightly around the middle, accentuating her unbecoming plumpness. From being washed countless times, the colors of the fabric had faded. The blue had taken on a lilac tint. In the presence of her father-in-law, she was careful to conceal any signs of wealth, constantly hoping to leave his house with a check tucked in her armpit.

"That's just how a man is, Dodô. When he's old, he dreams of being young. And what is youth if not a gallop on the rump of a horse with a mane and willful nostrils, and an unattached woman as well, ready to receive the proofs of our passion?"

Dodô was surprised at the old man's defense of Polidoro. Severe with his sons, he was the first to give them a good dressing down. Polidoro in particular, who often defied him and hadn't even appeared at the unveiling of his bust. All on account of the actress, who kept him under lock and key, at times at the Iris, at times in the suite at the Palace.

"Besides being a spendthrift, Polidoro doesn't have any feelings nowadays. He spends his nights immersed in sin and even looks down on his father, just to meet that woman's demands. How, then, can you defend him, instead of taking him to task?" When it came time for combat, Dodô put her hand to her waist. She readied herself to fight, even without her father-in-law's support.

"My son isn't irresponsible. He's from good stock. There has never been disrespect in this house. Magnólia herself never raised her voice against me. So you'd better watch what you say. What's more, no male is free of passion. A woman who doesn't understand that elementary truth doesn't reach her old age with her husband at her side. And since when is his marital state a reason to geld a male like Polidoro?"

Joaquim tried to get to his feet by leaning on the arm of the easy chair. He didn't see his cane anywhere nearby. He leaned on Dodô's shoulders, as though she were a wall. "Where did I leave that damned cane—that wooden leg I'm forced to use?" he grumbled, looking all around.

Dodô refused to help him. It would hurt his pride, make him feel obliged to walk around the room with the fear of stumbling, of falling to the floor.

"Even if someone offered me an arm, I wouldn't accept," he said, for the sake of some hypothetical onlooker observing him from one corner of the room. Thus he paid her back for her ill-treatment of him. When he reached the wall, he groped his way along it to the chest of drawers, in search of the cane he'd left there.

In control of his movements once again, he impudently confronted the woman.

"What are you complaining about? The main purpose of your marriage has already been fulfilled. The two of you now have more than enough daughters and money. Don't tell me that you and Polidoro didn't reach a firm settlement when you married. And a lucrative one at that. Or did you choose to trade all that for a tempestuous love, with no guarantees, and end up in the same fix as that actress?"

This act of retaliation restored his energies. He wanted to have Dodô as a victim. To subject her to some caprice that would wound her pride. His daughter-in-law came to see him only out of self-interest. On these whirlwind visits, she upset the equilibrium of the house, attaining the level of everyday emotions only through resignation to the need to show him a minimum of courtesy. She never brought a box of candy or a basket of fruit gathered from her orchard. She of all people, whose larder was overflowing. At her table, always set, there was everything from salty appetizers to caramelized sweets, produced by cooks who smiled and wept at the same time on seeing the ironclad recipes handed down by deceased grandmothers and runaway kitchen slaves.

The abundance of Dodô's table was not aimed at satiating other people's hunger. It was meant simply to show off the power of money. Like a missionary regimenting pagans and annexing fertile lands, Dodô accumulated money and possessions in order to give her daughters the product of all that effort. The five girls, for their part, expressed their thanks by setting her against their father.

Rebelling against her lot, she dreamed of crossing swords with her father-in-law, thanks to whom she had so often had to swallow spittle and frustrations. He had never had the least respect for her. He never asked her advice, even about a cake recipe. To him she was only a source of domestic order and human reproduction, though he had appreciated the lands and cattle that she had brought his son as her dowry.

"I thought that the presentation of the bust would spur you on to put the city in order. Above all to correct the excesses of your family."

She confronted the old man bravely, refusing to be humiliated. For a long time, she had wanted to experience the taste of vengeance; it had the flavor of Surinam cherries, as her father had emphasized.

Joaquim unobtrusively straightened his collar. Despite his advanced age, the gleam in the man's eyes grew brighter in the presence of a woman. She thought of seducing him with sweetness. However, since she had lost the habit of emphasizing the tender sentiments, her face contorted, forming deep furrows. She was incapable of cultivating even the ritual displays that are an intrinsic part of affection.

Joaquim noted her change of mood. He didn't know what to cope with first: his son's defense, or his daughter-in-law's need for drama.

"Do you want me to have Caetana thrown out of the hotel and chained to a seat in the bus to São Paulo?"

"If that's what's necessary, I don't see why not," she said, matter-of-factly.

"In that case, summon Constable Narciso. Perhaps he can solve your problem."

Joaquim sank down in the easy chair, wanting nothing more than to make that hollow his tomb. His desire to stay on amid enemies and members of his family was fading by the hour. Dodô, for instance, made him all the more eager to set sail without a fixed course, on an endless Atlantic voyage.

"Are you serious?" Dodô was alarmed, afraid that she had made a mistake. Every time she tried to figure out the Álves family, with their impulsive and aloof temperament, she was wildly off the mark. They were different from her own relatives in every way. Of course, no two families were alike. Not one of them had been begotten in the paradise widely proclaimed to be common to all of them.

"May I call the constable from here at your house?"

Dodô frequently went to extremes. She lacked tact when it came to handling delicate matters: she had no patience for bowing and scraping and courtly distractions. Like her father-in-law, she was reborn when she smelled cow dung.

"With so many vast country estates, you don't need my roof over your head. Besides, your brother is the governor's favorite. What more do you want?"

He lowered his head, his eyes closed. He was going to take his afternoon nap right there and then. He had ended the discussion. He was no longer acting like a bird of prey: his degree of interest in human intrigues had been appreciably reduced. And Dodô's land holdings, once considered precious, had now merged with his own, since the blood of his son and that of his daughter-in-law had formed between them a miscellany of plasma and ambitious genes.

Joaquim's attitude was an insult. Dodô felt as though she'd been driven out of his house. There was nothing more she could do. If the old man were remiss in his defense of his son, she would not spare him her revenge. She needed to act quickly.

As she reached the gate, a slight uneasiness came over her. Feeling it expedient to gather her strength together, she called to the gardener who was taking care of the wild roses. "Everybody has a talent. Yours is to grow beautiful roses. Mine is to note down details of the week on a pad of paper. When I was a little girl, I thought I'd like to be a reporter."

As her hand slid along her belt, she regretted the fat she had put on in those inprudent years. She immediately leaned against the palings of the fence in order to write a few words on the sheet of paper torn off the pad, faithful to her old habit of noting things down. Anyone who leafed through her notebook would find lists of things she had bought, reminders, even little notes never sent to the persons to whom they had been written. On occasion, she would forget whom they were meant for, so avidly did she resort to this means of chastising her neighbors and her adversaries.

"Hand this note of mine to Seu Joaquim before dinner. It's going to spoil his appetite," she said, interrupting her reading of it.

The wording of the text, written on the spur of the moment, gave her pleasure. Nodding her head, she approved of her own talent. Even in grade school, she had been outstanding when it came to dictations and compositions, as long as the subject of the exercise had a rural setting. Nobody in her class could better describe the state of mind of cows, whose apparent passivity concealed a sly nature, given to dissembling, with which she felt a sincere kinship.

The title of "Excellency," with which she had chosen to address her father-in-law in the note, seemed exactly right to her. Such ceremoniousness would have the merit of confusing his mind and upsetting his feelings. Her sole aim, however, had been to give discreet vent to her outrage. She read the text once again, aloud this time.

"Your Excellency, Seu Joaquim, I beg you to forget my visit. I for my part forgot it on the threshold of your house. Rather than your aid, I sought your advice. When the latter was not forthcoming, I felt myself to be all alone in the world, as though, in the course of my passage through the civil registry, the surname of Álves that became mine through marriage had been expunged. For many years now, I have appended that name to my own as an additional surname. Given these circumstances, I therefore find myself obliged to defend myself and my offspring from the attacks that are being launched against us by people of your blood. I hereby warn experienced mariners that there is a storm coming from the portside. Signed: Dodô Tinoco Álves."

No one in that family had protected her even in scandalous episodes. Yet Polidoro regarded himself as duly authorized to commit every sort of folly. The voice of his conscience had long since fallen silent.

Only once had she seen him flush, when she waved in his face the undershorts that he had brought from Rio, hidden in his suitcase. She had stumbled on this article of clothing only by chance. How could she have suspected the pleasure it would give a man such as Polidoro to bring back cotton undershorts embroidered with a masochistic motto that bared his sentiments? But Dodô had not been deluded by the episode. She herself had made a point of washing the undershorts with coconut-oil soap and rage in her heart, thereby coming to be on intimate terms with each word embroidered on the cotton.

Not one of them had come out in the wash. They had remained intact on the fabric and in her memory: "I was born to suffer." Near the fly, through which Polidoro, taking out his member, relieved his urge to urinate, she had also read in tiny letters: "Caetana."

Once she reached home again from Joaquim's, Dodô decided that the hour had come to provide Trindade with the flames of doubt and the hard stones of intrigue. She immediately sent for her eldest daughter, the accomplice of her ruses.

"Are you sure you're doing the right thing?" After hearing her mother out, Isabel obviously had scruples about an act that surpassed her imagination.

"I didn't send for you to have you preach moral sermons to me. Or would you rather be poor? Without a penny to leave your children?"

Isabel was alarmed. At the chaotic vision of ending up a pauper, she lined up on her mother's side.

"Is the constable going to go along with the plan? Isn't he a friend of Papa's?"

Dodô paced restlessly up and down the living room. She kept kicking up the crumbs around the table, unquestionably left by Polidoro, always a sloppy eater.

"Since when does a friend accept tips? The one who gives the most gets the man," she said emphatically. Her worries were of another sort, although she wouldn't have been able to define them.

"At least have a talk with Ernesto, Mama. He's more sensible than the rest of the bunch. Maybe he can dissuade Papa."

Isabel kept insisting. She was displeased with the public war between her father and her mother, exposing the family to a network of gossip that would already have spread through the whole town, perhaps even reaching the capital.

"Have you had a close look at a male overcome by passion? With a raging fever, and his entire body infected? May God deliver you from excesses like that, daughter. It's a good thing we women are safe from such torments. No, no, it's not worth the trouble of calling on the pharmacist for help. He too experiences passion, in an indirect way, and so he clings to your father's coattails."

The two women dipped their biscuits of fine manioc flour into their coffee, then quickly raised them to their mouths before they melted altogether.

"Shall we send a note or call the constable on the phone?" the daughter said, breaking the silence.

"Nothing written down. Such things are always compromising. I'm going to walk down the street past the police station, as though I were out shopping. Narciso is always somewhere around there. He doesn't let his rear end warm up in the chair of his office. Only in the ones in bars."

"All right, then, go ahead. What will you ask him to do?"

Dodô suddenly grew fidgety. Already on her feet, she didn't want to finish the snack she'd just begun. She grabbed her purse and headed for the street.

"I'm in a hurry. I can't waste a minute more."

"Tell me first what you're going to propose to the constable."

Her daughter accompanied her as far as the street. Dodô refused to let her go along to police headquarters with her. For such tasks as this, she asserted her authority as Polidoro's wife.

"You'll find out when the time comes. I want to keep it a secret."

"You won't even tell me, Mama?" Isabel said in a sad voice.

"Anybody who shares her bed with a husband or a lover isn't to be trusted. When it's time to fuck, she doesn't keep anything a secret."

Dodô turned her back on her daughter without further ado. She didn't want the chauffeur to take her to police headquarters in the car, preferring to arrive there panting for breath, a good pretext for resting for a few seconds in front of the yellow building where for years Narciso had spent his days with no hope of leaving Trindade.

THOUGH he was known as Balinho, his baptismal name was Aníbal. Caetana accepted the nickname under protest, at Balinho's own insistence.

"Why give up a historical name?" she lamented, knowing that "Balinho" was most likely a diminutive form of "Hannibal."

Balinho tempered his words. He did not want to reprove her, or tell her that the name, despite calling to mind a warrior with delirious dreams, was not especially to his liking. He treated her with the care owed a princess, despite the fact that the two of them had often spent their nights in cheap boarding houses and had no permanent abode. He had never robbed her of the illusion that she was a real actress, even if fortune had not favored her.

He avoided the discussion with her of certain feelings, confused from the beginning, preferring to have as his job the inventing of stories, in the hope that, entertained by some dizzying plot, Caetana would applaud the truth of imagination instead of that other truth, born of heartbreak.

"I saw your father only twice," Caetana said. "Both times he flew, now gripping the trapeze, now flying through the air without a safety net. He looked like a bird that doesn't want to alight on land. I never saw the color of his eyes from close up, or his undershirt soaking wet from sweat and fear."

Balinho suspected that he owed his nickname to Hannibal's decision to take African elephants to the heart of Rome to bewilder its legions, neutralizing all their strategic initiatives.

In order to get this plan under way, the general obliged the pachyderms, with their melancholy gaze, to negotiate steep slopes and narrow passes and to resist the magnetic attraction of abysses. He demanded, finally, that they go against their instincts and the limitations of their enormous bulk. Prepared to disregard any obstacle, the warrior made them fling themselves into the air like real trapeze artists, though without their gracefulness.

"I learned of the death of your father long afterward," Caetana said, deeply moved. "They say that, before hitting the ground in the circus ring, his body retained all its imperturbable elegance as it fell. Uncle Vespasiano told me that the owner of the circus, seated in the first row, noted the smile on your father's face, in the fraction of a second before he hit the ground."

Caetana made a point of insistently repeating the tragic theme, so as to promote in Balinho the pride of occupations that required a close acquaintance each day with the proximity of death, the better to enjoy to the full the pleasures of the senses.

She admired the trapeze artist who, possessing only the most superficial knowledge of history, had sensed Hannibal's delirium, so similar to his own, subjecting drowsy pachyderms to the vertigo of height and implanting wings in their stony backs.

Prince Danilo often interrupted these dialogues. By means of antagonistic addenda, he offended Balinho.

"And where did his elephants end up? Is it true that, once they'd been grilled, they served as tasty delicacies at exotic banquets? Wasn't there a single one of them left to tell the tale?"

With Caetana to defend him, Balinho jocosely admitted that pachyyderms were part of his paternal inheritance. After his father's estate had been divided, and his elephants were sold to a circus in Juiz de Fora, he had seen them leave with a heavy heart.

"Today they're the best circus act in Brazil. Maybe in the whole world. They're the only elephants who aren't afraid of heights. They can be hoisted up to the trapeze. They never feel dizzy, and they regard precipices with scorn."

Danilo envied him the promptness of his counterattack. Ever since he'd been a little boy, Balinho had wanted nothing to do with vulgarities. Imagination, always free and spontaneous, guaranteed the elegance of his language. Prince Danilo regretted not having this virtue. Life would have been more pleasant for him if he could have fought his enemies with sharp-honed verbal blades.

Balinho's lively impudence found fertile ground, in fact, in wretchedness. Installed now in the Iris, which never seemed to him an ideal setting, he made the slackers work, keeping them a long way away from Caetana: the actress mustn't wear herself out before the premiere.

Caetana, who until that moment had carefully refrained from revealing the type of opera in which they would be participating, ordered them to jostle one another onstage as she watched. Following her regal direction, they were made repeatedly to cross the stage nervously. She forced on them an unthinkable exercise for bodies that, unaccustomed to the discipline of the theater, kept colliding with one another as a consequence of Caetana's hastily decreed orders.

No one protested. Despite Caetana's vast annoyance with them, they sensed that each gesture corresponded to an action she had blocked out to be performed onstage. And that, even though she had not let them in on the secret of the roles they were to represent, she was already training them. In one way or another, she guaranteed that each of them would play a dramatic and poignant character, of the sort that awakens ghosts and varied emotions in the memory of the audience.

After the session to warm them up, they sweated, feeling satisfied, eager to talk with her. But Caetana simply smiled and shut herself up immediately in her dressing room. At the door, Balinho allowed no one to go in, unmoved by Ernesto, who had brought an assortment of canapés and a bottle of red wine from his own house.

"We're most appreciative of your thoughtfulness, but leave everything at the door," Balinho said.

Ernesto was indignant.

"Why can't I come in? I'm Polidoro's best friend and the owner of the Bom Espírito pharmacy. Who can say for certain that none of you will require my services?"

He was having difficulty keeping the tray balanced, his hands trembling from the effort of the strenuous exercises. Nonetheless, Balinho did not back down.

"I see you've lost your good manners from all that wandering around Brazil you've done."

Ernesto's voice attracted the attention of Danilo, who came to the pharmacist's rescue, scolding Balinho.

"Are you reprimanding me, by any chance?" Balinho said.

Prince Danilo took off his sweater. His low-cut undershirt showed his hairy chest. He knocked on the door, defying the young man's authority.

"Oh, it's you, is it?" Caetana said, in the middle of doing breathing exercises, annoyed at his presence.

"We've been together for years now. I refuse to be humiliated in public by a mere brat. Either Balinho mends his ways, or we each go our own way."

Gesticulating emphatically, he convinced her of his lofty pride.

Caetana's fingers, stroking her face, circled her eyelids and descended to the folds in her neck.

"Who's going to assure you of food and lodging?" she said, disheartened, sitting in front of the mirror. "If I were only forty, I'd try my luck in Rio, with my name taking up a whole column of the daily paper. Why not, if I still had the talent?" This venting of her feelings aloud had its origin in phrases rehearsed in her mind, hence accessible only to herself. The thought that inspired them tormented her, now that Danilo had forgotten all about her.

He had stopped paying attention to her because he was overcome by the certainty that in order to survive he depended on
Polidoro's passion for Caetana. As long as such ardor lasted, all
he need do was to go to the hotel café, ask for codfish stew with
Portuguese wine, and sign the bill.

In order to justify his appearance in the dressing room, he
changed the subject. "I'm here to say that Gioconda sent me. She
would prefer to have you summon her, rather than come knocking
on your door."

Caetana was annoyed. She refused to be intimidated. On the
eve of her triumph, she would not yield to Gioconda's entreaties.

Danilo, however, in egregious disobedience, led Gioconda in
by the hand. Her recent physical exercises, together with the
emotion of the meeting, made it hard for Gioconda to breathe.

Caetana looked at the woman in the mirror. "I myself gave
you that name, Gioconda, which comes from an opera. I only
hope to fight over the same love with you, as Norma and Adalgisa
did," the actress said, with a sigh of nostalgia for the old days. At
times, under the impulse of the talent granted her by the gods,
she felt as though she were Callas. All she had to do was open her
fish gills, and out of that great grotto would come pouring notes
of music—nacre and pearls.

"Don't leave me at this crossroads. If necessary, I will follow
you on foot to the end of the world," Gioconda said, precipitating
events. "Who am I in the realm of art, and who am I in your life?"

Danilo backed away. Lofty sentiments, even if set like tiles in
perfect symmetry, revealed the emptiness of his heart. It was far
too late now to envelop himself in a shroud sewn by passionate
hands. In the cramped rooms in which he slept, there was no
place for furniture, bibelots, souvenirs, or a woman.

"Where are you going?" Caetana shouted as she saw him take
to his heels.

He faced her squarely, unable to bear his loneliness any longer.

"I'm going to fulfill an animal duty. I'm just going off to piss,"
he said in retaliation, though he wanted her to caress him, to take
pity on him for his barren future.

"And what about me?" Gioconda persisted.

"I gave you your name to save you, that's all." Caetana felt trapped. They were trying to take from her the incurable plague of dreams.

"You gave me hopes that I'd be happy. When you named me, I thought you'd take me with you wherever you went. You'd never leave me behind, anxiously waiting for you!"

Caetana rose to her feet. She could no longer flee from this clash of wills. The two women looked at each other and gave every indication that they would trade answers swiftly.

"You were fooling yourself, Gioconda. I never belonged to anybody. Life alone held me. It clipped my hair. In a few weeks, I drove away anyone who saw my body."

Gioconda advanced resolutely upon her. She gripped Caetana by the shoulder. The actress sought to avoid her penetrating gaze.

"Admit that you fled so you wouldn't have to take me with you. Tell the truth! It will be my one consolation." And she dug her nails farther into Caetana's flesh, as the actress stoically resisted her onslaughts. She did not appear to be suffering, though she was growing faint from Gioconda's attack.

"You and Polidoro are up to your necks in the shit of illusion. You keep on being hoodwinked by life. I never loved either of you. Never, do you hear!"

Caetana freed herself from Gioconda. Once the latter had let go, she paced endlessly back and forth in the dressing room. She missed Riche's curling around her legs. Freedom was beneficent, she thought, pitying the misery in which everyone was immersed. No one could rob her of the right to approve of her own destiny as a wanderer.

"Do you mean to say I waited in vain?" Gioconda tried to follow the actress's nervous pacing.

Caetana almost didn't see her. Absorbed in the theatricalization of everyday life, she sought an excuse for sweeping away the past. She confused Gioconda with Balinho, or even with Danilo.

"Every morning, when he brought me my mug of coffee, Uncle Vespasiano guaranteed that I'd be a success. Despite his daydreams, my life was timed for failure, down to the last second.

How could I make good if we only put on shows in the sticks, peopled with souls suffering from leprosy, from Chagas's disease, mere ghosts? Damn it to hell!" Caetana exploded, heedless of the effects of her lack of restraint.

In her distress, she collided with Gioconda. She took her by the hand, but immediately let go of it when she felt her burning-hot skin, her fingers clutching her.

"If I was meant to fail, why did my uncle bring me up to dream? What right did I have to imitate Callas when no one even taught me how to sing? I was nothing but an apprentice with rusty vocal chords."

Gioconda trembled. She could scarcely hold back her tears during this confession. Caetana was forcing herself to offer her an apology for telling her lies.

"Stop, Caetana. Come off the stage. Come back to real life. Talk about us. About Polidoro, if you like. But enough of this mixing up of scenarios. Are you playing a role when you shit? Will you be acting when the time comes for you to die?"

Gioconda was restoring to her body a dignity that Caetana's presence easily took away from it. She wanted to free herself from the shackles of feelings, sharp barbs that wore her nerves to a frazzle.

"Illusion is my fate. I am doomed to pass judgment on life without writing out a receipt for it. Life, that pile of shit, isn't going to catch me unawares again. This damned life I've had to put up with owes me everything. I don't want failure to be the only stage direction in my old age. I prefer death."

"Who's going to keep you company to the very end?"

Gioconda had lost her gruffness. She grabbed the actress's hand, warming it against her sagging breasts without a brassiere. She felt Caetana's vague shudder at having no future. Her emotions, even though carefully hidden, had no one to belong to. Perhaps Caetana no longer counted on the delights of another's body. The delights that make a shambles of a bedroom and give forth, through the open slats of the window blinds, the strange perfume of passionate vitals.

"Say that you came back to take me away," Gioconda murmured, capturing her attention.

Caetana submitted to Gioconda only long enough to put her own anxiety to flight. She withdrew her hand. Clinging to her skin like glue, the woman's heat did not free her from the sensation of failure.

"The chaos of art runs in my veins. What good is love or the flesh to me if the soul is immortal? And my soul is the stage! It means success!"

Gioconda recovered her energy. Caetana's gaze, intense and oblique, was banishing her from the dressing room. It was worse than the twenty-year exile. The woman, her body filled out with surprising deposits of fat, had eliminated human passion. Her pores had closed like a curtain that blacks out the light of the sun.

The hope of being with Caetana, which caressed each day with feverish fingers, had dissolved. Gioconda no longer had anyone to wait for in the future, nothing but the raw truth, filtered through dejection. In an unpremeditated gesture, she went for Caetana's showy turquoise necklace. As she grabbed a fistful of the stones, she scratched the actress's neck, already the color of papyrus and beginning to wrinkle.

"What is it you want from me? Have you gone mad?"

"I want to see myself in your eyes!"

She put her arms around Caetana's shoulders, the object of her covetousness. Caetana could not escape, or seek aid from Balinho, who was busy at some task. Gioconda had never held her so close.

"I wasted twenty years waiting for you. Amusing myself with Polidoro on Fridays. A meeting under the sign of a horrendous religion in which you were the one to whom our prayers were addressed. Polidoro and I grew older by the year, along with the map of Brazil. Trying to guess where in this damned country you were fulfilling your destiny as an actress. An accursed actress, who went from region to region, setting foot in circus rings and on portable stages to show off your talent, almost in the dark, since they were lit only with a kerosene lamp. At times, impelled by melancholy and boredom, Polidoro and I used to fuck. We came at odd moments, and avoided looking at each other. We both knew that you stood between us. And we didn't have the courage to speak up against your presence."

She let Caetana go with unexpected gentleness. Her abandonment of her was an enigmatic, indecipherable sign. The flesh of the two women, which Polidoro had found so attractive, had faded. They lacked the vice of passion.

In a corner of the dressing room, Gioconda turned her back on Caetana. She hid her face between her hands, her body shaken by sobs.

Caetana was alarmed. Accustomed to drama experienced onstage, the only sort of plot that succeeded in taking her unawares, she rejected life that came to her disjointed, in spurts. Life to her was suitable only for the stage. Outside this domain, everything seemed false, insufficient, in dubious taste.

"Why are you crying?"

The words emerged from her chest like a musical phrase. Listening to her own voice, which was doing its best to be faithful to the registers of the melody, Caetana smiled, satisfied at not being off-key in the middle of her torment. She was a born artist. Daily life did not corrupt her. She had, therefore, to go on with the breakdown of humanity, personalized at that by Gioconda, who was claiming her soul.

"Now I'm the one who's going to say to you: that's enough drama. I didn't give you your name so you'd forget the stage and weep without witnesses. The only way of erasing the oily stains of tears is to garner the applause of the multitude."

Gioconda dried her face with the sleeve of her dress, wiping off her makeup. She wanted her toughness back. That was the suit of armor with which she had confronted the men of Trindade and put money aside.

"I apologize if I've bothered you," she said resentfully. Her false pride appeared amid broken trills that were not at all convincing.

She was just leaving when Caetana called her back. "Where do you think you're going with that offended face? Do you plan on exhibiting it like a war trophy?" she screamed, not caring if she was heard out in the hall.

"I'm the mistress of my destiny," Gioconda retorted, still drawn up to her full height. "You're not giving me any more orders. You've lost the right to rule my future."

The phrase boomed out, leaving no room for doubt. The sincerity of her intentions gave her a subtle beauty.

Caetana envied her sudden dignity. The mantle that she herself was wearing that night had been temporarily usurped by her recent enemy. At the threat of an artistic theft, she blocked Gioconda's path to the door.

"You and Polidoro never had grandeur. That's why the two of you stayed in Trindade waiting for me. You didn't know where to go. You lacked the courage to roam the world, to sleep in haystacks, to eat scrapings of raw brown sugar, to lose your teeth. When I remembered you, I pitied you," she proclaimed, relieved at venting her feelings.

"We never asked for your pity," Gioconda confronted her, undaunted. The certainty that she had come out the loser gave her the strength to resist.

"Do you remember a night at your house when I smeared my fingers with garlic and demanded living proofs of love or desire from you and Polidoro? Polidoro was scared; he was afraid to repeat that test in front of you. He was sorry he'd given in and passed it once before, in your dressing room. His ambition was limited to making me come in bed, something that merely caused my desire to grow old more quickly. You were different. Your fantasy was to please me. You didn't know, though, exactly where my heart was located—whether it lay in a hothouse of orchids or in a big bed with rumpled sheets. Both jealous, the two of you fought over me, heedless of the world of illusion. And to me illusion was more powerful than orgasm. Orgasm was no more than a loose stone thrown into the river. It broke to pieces in the current and was lost from sight in the gravel bed on the bottom."

She was about to go on just as impetuously when Gioconda blocked her path and cut her short. "And what proofs did I fail to give you? What are we talking about? Why didn't you object before this?"

Her serenade was spent. She was struggling now to recover the trail of the past. Perhaps there was still time to nourish certain illusions, despite deposits of fat making a build that had once been firm and delightful ugly now.

"I said to you jokingly: 'Kiss my fingers smeared with garlic. I want both your tongues to reek of garlic when the time for kisses comes.' The two of you laughed. You couldn't believe that I was asking for help, for you to deliver me from my wanton fantasy. Or for you to become part of it and take to the open road with me. Back in those days, I wanted to drag you all over Brazil."

At each word, Caetana struck a series of blows at a ruined memory, incapable of properly stitching together facts swallowed up by the years.

"Why didn't you tell us the truth?" In her distress, Gioconda ran her fingers through her hair. She could not resign herself to a fate based on unexpected, meaningless events. Their anticipations of what life would bring, reduced to someone else's dream, highly uncontrollable, cast them into a dungeon and degradation.

"You wouldn't have put up with the conditions of life in which an itinerant artist lives. The two of you always dreamed of a bed, a table, a pot on the fire. My house was the open air. By going my own way, alone, I would have all of Brazil to myself. I was never surprised at the wretchedness or the fantastic dreams of my country, always dressed in rags, nothing but skin and bones, yet inexhaustible. Uncle Vespasiano agreed to steal out of Trindade as though we were thieves. Without formal farewells, without first tearing up our feelings as though they were pieces of paper. Who can tell: we might thus have freed you and Polidoro of the thorns of possessive sentiments, which demand revenge and collect losses."

"It's too late now, isn't it?" Gioconda said disconsolately.

Caetana avoided answering. She had gone too far. It was not right to fracture the vertebrae of Gioconda's illusions, which were the only thing she had to shore up her dignity anew each day.

Caetana toyed with the objects on the dressing table. Balinho had brought to the Iris certain belongings of hers, to assure her of a feeling of permanence, to provide her with a daydream that Trindade had not foreseen. She snapped her fingers, producing a sound like a castanet. Balinho suddenly appeared at the door.

This snap of her fingers was the sign that Gioconda's visit was over.

"Shall we go back to the hotel?" Balinho shook her cape, hung up behind the door. "We'll never rid the Iris of the dust of so many years," he said as he enveloped Caetana in the cloak. She allowed the young man, shorter than she was, to put his arms around her.

"What am I to do now?" Gioconda asked, all adrift.

"Have everybody stay awake the whole night here at the Iris. Make them take a good deep breath of the atmosphere of a theater. Have they ever thought of the artists who shed blood on this stage?"

Gioconda paid no attention to her, blinded by her emotional impulses.

"Is this a farewell?"

Caetana headed for the exit.

"It's been a long time since I said goodbye to you."

Caetana hoped Balinho would open the door. Standing tall and straight, she took on an air of solemnity rare for her. Before leaving, she stared Gioconda straight in the eye once again.

"Look at my fingers. I never again rubbed garlic on them."

And, without gathering together the shards of Gioconda's shattered face, she left the dressing room, followed by Balinho.

POLIDORO was hurriedly summoned. Having shut himself up in the Iris, he refused to open the door. His daughter's voice persuaded him to leave his refuge.

"What is it you want at this hour, my girl? You should be in bed with your husband."

With his car at the door, he went to his father's house. Joaquim was breathing his last after having eaten a pork-and-black-bean stew. In an act of rebellion, he had demanded a royal repast as his farewell.

"I'm not going to return this meal to the earth in the form of dung. I'm going to take it with me, in my stomach, at the hour of my death."

Nobody believed that he'd made up his mind to part company with them. Dodô's visit to the house had left in the air the unmistakable, repellent scent of musk that his daughter-in-law insisted on wearing.

"Has the doctor been called?" Polidoro's drowsy voice bore no trace of the emotion of bidding his father a final farewell. It suddenly seemed to him that Joaquim had long since left this world, forgetting to take his corpse with him.

In the semidark bedroom, lit by two silver candelabra, the brothers kept their spirits up by following the ritual sequence called for when death was imminent.

"So you've come at last, Polidoro."

Envy had imprinted itself on the family confraternity. They would far rather have played the role of artist, now assumed by their brother, than drive cattle over grazing grounds.

"Can you hear me, Father?" Polidoro asked, beneath Dodô's reproving gaze.

"Of course I can, but I'm not interested in talking," the old man answered.

The question that their father had thus put an end to by his reply came as a relief to those present. They took turns now at staying in the bedroom and going down to the unpretentious dining room. Joaquim himself had ordered that all the ostentatious ornaments be taken down into the cellar.

"The more you know I possess, the sooner you'll want to see me dead," he opined.

The table was loaded with sweets, salty appetizers, and a ham hock provided at the last minute.

Dodô followed her husband into the garden. As he waited for dawn to break, Polidoro studied the effects of the moon on the human heart. His bladder ached, and he relieved himself right there, disregarding his wife's presence.

"That's all you have to show me you're still a man," she said cuttingly, wanting to offend him.

Polidoro immediately drew away. He was always careful to preserve his privacy.

"Aren't you satisfied, Dodô?"

"Not ever, where you're concerned. I'll be at peace only after you've died."

She walked over closer to Polidoro, taking advantage of the moonlight to look at her husband.

"Whether we like it or not, we're getting older by the minute. And your actress is older than ever," she said emphatically, with heartfelt satisfaction.

"Respect my dying father at least."

Polidoro comported himself with unheard-of aplomb. He pulled the wicker chair over so he could sit down in it. The early-morning breeze restored his muscle tone. He was mastering the pleasure of being alive, in contrast to the rite of death so close at hand.

"It won't do you any good to run away, Polidoro. Vengeance is nigh. This time the gods are going to be on my side. Above all Our Lady of Aparecida."

Polidoro was alarmed, despite the shield of serenity with which he was gifted. Enameled bright red, Dodô's fingernails seemed to grow longer as they aimed straight at him.

"Well, let it come. I'll be waiting. I too will use my weapons," he said in a low voice, his jowls trembling. He was wearing suspenders instead of the curried-leather belt that had been a last present from his mother. He stretched them out, then immediately let them fall back into place. The sharp slap they made against his chest was a sign of his contained fury.

"If you keep doing that, your trousers are going to fall down," his wife declared in the same tone of voice she employed at home, one to which they were all accustomed, which meant the final consolidation of a state that had always been immutable.

Polidoro accepted the ham sandwich brought by one of his sisters-in-law. He took the first bite and thought of his father, who would never again enjoy the delicacies from a pig that had met its end in the midst of an unequal combat.

"Thanks, Junca. I was hungry and didn't realize it." With that phrase, he managed to get rid of his sister-in-law and remain alone with Dodô. Perhaps she would reveal the plans devised against Caetana.

"When all is said and done, what is it you want?"

"The return of what belongs to me," she answered.

Polidoro got out of the chair. His fingers were smeared with fat. Angrily, to provoke her, he wiped them off on his trousers.

"Isn't a fortune enough for you? A whole world of land and cattle? A whole damned pile of gold on your bed?" He hinted at her wretched loneliness, her empty body that no one sought out.

Dodô did not lose heart. She was prepared to take him back home with her at any price. If her body had long since made her soul turn cold, she still had a woman warrior's spirit. Polidoro feared her determination. He prepared himself for the fray.

A voice coming from the kitchen took their breath away.

"Hurry, Seu Joaquim just died."

The sister-in-law who had given him the ham sandwich had taken it upon herself to bring the news of Joaquim's death.

Polidoro ran to the kitchen. Dodô lingered behind for a moment.

"It's no use trying to run away. Not even with Joaquim's death as your excuse. From today on, expect me to be waiting for you at every corner. I'll be there, on the lookout for you."

With its tiled walls and floor, the kitchen seemed even colder in the winter months. He trembled, feeling his joints creak as he ran. For the first time, he would see his father in a state that would strike fear into his heart, the same state that would fall to his own lot in the years to come. He looked behind him.

"Well, then, so be it," he said, and disappeared inside the house.

The hubbub grew. Neighbors came running to help organize the wake. Contrary to the usual custom, Polidoro recommended an immediate funeral, the very next day, at noon perhaps.

To everyone's surprise, Dodô was opposed.

"The body isn't cold yet and you already want to fling it into the ground? That's an insult to Seu Joaquim's memory."

Polidoro motioned for her to shut up. His face slightly flushed, he felt ashamed to be ordered about in public by his wife. Dodô, however, possessed a power that the other wives in the family did not have. When she had joined this rustic flock, she had brought money and unavowable dreams with her. Wisely, the brothers steered clear of the argument.

"My daughters and I will go to the funeral alone if it's after four in the afternoon—the hour when darkness sets in. Before that, the coffin isn't going to leave this house."

Forgetting the circumstances, Polidoro looked at his watch. He was disturbed by the presence of Ernesto, who had deserted the Iris.

In order to humiliate his wife, Polidoro feigned indifference, appearing to pay no attention to the argument. "How is everybody at the Iris? Are they surprised I'm not there?" he worriedly asked the pharmacist.

Ernesto looked at Dodô's pale face. The public humiliation, with the family as witness, made her ache all over. Ernesto avoided answering Polidoro, precisely because Vivina had arrived, and instantly put her arms around Dodô in a long embrace.

Ernesto was afraid that, under the pressure of the death of his father, already turning slightly blue inside the coffin, Polidoro might suddenly bring up the name of the actress. Dodô and her daughters, moreover, shared that fear. Standing in the middle of the living room, near the coffin, they formed a nervous thicket whose branches shook with greed.

"You're the oldest one of us and the richest, but your word isn't law when it comes to death," the youngest of Joaquim's children spoke up. "The funeral procession will go, just after sunset, to where our mother is buried. Dodô is right. We can't confuse sweat with tears that are shed."

Polidoro eyed his father for the last time, his thoughts far away, wondering what was taking place at the Iris. Life was going on despite his absence. The same thing was happening to his father. Joaquim had just departed, and everything was flowing on with the same vigor as always.

"I'll meet you at the graveside. I'll choose the hour that I'll be there," he said sullenly, without fixing his eyes on Dodô.

At the cemetery, Narciso avoided Polidoro's company. He didn't even come forward to give him a hug, and seemed ill-at-ease on seeing him. Polidoro noticed that Narciso's hands were shaking so badly he hid them in his pockets. He had pulled his hat brim far down, so no one could see what direction he was looking in.

"That man's a Judas," Polidoro said to Ernesto, who was standing next to him. He was sorry that Virgílio, in charge of the Iris, wasn't present. With his flair for history, he could trace down the origin of Narciso's betrayal.

"You're out of your mind, Polidoro. You're starting to have a persecution complex. Narciso's always proved that he was a friend of yours; besides, he shits in his pants out of fear of you."

Polidoro had forgotten all about his father. With his eyes riveted on Dodô, not a single one of her movements escaped his attention. He might catch her passing a wad of bills to the constable by way of the handkerchief, wet with fake tears, pressed to her chest. The police officer had always appreciated furtive acts, subject to the condemnation of society. He was nothing but a man living on the edge of things, Polidoro thought, disconsolate at the treachery of his old ally. How had he failed to suspect an alliance between Dodô and Narciso, which now looked so obvious? He even suspected that the friendship between the two was a long-standing one. Perhaps Dodô and Narciso had met more than once in the dead of night, failing to succumb to the flesh only because they were busy exchanging complaints, Dodô coming out with every sort of calumny against her husband, and the constable, for his part, complaining bitterly about his family in Rio, with no sympathy for the calvary that he was suffering, not to mention his failure to be transferred out of Trindade.

The gravediggers applied their shovels swiftly and precisely.

They flung dirt on the coffin, making the ceremony a brief one in the interests of the family. From the burial site the men would go off to drink beer in the city's bars.

"I already know how Dodô bribed the constable," Polidoro whispered in Ernesto's ear. Polidoro too, handkerchief in hand, was feigning a grief that in fact he did not feel. In latter years, his father and he had regarded each other with growing impatience, bordering on rancor.

"It's not because he's passionately in love that Narciso is going to betray me," he said insistently. "I suspect he can't even get it up. He hasn't gone to Gioconda's place for a long time."

"I beg you, Polidoro, keep your mind on the funeral ceremony. They're already lining up to offer condolences."

Polidoro passed his fingers over his chest, near his heart. There were no roaring sounds forthcoming from that area. He wished that Caetana, in the solitude of the bedroom, were sinking her teeth into his nipples, sucking them with the vulgar words of a red-hot whore, lacerating his flesh only to exact from the man signs of weakness, thus assuring him that his feelings had not gone dead.

"Thank you," he repeated with each embrace. The funeral guests were eager to enlist his help in combatting their respective causes for weariness and displeasure. He was the most powerful of Joaquim's sons.

Dodô confronted him at the very end of the line, as though she were not a relative.

"I've already warned you to watch out, Polidoro. Unless you beg my pardon."

Before her husband could demonstrate his dissatisfaction in public, Dodô's daughters surrounded her for her protection. That army of skirts held the man's ill-humor in check for a short time.

He stared at his watch once again. Should he go on home or head for the Iris, regardless of the consequences? His ill-shaven beard made him uncomfortable. He frantically scratched his face with his fingernails to rid himself of the sudden itch.

"Do you want an ointment for your face?" Prepared as always, Ernesto held the tube out to him.

Polidoro followed Dodô from a distance. Her backside wiggled with self-assurance. Unfortunately, he had lost sight of Narciso.

"Funny, I was able to sow only girls. I suspect I've got weak sperm. Fate didn't see fit to give me a boy."

He still didn't know which way to turn. After all, burying one's own father had inevitable consequences. He thought of the sensual pleasures of the years, all of them inelegant and crude, that had been responsible for shattering his illusions. They had soon drained away, leaving behind as a reminder wrinkles, despair, and white hair.

"Getting through each year is a Herculean task," he said, smiling for the first time that week.

He accepted a lift from Ernesto, who had taken the car out of the garage. Meticulously, the pharmacist cleaned off the windshield and tested the wiper. The way machines worked always escaped him.

"I'll still be the Juan Fangio of Trindade some day," he said, to cheer up the passenger slumped over in his seat alongside him.

Polidoro had plunged into the dark shadows. He was not available. Surrounded by enemies, his heart was disappearing.

"From now on, nobody leaves the Iris without my permission. In fact, the theater is going to become a citadel."

Though it had grown unfeeling, his voice did not hide the hurt of having done battle with his wife and his daughters.

"That's the only way we'll enjoy ourselves in Trindade," Ernesto concluded, starting the car. The roar of the engine kept him from noticing Polidoro's discreet sigh as he sat slightly hunched over in the seat.

ERNESTO HAD rarely seen Palmira except at Gioconda's place. The conviviality established at the Iris erased in his memory the times that he had frequented her bed, as well as the pleasant memories he had taken away with him from her sweat-soaked mattress.

Palmira seemed different and inaccessible to him all of a sudden. The sensation that he could begin a love affair containing a relative proportion of innocence set his imagination afire, placed his affection in jeopardy. When he went away from her, even just a short distance, he suffered a sort of sadness that came from a zone whose mission it was to bring back to him scenes of his adolescence.

Palmira noted his emotion. Although unused to appreciating men because she served their needs in bed, receiving absent-minded kisses along with their acid semen—she deliberately fled Ernesto's gaze to entice him into following her. Every isolated corner that they searched for and finally found turned, for both of them, into a bewitched hiding place: almost the moment they settled down in it, they hastily left it, perhaps moved by the fear that boredom, stemming from habits that had become routine, would single them out as victims.

Diana noted the sentiment that kept bringing sudden blushes to Palmira's cheeks and sending her into nervous bursts of laughter. Even her avarice, her habit of bringing home with her leftover cake and useless bits of string, was gradually tapering off.

As soon as the sweets, the salty appetizers, and the drinks were served, Palmira was the first to pass up her share, giving it instead to Ernesto, who, for his part, was proud of having a woman make sacrifices for him in public. In his eyes, such an attitude represented a veiled promise that some day she would wash his undershorts, his shirts, and even his soul, so frequently downcast.

Indifferent now to the fervor of Venieris, the man without a country, in his artistic crusade, Ernesto was afraid that he had aged, that there was no longer enough time left for him to experience his passion to the full. When he looked at Palmira, though, he immediately became reconciled to his body, now crisscrossed with wrinkles.

His joy made him forget his own home and fireside. It had never seemed so easy for him to unload his family, who usually clung to his back like a heavy burden. This feeling of lightness was due merely to the illusion that he desired Palmira. The woman's body, contemplated from afar, produced the same effect as a little night-light on the veranda of his mother's house.

Constantly keeping a close eye out, Diana did not approve of this recently-begun romance. The radiance emanating from Ernesto and Palmira clashed with the years engraved on both their faces. Such delirious excitement was better suited to young people. Diana especially mistrusted the fateful consequences of love. Once in flames, bodies diffused all around them false illusions and pernicious effluvia.

She drew Virgílio's attention to the problem. Bent on forming an active and competent social cell, the professor had not perceived the perfidy of the pair of lovers. He was alarmed. Subterranean movements, amorous in origin, might well undermine his theater.

"If it's as chaotic as you say, we risk not putting on a show," he lamented contritely.

Diana was grateful for his support. Having a friend to whom she could pass along her anxiety, she would be able to throw herself more wholeheartedly into whatever role it would fall to her lot to play at the premiere.

"What shall I do about this romance?" Virgílio asked her.

Polidoro overheard the conversation. Informed of what was going on, he deemed it to be a trivial matter. He came to Ernesto's defense, advising that it was better to drop the subject.

"If you like, we'll provide them with a corner for them to calm their ardors in."

Because he was still suffering from the shock of burying his father, his judgment was implacable: "In a few hours, that love will be nothing but ashes. Life is a bunch of shit!"

Virgílio was opposed to dismissing it in such terms. He, for his part, took certain moral teachings into account. Life, the supreme good, ought to be treated with respect.

"Why are you so scandalized, Virgílio? Isn't your name that of a poet who didn't like anything but cow manure?" Polidoro was annoyed. His voice, an octave higher, attracted the attention of Gioconda, who had fallen into the habit of shunning human conviviality. Between deep drags on a cigarette, she approached them.

"Virgil was both a lyric and a bucolic poet," the professor broke in, overweeningly proud at being the only helmsman of a boat loaded to the gunwales with books and dreams.

"That may be. But if he wanted to sing of the delights of life in the country, he had to love cows. The way I do. He needed to talk of manure, chiggers, cattle ticks, and God knows what all. Or are you of the opinion that rural life is always poetic?"

Virgílio beat a retreat. Polidoro's evident impatience could not be attributed only to his sorrow at losing his father. The black armband on his shirtsleeve served to placate his conscience, his attention being centered wholly on Caetana. To the point where, immediately after the funeral, he had sought out the actress. She, however, had already gone back to the Palace. Polidoro had exploded at the mere idea of this supposed abandonment of him.

"Caetana has gone out of her mind! We have only three days to go before the first performance, and we don't know one thing about it."

Ernesto received precise instructions.

"Enough of that idyll of yours right now, you hear?" Polidoro pretended not to see Palmira standing next to Ernesto. "Bring Caetana here this very minute. If necessary, drag her here by the scruff of her neck."

Polidoro took a deep breath, puffing out his chest with pride that he could at least face up to the risk of losing her. Or at least pretend, before this select audience, that as a male he had the city, the theater, and, consequently, the actress under his thumb.

"In the past, I mounted her hips. I was an expert rider, a wild stallion. An untamed animal. Has she perhaps forgotten?"

The last words, betraying a love that came back to life in the warmth of the least mention, had been uttered in Ernesto's ear. His friend, sensitive now to the claims of love, embraced him with heartfelt sympathy.

"I'll do anything for you. And I'll have the joy of seeing you two together in bed again."

Venieris, seeing Ernesto leave, presumed that when Caetana returned to the theater she would weep with emotion at his artistic handiwork.

"How are we doing?" Virgílio asked, inspecting Venieris's work.

"The blue paint is all used up. There's still some red and some yellow left. I'll perform other miracles with them."

Convinced of the merit of art, Venieris was reluctant to take time out to sleep. He refused to be looked down on, and was pleased to allow Virgílio to inspect his work, which was well along. Various panels of painted cloth were hung up to dry from the ceiling. When put together, they would form a single scene, the façade of a theater, with the words CAETANA TODAY at the top.

The fake doors, lacking a rigorous symmetry, offered anyone who looked at them the illusion that they were all easily opened and shut. In fact, only one of them opened, the one through which the audience would enter. In decorating the doors, Venieris had not forgotten to paint huge handles on them, larger in diameter than any open hand.

"Aren't these panels of cloth stretched across the façade of the Iris going to make it hard to get inside?" Virgílio asked worriedly. For him, efficiency went hand in hand with aesthetics. "They're certainly beautiful! But will they be practical?" And, forgetting his duty to observe events in order to record them on paper some day, he left Venieris.

The Greek resented the lack of attention being paid him. Who would remunerate him for his sleepless nights, his paint-stained trousers, the crust of illusion growing thicker and thicker in his soul? Fearing the future, in his idle moments he asked himself what fate he could reasonably expect, once the dream of art had come to an end. Who else would commission a work of these dimensions from him? It would have to be of the size of the façade of the Iris. And then there was the stage set, which he had invented without regard for the sort of performance to be put on. An effort such as that was equivalent to building a city all by himself.

"Anyone who once lives on intimate terms with grandeur never again gives it up," he said uneasily. He looked at himself in an imaginary mirror, wanting to hear from inside the glass a voice that would assure him of his genuine vocation as an artist. "Who's a better painter than I am?" And the echo came back, full, round, rich: Venieris.

Sebastiana, for her part, suffered from Virgílio's indifference. Though he was often a lover who was a failure in bed, something to which she was accustomed, she did appreciate not only the professor's caresses, but above all the fact that she was the favorite of a man whose specialty was books, objects that previously had never come into her hands, not even in her dreams.

The Greek's remark, made on the sly, reached her ears. Left to herself now, she held his hand, to spare him from unhappiness. But how to inhabit the body and mind of a man who refused to have anything to do with a woman?

"Is it only art that interests you these days?" She covered her mouth so he wouldn't see her missing teeth.

Venieris nodded. For a long time now, the thought of a woman's genitals had been tormenting him. He was afraid of curly black hair that grew with tropical luxuriance, unlike his own hair, which, being less kinky, was in harmony with his discreet member. He would never allow his testicles to be weighed, as Virgílio assured him was done in certain mountainous regions of Europe. If nature had not endowed him with a bigger-than-average member, it *had* provided him with the boundless destiny of dreaming.

"I'm not a cultured man. But I inherited the ability to bargain from the Phoenecians. I was furious, though, when I left the Aegean and the Mediterranean for this country, where a woman's genitals are a mouth that devours serpents and scorpions. Aren't all you women ashamed of that really desperate state of affairs?"

Diana came by in time to note Sebastiana's embarrassment, since she was incapable of pursuing a conversation on a deeper level. Her store of knowledge being only skin-deep, life came to her by way of a mere handful of words. By the third sentence, she practically implored the person she was speaking with to halt the march of events.

"Do you mean to tell me that on the day of the premiere the façade of the Iris will have those panels of cloth over it?"

Diana looked closely at Venieris's work. Though she had no critical sense, she longed to be admired for her intelligence. To have her accesses of passion, regarded as unrestrained in bed, be forgotten, at least at certain times.

Venieris shivered. His chest rumbled at the thought of Diana swallowing the penises of Trindade with the precision of one who possessed the knowledge of how to keep them hard for long minutes inside her vagina. Luckily, he had never landed in her bed. She always made love parsimoniously, whereas he yearned to be devoured some day by a woman who would sprinkle his body with nutmeg, oregano, hot pepper, rare spices, even though he feared that the feverish practice of sex might turn into a vice or an obsession.

Diana caressed her bosom. She felt her hard nipples, sensitive to the amorous destiny being played out around her. She had spirit when it came to awakening appetites in a body lulled by the fear of passion.

"Isn't it true that the audience will have the illusion that it is entering a luxurious theater?"

In mentioning the fake façade, Diana was out to charm the Greek so that he would ascribe to her the gift of being a muse. He had told Virgílio that in Greece, on giving birth to a son who was to be transformed instantly into a god, the woman enjoyed the same benefaction.

"Ah, how much I want the benefits of life!"

Waggling her hips, she dreamed that the Greek brought to art, at the whim of his mixed colors and his paintbrushes with almost no hairs left, the beauty of the woman born in the tropics. Dark-haired like her, with the swarthy skin of a wandering gypsy, black eyes that could be blinding on melancholy mornings just as it grew light.

Venieris let go of his brush for a few seconds. He leaned the ladder against the wall. With art as their excuse, the two of them scrutinized each other carefully. Diana took pleasure in being an artist without giving up the attributes that drew a partner into bed.

"What are we doing here anyway?" Venieris said in a choked voice, his words coming out in a rasping foreign accent. He felt tempted to go back to Greece, taking this woman with him inside his suitcase, dressed in red silk to enhance her dark complexion. She would be living proof that he had really been to America.

Diana's pleasure in being seductive vanished. Disillusioned by the Greek's words, which had not made her desire any stronger, she pointed at the stage.

"It's three days before opening night. When are you going to fill this empty stage? Or will we be the only ones to occupy such a dreary flat surface?" she asked sternly.

Venieris brought her a series of sketches showing that he was making progress in his work.

"Since Caetana refuses to describe what opera we're going to stage, I've thought up several settings. A bed, a dining table, a salon, all together, suitable for any artistic situation."

Polidoro, who had not taken part in the conversation about the purpose of art, inspected the seats intended for the audience.

"Some of them are broken. They're going to do damage to the richest backsides in the district. But that's not important. They deserve it."

He laughed, satisfied with the progress of the group. Virgílio had good administrative judgment. He took better care of reality than he did of history.

Flattered by the cattle baron's appreciation, Virgílio in fact took great pride in doing his work well, since his express intention was to garner praise. He wanted to be indispensable for once in his life.

"Who's going to send out the invitations for the first night?"

His vest and tie impeccable, the professor assumed the pose of a senator of the republic.

"We don't need announcements or invitations. Dodô took charge of spreading the news of the show. Don't forget that she's the cleverest schemer in Trindade."

He neglected to mention his own prestige. He had sent his farmhands in secret all over the district to invite the most representative men, suggesting that they bring friends and trusted employees. It would be best if they left their wives at home. With their wives at their sides, men became inhibited, which confused things, and made their womenfolk falsely happy.

Virgílio was relieved. He wanted the theater to be chock-full, the human warmth radiant. He imagined what the audience at the theater in St. Petersburg would have been like before the Revolution, the gentlemen and the ladies getting through the sleepless nights after having attended an elegant, spectacular opera.

"It will be a success. The carnival for the next victory of Brazil in the World Cup matches is going to begin right here. But what is going to happen to us after Brazil has won the gold cup?"

Virgílio's faraway look had shifted to Polidoro, plunged into a gassy sphere at the mere mention of the future, when noises at the door attracted his attention.

"Look who just arrived!" Virgílio exclaimed.

Caetana came in, followed by Ernesto and her retinue. She was carrying Riche on her bosom.

"Who's that over there?" Polidoro, daydreaming, had difficulty letting go of the reins of the imaginary steed on which he was mounted. Clinging to its high-strung neck and nervous mane, he was riding across meadows and rivers full of famished piranhas.

"Everybody gather together!" Caetana shouted. "The time has come to assign you your roles."

Without her cape and buskins, Caetana's movements were more agile, despite the weight of Riche nestling on her chest. The cat had curled up between her opulent breasts, stealing heat that Polidoro was dreaming of storing up for his senses to consume.

Even in the Iris, Polidoro was intoxicated by the odor that came to him, in waves, from Caetana's private parts. An aroma that helped him fall asleep, convinced that his nostrils had absorbed it forever. Hence, even if Caetana were to leave, he need only smell his own body to bring the woman back, whole and flourishing.

The dark circles under Caetana's eyes betrayed sleepless, restless nights. Above all the latter, when, alarmed by her unpredictable future, she had gone into the living room in search of Balinho, who slept on the sofa with Riche at his feet.

Balinho thought he was dreaming, feeling Caetana stroking his hair with a delicacy that was unexpected, coming from those hands, which had become far fatter. He gave a start.

"Don't panic. It's me."

She did not dare ask him anything about the opening night. Or about things that had happened in the past, capable of allowing her to tread the boards with a serenity whose origin was the secret passion of living like someone who, a long time ago, had left hope behind without the least regret.

Balinho leapt up from the sofa. He had taken off his pajama bottoms. Standing there in his undershorts, covered with shame, he hid his penis with his hands. The innocent gesture diverted her attention from her anxiety.

"Don't worry. You could be my son."

She stopped stroking his hair. Her maternal gesture had suddenly got all mixed up with the follies provoked by the viscous desire of another's body.

After buttoning up his pajama top, which he picked up off the floor, he brought her wine. Ruby-red in the goblet, like the fear that assailed them in these wee hours just before dawn.

"What name to give to such profound distress?" she asked. Not waiting for a reply, she seemed to be thinking over what she was about to say. "If only Uncle Vespasiano were alive! He would take me personally to the stage entrance, just to confirm that the whole thing was real. How many times he used to tell me that there's no need to fear playing a role onstage. Besides, what is there left of the actor far from the footlights? He himself had a fear of surviving were he to be banished from the wretched circuses or from the tumbledown shacks, with practically no roof and lined with palm fronds, that served us as theaters."

Caetana hid her face, not wanting Balinho to see her eyes. He remained standing there, as rigid as a soldier at attention.

"We still have Brazil left to conquer!" In his enthusiasm, he forgot about his thin, hairy legs, exposed to the breeze that was coming in through the open window.

"We'd better get some sleep. We might come down with colds." Downcast, Caetana began to walk away.

"Where are you going?" He wanted to bring her back, to force her to smother the emotions that she had aroused in him.

"I'm going off to dream, Balinho. To dream the way I always do."

Caetana shuffled to the bedroom in the slippers that she had worn for years, as Balinho, wide awake, looked out the window, on the alert for Dodô and her wraiths. He was old enough to safeguard himself against the failures that Caetana had mentioned. Every step up on a ladder offered at the same time a descent into hell.

Suddenly there were repeated knocks at the door. He was unable to distinguish enemies from friends at that hour, just as dawn was about to break.

"Who is it?"

Ernesto came in, all out of breath, wanting to take them to the Iris. The group there could no longer bear the tension of the many decisions that still had not been made. If Caetana refused to come, Polidoro would cancel the contract.

At the Iris, all of them drowsily crowded around Caetana. She brandished sheets of paper like weapons. She had brought precise notes with her from the hotel.

"Let's not fight, I beg you," Virgílio spoke up first—he who proclaimed himself an expert when it came to knowledge of the human heart, wherein lay deposits of mire, rotten roots, and strange, loathsome creatures.

"Where's Gioconda?" Caetana noted that she was missing.

Brought on the scene by the Three Graces, Gioconda sat down between Ernesto and Virgílio. Their masculine shoulders supported her with the steadfast strength of a mountain.

"Are you all right?" Ernesto turned his attention to the woman in hopes of making Palmira jealous, since she was keeping a close eye on him. She had her doubts about the power of emotions that had been aroused only a few minutes before.

Balinho glanced at the clock on the wall, looking down upon them impassively. He hoped that sensitive instrument would bring Saturday around as quickly as possible.

"Very well," Caetana said with a sigh, trusting in the acoustics of the Iris. "Here are the roles."

She handed them out slowly, indifferent to the wounds that she might well be implanting in each one of those anxious hearts.

DODÔ PROWLED about the Iris, followed by Narciso, who kept his distance. She had forbidden him to get anywhere near her. "I'm a decent woman. I don't want to be taken for one of those whores on the loose in Trindade."

Put on his guard, Polidoro unleashed his dogs against such an onslaught. He appointed Mágico the leader of the pack.

"Follow my wife, or else you'll lose your job at the Palace."

As the night of the performance approached, Polidoro abandoned any pretense of politeness. Unable to sleep, practically camping out, he was all on edge. The one thing that kept him going was the dream of having Caetana beneath his body, on the point of writhing in sensual agony.

"It doesn't matter if I'm impotent at the time," he confessed to Virgílio. "It doesn't make any difference. I want to possess the woman naked, and learn the secret of her odor."

As soon as Caetana had handed out the roles, two groups formed. The first, prepared to die for art's sake, followed Caetana's lead, no matter where she went. The other, allying envy with the melancholy hope of reversing an apparently final situation, feigned independence. It no longer was of any importance to those in this group, as it had been before, to represent onstage life's various dramas.

"What happens onstage is sheer pretense. If that is art, then what is life, which contains within it blood, hatred, and hunger?" Palmira inquired. Her question was ignored by the actress.

Nobody was willing to reply, to run the risk of arousing Caetana's anger.

"It's best not to have her as an enemy," Balinho warned them as, with patient resignation, he cleaned the Victrola, using cotton brought from the Bom Espírito pharmacy.

"And does this Victrola have a name?" Sebastiana handed him the cotton with the tips of her fingers, afraid of dirtying it with the grease from the canapés. She kept on eating nonetheless, especially since she felt that she was the object of Virgílio's indifference.

"The less I fuck, the hungrier I am," she confessed in the morning. Regretting having made an inane remark, however, she explained: "Art alone isn't enough. I think I began this career too late. So I'm anxious about certain things in life. All that shameful behavior I can't get out of my head. I'm as delicate as the ripe persimmons we have there in the back yard at Estação."

Concentrating on his ticklish task, Balinho asked her insignificant questions that didn't require answers.

"So you prefer life to art?"

Sebastiana probed her gum, which was receding because of the three missing teeth. She had not been brought up to filter out words that might wound her sensibilities. Her vital impulse was restricted to washing her private parts carefully—out of fear of diseases that assail human beings like a whiplash—and, when it was time for a break, to drinking coffee with cornmeal cake. As dusk fell, however, she whiled away her time in vague conversations. She especially liked hearing the professor talk. She answered with nods and exclamations, a repertory that was more than enough for Virgílio until the following week.

"Are you making progress at the rehearsals?" Balinho had already gotten rid of the crust of dirt that had been allowed to accumulate on the Victrola through neglect. He was now reaching the cotton down into the secret apertures near where the gears themselves lay. Every so often, he stroked the phonograph records on the table. "If one of these records breaks, we're lost," he said in a panic. Then, perceiving his lack of verbal self-restraint, he dissembled. Sebastiana, luckily, had not heard the remark.

Palmira, sitting on the floor, felt full of resentment. The tears that streamed from her eyes seemed light, as if they had lost all their salt.

"What's happened?" Sebastiana was startled by her friend's disheveled hair.

"A disaster," Palmira replied ruefully.

Venieris kept his distance from the women. They embodied a passion that the gods of his homeland had always condemned. It was a fire for their exclusive use. Hence he safeguarded himself from uncontrolled anxiety over those creatures that he saw floating in the basin of water where he cleaned his brushes. Staying away from them, his energies devoted to the trials and tribulations of art, he wanted only to finish his work. To garner applause even before the night of the performance. Caetana's success, planned for Saturday, threatened to obscure his artistic merits. He had learned, during these days at the Iris, that secrets bore within themselves betrayal and bad omens.

"Tell me!" Sebastiana persisted.

"Ah, how I miss Estação! Life there was never boring."

Sebastiana exhaled her expectations onto Palmira's bosom, whose cleft her mouth brushed with a whiff of beer.

"Life spared us from love there!" Palmira's manner of speaking seemed to be the handiwork of one of their neighbors at Estação, a carpenter who, in his zeal to get materials to build stools and hatracks, lopped off branches of trees with sharp-honed but cruel pruning shears. "How sad love is! People think it's honey, but kisses seem like brine." Palmira tried to hide the damage to her makeup and her apparel.

"Where in the world have you been, to come back in such a state?" Sebastiana didn't go along with the idea that people should be left by themselves in their hour of affliction. "We were always together at the brothel. How many times we shared the same room! Now that life is bleeding you, don't leave me out."

The sole person responsible for her troubles was the pharmacist. Impelled by feelings that were roiling his insides, forcing open his inner doors, Ernesto took Palmira to the empty space underneath a stairway that led to the second floor. An area where, despite the intransigence of Virgílio, who demanded of them all that they keep the public parts of the theater absolutely spotless, dust and spider webs had been accumulating for many years. Because of their passion, they regarded this circumstance as negligible. Palmira smiled happily at recovering, if only fleetingly, her lost youth. Especially since, despite their age, they acted like fools.

On being kissed, however, Palmira was overcome by doubt. She didn't know whether or not to return Ernesto's kisses with equal impetuousness, as he put his tongue between her teeth, sucking her gold fillings, using his ardor to fill the other cavities in her mouth. Was the man's desire founded purely and simply on her supposed innocence? This was undoubtedly a false state, but one in which they both believed.

The more aloof Palmira showed herself to be, the more persistently Ernesto kissed her. The man's saliva spread out across the woman's face and dribbled down into the pupils of her eyes, blinding her.

"They'll see us," she tried to protest.

Ernesto rudely shook her. "Don't talk, or I'll lose my erection." He nervously coaxed along his own desire, oblivious of the woman in his arms.

Thrown to the floor, Palmira found her nostrils invaded by dust and began to sneeze, each gesture of love costing her a dramatic effort.

"Spread your legs, or else I won't make it." Annoyed, Ernesto tried to pull off her panties.

"Wait a minute," she said, ready to collaborate, despite her sneezing. But their worry about solving so many difficulties gradually put an end to the amorous impulses of both of them.

As she experienced the emotion of reliving the scene, Palmira began to speak more and more haltingly. The story came out without any flavor to it.

"Don't leave me on tenterhooks, Palmira. Did the two of you finally fuck or didn't you?" Sebastiana asked beseechingly.

Palmira looked at herself in her pocketbook mirror. She brushed her hair and put powder on to remove the shininess from her face.

"The man couldn't get it up. That wasn't the worst moment, though. It was when we looked at each other, altogether ashamed of ourselves. We wondered what we were doing under that stairway reeking of urine."

"And where is Ernesto?"

Polidoro had sent Ernesto to see Narciso. He was prepared to top anything that Dodô proposed. For this mission, Polidoro had every confidence in the pharmacist's cleverness.

"Are you listening to me?" he asked.

His will sapped, Ernesto had difficulty answering. His body was feeling the effect of the recent damages done to it.

Faced with Ernesto's visit, the constable was firm. His services ought not to have been called upon. He now felt fortified by the certainty that his wife, in the working-class district in Rio de Janeiro, could never get along without his help.

"How much do you want, to leave us in peace?" Ernesto asked, giving up his much-vaunted diplomacy.

"I don't have a price any more. You two showed up too late."

The constable coldly ended the interview, picking papers up off the shelf and piling them in one corner of his office, beneath the noble gaze of General Médici's portrait hanging on the wall.

"It looks like something's going to happen," Ernesto said, not knowing how to take his leave.

Narciso didn't say a word. He was enjoying wreaking his revenge. It was good that Dona Dodô had her mind definitely made up. Retaliation tasted like Surinam-cherry sherbet.

The message, when it came back to Polidoro, left no room for doubt. He could no longer count on the services of Narciso. His system of bribery had undergone changes. The constable had gone over to Dodô's side once and for all.

"It wasn't for money. I've got more of it than Dodô. The advantages that in fact carried the most weight with Narciso were guaranteed by Dodô's brother."

"I've never seen Narciso that happy!"

Ernesto was eager to flee the memory of the fracas with Palmira. When he urinated, however, he fingered his penis, feeling discouraged. The most sensitive human machine had failed him.

"That means he may leave us in the next few days."

In the town hall, Polidoro sounded out Pentecostes on the subject of Narciso's transfer. If he had really received one, could they still block it? Pentecostes, finding himself in an area above partisan interests, declared his neutrality. He intended in this instance to limit himself to applauding Caetana in the middle of a scene.

"How long it's been since I've been to a good show! Nothing is more comforting than art."

The mask of falsehood was glued to Pentecostes's face; his tiny, invariably sly eyes simulated emotion.

"Another bastard," Polidoro commented on his return to the theater.

Ernesto examined his fingernails, violet-colored from a vitamin deficiency.

"How quickly old age comes!"

That was the mood they were in when Gioconda burst in on them. "Caetana has decided to make changes. She's trying to steal the role that was Diana's from the beginning. She insists that the parts have to be rotated. I don't object to exchanging roles, but only after the first performance." She was visibly perturbed. Caetana's return had brought on in her a decided mental confusion bordering on chaos.

At the mere mention of a future project, Polidoro shivered. The future, in his eyes, was a brick that, even though fired at a high temperature, betrayed its origin as clay, fragile and gritty.

"What guarantees do you want from me, Gioconda?"

"You and I have spent twenty years in need of Caetana. That being so, ask her. It's Caetana who has the key to the secret."

In an eminently theatrical gesture, typical of Caetana, Gioconda turned her back on them.

"Look what we're turning into. We still haven't given our first performance and we're already beginning to fight. If we go on this way, we won't leave anything for Dodô to do. She'll end up pitying us," Polidoro said.

He was parading these thoughts past Ernesto when Prince Danilo summoned him, on Caetana's order.

"Why doesn't she come here?" Polidoro said arrogantly.

Danilo owed him for codfish stews and succulent plates of beans. He preferred, therefore, not to mention to him the coming of age of art. Though artists suffered torture at the hands of men like him, they constituted the vanguard of the human conglomerate.

Polidoro ended up going to see her. She was in her dressing room, mopping her breasts, which heaved in constant desperation, especially during rehearsals. Desire penetrated her consciousness like a harpoon.

"We have just two days left, Caetana, and we still don't know what the musical background of our story will be," he protested, his eyes riveted on the actress's shocking bosom.

Caetana, like an alpinist, moved in rarefied altitudes. She resisted anyone's taking away from her the purity of mountain heights. Without returning his look, she occupied herself with minor details.

"We don't need scores," she replied firmly. "Because we won't have an orchestra, not even a violin. Balinho will be responsible for the music."

Virgílio burst into the dressing room, filled with emotion at the thought of being transfigured onstage into an intolerant French nobleman, prepared to destroy the amorous dreams of his son, who was devoted to a celebrated courtesan. This role, fought for in the beginning by the pharmacist, was made to measure for him. Ernesto was at least five years too young to fit the physical characteristics of the character.

"You're too young, Ernesto, in addition to being very vigorous," he said, hoping to make him give up the role willingly by uttering words that Ernesto longed to hear.

Each time there was a dispute, Caetana calmed everyone down.

"Don't be in such a hurry. You're not going to begin action till the very moment you step onstage. The truth is that you're not going to utter a single word. Just move your lips and pretend you're saying what I'm saying."

Polidoro refused to be one of the actors. Theatrical illusion wasn't his cup of tea. In that part of the country, where he was known as Polidoro Álves, he couldn't be anyone except himself. So he chose instead to take care of questions from outsiders. Such as, for example, those of his enraptured friends who, overcome by Caetana's talent, wanted to send her flowers and other gifts.

Caetana interrupted his daydream. She announced with conviction: "I'll be the heroine. Violetta herself!"

She had long had ambitions to perform the role. No one would be able to take it away from her. She embodied it to perfection, even though physically her proportions were not at all those of the demimondaine attacked by a microbe whose origin was orgies and unbridled love.

"Any body will do to experience human emotions," she said, to banish all doubts.

Without asking permission, failing to observe the rules laid down by Caetana, Diana opened the dressing-room door. "Come right away!" And she disappeared as swiftly as she had come.

Caetana did not budge. She had tamed so many convulsions

of those around her that she paid scarcely any attention to them. Polidoro, who for twenty years had kept a tight rein on his emotional reserves while waiting for Caetana to come back, was immediately galvanized into action. He rushed out at Diana's heels, carping at Caetana's indifference when it came to confronting realities that she judged to be mere everyday occurrences.

The procession following Diana grew longer and longer as she headed toward the street. Even Venieris—obsessed by the stage sets, which were not always in accord with what Caetana had in mind—joined the group.

Pentecostes was waiting for them out on the sidewalk. Feeling self-conscious, he limited himself to straightening the knot in his tie as he pointed to the streamers festooning the streets. In his capacity as mayor, he did not see how he could go against popular dictates.

"I'm very sorry, Polidoro. Just see what was left in our streets. They looked like a plague of locusts from Egypt. There was nothing I could do."

Full of affectations, Pentecostes blew his nose, making as if to disappear from the great landholder's sight. Only the solemnity of his office and Polidoro's fortune held him back.

On Friday, Trindade woke up adorned with streamers, specially prepared to celebrate the performance of the Brazilian team in Mexico City, on the eve of their winning the world championship for the third time.

"How pretty a street adorned with streamers is! It's almost a Pentecost Sunday," Virgílio said in a fawning voice, unable to fathom the reason for the politician's visible discomfort.

"Just look at those streamers: LONG LIVE MÉDICI! THE CHAMPION PRESIDENT." Mágico's joy betrayed his sympathy for the military. Ever since the 1964 coup, he had stopped worrying about the fate of Brazil.

"Trindade is full of toadies," Diana shot back disgustedly.

The streamers, stretching across the streets, were reminiscent of the same decorative spirit as the little flags for the June holidays. Each of them, bearing an individual motto, deified a player. The athletes, come down from Olympus, were part of an epic configuration. Under the aegis of Neptune himself, amid sea sprays of fame, the name of Pelé stood out.

"But what's that?" Polidoro stammered, pointing to the streamer squeezed in between Médici's and Pelé's.

Though naturally timid, Sebastiana, wanting to test the precarious progress in reading she'd made thanks to Virgílio, began to decipher it letter by letter.

"T-h-e w-h-o-r-e i-s b-a-c-k. G-i-v-e h-e-r a b-i-g h-a-n-d!" she read finally, in one go.

Despite Sebastiana's satisfaction, she had failed as yet to form a perfect union between the act of reading and that of understanding, so she stood straight and tall to garner her laurels. When she turned back toward Polidoro, she saw that he was pale, about to burst into sobs. Only then did she begin to mistrust the message embedded in the words.

"But what whore do they mean?" she asked with genuine naïveté.

Ernesto went over to Palmira, eager to show her how brave he was.

"This is Narciso's doing. The war has now begun. But we'll be ready for combat."

Imbued with the spirit of art, Sebastiana, like a courtesan of bygone days, did not feel offended. Even in the land of Christ, far from Trindade, many women had been stoned to death, victims of the same accusation. In any era, puritans and those who were repressed demanded human scapegoats to sacrifice.

"It's Trindade's turn to show its intolerance," she said, borrowing from one or another of Virgílio's phrases.

Pentecostes, who had not left yet, was waiting to see how things turned out.

"And do you have proof of these accusations, madam? Since when can you compare us to savage peoples? If you have doubts as to our degree of civilization, why not take the matter to court and swear out a complaint?" he challenged her pretentiously.

Pentecostes's intervention threatened to precipitate a heated discussion with Polidoro. They now had the rare chance to dig up old quarrels.

"Why this idle chatter, Pentecostes? Who is it you're trying to fool, other than whores and thugs?" Polidoro shot back, practicing for the lists. He didn't place the slightest trust in the words of that man to undo the knots of the insult.

Pentecostes temporized. He tried his best to hide his embarrassment. His friendship for the Álves family, and Polidoro in particular, obliged him to contain himself, even more than did the demands and the self-restraint imposed upon him by the official post he held. Besides, time was of the essence. In the interests of the community, it would be better for him to hide himself away in his office.

Pentecostes's withdrawal impelled the others to return to the Iris. His mind on the streamer, which no one had thought to take down, Polidoro did not notice that he was all alone. He presumed that Virgílio—an expert when it came to strategy, having read so many books on war—was alongside him.

"The enemy has begun to close the ring," Polidoro said. "They're trying to reduce us to living on bread and water, Virgílio."

The image drawn from the Bible consoled him. The Hebrews too, in defense of the one God, had sacrificed their own lives.

Preoccupied with the accusations vilifying Caetana, he was not surprised by Virgílio's silence, though generally he was a real chatterbox. He was no doubt doing his utmost to extract from his memory appropriate examples to apply to their enemies. Polidoro would have to agree with him that, as soon as they isolated Dodô, the other adversaries would surrender.

"What shall we do to stand up to them?" Polidoro went on doggedly.

The historian continued to hold his tongue. His failure to speak bordered on egotism, a lack of solidarity.

"Are you listening, Virgílio? Take steps to ensure the immediate withdrawal of the enemy. If necessary, we'll make a traumatic incision in the tumor."

With his eyes still fixed on the streamer, Polidoro offered Virgílio the chance to redeem himself. Especially since he had persuaded himself that the human drama could not dispense with alliances and accomplices.

Virgílio refused to speak. He was revealing his indifference and his cowardice. Abandoned by his friend, Polidoro made up his mind to confront him. Would he be capable of tolerating Virgílio's gaze? When he turned his head around, he didn't see him. Everyone had disappeared.

"Where have those worthless bastards and bitches taken off to?"

He suspected that the group had fled through the side door of the Iris, which the wind was blowing back and forth. A storm was about to break.

Polidoro did not budge. Besides the weight of his loneliness, he was afraid to retreat into the theater. He had no way of foreseeing the plots woven separately by Dodô and Caetana, each aiming at imprisoning him. Whatever the circumstances, he felt himself to be the victim of the two women. Caetana would never call him to her dressing room to embrace him and restore him to life. Or even agree to shed a few tears with him in memory of the love that lay behind them.

"Very well, let the streamer stay there. So everybody can see it," he said vengefully.

He had started to leave the scene when suddenly he changed his mind. As the chief of a tribe that had gone astray, he was duty-bound to goad it, to answer for its follies. Defeat at the Iris would land him back in Dodô's arms.

With these prognostications in mind, he ran into Francisco, who was bringing him the consolation of admiration.

"May I ask why?"

"I've always admired winners," the waiter said, certain that this would please his employer.

It seemed to Polidoro that an angel had lowered its wings to envelop and protect him, even though it had appeared in the form of Francisco, that schemer. It was not always possible to choose perfect human warmth to cover us like a mantle of thistledown. The good omen nonetheless cheered him. It behooved him to forget his loneliness, no matter what the price. Immersed in brine by his friends until just a short time before, he was now drying in the sun of hope. He offered his arm to Francisco.

"Come with me to the Iris. You're my guest."

VIRGÍLIO FELT noble-minded that Saturday. Unlike the poet Homer, whose name was always associated with his own, and who depended on a little oil lamp in order to perceive no more than a few vague shadows, he was in charge of all the lights of the Iris theater.

He had been rehearsing since the evening before. The play of light and shadow obtained that night had turned his imagination topsy-turvy. For he, who had always depended on a transfusion from others to make his way across borders, to enjoy new sounds and unusual landscapes, could now accentuate Caetana's eyes, her distressed mouth, her bounteous breasts. Or even the little glass jar, one of the props for the stage set.

Caetana forbade him to allow the light to fall directly on her face.

"For an artist such as Caetana, it suffices to illuminate half her face," Prince Danilo said to guide him; he himself was reluctant to become a victim of the deformations produced by the direct beams of light.

Knowing how delicate a matter it was to fight against the opposite of darkness, Virgílio asked them to show him how to change the fuses. He failed every single lesson, however, then finally resigned himself to the meager resources of the Iris Theater and to the limits of his own talent.

Venieris anxiously awaited the moment when the public would acclaim his work.

"What time are they going to open the door to let people in?"

In the sleepless hours as dawn was breaking, with the help of

Mágico and Polidoro's farmhands, the painted panels were suspended from the roof, firmly attached with ropes. Hanging loose,
without counterweights on the ends of them, the lengths of fabric
swayed against the walls, transfiguring the appearance of the old
building. The false façade turned the modest movie house into a
miniature lyric theater.

Mindful of the danger that some enemy prowling about might
damage the fruit of so much labor, Ernesto examined the effects
of the fake front from the sidewalk. He was not moved by moral
scruples. In art it was constantly necessary to commit transgres-
sions, as Caetana had explained to him amid sighs. Like Palmira
herself, between carnal faults and coital fiascoes, he too had taken
such a concept to heart.

Still suffering from the disillusionments of the fleeting love
that was stifling his innermost cries of protest, he rebelled at the
stairs painted red. In the midst of this aesthetic contemplation,
he was suddenly overcome by the memory of Vivina at home,
from whom he no longer had any way of escaping, no matter what
wild dream he might fall back on as a pretext.

"And what if the ticket-holders tried to go up the fake stairway
instead of using the real door?"

Not wishing them to think him lost in absurd daydreams, he
tried to justify himself. "What's troubling me is my Samaritan
spirit. I don't want any accidents to happen on opening night."

Polidoro kept pacing back and forth on the sidewalk in front
of the Iris. On guard against suspicious movements, he feared a
treacherous attack. When they were least prepared, absorbed in
the exercise of art, the murderous hand would strike from behind,
robbing them of their illusions.

"What an obsession!" Virgílio exclaimed, refusing to work
under the ministry of fear. "Dona Dodô is a generous soul. Why
would she raise a hand against her own husband?"

Such naïveté upset Polidoro. Having meticulously blown off
the dust from so many documents, and being in the habit of
proceeding at the same slow pace with which silverfish devoured
papers, Virgílio could not properly judge the maneuvers of a blood-
thirsty enemy.

"She's not your wife. What do you know about that viper?" Polidoro lost control of himself, not noticing the damage he was doing to the sensibility of his friend, a credulous defender of conjugal harmony.

"I never married, but if I ever were to change my mind, I'd look for a lady like Dona Dodô."

The professor's sudden pallor plunged Polidoro into doubt. "All that for Dodô?" he said, overcome by the black suspicion that the historian's fierce defense of his wife was owed to a hidden love for her.

"It's only art that's giving me a reason to live now," Virgílio said, causing Polidoro to dismiss his gloomy thoughts. "How am I to go onstage if you keep warning us about the enemy?"

Virgílio went back to work as Polidoro, wishing to give to one and all an example of steadfastness, toyed with his suspenders. He was wearing the striped trousers of a street vendor of old bottles and had his shirtsleeves rolled up. That night, when he turned up in a lead-gray jacket and a bow tie, they would easily take him for a cosmopolite. Caetana herself would be unable to resist his surprising elegance.

His mind at ease, he decided to extend his compliments to the Greek. To tell him in person that his great artistic merit, from that day forward, might possibly condemn him to social maladjustment. After the performance, who would buy a length of material from him without fearing to wound his sensibilities as a painter? In such a case, perhaps the only solution would be to leave Trindade. Polidoro hoped that after so many years in Brazil Venieris had not forgotten the way back to Greece.

Overwhelmed by this speech and in tears, the Greek accepted the possibility of changing course, seeking out once again the homeland of his forefathers, and giving up being a tradesman.

"I am prepared to obey what my destiny commands," he said in heartfelt reply, grateful and deeply moved, looking at his paint-stained hands.

At the moment, however, Polidoro's plan was to immobilize the enemies lying in ambush, to refuse to yield them territory for an unexpected attack.

"And where can Dodô be?" He had brought up the feared name.

Mágico, who had been charged with the task of tracking Dodô and Narciso, was ashamed to list his failures. Suspecting that they were being followed, Dodô and Narciso had taken off in opposite directions. When Mágico had Dodô in sight, he lost track of the constable. Moreover, they behaved with perfect innocence. Not one of their gestures betrayed the least intention of deception.

"Everything is under control." Mágico drew himself erect, beaming, foreseeing a reward.

Polidoro was bitterly brooding over a secret frustration. That afternoon, when he had knocked on the dressing-room door with the illusion that Caetana would gratefully throw herself into his arms, thanks to his effort to transform the Iris into an auditorium that still smelled of wild lavender, Balinho, to his displeasure, suggested instead that he come back just before the curtain went up.

"What are you talking about?" Polidoro shouted, indignant at the worship of a fantasy that, in order to be upheld, made him its sacrificial victim. Particularly since he himself had arranged to buy, in Venieris's shop, a fabric that fell properly and was not transparent. On that occasion, when the Greek had offered him a reduced price, he, with profound pride, had refused, at which point money had lost all importance. The possessor of a fortune, he was bending every effort to spend it forthwith, for the pleasure of at least impoverishing Dodô and their five daughters.

Unbendingly, Balinho informed him that Caetana, in her eagerness to be fair, would admit people at the door only in the strictest of shifts. Those who were in the cast would be allowed in one by one before the opening of the curtain so that she could communicate her final instructions to them. "It's just a precaution, since we're certain we'll be a success." And he went on, in a solemn voice: "Caetana has confidence in everyone's talent, including her own."

Indignant at first, Polidoro gave in almost immediately.

Against his will, the fear of failure haunted him. Not that he attributed the ruining of the show to Dodô's lack of moderation, but, rather, to its structure of daring imprudence, of pure improvisation, as Caetana had demanded. He was a man who took good care of pasturing his cattle, but everything onstage seemed to slip through his fingers. Although Caetana preached the powers of imagination, he was not of the opinion that with imagination alone it was possible to build a sand castle and live inside its walls.

"Are you certain everything's in order?" Polidoro insisted, prepared, if necessary, to send to the capital, even at that late hour, for certain decorative touches that might be missing so as to enhance the stage set, or perhaps even have an entire orchestra, of the sort that enlivened debutante balls or senior proms, dispatched to Trindade.

Balinho's terseness did not convince him.

"Is Uncle Vespasiano's Victrola really going to work all right? Without it we're lost."

For the first time, he treated Balinho with the same affection he'd given his daughter Isabel before she fell under Dodô's domination.

This change in the way Polidoro was dealing with him had its effect on Balinho. He felt intimidated, and avoided getting on more intimate terms with the cattle baron. His boundless loyalty to Caetana did not allow him to be the accomplice of the actress's former lover. Polidoro was a fleeting presence in his life. He therefore owed him no heartfelt wishes for good fortune. Nor did he need to favor him with friendly overtures.

Such coldness, unusual in a young man, struck Polidoro by its very power. Subject to dreams of love, whose one source was Caetana, he thrust his hands into his trouser pockets in humiliation, giving up all claim to a heroic stance.

"Tell Caetana that most of my claims are paid up. I'll settle the last debt of all tonight, as soon as the house lights of the Iris go down," he said circumspectly, overcoming with genteel elegance his desire for vengeance.

Gioconda arrived in time to hear the last sentence. The words floating in the air had no effect on her. She bustled through the theater like a familiar shade. Appearing on the same stage with Caetana provoked in her a strange sensation of weakness. She was

n her dry skin, no longer lub.
bed against her own.

ms of light directed her way
But fearing that she might
ngs, she clapped her hand
she accused the stage of
high price in exchange
aranteed that in that rectangle
eeding.

ore than love?" Gioconda had proclaimed
one now, Virgílio's victim, she was obliged to
rself. "Beam the infernal light on our enemies!"

In his haste to pacify her, Virgílio turned out all the lights.

"How could I harm her if I gave life to her onstage?" he exclaimed. "Didn't you hear what Danilo said? Without the proper lighting onstage, there is no fantasy; nobody sees us. We turn into mere ghosts."

In the darkness brought about by Virgílio, Gioconda tripped over a chair, falling flat on the floor. Taken unawares, fumbling about in empty space, Virgílio managed to reach her. He tried to help her to her feet. Gioconda didn't want any help. Her affronted pride would be restored only by means of proofs that Virgílio was unable to offer.

"What do you know about me? Are you perhaps laboring under the illusion that art is my main ambition?"

With the lights on again now, Polidoro helped her to her feet. She sympathized with the cattle baron's mood. She feared that there would not be a single winner at the Iris.

"What's the matter?" she asked, trying to be helpful.

"It's Balinho. He's acting as though he's the owner of my country properties."

The moment his name was mentioned, Balinho appeared, looking gaunt; his complexion had lost its color in the last few days. He inspected the surroundings. Consulting his watch, he addressed Polidoro.

"It's not your turn yet." He looked at Gioconda. "As for you, you're exempted from having to consult Caetana."

On noting the havoc that this informati
woman's face, Balinho did his best to correct h

"Caetana never tires of saying you're a born ac
a vocation to direct others."

This flattery, instead of puffing her up with pride,
of the theatrical props she bore within her soul as a coun
In the last few hours, she had opted for a straightforwardn
had come from her loneliness, which she had recently b
aware of. She no longer wished, as she once had, to be part
group whose aim was to wander superciliously in the world
dreams.

"Don't worry, Balinho. I'll be the last one to abandon ship.
To me, Caetana will be Callas, for tonight at least."

Hoping that Polidoro would notice the degree of self-denial of
a former courtesan, she repeated the sentence. He, however, in
addition to not noticing her altruism, was irritated at the hint that
he too should forsake Caetana, to give proof of equal grandeur.

"Women never know what they want. That's why we dream
in your place, and reform the world without consulting you," he
said, and wandered off proudly in his high boots, making a great
racket.

Considering this to be a state of emergency, Gioconda summoned the Three Graces.

"We've very nearly become actresses for good! This profession
is like a priesthood. It leaves indelible marks on a person's soul.
While we've been encamped in the Iris, I've contained myself, so
as not to give orders. You don't know how hard it was for me to
give up command. I hope you appreciate my sacrifice."

The declaration brought Sebastiana back to the homely reality
she'd been escaping from. Feeling forsaken, she embraced Gioconda.

"What will become of us after tomorrow?"

Gioconda shook her head, preferring to take her leave. But
Palmira, whose feelings for Ernesto were growing weaker by the
minute, refused to let her go. The expectation of the performance
provided her with lively emotions and attitudes.

"What right do you have to throw us off balance, when the

aware of the death of all feeling in her dry skin, no longer lubricated even when another body rubbed against her own.

Onstage, beneath the erratic beams of light directed her way by Virgílio, Gioconda let out a cry. But fearing that she might pour forth her most closely guarded feelings, she clapped her hand over her mouth. Caetana was right when she accused the stage of mercilessly enslaving them. It exacted a high price in exchange for the magic it offered. Caetana guaranteed that in that rectangle their bodies ran the risk of bleeding.

"What can bleed more than love?" Gioconda had proclaimed spitefully. All alone now, Virgílio's victim, she was obliged to defend herself. "Beam the infernal light on our enemies!"

In his haste to pacify her, Virgílio turned out all the lights.

"How could I harm her if I gave life to her onstage?" he exclaimed. "Didn't you hear what Danilo said? Without the proper lighting onstage, there is no fantasy; nobody sees us. We turn into mere ghosts."

In the darkness brought about by Virgílio, Gioconda tripped over a chair, falling flat on the floor. Taken unawares, fumbling about in empty space, Virgílio managed to reach her. He tried to help her to her feet. Gioconda didn't want any help. Her affronted pride would be restored only by means of proofs that Virgílio was unable to offer.

"What do you know about me? Are you perhaps laboring under the illusion that art is my main ambition?"

With the lights on again now, Polidoro helped her to her feet. She sympathized with the cattle baron's mood. She feared that there would not be a single winner at the Iris.

"What's the matter?" she asked, trying to be helpful.

"It's Balinho. He's acting as though he's the owner of my country properties."

The moment his name was mentioned, Balinho appeared, looking gaunt; his complexion had lost its color in the last few days. He inspected the surroundings. Consulting his watch, he addressed Polidoro.

"It's not your turn yet." He looked at Gioconda. "As for you, you're exempted from having to consult Caetana."

On noting the havoc that this information brought to the woman's face, Balinho did his best to correct himself.

"Caetana never tires of saying you're a born actress. And with a vocation to direct others."

This flattery, instead of puffing her up with pride, stripped her of the theatrical props she bore within her soul as a counterweight. In the last few hours, she had opted for a straightforwardness that had come from her loneliness, which she had recently become aware of. She no longer wished, as she once had, to be part of a group whose aim was to wander superciliously in the world of dreams.

"Don't worry, Balinho. I'll be the last one to abandon ship. To me, Caetana will be Callas, for tonight at least."

Hoping that Polidoro would notice the degree of self-denial of a former courtesan, she repeated the sentence. He, however, in addition to not noticing her altruism, was irritated at the hint that he too should forsake Caetana, to give proof of equal grandeur.

"Women never know what they want. That's why we dream in your place, and reform the world without consulting you," he said, and wandered off proudly in his high boots, making a great racket.

Considering this to be a state of emergency, Gioconda summoned the Three Graces.

"We've very nearly become actresses for good! This profession is like a priesthood. It leaves indelible marks on a person's soul. While we've been encamped in the Iris, I've contained myself, so as not to give orders. You don't know how hard it was for me to give up command. I hope you appreciate my sacrifice."

The declaration brought Sebastiana back to the homely reality she'd been escaping from. Feeling forsaken, she embraced Gioconda.

"What will become of us after tomorrow?"

Gioconda shook her head, preferring to take her leave. But Palmira, whose feelings for Ernesto were growing weaker by the minute, refused to let her go. The expectation of the performance provided her with lively emotions and attitudes.

"What right do you have to throw us off balance, when the

show is only two hours away? What did we do to you to make you leave us abandoned like orphans?"

Sebastiana asked to have a few discreet words with her alone. "The thorn in my heart doesn't matter. We'll never be the same after tonight." She stumbled over her words, partly because of the teeth she was missing. She had, however, rid herself of the feeling of ugliness that had plagued her since she was a little girl. If, on the one hand, God, for some odd reason, had deprived her of beauty, it was, on the other, a relief to think that, at least once in her life, she had assumed the dimension that is the hallmark of great performing artists.

Her heart touched, she took the initiative and enfolded Palmira in her arms. Her friend instantly experienced the shock of human warmth. And the nostalgia that immediately ensued accentuated her flushed features.

Sebastiana prided herself on being able to touch her companion's heart with the strength of her thin arms, making use of a subtlety that, in the end, opened vents of fresh air between their respective bodies.

Diana, for her part, observed impassively the grimaces on Gioconda's face, which had aged her so strikingly in such a short time. The exile they had endured inside the Iris had affected them all. Each of them, flooded with destructive hopes, had become an easy prey of illusions. This carrousel, going round and round from the impetus of emotions, left them adrift.

In order to escape from Diana's furious silence, Gioconda thought of going over a few of the scenes onstage. In a little while, acting with Caetana, she would be witness to the actress's emotion as she lent to Callas, whose voice would emerge from the records being played on Uncle Vespasiano's Victrola, the lips that the Greek diva lacked in order to be majestically present at the Iris Theater.

Onstage, like mutes, they all moved their lips, pretending to sing. Balinho had sworn that the effect of this pantomime would be convincing, perfect.

"I'll be responsible for synchronizing the voices. When Caetana moves her lips, Callas's voice will come out, with the orchestra in the background," he said, with no fear that he might be mistaken.

"And how about us, who don't know the first thing about music?" Diana inquired worriedly.

"Just keep moving your lips and everything will come out fine. You don't need to know the music, which you're going to forget right away anyhow," Balinho said.

Tempted by vanity, which brought to her face an expression that was reflected in the gleaming crystal vase on the table, brought from the Palace, Gioconda imagined herself fighting with Caetana to take over certain scenes, just to tear the latter's heart out. The sound of Polidoro's boots stamping on the dry boards put a stop to her daydream.

At the sight of Gioconda and the Three Graces all together, a strange family that squandered among its members emotions that they alone knew the names of, the cattle baron wondered how he could warn them against the inordinate ambition that had come over them in the last few days. They actually ran the risk of intolerance and smugness, and of turning a deaf ear in the future to the appeals of men who, overcome to the point of nausea by desire, knocked on the door of Estação. All in the name of art, a lunar eclipse of brief duration.

Ernesto drew Polidoro over to the circle of women. Sitting on the floor, they went over the performance in detail. The cattle baron leaned against a packing case. Seen from there, the stage, with its improvised furniture and Venieris's sets, was more beautiful. Above all because of the flower arrangements brought from the Suspiro estate, set out on the table around which the flighty Violetta in her Paris salon would flit about.

"We've accomplished a miracle, Ernesto." Polidoro was referring to the party decor set up onstage.

"Do you think we'll convince the audience that they're really going to see the opera called *La Traviata?*" Ernesto asked.

Polidoro read his few scattered notes. The sheets of paper had grease marks on them from the sandwich he was still eating.

"According to Balinho, everything is in order. We went over everyone's duties yesterday. We won't have any excuse for failing.

What's more, it's neither Paris nor Rio de Janeiro here. What more can an egg-sized city like Trindade ask for?" His voice sounded false as he tried to dominate the situation.

Venieris was putting the finishing touches on his handiwork with his paintbrush muddied by various colors. Of his entire stock, all that he had left was red, which he had used far too much of, without considering the consequences. Beneath Virgílio's lights, the color of passion was heightened, dulling the marble hue of human skin.

"Who are you going to be?" Francisco asked the pharmacist.

After becoming part of the group the day before, the waiter kept asking one question after another, maintaining that it was safe to answer them all, since Polidoro had forbidden him to leave the Iris, so as to avoid any information leaking out.

Ernesto jauntily assumed the youthfulness of Alfredo, the heroine's lover.

"I shaved my beard just a minute ago, so as to look younger. Before going onstage, I'll coat my face with a cream that will make me several years younger. I won't even recognize *myself* in the mirror! Do you want to know about the other roles? Except for the chorus—which we decided to cut out?"

The exclusion of his name from the cast of characters as read off by Ernesto wounded Danilo's sensibilities. No voice, moreover, had been heard revealing his status as Alfredo's father, the moving force behind the tragedy they were about to take part in, a role Virgílio had been forced to turn down he could attend to the lighting effects.

"Everyone to their places," Virgílio shouted, breaking up the group of actors. The others had to take refuge in the aisles. In the next thirty minutes, Venieris would be letting the first spectators into the Iris.

Polidoro trembled as though he were knocking at the portal of heavenly bliss. In less than five hours, he would be taking Caetana to bed. In the whirlwind of desire, he would lose, once and for all, his fear of growing old after being robbed of his dreams and fantasies.

He hurried to Caetana's dressing room. In that cubicle, fragrant with the scent of wildflowers, Balinho was helping her get ready to go onstage. He handed her the mirror, the creams, and the fake jewels.

"May I take part in the festivities?" Polidoro said, trying to make a joke.

Caetana touched the objects with pious devotion. They were from the days of Vespasiano. Her uncle had harbored strange beliefs. In the minutes just before going onstage, he would avow that there existed out there on the boards, completely outside of the text that was about to be recited, a universe on the move that did not obey people's familiar notions of time and space, yet was capable of bestowing on the words, when joined to the theatrical gestures, their one and only chance to trigger a nameless fervor, the complete opposite of the colorless and repressive daily life of most people.

"Is the theater full?" Anxiety suddenly brought back Caetana's youthfulness.

Polidoro was elated at the beauty that the effects of art had restored to her.

"There's not a single vacant seat," he lied, certain that no one would miss that perfect night.

"It's best that way. Art is the only thing that thwarts mediocrity," she murmured to herself. And she ordered in an imperious tone: "Hurry up, Balinho, it's time to take your place next to Uncle Vespasiano's Victrola."

Under his arms were the phonograph records, which he had carefully dusted the night before. He was prepared to save them from the terrible wrath of some buccaneer. Everything about Balinho inspired confidence.

"I'll be back at the end of the first act."

Alone again with Caetana, Polidoro sighed.

"After the performance, will you agree to be my wife?" He failed to take into account the nervousness that precedes all opening nights. Her mind was elsewhere as she sat before the mirror.

"I'm like the bullfighter who prays to the Virgin before facing the bull."

Closely eyeing Callas's portrait, she made every effort to imitate the diva's felicitous image. "Callas is my Virgin," she said, moved. In the photograph, the Greek singer was enveloped in the black of heroines doomed to be sacrificed. Caetana was warming up in the mirror now, opening and closing her mouth in swift movements. By so doing, she would convince the public that her voice was Callas's, which would emerge from Uncle Vespasiano's Victrola.

"Nobody will have any doubt that my art is being conjoined tonight, and forever, with Callas's!"

In his role as stage manager, Virgílio appeared at the door. "Your attention, please! We're about to begin this minute."

Polidoro straightened his bow tie. His status as the lover of the principal actress would make him the object of the public's curiosity.

"Listen to the orchestra!" Caetana hugged her chest for fear that the chords sounding in her memory would suddenly vanish. "It's *La Traviata*, right?"

Wishing to take advantage of the actress's uncontrolled emotions, Polidoro inhaled her perfume with a turgid expression. "Are you happy, Caetana?"

Mounted on her buskins, the actress headed for the entry to the stage, oblivious of Polidoro. The curtain would open the moment Balinho changed the record.

"My hour has come!" Caetana said, her heart moved, looking at the man.

He stroked her face, feeling pity that dreams came true only to leave an emptiness in one's heart. Caetana, her head slightly lowered, accepted the caress.

"Say that you'll be mine," he pleaded in her ear.

On the brink of allowing herself to be carried away by a fancy enveloped in the mysterious patina of time, Caetana smiled.

"After my triumph, I can be anything I want."

Drawn up to her full height, she was heading for the stage when Gioconda blocked her path. Though she was disconcerted at first, Caetana regained her composure, concentrating only on the music.

From his seat, Polidoro was proud of attracting attention. He watched as the curtain opened, revealing the actors. In bright costumes, they moved back and forth in high spirits, in an attempt to reproduce for the audience's imagination many of the characters in the opera who were not present onstage. Their improvised attire rustled at each disorganized movement they made. With utter naturalness, Caetana took a step forward so as to stand out from the group. She used her fan as if it were a worldly device whereby she had replaced Paris with love for Trindade.

The exclusively masculine audience applauded her as she stood center stage, obliging her to bow.

An anxious voice bawled out amid the applause. "Long live Brazil, long live the triple world champions!"

Another voice, a facetious one, shouted enthusiastically: "Encore!"

"Why an encore, if she hasn't even begun to sing?" the man sitting next to Polidoro broke in.

Under Balinho's baton, backstage, the voices of the chorus, coming from the Victrola, drowned out the laughter and the incipient pandemonium.

Obediently keeping time with the orchestra, Caetana pretended she was singing, surrounded by the cast. Gioconda, in the role of Flora, danced attendance on her friend, smothering her in exaggerated signs of affection. She too was out to attract all eyes. They would soon arrive at the scene of the toast proposed by Violetta's lover. Ernesto, in the role of Alfredo, would have the pleasure of extolling in public the love of which he had dreamed in the long afternoons that he had whiled away in the Bom Espírito pharmacy.

Polidoro gave a sigh of relief. Besides beating Dodô in her chosen territory, he had tied her hands forever. He would now be able to celebrate a double victory, Caetana's and Brazil's. To him, life was in apple-pie order.

THE CHIEF referee whistled at three in the afternoon, beginning the match. Certainty reigned that the Brazilian team would be the winner, there in the Mexican capital, on this Sunday in June.

Polidoro looked at his watch. He hadn't slept. Since the evening before, following the events at the Iris, he had been making his escape from family and friends, like a fugitive from justice. When he was thirsty, he went by car out to Suspiro, his country estate, where he did not fear ridicule or cruel laughter. As soon as he set the empty cup of water or coffee on the sink, he hurried back to the city. The headlights of the car lit up the road in the dark but did not relieve the torment in his breast.

In Trindade, his spirits were lifted by the hope that Caetana, after her disappearance, might again turn up at the Iris or on the fifth floor of the Palace.

He was guided by the moonlight as he walked to the center of the public square. Half hidden behind the columns of the familiar busts, he inspected the hotel and the neighboring streets. The two statues, both of them in bronze, representing Eusébio and Joaquim, awakened bitter memories. Following their example, he ran the risk of being the third some day in a series that threatened to be endless.

At the end of the game, which Brazil won, a carnival procession never before seen in Trindade invaded the streets. There was such a commotion that Polidoro, no longer able to remain in the square in safety, hurriedly sought another refuge.

His hat brim pulled down to hide his face, he went by car to the old train station. The building would be a crèche where he could get some rest for his soul in despair.

Having been forced open, the door was ajar. Some malefactor or bum, in search of shelter, far from the police, had gotten there first. He entered cautiously. He was afraid that Narciso might be lying in wait, discharging the full charge of his revolver at him. Or Dodô, with a kitchen knife, finally fulfilling her long-standing promise to cut off his balls, those great insults to her honor.

As he came through the door, he felt the impact of an object landing on his chest, as though Riche were attacking him again with the intention of taking Caetana away from him. Yet he felt neither an acute pain nor the blood of a wound incautiously incurred.

"Come out from wherever you are, Narciso! Confront me face to face, you coward! We've got accounts to settle," he said when he saw on the floor the banana that had hit him.

The echo sent back an almost epic wave of sound, intensifying his eloquence. He was eager now to assume once more a demeanor appropriate to a belligerent male capable of confronting a clever enemy, thereby relieving him of his constant anxiety. At that instant, he understood the meaning of war in the lives of various peoples, the interest of generals in bringing about conflicts as a means of easing tensions and relieving collective frustrations.

Love, which was a trap, toned down his aggressiveness. His feeling for Caetana had mellowed him. He realized, there in that building reeking of urine, that in recent years Dodô had turned into the man of the house; hence she had reason to complain.

Narciso did not want to meet Polidoro face to face. He was hiding his own shadow. Like a samurai, the latter turned round and round in a circle of a minimal diameter, not offering his back to the enemy. He heard a noise coming from the platform. Narciso had decided to duel with him.

"What are all of you doing here?" Polidoro said in terror, not catching on to the fact that the people who were there were Gioconda and the Three Graces.

"Whoever got here first is the one who has the right to ask that question. Tell us why you've come to disturb our solitude, to invade our refuge?"

The women, clinging tightly to each other's hands, were dragging one another along haltingly. Each of them was afraid she would get separated from the group. They were still dressed in their costumes from the Iris, as though awaiting the signal to come onstage again. There in the station they missed the shivers up and down their spines of the night that had just passed and the voice of Callas, whom they were beginning to appreciate.

"Where have you been on this accursed night?" During his goings and comings back and forth to the country house, Polidoro had not seen a single light on when he drove by the brothel.

"We fled from the Iris and came directly here," Sebastiana informed him. She had just woken and was wiping the sleep from her bleary eyes.

Palmira was upset. Polidoro reminded her that Ernesto was now in Vivina's arms. The fleeting love affair between them had not lasted a week.

"My hunger is even worse than that," she said thoughtfully, searching for objects on the floor, till she found the five doves and the stubs of the candles from the birthday cake on the cardboard plate.

"If I just had one piece of that cake left!" And she sucked in her belly, burning with hunger.

"What a shame—the ants ate the whole layer we forgot to take home with us, in our hurry to go visit Caetana," Sebastiana lamented, turning toward the entry. She sensed that Virgílio, permanently contending with Ernesto for the cattle baron's friendship, was about to arrive.

"Even if I wasn't sure they were machos, there'd still be good reason to be suspicious of them. Those two seem more like Polidoro's women," she had maintained, by coincidence, during the long hours before daybreak.

Sleepiness was making Polidoro's eyelids heavy. He flung himself down on the bench. Sitting alongside him, Gioconda hung her head dejectedly. In that same building, even before the train whistled at the curve, she had begun to dream of Caetana, who would bring her illusions and hope.

"Move over," Diana said, making Polidoro slide farther down the bench, wanting to sit next to the two of them, she too needing the warmth of drooping bodies.

Polidoro consoled himself by remaining jammed in between the two women. He counted only on the smell of those creatures.

He remembered Dodô. He had retained no memory of her body. In his torpor, that thought startled him. For the first time in all those many years, he admitted that his nature was the same as Caetana's, with the same orifices, through which in the past he had indulged his incontinent virility.

"If only Virgílio had a hunch we were here!" He felt a claw in his heart.

"That's the only way we'd find out what happened at the Iris," Sebastiana said, confident in the reality that the professor had been passing on to her little by little. He gave her continual proofs of his profound love of the truth, although later events almost always belied his version.

"Weren't you there to see?" Diana was critical of Sebastiana's submissiveness, her stubbornness in not learning to read. How resignedly she embraced men, in the almost religious belief that they were the only ones who could assure her of her daily bread.

"I was watching the audience. How could I tell what was happening in the wings?"

She smiled, proud of her correct use of the word that best defined the corridors and the narrow passageways backstage, through which the artists, beneath their halo of suffering and ecstasy—which moreover, left them insecure and unstable— passed immediately before going onstage.

"How I suffered on that stage, forced to open my mouth so that a dead person could sing, with me as her medium!"

Nervously, Sebastiana walked round and round the bench. Only half her distress, more evident each time she spoke, reached Gioconda, Diana, and Polidoro. Palmira alone, far distant from the bench, could see the whole of it.

"Who told you that dead people were singing, using us as intermediaries? I'd rather have Dr. Know-It-All here with us than allow you to talk," Diana said to her harshly, without thinking twice.

Sebastiana turned resolutely toward the bench and confronted her.

"I've played onstage, and I'll be an actress till I die. Even though the performance isn't over yet. I'm proud of this profession!"

"It's goodbye to art. We're nothing but whores now," Diana said in a biting tone of voice, her claws bared.

Each minute made Polidoro and Gioconda more weary on that interminable, sleepless night. Slowly, they leaned their heads on each other's shoulders. The mutual support gave them the sensation, helped along by their drowsiness, of being on the sofa in their respective houses. The pleasant illusion that a home and hearth, and the comforts they offered, were not such an impossible way of life after all, or one to be forever condemned.

Palmira woke up Gioconda, oblivious of Polidoro's head, jolted by her vigorous shaking.

"Those two are going to kill each other yet, Gioconda."

"Leave me alone. Isn't what's already happened enough?" Gioconda woke from her lethargy with a bitter taste in her mouth.

Palmira began to pick up the doves and the candle stubs and stowed them in her purse. Since she had come out of the Iris, she was once again horrified at any form of waste.

"I want the truth," she said, in the midst of the litter.

"What truth? The fact that we were a failure?" Trying to get to her feet, Gioconda pushed Polidoro away. Deprived of the balance that the woman's head offered him, he toppled over onto her.

"Wake up, Polidoro!" Her spirits were reviving.

Thrown out of the nest, Polidoro was frightened. As darkness fell each night, life had always reached him through the warmth of a woman, a boiling fountain of water in which he bathed every time he dreamed. Not knowing where to turn, he forced himself to observe details all around him that had previously gone unperceived. In the future, in his leisure time, he urgently needed to reconstruct certain facts that seemed so obscure today.

"I bet Virgílio's going to turn up," Sebastiana said. She could no longer live without the professor. Thanks to him, life could suddenly smile on her. Especially when he stuffed her full of stories that Sebastiana acknowledged she had experienced only because they came from his mouth. Stories as bright as sunny days. They were almost the same as a trip to Rio de Janeiro.

In the midst of all the commotion, Virgílio appeared.

"I had a feeling that you wanted to see me."

Always so careful about his appearance, never forgetting the clean handkerchief that adorned the outside pocket of his suit coat, ever ready to dry the tears of any lady who was weeping, he impressed those present by his negligence.

"Where have you been, to get here so late?" Polidoro said impatiently.

"Back there, pursued by ghosts and the lights of the theater, which still blurred my vision. Since I was the last one to go, I turned out the lights, leaving the theater in darkness. How painful it was to disconnect the projectors that illuminated such an imposing spectacle."

"How did you know we were here?" Diana asked, reacting to the presence that was monopolizing everyone's attention.

"Where else would we go, if we lack the courage to go home?"

"Is Ernesto also back there, wandering around all by himself?" Palmira didn't want to hear any more about the needs of that love. As far as she was concerned, her feeling had been drained dry at the Iris. All she hoped was that the pharmacist would be discreet and not try to revive those memories.

"If only I understood what happened!" On the point of catching cold, Virgílio blew his nose. He ran his fingers through his hair, trying to make himself look presentable. He was ashamed that the proofs of his thoughtlessness and his disillusionment were imprinted on his friends' retinas forever.

His melancholy but genuine declaration disconcerted the group. For the first time, the professor admitted that he had no knowledge of a reality to which he had been a witness. He was giving up his cleverness at improvising explanations of a recent history that was still only skin-deep for all of them. Virgílio didn't even have the heart to justify the tumultuous happenings of the present by way of some fact from the past, as was his usual practice.

In this emergency, Polidoro took over the professor's function. Exhaustively clutching his sweating head, to which there clung a few hairs coiled like a snail, he forced himself to remember. "It all started shortly before the end of the first act. I was in the front row, so moved that the thought never went through my head that Narciso, carried away by an insane impulse, would use the back door in order to commit a criminal act and silence Balinho."

"Why would he want to rub out Balinho? It would have been better to kidnap Caetana at the end of the opera, as she was acknowledging the applause. Had they thought of the consequences if he were to disappear with Caetana? The diva of the company! With the aggravating circumstance that she was making use of the voice of a star that's worth a fortune in dollars." Virgílio thought it all over carefully, though still inclined to accept the cattle baron's version of the matter.

"So who was the guilty party?" Diana made a move as if to leave the building in search of her bed, without a man mounting her haunches.

"Any one of us," Palmira said, instilling doubts in vainglorious hearts tarnished with verdigris.

Having returned to his memories, Polidoro took no notice of the women.

"All I know is that suddenly, even though Caetana was moving her lips, neither the voice of the Greek singer nor the orchestra was heard."

At first Caetana didn't notice. But when she realized that she had no accompaniment, she seemed unable to believe it—opening her eyes wide, forgetting to close her mouth. The others, noting the state she was in, also froze, except Ernesto, who, amid the rapture of his love, gave living proof of his passion for Violetta, not perceiving that Uncle Vespasiano's Victrola had ceased to provide the music indispensable to the scene.

Gioconda, in the role of Flora, signaled to Ernesto to warn him, pulling on the tattered suit he was wearing as a substitute for a cutaway coat. She was in despair over the pharmacist's self-conceit. He would not bow to the evidence. So then Gioconda latched on to Caetana. She hoped that Balinho, being only temporarily deprived of his senses, would start the music up again. In their embrace, which lasted for some two minutes, Gioconda whispered a few words in Caetana's ear. With a violent jerk, Caetana freed herself from her, as though struck by an unbearable truth. And she heard the catcalls. The audience had finally caught on to the trick. Instead of singing, Caetana had borrowed a voice coming from backstage. The actress cringed. The shabby behavior of Polidoro's friends was unpardonable. Humiliated, she hurried offstage, not falling in her lofty buskins thanks only to Ernesto, who, finding himself deprived of his fervent mistress, demanded that she come back onstage, where love, represented by him, awaited her. In no way would he go on loving without the presence of the object of his passion.

"Come back, Violetta, come back! What will become of this little French nobleman without you!"

Convinced that he was speaking a truth that the audience would easily understand, Ernesto grabbed her by the arm. Caetana struggled against this interference. She very nearly stumbled, but, with great effort, Ernesto managed to keep her on her feet, a heroic deed that he performed above all because he knew he was the object of the gaze of the males in the audience, who, envying him his insane love, were itching for him to fail. He therefore helped her leave the stage with the same dignity with which she had made her entrance.

Once they were away from the eyes of the audience, Ernesto, who had a family to support and hence a duty to beware of a heart attack and a wrenched arm, let go of her all of a sudden, without the least pity. Leaning against a column, anxious to recover, he lost sight of Caetana. The one thing he remembered was that Danilo, ready and waiting to enact the role of the jealous father in the next act, was at his heels. The prince had bared his canines, all set for revenge.

"It wasn't like that at all. That's nothing but a bare-faced lie!"

Gioconda interrupted the sordid version at an untimely moment. They were attributing to her an ungrateful and deceitful role in the fiasco. What could she have whispered in Caetana's ear that the actress didn't already know? On other occasions, she had succeeded in opening her heart to her, desperately in need of pouring itself out. She had, however, certain observations to make. It had not been Ernesto who had guided Caetana to the aisle. She, Gioconda, had been the one who, noting the actress's distress, practically blinded by tears, perceiving before her only ditches, crags, and cliffs, had taken forceful measures.

"Ernesto tried to take her away from me. What does he know about women? Going to bed with them doesn't give him the authority to argue about shaky and desperate feelings."

She plunged to the bottom of her memory. The journey was a painful one for her.

"At the door that led outside, Caetana may have wanted to thank me. To confess, perhaps, that she was boiling with rage. We were enveloped in shadows. Virgílio's spotlights weren't there to light up her face. But even in the half-light, Caetana's gaze was so intense that I feared I'd be penetrated. It went all the way through me and the wall behind me and then returned to her own eyes.

" 'It won't matter at all, Gioconda. I've been defeated yet again. Except that I don't have Uncle Vespasiano to console me now,' Caetana said, knowing beforehand that I was fervently memorizing her words. Unable to hide my despair, I felt like taking my vengeance on whoever it was who had destroyed her last illusions.

"Caetana lifted her chin high. She did not seem to be present. There was a long road ahead of her. She would once again swallow dust, fried cassava, manioc meal, chunks of pork fat, and jerked beef. Every gesture of hers was that of a queen who had been dethroned, surrounded by traitors who hated her but could not take her title or her dignity away. They demanded that she leave the country; otherwise, should she choose to remain, she would be imprisoned in a stairless tower.

"Caetana wrapped up the cape that she had brought offstage with her and hid her face with it, till only her eyes were visible. The red velvet glowed.

" 'It's life that betrayed us! Nobody betrays us all by himself. Men are mere tools of destiny. Besides, we still have the taste of raw meat in our mouths. We've barely left the age of the cave dwellers, Gioconda. And that's still your name, isn't it?'

"She gave a forced smile," Gioconda continued. "She was getting ready to leave me all by myself. I didn't know what to do, torn as I was between her and the Three Graces. I walked toward her."

Sebastiana interrupted Gioconda's account to embrace her, out of compassion. She could not bear being by herself. She had the impression that she was saying goodbye forever to Gioconda and Virgílio. She would never see them again once they took the train. "I already know what you said to her." Sebastiana seemed to be racked with sobs.

"What can Gioconda have said?" Palmira asked, weak and defenseless on confronting the world of words. She clung to Sebastiana as though the feeling of security that she so badly needed would be forthcoming from her. Once again, poverty terrified her.

"It's obvious that Gioconda offered her our house. She said to her: 'Come to the brothel. I'll make dinner for us. We're famished for salt and for love. While I'm in the kitchen with the pots and pans, the Three Graces will look after you. After that, we'll tuck you in bed. And you'll never feel cold again.' Wasn't that what you said to her, Gioconda?" Sebastiana had begun to cry, moved by the poverty that was already knocking at their door. The years of splendor were over. She held on to Palmira's hand so that they would grow old together. Fear must not thrive among them.

Gioconda felt exhausted, without the courage to go on. Polidoro had lost interest in her. He was demanding that Virgílio speak, but the professor was reluctant to do so. Nonplussed, he found himself, like the others, beneath the sign of passion and of hatred closely interwoven.

"What hatred are you talking about?" Polidoro said to Virgílio when he finally spoke. Such distrust was of deep concern to Polidoro. It was as though the professor were fostering the baser feelings just so he could compare all of them to his enemies.

"The only thing I remember is that, having just barely recovered from the scare I'd had, I forgot to switch off the spotlights onstage. Beneath that intense beam, the characters seemed like butterflies, winged creatures, prisoners in a net of light. At the same time, as I saw how terribly frightened they were, I felt as though I were an Englishman in India. After trapping them in a blind gorge, I was proposing a surrender whereby their lives would be spared in exchange for giving up their religion."

Onstage, however, they were all up in arms.

"Hurry up and turn those lights off, Virgílio. Get us off this damned stage, please!" Abashed, they would leave the stage only under cover of darkness.

Virgílio immediately plunged the theater into pitch-darkness. He left on only the light of the stairway leading down to where the audience was sitting. For anyone who wanted to make his escape, that was the ideal way. The Iris was empty in a few minutes. Everyone was in a hurry to go home and forget the fiasco. No one had any desire to witness embarrassing scenes.

Polidoro was indignant at the disorderly flight. He raised his voice so that they could all hear. "This isn't an animal pen, or a pasture for a cattle stampede. Behave like gentlemen or you're going to have me to settle accounts with."

In silence, they now looked for the exit. A threat of an almost spiritual nature was hanging over their heads, originating in imposture. Failure might come their way too some day.

Feeling his way along, Virgílio reached the wings. The Three Graces bore a grudge against Gioconda, being afraid she'd follow Caetana wherever she went. Gioconda had sworn never to leave them without a roof over their heads, especially now that old age was swiftly creeping up on them.

"Where's Balinho? Go get him, Ernesto," Gioconda said.

Ernesto refused. He was on his way out. Vivina was looking all over the streets of Trindade for him. He couldn't sacrifice his wife's life on this night of thunderclaps and storms.

Worried about what might have happened to the young man, Gioconda turned to Virgílio. There had surely been some sort of accident. That was the only possible explanation for the silence of the Victrola, which Balinho was prepared to defend with his very life. Wherever he might be now, he was feeling contrite. Responsible, perhaps, for the disaster.

At Sebastiana's side, Virgílio glanced at the moldy walls of the train station.

"I'd become reluctant to take on the responsibility. I'd been afraid I'd catch Balinho by surprise backstage in some act of a dubious nature. I suspected that, undermined by unpremeditated feelings, all of them come from outside and bent upon strangling his soul, he had been unable to put up any resistance against them. Despite his innocence, he had harbored villains; he had lent them his soul."

Amid sighs shared by the faithful Sebastiana, the compassion awakened in Virgílio by the destiny of others was redoubled. "Poor human soul! No matter how honest and hardworking, it always slips and falls on slimy stones."

Diana could bear the professor no longer. Besides being ungrateful, never giving her affectionate embraces on Christmas Day or bringing her even one present, he was exploiting docile Sebastiana.

"The truth is that you were afraid to go to the Victrola," she said, fanning herself with the warped pages of a newspaper that bore the date 1963.

"I've never been a coward! Point out to me a single instance when I fled the rostrum or ran away from pupils who were threatening to throw pebbles at me!"

He reacted in the face of aggression. As a matter of fact, he had never killed a man, but it wasn't necessary to pass that test in order to show one's bravery. Nor provoke expensive wars with the intention of inculcating rudimentary notions of patriotism.

"You were afraid nonetheless. I offered to go along with you, seeing as how Ernesto, the scaredy-cat, ran to Vivina's iron arms."

Loyal to his childhood friend, Polidoro tried to put a stop to this libel against Ernesto.

"And where was our Greek? He tried to divert everyone's attention to a character possessed of aims and purposes that were probably of epic proportions."

"Don't interrupt me, Polidoro," Diana said, feeling outraged.

Surprisingly, he accepted the reprimand. As though it would do him good to be on intimate terms with humility.

As an actress, Diana struck poses that were superb, in sharp contrast to the moldy walls of the building.

"I went to look for the candle and the box of matches, fumbling about in the darkness. Ernesto and Palmira had hidden them underneath the stairway on the second floor—the isolated corner that had turned into their love nest."

The feeble light of the candle guided her to where the Victrola was. Diana made a loud noise with her shoes, wanting to warn Balinho that she was coming. But he wasn't there. He had been abducted or, tired of the theater, had simply disappeared. Life in the Iris, where delusions cropped up with unprecedented violence, brought out in clear sight sentiments that went from love to envy, by way of contempt, bitterness, resentment. Perhaps Balinho felt an urgent need to live on his own, abandoning Caetana's shadow, which was suffocating him.

The Victrola had also disappeared. On the table there was nothing but broken phonograph records.

"What records were they?" Gioconda sounded apprehensive.

"The records of the opera we were staging."

"Do you mean to tell me that Balinho broke the records before he disappeared?" Sebastiana said in amazement.

Virgílio rejected this version.

"That wasn't his doing. Why would he act against the interests of his mistress?"

The professor's spiteful remark, which reduced Balinho to the status of a domestic animal with a collar, delighted Polidoro. He had no esteem for the young man. Because of him, he had not managed to kiss Caetana, or take her to bed with him.

"Balinho had reasons to betray her. He would never agree to Caetana's staying with me in Trindade. Especially after the triumph offered her by me," Polidoro stated with conviction.

With a gesture, Gioconda brought the delirium under control. Madness had spread throughout the abandoned station, as though ghosts, hugging the walls as they waited the train that would come through there some day to take them away, spoke of facts that they had not witnessed. The contradictions accumulated. She, for her part, could only attest to the fact that, after Diana's return, Venieris had suddenly appeared, downcast.

"Is it some new trouble?" She suffered for the painter, who

spoke incomprehensible words to her, in Greek sometimes, as though he could find comfort only in that way.

Venieris was unable to forgive Virgílio for having plunged the theater into darkness without consulting him. Nobody could then appreciate the stage sets built for the express purpose of conferring on the old Iris an extraordinary aesthetic. As though that displeasure hadn't been enough for him to have to swallow, another one, more serious still, had occurred. Dragged along by the men who were rushing out of the auditorium like a herd of buffalo, he found himself in the street. In the midst of cars that were fleeing at top speed, threatening his life, he discovered that a certain criminal hand, doubtless in the pay of someone, had arranged for the removal of the drop curtains on which he had painted the theater's false façade.

"It was the death blow to our dream," Venieris said in distress. "We don't have a single souvenir left. Even if I wanted to make those paintings over again, I wouldn't be able to. The one thing left for me to do now is go to Greece and paint a real theater there. It's the only way to be happy again."

On seeing the evidence of the theft, Venieris started shouting for help. Francisco, along with Mágico, patted him on the back. "What a pity. It was so pretty!" And Francisco politely asked to be excused. The Palace bar was crowded with customers.

"I consoled Venieris and asked if he'd seen Balinho, who'd been carried off by kidnappers," Gioconda explained, leaning against the bench at the train station.

"Nobody said a word to me," Venieris answered, unable to think about anything except the theft of his paintings.

As Gioconda was recounting the story, she relived the haste with which they had knocked on the door of Caetana's dressing room. Though Caetana didn't answer, they went on knocking. Virgílio tried to batter the door down.

"If only we could count on Danilo for help," Palmira said, longing for a superb body after having lived on intimate terms during all those days with a man as frail as Ernesto.

"Turn the handle. You'll see that she didn't lock herself in."

The professor opened the door gently. He was afraid of Cae-

tana's anguished reaction to what had happened. Gioconda, however, went on in first, finally prepared to plunge into madness.

Caetana had disappeared from the dressing room. While they
were arguing, she had taken her costumes and the fake jewels with
her. The dressing table was empty.

Palmira sat down on the bench next to Polidoro. She felt pity
for the sorry figure he was making, repeating the same thing over
and over. "They've flown the coop again. Just the way they did
twenty years ago."

"Where have you been all this time, since you left the Iris?"
Mistrustfully, Gioconda interrupted his monotone. Polidoro too
had motives for committing a base deed. Failure would leave Caetana at the mercy of his compassion.

"Don't force me to speak, I beg you," he answered in a hoarse,
feeble voice.

"Where would Caetana head without money and without a
future except for Polidoro's arms?" Gioconda was bitter, not even
trying to control her temper.

Virgílio was opposed to this line of argument.

"Caetana would kill herself rather than depend on Polidoro's
charity."

The cattle baron freed himself from Palmira, who was clutching his hand. "It wouldn't be charity but love!" His thunderous
voice was a sign that he was recovering. He fought furiously. What
did they know, after all, of his despair at the Iris, when from his
seat he perceived that the mist of dreams was blending into one
with the film of light beamed down on the stage by Virgílio. For
a long time, he didn't budge. He sympathized with Venieris's
woeful protest, his art discredited because of an underhanded game
of plots and counterplots. What homeland did he have left after
having discovered the imperatives of art? He saw Ernesto, fleeing
from Palmira, trip on the stairway leading from the stage, in his
hurry to return home. He walked past him and pretended not to
notice him. All alone in the auditorium, Polidoro approached the
stage. He heard the cries of the Three Graces behind the curtain.
And he noted the disappointment of the group when they opened
the door of the dressing room, with no idea of what had become

of Caetana. It was then that he decided to confront Dodô, but she wasn't home. He grabbed the shotgun he used to hunt pheasant, and ran to the police station. The building, with just one light on, looked empty.

The corporal on duty received him. "Dr. Narciso went off to Rio de Janeiro about an hour ago. He wanted to be with his family in front of the television set, to celebrate Brazil's winning the World Cup."

The corporal offered him a cup of cold coffee with sugar. He was sorry not to be able to be of more help. Polidoro shouldn't count on Constable Narciso in the next few days. When he returned from Rio, he would be staying in Trindade only long enough to hand his post over to his successor. He had finally been assigned to duty in a district on the outskirts of Rio de Janeiro—a reward for his services as a servant of the state. With a look of complicity, the corporal hinted that Polidoro knew the favor that had been done Narciso. It was to Polidoro and to Dona Dodô that the constable owed his transfer and his promotion.

"I tried to hide the truth!" Polidoro buried his face in his hands. "It hurts me to think that Dodô is the guilty party."

Polidoro was shivering from the cold, the same cold he had felt as he went upstairs just after dawn to the fifth floor of the Palace, in the hope of still finding Caetana. He wouldn't know what to say. He found the door wide open, the drawers emptied out, papers strewn all over the floor. The move had been made in a hurry. They were old hands at packing and unpacking suitcases. The only thing they had left behind was a photograph of the Greek diva on the wall. From the neck of the foreigner, dressed all in black, there hung the cross of the Orthodox Church.

At the sight of the singer, he threw himself on the bed, sobbing. The sheets still retained the odor of Caetana and a remote warmth. In desperation, he nestled his penis against the mattress. He pressed down hard on it as though he were penetrating her. He felt ashamed of himself, however, and did not complete the act. It was like making love to a corpse that had been disinterred merely for his pleasure.

"How did they get out of here with their baggage?" he asked Mágico, who was sleeping on the sofa.

Mágico had a hard time coming to. Awakened with a start, still sleepy, he begged Polidoro's pardon.

"They climbed into the same truck that brought them here. Danilo went off to look for the driver, who was having a drink at the café on the corner. By coincidence, he was just on the point of leaving."

"And what about Caetana?" He was afraid that Mágico would recount a dramatic scene, plunging a nail into his heart.

"She acted as though nothing had happened. Her gestures seemed theatrical. Maybe she exaggerated her tone of voice when she gave orders, urging everybody to get a move on."

Mágico concentrated all his attention, in an attempt to fish up some memory that would be of interest to Polidoro.

"Oh, yes, she looked at me as she always did, hardly seeing me. She also ordered the chandelier lights turned out. She didn't want the cat purring on her bosom to be disturbed. She looked all around the lobby. A metallic look. Do you know what she said?

" 'Tell the people of Trindade that I'm coming back twenty years from now. If I'm still alive and they are too. I hope to bring with me then my old age and my last illusions. To a city that dreams only of cows, it'll be worth waiting for me.'

"She climbed into the cab of the truck in her stage costume from the Iris, the cape, and the tiara on her head. Balinho helped her in, settling down alongside her."

The account he'd given exhausted Polidoro.

"She promised to come back some day," he concluded.

Gioconda's gaze was fixed on the horizon. What was missing in the scene before her was an avenue adorned with leafy trees on which to rest her eyes.

"It won't be easy to wait twenty more years."

"As luck would have it, there are lots of us who won't be alive then," Virgílio said, apparently resigned to this denouement.

They heard the skyrockets and the din in celebration of Brazil's third World Cup victory.

"How many points did we win by?" Taking his time, Polidoro was coming back to life.

Diana felt relieved at the possibility of going back home soon.

"If we had a map, we'd know where Caetana went," Virgílio said. Sitting next to him, Sebastiana pressed him to talk about Brazil.

"Brazil is too big, Sebastiana. That's why we're fated to be lonely," Gioconda said, sitting down next to Polidoro.

All of a sudden, the cattle baron was overtaken by a strange emotion. At a signal from him, they headed for the platform, hoping the train would appear, rounding the curve.

"When will she arrive?" Palmira had no idea from which direction the train for happiness pulled in. From the right or the left?

"Didn't you hear? Twenty years from now!"

Polidoro had his eyes glued to the dirty rails. He was certain that illusions also jumped the track, mutilating travelers who had inadvertently boarded the impossible dream.

"Caetana!" he shouted, his hands cupped around his mouth, turned toward the south, the direction the wind was coming from.

"Here I am," Gioconda answered.

Polidoro offered her his arm. It was time to leave the station. The Three Graces and Virgílio went on ahead. With each step she took at Polidoro's side, Gioconda assumed more confidently the pose that she had finally stolen from Caetana.

Nélida Piñon was born in 1937 in Rio de Janeiro, where she now lives. Since 1961 she has published eight novels and three collections of stories. She has taught at universities in Brazil and at Columbia, Johns Hopkins, and the University of Miami, where she is the Stanford Professor of Humanities. In 1989 she became the fourth woman to be elected a member of the Academia Brasileira de Letras. Piñon's work has been translated into Spanish, French, Italian, and Polish, and some of her stories have appeared in American anthologies. *The Republic of Dreams* was her first novel to appear in English.

A NOTE ON THE TYPE

The text of this book was set in Goudy Old Style, one of the more than a hundred typefaces designed by Frederic William Goudy (1865–1947). Although Goudy began his career as a bookkeeper, he was so inspired by the appearance of several newly published books from the Kelmscott Press that he devoted the remainder of his life to typography, in an attempt to bring to the printers of the United States a better understanding of the movement led by William Morris.

Produced in 1914, Goudy Old Style reflects the absorption of a generation of designers with things "ancient." Its smooth, even color, combined with its generous curves and ample cut, marks it as one of Goudy's finest achievements.

Composed by Crane Typesetting Service, Inc.,
West Barnstable, Massachusetts

Printed and bound by The Haddon Craftsmen, Inc.,
Scranton, Pennsylvania

Designed by Dorothy S. Baker